P9-DXC-741

A JOURNEY BEGINS

"You'll probably be wanting fresh water," said McGuire, "so you might as well go on into the center of town to the well . . . Then take the left fork past Stidham's store, and you should find yourself a decent place soon after that. Go too much farther, and you'll be among the Indians and the coloreds. You won't want that, of course. Not with your daughters being with you."

"Thank you, Sergeant," said Thayer abruptly. "Come on children, let's be going." He offered the reins to Nimbus back to Creed and the reins to Payday to Drake.

"Good luck to you, Reverend," said McGuire. "I wish you a safe journey."

"Thank you, Sergeant," said Thayer. He snapped the lines over the mules, and the wagon lurched forward.

As the second wagon passed him, McGuire repeated his good wishes to Tyler and Louise, and then he did the same when Creed and Little Bee rode by him. They, in turn, bid him a forced but polite farewell.

As soon as McGuire and his men were well behind them, Creed said, "What do you make of those men back there, Little Bee?"

"Including the sergeant?" asked Little Bee.

"Sure, him, too."

"Horses' asses," said the boy succinctly.

Creed laughed and said, "You got that right."

This book also contains a preview of the exciting new western novel *Sixkiller* by Giles Tippette.

CREED

TEXAN'S HONOR

BRYCE HARTE

BERKLEY BOOKS, NEW YORK

TEXAN'S HONOR

A Berkley Book / published by arrangement with
the author

PRINTING HISTORY
Berkley edition / May 1992

All rights reserved.
Copyright © 1992 by The Berkley Publishing Group.
Sixkiller excerpt copyright © 1992 by Giles Tippette.
This book may not be reproduced in whole or in part,
by mimeograph or any other means, without permission.
For information address: The Berkley Publishing Group,
200 Madison Avenue, New York, New York 10016.

ISBN: 0-425-13266-8

A BERKLEY BOOK®TM 757,375
Berkley Books are published by The Berkley Publishing Group,
200 Madison Avenue, New York, New York 10016.
The name "BERKLEY" and the "B" logo are trademarks
belonging to Berkley Publishing Corporation.

PRINTED IN THE UNITED STATES OF AMERICA

10 9 8 7 6 5 4 3 2 1

To my son,
Tory,
with all my love

REAL HISTORY

The Indian Nations that eventually became the state of Oklahoma were a minor theater of operations for both the Confederacy and the Union during the War Between the States, but several battles and skirmishes were fought on Indian lands by forces that included soldiers from several tribes. Some of these battles and their combatants are described herein; they are related as accurately as possible.

Every geographical feature mentioned in this story has been given the name that it had in 1866. Some of these places no longer exist, such as Alberty's Store and Doaksville.

In Chapter 4, Creed is confronted by a ball of eerie light, a phenomenon that he can't explain. This oddity is real—it's known to the people in present-day Ottawa County, Oklahoma, as the "Spook Light." They invite visitors to come see it on almost any summer night, especially in July.

The Texas Road that Creed travels through the Indian Nations is still in evidence. Its general course is the same as that of U.S. Highway 69 from Baxter Springs, Kansas, to Denison, Texas.

Every piece of history described herein as having taken place prior to 1866 is true, including the genealogies and family histories of every character with the exceptions of Creed, Little Bee Doak, the Thayers, and Britt Tyler.

PROLOGUE

The voices and footsteps of several men awakened Creed. He opened his eyes to dim light, and it took him a few seconds to realize where he was and the predicament that he was in. He was scrunched up in the corner of the room, bound hand and foot, fully clothed with a blanket over him, and he hurt all over from the tight bindings. He was in the custody of U.S. Deputy Marshal Jim Kindred, who was just then stirring in the bed, and they were in a room in the Mounts Hotel at Lee's Summit, Missouri.

"What the hell is that?" groused Kindred as he was awakened by the noise in the hall. He sat up in bed to get his bearings.

Before the marshal had time to think, the door burst open, and five hooded men entered the room.

"Who the hell are you?" demanded Kindred.

"Shut up, Marshal," said the first man, his voice muffled by the grainsack over his head, "and don't get in the way. We don't want you. We're after him." He pointed toward Creed on the floor.

"He's all tied up," said another intruder.

Creed was more alert now, and he thought that he recognized something familiar in the voices of the two men. The first sounded like Jesse James, and the second seemed to belong to Frank James. One enemy and one friend. He wondered which of the two was in charge.

"What are you doing there?" demanded Kindred. He tried to stand but was pushed back onto the bed by the first man.

"I told you, Marshal," said the intruder. "Just shut up and don't get in the way, and you won't get hurt."

1

Creed was certain now that the speaker was Jesse James. Damn! he thought. What's he doing here?

"Who are you?" demanded Kindred again.

"Get him up, boys," said the second man. He grabbed Creed's coat and hat off the floor.

Creed was equally positive that this man was Frank James. That's a break, he told himself.

"Never you mind who we are," said Jesse. "Just be grateful that we're only gonna hang *him*."

The other four men got Creed into a standing position.

"That man's my prisoner," said Kindred, "and I'm taking him back to Texas to hang."

"Well, we're gonna save you the trouble," said Jesse. "You got him, boys?"

"Wait a minute," said Frank. "His feet are tied." He knelt down and untied the rope around Creed's ankles. "There. He can walk now."

"All right, let's go," said Jesse.

Two men flanked Creed, and they pulled and pushed him into the hall. Frank led the way, and the fourth man followed. Before they reached the stairs, Creed heard Kindred shout, "You can't do this! He's my prisoner! You can't do this!"

He heard Jesse reply, "We're gonna do it, Marshal, and there's nothing you can do to stop us." What happened after that, he could only guess, because Frank and the other three men took him downstairs and outside where ten mounted men waited for them. Lynch mob? wondered Creed. They had to be some sort of gang—even in the twilight he could see that they had the street to themselves.

"Get him on his horse," said Frank. They put Creed in the saddle atop Nimbus, then Frank placed Creed's hat on his head and his coat around his shoulders and fastened the top two buttons. "Wouldn't want you to come down sick again," he said softly in Creed's ear.

Jesse came out of the hotel carrying Kindred's shotgun. Since he'd heard no gunfire, Creed assumed that Jesse had taken the weapon away from Kindred.

Just as Jesse swung up into the saddle, Kindred came running out of the hotel shouting, "Hold on there! You can't do this!"

"We're doing it, Marshal," said Jesse, as he leveled Kindred's shotgun at him. "Now stand clear, and let us get this over with."

As Kindred backed off, Jesse kicked his horse and headed west out of town.

The others followed suit, taking Creed with them. They rode about a mile across the prairie until they came to a creek bottom that had several large oaks and cottonwoods growing in it, any one of which had a strong limb suitable for hanging a man. Jesse held up his right hand as a signal for them to halt.

Before anybody could do or say anything, Kindred came racing up out of the darkness, shouting, "Hold up there!" Kindred must have thought that Jesse and the others were obeying him because suddenly he acted like a wild man, charging Jesse and causing a collision between their horses. Both riders were thrown clear, but the animals went down in a din of wild, frightened whinnies and in a heap of legs thrashing crazily as they tried to right themselves.

"Crazy bastard!" screamed Jesse as he regained his feet. He saw Kindred struggling to get up on his hands and knees, ran over to him, and kicked him solidly in the ribs with the sharp toe of his boot. "Little bastard!" he swore again. "I ought to kill you for that."

Frank jumped down from his horse and stopped Jesse from kicking Kindred again. "Let him be," he said. "We've got other business here."

"Just let me kick him once more," said Jesse.

"No, let him be," said Frank. He pulled his brother away from the writhing, gasping marshal.

Creed figured Kindred must have been hurt badly by the way he rolled around on the ground holding his sides. In a way, he almost felt sorry for Kindred. Almost.

"All right," said Jesse, "let's get him strung up."

Frank took Nimbus by the reins and led Creed to a good-sized tree. The three men who had been in the hotel room joined them. Jesse and the others remained aloof, several feet away.

"Get him down," said Frank.

The trio helped Creed to the ground. Just then, one of them shouted, "Sonofabitch!" and knocked Creed to the ground. All three of them piled onto him, and although they cursed him and acted like they were hitting him, none landed a blow. One even said softly, "Stay down, Slate, and pretend you're hurt." Creed recognized Jim White's voice and did as he was told. The three men stood up abruptly and looked down at Creed, trying to appear menacing through their masks. Creed figured that besides White he was looking at the Shepherd brothers.

"Get a noose on him!" ordered Frank. "Let's get this hanging over with."

White and the Shepherds fell on Creed again, this time with a rope. When they finished, Creed felt one loop around his neck and another under his coat and around his chest. He couldn't be certain, but he thought that they were the same rope or that they were tied together at least.

"Get him on his horse again," said Frank. As White and the Shepherds put Creed atop Nimbus, Frank threw the other end of the rope over a limb of the cottonwood they were under. He grabbed the line again and tied it to a smaller tree. He remounted his own horse and moved it close to Creed so he could adjust the noose. As he did, he whispered, "Better pretend you're hanging for real, Slate, or Jesse or Arch will put a ball in your brain for sure."

Jesse walked up to them and said, "What's taking so long?"

"All set," said Frank. He moved his horse away from Creed.

"Good-bye, Slate Creed," said Jesse, his tone mocking and hateful. Without another word, he slapped Nimbus on the rump, startling the Appaloosa into bolting from under his master.

Creed dropped a foot or so, then was brought up short by a jolt on his armpits. At the same time, the noose tightened around his throat, gagging him but nothing more. Suspended above the ground, he remembered what Frank had said about pretending to be hung for real, so he began kicking the air violently, twisting, and swinging back and forth as though he were choking. He kept this up for a good minute or more, then fell limp, feigning death.

As soon as Creed ceased moving, Jesse pulled his six-gun and started to take aim at the Texan's drooping head, but before he could squeeze the trigger, Frank jumped down from his horse and stopped him by grabbing his wrist and lifting it skyward.

"No, Jesse," said Frank in a low growl that only his brother could hear.

Jesse wrenched his hand free and said, "I was just gonna make sure he was dead."

"No, Jesse," snarled Frank as he grabbed Jesse's wrist again. "He died like a man. He doesn't need to be shot like a dog."

After a moment to think about it, Jesse said, "All right, Frank.

I'll grant him that much, but that marshal deserves to be dead, too."

"No, Jesse," said Frank. "We made a bargain. If you don't stick to it, I'll never ride with you again."

Jesse thought about that, too, then said, "All right, Frank, I won't kill him. Let's go."

"No," said Frank. "We're gonna bury our friend first."

"Well, I'm not sticking around for a funeral," said Jesse.

"Then why don't you take the marshal back to town?" suggested Frank. "I think you hurt him so bad that he can't ride without help."

"All right, we'll do that," said Jesse. He shoved his revolver back inside his waistband, then walked back to the other men. A few of them helped Kindred to his feet and put him back on his horse. Jesse gave the signal, and they headed back to Lee's Summit.

"Follow them for a ways, George," said Frank, "and make sure none of them double back here too soon."

George Shepherd jumped onto his horse and rode after Jesse and the others.

"Let's get him down now," said Frank, as soon as George was out of sight. "Slate, are you all right?"

Creed opened his eyes and tried to speak, but all he could do was rasp out, "I'm alive at least."

Frank untied the rope that held Creed and lowered him gently to the ground. Creed wobbled, then dropped to his knees where Oll Shepherd caught hold of him before he fell over. White produced a knife and cut the ropes around Creed's hands and chest, freeing him completely.

"I'm sorry about this," said Frank, "but it was the only way we could think of to save you from Jesse and Arch. They were gonna kill you, Slate."

Creed cleared his throat and said hoarsely, "I sort of figured that much, Alex. Thank you for saving my life."

"You're welcome," said Frank, "but there's no time to waste. Jesse or one of the other boys might come back here soon, so we've got to get you out of here. Can you ride?"

"Sure, I can ride," said Creed.

"Then you'd best get mounted up and get on out of here," said Frank. He pointed and said, "Jesse and the others went east, back to Lee's Summit. That way is west."

Creed stood up and offered his hand to Frank. "How do I ever repay you boys for this?" he asked.

"Just remember us kindly," said Frank, shaking Creed's hand.

"Maybe say a prayer for us if you ever think of it," said White, as he shook Creed's hand.

"Lift a glass in my honor sometime," said Oll Shepherd, as he took his turn saying farewell. "And do the same for George if you think of it."

Creed climbed atop Nimbus and said, "Thank you again, boys."

"Go on," said Frank, "and get out of here."

Creed tipped his hat, then rode off in the direction that Frank had suggested without looking back.

At the first crossroads that he came to that night, Creed turned south. His search for Marshal Quade and the other men who had put the blame on him for their crime could wait. For now, he would return to Texas but not to his home in Lavaca County. He was needed elsewhere.

1

Spring was awakening the land when Slate Creed crossed the border between the Treaty Party Addition of the Cherokee Nation and the lands of the Quapaw Nation in Indian Territory. The black earth track of the road was damp from a recent late-winter rainstorm, but it wasn't so muddy that clods of dirt stuck to his horse's hooves. A bright sun lazed in the midday sky, and a gentle breeze from the south wafted warm air over the greening grama grass and the budding trees and bushes of the creek bottom that crossed the trail ahead.

Creed felt the same peace that sailors experience at sea: the serenity of being one with Nature, of being attuned to Creation and the Creator. The mood and the moment would have been perfect if only the woman that he loved were there to share them with him. He let his mind drift through his memories of Texas, of Lavaca County, of Hallettsville, of the Double Star Ranch, of Texada, of home, and he wondered whether he would ever see them again.

Before the pangs of forced solitude and loneliness could wrack him this day as they had for so many days gone by, Creed heard the shriek of a woman in distress. He reined in Nimbus and cocked an ear in anticipation of another cry. When a second scream came from the creek bottom one hundred yards ahead, he loosened his coat, felt the butt of the Colt's tucked securely inside his waistband, then urged the Appaloosa into a canter.

A black-haired, dark-skinned woman attired in a squaw's buckskin shift came running up the trail from the creek bottom. Her chestnut eyes were wide with fright until she saw Creed riding toward her. She stretched out her arms toward him, as if she were seeking a protective embrace, then she cried out, "Help me, sir! Please help me! He gonna kill me!"

In pursuit of the woman was a ruddy-faced, bearded man also on foot. Before he saw Creed, he shouted after the woman, "Come back here, you bitch!"

In the next instant, Creed closed the distance between him and the terrified woman. He jumped down in front of her.

"O lordy, sir!" she pleaded in the drawl of slaves. "You gots to help me! He gonna kill me for sure! Please help me, sir! Please help me!"

Creed took her by the upper arms, looked her straight in the eye, and said, "Hold on now. What's this all about?"

"He gonna kill me, sir," she cried. She glanced back over her shoulder.

"Nobody's going to kill you," said Creed, as he gave her a quick study. Her hair was braided Indian fashion, and she had the facial features of an Indian, but the brown tone of her skin was too dark for an Indian. Probably an Indian mulatto, he thought. He guessed her age to be around thirty.

She looked back at Creed and said, "Oh, yes, sir, he gonna kill me! You gots to help me, sir!"

Creed squeezed her arms tighter to reassure her as he repeated, "Nobody's going to kill you."

"Get your hands off my nigger," said the man who had been chasing the woman. He'd stopped in the road several feet away, fists on hips, glaring at Creed and the fugitive female.

Creed shifted his view to the man and sized him up as a farmer—a poor one, from the looks of his tattered slouch hat, patched coat, and homespun trousers, all a dingy brown. His shaggy hair and long beard were streaked gray and white, and his blue eyes had an iciness that put Creed's senses on guard.

"Didn't you hear me?" snarled the man. "I said to get your hands off my nigger!"

Creed gently guided the woman to one side as he confronted the hostile farmer. He forced a friendly smile and said, "Pardon me, sir, but who are you and what's the trouble here?"

"His name is Branch," said the woman.

"There ain't no trouble here," said Branch, "unless you bring it on yourself, mister. Now you just step aside and let me take my nigger, and I'll be gone from here in no time."

"Well, Mr. Branch, I can't let you do that," said Creed, as he stepped between the woman and the farmer.

"Is that so?" said the farmer. Without another word, he reached inside his coat and drew out a Bowie knife. He bent into a fighting stance as if to challenge Creed.

"Yes, sir, that's so," said Creed, as he spread his coat to show Branch that he had a revolver inside his waistband.

The farmer straightened up and said, "Now hold on, mister. I don't have a gun on me. That wouldn't be fair of you to draw down on me with that six-shooter. I just want my property, is all. I got rights here."

"Don't you know that slavery has been abolished?" asked Creed, giving Branch the benefit of the doubt.

"Sure, he knows it," said the woman, as she peeked around Creed's shoulder. "And I knows it, too. Peddler come by and say that the Tribes all had to 'bolish slavery and share the land with them."

"That was just for the Injuns," said Branch. "Don't have nothing to do with white folks in the Nations."

"That's not the way I understand things to be," said Creed. "The way I recollect it, President Lincoln abolished slavery in all the states of the Confederacy, and since the North won the war, it holds that the slaves in the South are free now."

"But this is the Nations," argued the farmer, "and what that Black Republican Lincoln said don't mean squat here."

"Don't listen to him, mister," said the woman. "Peddler man come by the farm and he say that the Yankee generals done made the Tribes give up their slaves and that all the slaves in the Nations is free now."

"She's lying!" spat Branch. "I tell you true, she's my property, and I'm gonna have her back." He raised his arm to throw the knife at Creed.

Creed was quicker to react. He pushed the woman to the ground behind him, while he stepped aside, drew his Colt's, dropped to one knee, and cocked the gun.

The Bowie knife flew through the air, missing its intended target.

Angered into reacting to the attempt on his life, Creed took a steady aim at arm's length and fired at the farmer. The ball struck its target in the chest a few inches above Branch's right breast, the impact knocking him backward to the ground. He rolled onto his left side, tried to move his right arm but couldn't, then used his left to push himself into a sitting position. He stared wild-eyed at Creed and swore, "You dirty sonofabitch! You've killed me!"

Creed stood up and walked over to the wounded man, keeping the Colt's ready in case the farmer had another weapon on him. He peered at Branch's wound, then said, "No, I haven't killed you, Mr. Branch, but I ought to, for throwing that Arkansas pig-sticker at me." He looked closer and said, "Don't worry. You'll live."

Because he'd been concentrating on Branch, Creed had forgotten temporarily about the woman. He received a rude reminder when he heard her shout, "Mean old sonofabitch! He need to die!" He turned just in time to see her brush by him with the farmer's knife raised high over her head. He reached out for her, but only managed to deflect her arm as she swung the blade down at Branch.

She missed her target, and her momentum carried her into the farmer. He fell over backwards with her atop him. She dropped the knife beside him. He saw it. He pushed her away, rolling her onto her back. He picked up the blade with his one good hand, raised it over his head, and cried, "Dirty nigger bitch!" then brought the Bowie down hard, jabbing it deep into the woman's abdomen, twisting the blade as he tried to withdraw it for another thrust. She screamed in terror and pain as she grabbed his hand.

Creed was too surprised by the woman's sudden attack and the farmer's instinctive counterattack to save the woman. He aimed quickly at the side of the farmer's face and fired.

The fatal ball entered the farmer's head between the left ear and cheek and exploded out the right temple. He fell back, quivered, gasped for air, and died.

The woman continued to scream in agony and fear, awakening Creed to the horror of the incident. My God! he thought. How did this happen? Why did this happen? That man's dead. I killed him. He's killed her. He dropped to his knees beside the woman. She stopped screaming, and with an incredible effort, she pulled the knife from her body, then cast it away.

"I'm sorry," said Creed, his face distorted with sorrow for her. "I tried to stop him."

"O lordy!" she cried. "I's dying, ain't I?"

Creed could only nod an affirmation. Her wound was too grievous; yes, she was dying.

With bloody fingers, she grabbed Creed's arm and said, "Mister, you gots to promise me. You gots to promise me."

"What?" mumbled Creed. "Promise you? Promise you what?"

"My boy," she gasped. "My boy. Take him. My boy. Take him to my brother. My brother Hum. Down to the Choctaw Nation. Down to Armstrong's. My brother Hum. My boy. Down to the Choctaw school. Armstrong's. Promise me, mister."

Her tone was so desperate that Creed could only stutter, "Yes, I-I-I . . . promise I'll take him . . . to your brother." He looked up and scanned the area quickly, then he looked back at her and said, "But what boy? Where—?" He didn't bother to complete the question.

The woman was dead.

2

The crack of a twig breaking underfoot caused Creed to whirl about, his gun aimed in the direction of the sound, ready to kill again. Someone was there. A short someone. A boy. The woman's boy? wondered Creed.

If he was her son, he didn't look like her. His straight hair had a brown tint to it. He had a golden complexion, Caucasian facial features, and hazel eyes that were filled with a mixture of fear, hatred, and sorrow as he stared at the body near Creed. He was dressed in leather trousers tied at the waist with a rawhide thong, a red woolen shirt, moccasins, and a low-crown, black felt hat. A charcoal gray army blanket was draped over his shoulders Indian style. He appeared to be about eleven or twelve years old. "Mama!" he cried suddenly, before he sprang forward and ran to the dead woman. He dropped to his knees at her side. "No, Mama, you can't be dead!" He threw off the wrap and shook her. "You can't be dead, Mama!" He wore no coat.

With his mind reeling with confusion, Creed lowered his gun and stood up. He wasn't sure of what to do. This was her son, he knew now; the boy that he had promised to take to her brother—what did she call him, the brother? Makes no difference right now, he thought. He looked around him. My God! How did this happen? he asked himself. What am I doing here? He looked down at the boy. What is he doing here? He saw the bodies. What are they doing here? This is too ridiculous. His head fell back limply, and his amber-flecked green eyes rolled skyward. Why do these things happen like this? he asked in painful silence.

12

"You can't be dead, Mama!" the boy wailed. He shook her again and repeated the cry. "You can't be dead, Mama!" Then he fell across her lifeless body and wept uncontrollably.

"It doesn't make sense to me either," said Creed aloud, although he didn't expect the boy to reply or even to hear him. He uncocked the Colt's and stuck it back inside his waistband. He heaved a sigh, scratched at the thick, strawberry blond curls at the nape of his neck, then walked over to Nimbus. Having been with Creed throughout the war and being familiar with the sound of gunfire, the Appaloosa hadn't run off but had taken the opportunity to get some nourishment, casually grazing beside the road. The stallion raised his head upon Creed's approach, but continued to munch on the green grass. Creed took the reins and led the horse down to the creek to let him drink. The Texan hoped to find some answers to all the questions plaguing him.

The water gurgled and swirled and churned as it flowed past man and horse. Two redbirds sang and danced in the air overhead as they played out a courting ritual. A swallowtail butterfly fluttered past. A water spider floated on the surface of the creek. A crawdad darted under a mossy rock in the stream bottom when Nimbus stuck his muzzle into the cool water and sucked up a long drink. A peaceful, idyllic scene if ever there was one, but for the tragic incongruity of a man and a woman in death's repose and a boy weeping over his mother's body.

Why? Creed asked himself. No answer. He looked heavenward and said aloud to his Maker, "I didn't want to kill that man." He let his head droop in apology as he said, "But I did kill him. I killed him, and I can't change that." The boy's sobbing penetrated his thoughts. He glanced over his shoulder at the youngster. "His mama's dead, too, and I can't change that either." An echo of the woman's voice exacting his promise to take her son to her brother in the Choctaw Nation haunted him. He looked skyward again and said, "But I can keep my word to that poor woman, is that it?"

A jayhawk, gliding over the treetops, screeched in reply.

Creed saw the bird and recollected how Grandfather Hawk McConnell had often told him that the Great Spirit was everywhere, that He was known by different names among the Tribes, that He was all mysterious and wondrous and powerful, and that He could be whatever it was that He wanted to be at any time, at any place, to anybody.

The bird of prey screeched again, as if to confirm Creed's thoughts. The Texan's head bobbed with understanding, with approval, and with thanks.

Creed tied Nimbus to a hickory tree, then he approached the crying boy. He stopped beside him, bent down, and placed his hand on the lad's shoulder. The child pulled away. Creed sort of expected that to happen. "It's all right, son," he said, as he tried to pat the boy's shoulder.

"Don't touch me, white man!" screamed the boy, as he shrank away again. He saw the knife on the ground a few feet from his mother's body. He lunged for it, grabbed it, and turned on Creed. His tears had stopped. His mother's blood was spotted on the front of his shirt; it looked like a badge of honor on him. "Don't you ever touch me again, white man, or I'll cut you up worse than old Hezekiah cut up my mama." He flashed the blade at the Texan.

Creed raised his hands in mock surrender and backed away a few steps as he said, "All right, I won't touch you, son. Just put the—"

The kid interrupted him, yelling, "I ain't your son, so don't call me that!"

Creed lowered his hands and said, "All right, what should I call you?" When he didn't receive an immediate answer, he repeated the question, but with more authority this time. "I said, what's your name?"

"Little Bee," he said defiantly. "What's yours?"

"Creed. Slate Creed." He smiled and tried to be friendly as he added, "I'm from Texas. Where are you from?"

"I ain't from no place," said Little Bee.

"You've got to be from some place," said Creed.

"No, I don't."

"All right, you're not from anywhere. So how did you get that name, Little Bee?"

"That ain't none of your business, white man."

"I'm afraid it is," said Creed. "You see, Little Bee, your mama made me promise her something before she died."

Little Bee's face twisted up with confusion and disbelief. "What's that you say, white man?"

"Before your mama died, she made me promise to take you to her brother in the Choctaw Nation."

"You're lying, white man. Everybody knows white men talk like snakes. You're lying to me, and I know it."

Only two accusations had a tendency to raise Creed's wrath. One was being called a thief, and the other was being called a liar. To refer to Creed as either was to invite instant violence without warning—usually, but not in this case.

Creed swallowed hard in order to control his anger, then said, "You're lucky you're just a kid, Little Bee, because if you were a man and you'd called me a liar, I'd be knocking your teeth down your throat about now."

"Go ahead and try it," snarled the boy.

Creed was amused by the lad's bravado. He chuckled and said, "Well, I do admire your sand, Little Bee. Of course, I think you know that I wouldn't do that. Hit you, I mean."

"Of course, I know you wouldn't hit me. Not as long as I got this Bowie knife in my hand."

Creed chuckled again and said, "All right, you can think that way if you want, but all the same, I wouldn't hit a kid."

"I'm not a kid, white man."

"No? Then what are you? A wildcat?"

"No, I'm a Choctaw warrior."

"A Choctaw warrior?" queried Creed. "You look like a kid to me, Little Bee."

"Oh, yeah? Well, watch this, white man." And without another word, Little Bee fell on the corpse of his mother's killer and proceeded to scalp the old farmer as Creed watched in horrified silence, unable to move and stop the boy from mutilating the dead man. As soon as he'd finished the morbid deed, Little Bee jumped to his feet in triumph, waving Branch's hair over his head and giving out with his childish version of a war cry.

Creed swallowed his disgust, squatted down, picked up a thumb-size rock, and scratched at the dirt with it. "So you think that makes you a Choctaw warrior?" he asked.

"I was a Choctaw warrior before scalping old Hezekiah," said Little Bee. "I was born a Choctaw warrior."

"Was that his name?" asked Creed, pointing at the dead man. "Hezekiah? Your mother said his name was Branch."

"Yeah, that was his name," said Little Bee. "Hezekiah Branch. He was the meanest old sonofabitch that ever lived. I'm glad you killed him."

"Well, that's the whole deal, Little Bee. I killed him. You didn't. His scalp belongs to me."

"No, it don't," said Little Bee, drawing away as if Creed had made a move to retrieve the grisly hairpiece.

"Yes, it does. You see, a Choctaw warrior can only take the scalp of a man that he's killed."

"How do you know that?"

"Because my grandfather told me, and he's a real Choctaw warrior."

Little Bee's face scrunched up again as he said, "You're lying again, white man. You ain't got no Choctaw grandfather."

Creed pointed a finger at Little Bee and said, "I warned you about calling me a liar, kid. You do it once more, and I'll forget you're just a little fellow."

"You're a liar, white man!" said Little Bee with all the daring and defiance that his small body could muster.

Creed stood up slowly, deliberately straightening to his full height of six feet in order to scare the boy. "I warned you, kid," he said. "Now you're going to get it." Seeing that the kid was unmoved, he took a menacing step toward Little Bee, but that didn't faze him either; he dropped Branch's scalp and readied himself for a fight. Another step brought Creed within striking distance of the knife, and the kid took a swipe at him. Creed jumped back, feigned another approach, and let Little Bee take a second lethal swing at him, this time backhanded. Quick as a cat, the Texan moved in, caught the boy's right wrist with his left hand, and took hold of the red shirt with his right, jerking Little Bee off the ground.

Little Bee fought back, kicking with both feet at Creed's legs and groin. His hat fell off as he landed a foot in the middle of the Texan's right thigh, forcing Creed to let go of his shirt but not the arm that had the knife. Being dropped to the ground off balance surprised the kid, and without thinking of anything except righting himself, he released the Bowie.

Seeing the knife fall, Creed pushed the boy away, sprawling him on the ground beside his mother. When the kid scrambled to retrieve the weapon, the Texan planted his foot firmly on the handle, thwarting and frustrating Little Bee into flailing madly at Creed's legs and finally at his groin, where he landed one firm blow. "Oo-ooh-nh!" grunted Creed, eyes bulging with pain and surprise from the attack. He grabbed his injured organ with one hand and slapped the kid across the face with the other, knocking him backward onto his buttocks again. Creed dropped onto his knees involuntarily, still holding his groin and sucking for air, while covering the knife with his legs. Little Bee came at him again, and Creed saw no option except to rap the kid with the back of his hand and knock him down again. This time he drew blood from the kid's nose and upper lip, and Little Bee stayed down for a moment as he assessed the damage to his face.

"Listen, you little piss-ant!" swore Creed, air hissing between his lips. He winced with pain. "Damn you!" A touch of vertigo struck his senses. He took a deep breath to combat the sensation. "Damn that hurts," he muttered through clenched teeth.

Little Bee sat up, holding his mouth and nose and feeling the warm blood trickle between his fingers. He looked down at the red flow, then glared at Creed. "Damn you, you white trash!" he screamed. He leaped to his feet and made another charge at the Texan.

Creed caught the kid in his arms and rolled over on him, pinning him to the ground, his own hat falling off. He put his forearm over the boy's throat and applied pressure—not enough to hurt the youngster, but enough to cut off his wind. "Just stop it!" shouted Creed in his face. "Stop it now, or I'll forget you're just a kid."

As soon as he realized that he couldn't breathe, Little Bee ceased struggling.

Creed eased off. "That's better," he said. He sucked in a breath, then continued. "Now get this straight, kid. Your mother's dead, and she left you to me. Now I know you don't see it that way. All right, that's fine with me. You can go your own way if you want. I won't try to stop you. As for me, I'm going to give your mother a decent burial, and I'm going to bury that man you just scalped. Then I'm riding out of here. With or without you. Have you got that? But if you get in my way, or if you try anything else with me, I'm going to forget you're a kid and put a ball in your brain, just like I did to that man over there. Have you got that now?"

"Yes," rasped Little Bee.

"All right," said Creed. "Now remember what I said. I'm going to let you up now, and if you try anything, that's it. You'll be joining your mother in the spirit world." He removed his arm from the boy's throat, then pushed himself onto his hands and knees. When the kid made no moves, he picked up the Bowie knife, then stood up again. His groin hurt really bad, but he decided against letting Little Bee see him in pain again.

He stooped to pick up his hat, grinding his teeth to hide the spiking pangs between his legs. He straightened up again, and the agony eased off. "All right," he said, "let's get those graves dug."

3

Digging the two graves was difficult, dirty, and depressing, but it gave Creed time to think and to question himself. He wondered about the boy, the woman, and the man. Who were they? What were they doing here? He wondered about himself. What am I doing here? Why did I choose to come this way through the Nations? Why did I arrive at this spot at this particular time? Why did this happen?

Finally, he gave up looking for causes for the tragedy, and he started thinking about the consequences. He considered reporting to a local lawman the murder of the woman by Hezekiah Branch and the subsequent killing of Branch by him. How do I tell the law about this? he wondered. Will they believe me? What if there's paper out on me, and they find out that I'm wanted back in Texas? Then what? What about their families? Did the woman and Branch even have families? They should be told. But should I do the telling? Damn! Why do these things happen?

He quit thinking and worked all the harder.

Creed chose a spot for Branch's grave that was far from the road, in full sunlight, and likely to be overgrown with weeds by the middle of April. For the woman, he picked out a shady, grassy site on a rise that overlooked the creek. If she were my mother, he told himself, this is where I'd want her to be, in a pretty place and as far away from Branch as possible. He used the Bowie knife to break up the earth, and Little Bee scraped up the soil with a tin plate that the Texan provided for the task. It took them much of the afternoon to do the digging, but putting

19

the bodies in their graves and covering them with dirt and rocks took less than an hour.

During this whole time, Little Bee was absolutely silent, neither speaking nor crying, not even a whimper. He obeyed Creed's few orders without question or hesitation, performing efficiently and completely. Creed was surprised by the boy's attitude. The kid had agreed to co-operate, but he was still a kid, which meant he would probably go back on his word—or so Creed figured. When he didn't, Creed had to admit to himself that he was impressed by the youngster's integrity.

Funerals were nothing new to Creed. He'd attended family burials during his youth, and he'd helped to bury several men during the war. This, however, was the first time that he had to speak over the departed.

Being nervous and conscientious of this duty, he stepped up to Hezekiah Branch's grave but didn't speak right off. He tried to call up the words from his own mind, but they wouldn't come. At last, he heard a voice deep within him telling him what to say: "Lord, I killed this man because he tried to kill me and because he killed this woman. I didn't know him or anything about him except that he abused this woman and her son. He's Yours now, Lord. I suppose it's my Christian duty to ask You to forgive him for his sins and to have mercy on his soul, so that's what I'm doing. He's all Yours now. You do with his soul what You will. We've buried him proper so the wild critters won't dig him up and pick over his bones." He paused, unsure of what to say next. When he heard nothing more from the voice, he said simply, "Amen."

Little Bee had stood beside his mother's grave the whole time Creed was speaking over Branch. When the Texan joined him, he looked up at Creed, then back down at the mound of dirt and stones, but he remained silent.

Creed cleared his throat, wishing to speak but couldn't. He was just the same as when he stood over Branch. Nothing would come out of his mouth, until he heard the voice and began repeating its words. He said, "Lord, this woman—" He stopped there because it suddenly dawned on him that he didn't even know her name. He looked down at the boy and asked, "What was your mama's name, Little Bee?" When the kid didn't reply right away, Creed added, "It would help me to pray for her, if I was to know her name."

"Martha," said Little Bee softly, without bothering to look up at Creed. "Martha Doak."

Creed nodded, then continued with the prayer. "Lord, Martha Doak was killed by that man Branch. She tried to kill him first, but from what little I saw of the two of them together, I guess she thought he had it coming. Anyway, she's dead and in Your care now. I hope You can forgive her for trying to kill Branch, and maybe You can show her a little mercy and give her a better life than she had here on earth. You see, she was a slave here, Lord, and not many slaves ever get a chance for a good life. She did bring this boy here into the world. That ought to count for something, Lord. From the way she made me promise to take him to her brother down to the Choctaw Nation, I'd have to say that she loved this boy a whole lot, Lord. And that ought to count for something, too. So maybe You could go easy on her for wanting to kill Branch back there. She just wanted to do it, but she didn't do it. I did. So don't go blaming her for it, please, Lord?" He paused for a second, then said the few lines that he could recall from the Christian burial services that he'd witnessed. "Dust to dust, ashes to ashes. We commend her soul to You, Lord. We've buried her proper, so now she's Yours." He glanced at Little Bee, wondering what else to say. He shook his head and added, "I don't know, Lord. I suppose You needed Martha more than this boy needs her. Well, she's all Yours now. Amen." The voice within him fell silent. He waited a moment to make certain it would remain still, then he asked, "Would you like to say something for her, Little Bee?"

The boy looked up at him and said, "Would it be all right?"

"She was your mama," said Creed. "The only one you'll ever have. Don't you think she'd want you to say something for her?"

Little Bee shifted his view back to the grave and said, "I ain't so sure what to say."

"This is one of those times when you let your heart speak for you, Little Bee," said Creed without thinking. But when he did think about it, he realized that he was repeating the same words that his Grandfather Hawk had said to him when his father was killed. Recalling that moment brought a tear to his eye.

The boy looked at Creed again and asked, "Do you think the Great Spirit is really listening to us?"

"He's listening," said Creed, trying to blink away his own tears. "You just talk. He'll hear you all right."

Little Bee nodded, reassured now. He let his view drift toward heaven but said nothing. He looked down, then began crying again. "Oh, Mama," he wailed. "Oh, Mama." He fell down across the grave and bawled.

Creed let the boy alone. He walked away to find some solitude of his own.

The day was growing late, too late for Creed to be thinking about going any farther into this strange land. He decided to make camp for the night. This was as good a place as any for it. Running water, plenty of wood for a fire, protection from the wind. A good place for camping.

While he was unsaddling Nimbus, Creed began wondering again about how Branch, Little Bee, and Martha Doak came to be out here on the prairie, so far from who knew where. He hadn't seen a house or a cabin or even an Indian hut since crossing into the Quapaw lands. Where had they come from? Were they traveling together? Was the woman running away with the boy? Was Branch chasing them? Hunting them? All three of them were on foot. Was that how they got there? He had a lot of questions to ask, and only Little Bee could answer them. But first things first—a fire and some food.

Figuring that he would be spending a lot of time on the trail and that he'd be traveling through territory that was sparsely settled and even less civilized, and because he had a strong desire to avoid people for a while, especially after what had happened to him up in Missouri, Creed had gone to the bother of buying some much needed cooking and eating utensils at a general store back in Missouri. They included a small boiling pan, a frying skillet, a coffee pot, a tin cup, a tin plate, a spatula, a spreading knife, a fork, and two spoons—a small one for eating with and a bigger one for stirring and serving. He hadn't figured on having company, though. Well, we'll just have to share for now, he thought as he looked at Little Bee sitting beside his mother's grave.

He started a fire, then filled his coffee pot and cooking pan with water from the creek and set them beside the fire to heat up. He poured some dry beans into the pan and added a few strips of beef jerky for flavoring.

As he made some coffee, Creed heard a mule bray. His first thought was that somebody was coming up the road from the south and that he would wait for him or them or whatever. When no one came along in the next few minutes and the animal brayed again, he concluded that the mule was either wild or that it had belonged to Branch and that he had left it somewhere while he chased after Martha Doak and her son. Either way, the beast would come in handy now. He went looking for it and found it tethered to an oak tree on the other side of the creek and twenty yards off the road. He surmised it was Branch's animal. It was saddled and carrying much the same gear that he had, including an old .54-caliber Mississippi percussion rifle. He untied the mule and led it back to the camp, where he tied it up again beside Nimbus; then, he returned to his cooking.

The odor of food cooking reached Little Bee's nostrils and stirred his survival instincts enough to make him forget his grief and to seek sustenance. He joined Creed at the campfire.

"Hungry?" asked Creed.

"I could eat a horse," said Little Bee with controlled enthusiasm. "Mama and I didn't have much to eat after we left Mr. Vann's three days back."

"Mr. Vann's?" queried Creed.

"Yes, sir," said Little Bee. "Mr. Vann was a slave like us. He told Mama and me that his master took him and his other slaves down to Texas when the war came, but they came back to the Choctaw Nation where Mr. Vann and his wife Hannah was set free by the Union soldiers. They moved to the Grand River near Brushy Creek a few years back and made them a farm there. Mr. Vann gave us some food, and we got this far before old Hezekiah caught up to us this morning just before you come along."

"Were you and your mother Branch's slaves?" asked Creed.

"We was, but a peddler come along some time back and told Mama that the slaves was all set free and that old Hezekiah had no right to keep us no more."

"So you ran away from him?"

"That's right," said Little Bee. "Mama said we could go find her brother, Uncle Hum. Mama and him were born in the Choctaw Nation. Their mammy was a slave named Tabby, and their daddy was a Choctaw man named John Doak. Mama said that Uncle Hum was called Humma when he was born because he had red hair like his daddy. Humma, that's Choctaw for red."

Creed studied the kid for a moment and wondered if Little Bee had gotten his name because of his yellow complexion and dark hair, the coloring of a bee. Probably. "Is that how you got your name?" asked Creed.

"No, sir," said the boy, his head drooping a bit. "Mama named me that 'cause she said I was so sweet when I was a baby, that I brung her honey like a little bee." He looked at Creed, expecting him to laugh.

"Well, now I see why you didn't want to tell me about it earlier," said Creed quite seriously and much to Little Bee's relief. "You say your mother and Uncle Hum were born in the Choctaw Nation. Where were you born?"

"I was born there, too. My daddy was John Doak's son Titus Doak. When my grandma died, Mr. Titus sold Mama and me to old Hezekiah, who took us to his farm on Spavinaw Creek in the Cherokee Nation. That's where we was when Mama and me ran off last week."

"Did Branch have any family at this farm of his?"

"No, sir. There was just him. And me and Mama."

The Texan nodded, then said, "Your mother said your Uncle Hum was down in the Choctaw Nation yet at some place called Armstrong's. Do you know anything about that?"

"Yes, sir," said the boy. "Mama told me that she and Uncle Hum was split up when they was younguns. Uncle Hum was sold to some missionary folks who took him to this place called Armstrong's. Mama said we was gonna find this Armstrong's and look for Uncle Hum."

"If you were looking for this Armstrong's that's supposed to be in the Choctaw Nation, why were you going north?"

"Mama said we could throw old Hezekiah off the trail if we was to go north first then backtrack later on when it was safe."

"That makes sense, I suppose, but Branch didn't fall for the trick, I see."

"No, sir, I guess not," said Little Bee, tears welling up in his eyes again as he let himself remember that his mother was dead now.

Creed felt sorry for the boy. He wanted to touch him, to comfort him, but he was afraid of a repeat of his earlier attempt to console the kid. "Well," he said, "we'll eat some supper and get a good night's sleep before we push on tomorrow."

"Thank you, Mr. Creed," said Little Bee, "but I believe I'll be going my own way tomorrow."

"Your mother wanted you to go with me," said Creed.

"That's not what you said before," said the boy, his voice toned with belligerence again. "You said Mama made you promise to take me to Uncle Hum down in the Choctaw Nation. Well, you don't have to do that. I'll just find him all by myself."

Creed realized that it would be foolish to argue with the kid. No matter what he said, Little Bee would reject it. "All right," he said. "Have it your way. Tomorrow you can take that mule and all the trappings on it and go your own way." He smiled and added, "All right?"

Little Bee looked at him suspiciously, then said, "Do I get old Hezekiah's rifle, too?"

"Do you know how to use it?" asked Creed. "I mean, if you can't use the rifle, then why take it?"

"I know how to shoot it," said Little Bee.

"No, I said use it, not shoot it. Any damn fool can load a rifle and point it at something and pull the trigger. But it takes somebody with a good head on his shoulders to use a rifle properly. It takes somebody with good sense to know when to use that rifle and when not to use it. That's what I'm talking about, Little Bee."

"Well, I know how to use it then," said the kid.

Creed studied the boy for a moment, then said, "I don't think you do. The rifle goes with me."

Little Bee glared at Creed, but he didn't argue; he had other plans to work out instead.

4

Two hours before dawn the next morning Creed was awakened by the sound of a twig breaking underfoot. Without opening his eyes, he reached slowly with a stealthy right hand under the saddle sitting on the ground beside him and gripped the Colt's that he had put there the night before. Then he allowed one eye to open, and he scanned the camp.

The fire had burned down to a pile of embers, and Little Bee was gone. So were all the trappings that he had given the boy.

Creed opened the other eye and looked in the direction of Nimbus and the mule. No mule either.

So the kid lit out in the dark, thought Creed. Not real smart, but pretty bold. He moved and was given a reminder of his tussle with Little Bee the day before. Tough kid.

Creed sat up gingerly and took a closer look for Little Bee. Yes, he was gone, and he had taken the mule—and Branch's rifle. Well, I guess I'll be riding alone after all, thought Creed. But what was it that woke me up? he wondered. The kid leaving? Probably. Do I stop him? Why bother? Before he could formulate an answer to that question, he heard an owl hoot in a nearby oak tree, which made him recall the hawk screeching at him, and he was reminded of his promise to Little Bee's mother. He won't get far in the dark, he thought. I'll go looking for him after sunrise. He started to lie down again, but he stopped when he caught sight of something out of the corner of his eye. He turned his head and strained to see in the darkness. What's that? he wondered.

Downstream from the camp, a giant sphere of silvery white light, something akin to the full moon, bounced like a lopsided ball among the trees, almost as if it were ricocheting from one tree to the next.

What on earth is that? wondered Creed, as he bolted upright again, the Colt's still in his hand. In the next instant, he was on his feet and moving toward the eerie glow, wondering if someone was out there carrying a lantern. No, not a lantern, he thought. Lanterns glow yellow, not white.

Nimbus whinnied and danced nervously at his tether.

Creed halted. That light sure has him spooked, he thought. "Easy, Nimbus," he said softly to reassure the Appaloosa, but not to alert whoever or whatever it was that was making that light. "Easy, boy." He walked over to the horse and stroked his neck, all the time watching the light on the horizon. "Do you know what it is?" he asked the stallion. "I sure don't." He watched it another few seconds, then said, "But I'm sure going to find out."

Creed picked his way along the creek bank toward the light, but he didn't seem to get any closer to it. As he moved, it moved. What the hell? he wondered. He continued to follow it for some distance, but after half an hour of walking, he could still draw no closer than the original distance between him and the light; he gave up the chase and started back to camp, occasionally looking back over his shoulder to see if the light followed. It did.

When he got back to the camp, Creed found the mule tied up to the tree next to Nimbus. Little Bee was sitting beside the campfire that was now burning brightly. He was wrapped in a blanket, shivering, although it was quite warm, and the kid was staring at the ball of light behind Creed.

The Texan turned around for another look at the strange glow. "Do you know what that is?" he asked, waving the revolver at the light.

Little Bee didn't answer.

Creed studied the boy and saw the fear of the supernatural in his face. "Have you ever seen anything like that in these parts before?" he asked. When the boy didn't answer again, he said, "No, I guess not. You're a stranger here, too." He looked up at the light and thought he could see it changing shape, mutating from a ball to an oval then becoming elongated, with short beams extending from it like two arms and two legs but no head. "I can't say that I've ever seen a ghost before," he said, "but maybe I've seen one now."

Panic seized Little Bee. He grabbed Creed's leg and clung to it like a small child would hold on to a parent in the presence of something frightening.

Damn! why did I have to say ghost? he wondered. Poor kid is scared to death. Then another thought crossed his mind. "That's your mother's spirit out there," he said. "I think she's trying to tell you something, Little Bee. I think she's unhappy because you tried to run off like you did."

"No!" cried the boy. "It's old Hezekiah! He's come to get me because I took his scalp!"

That was a thought that hadn't entered Creed's mind. Hezekiah Branch, a bogeyman. At least he was to Little Bee. "No, it's not old Hezekiah," said Creed. "It's your mother's spirit. I just know it's her."

"No, it's him!"

"No, it's not," said Creed, pulling the boy into a standing position and looking him straight in the eye now. He remained bent over to let the kid see him better, and he held on to Little Bee's arms as the light of the campfire washed eerily over their faces. "It's your mother. I think she's unhappy with both of us, Little Bee. You, for running off like you did, and me, because when I woke up and found you gone, I was glad that I wouldn't have to take you to find your Uncle Hum down in the Choctaw Nation."

Little Bee studied Creed's face and realized that he was quite serious. "Do you really think it's Mama's spirit out there, Mr. Creed?" His eyes shifted back to the light.

"Yes, I do," said Creed, as he too looked sideways at the light. "I think it's her, and I think the only way her spirit's going to find peace is for you to promise to stick with me until we can find your Uncle Hum and for me to keep the promise that I made to her before she died."

"Do you think that will work?" asked Little Bee, his gaze fixed on the light now.

"It's worth a try," said Creed. He released the kid's arms and straightened up, and both of them turned to face the light directly.

Little Bee swallowed hard, then said, "Mama, I promise to go with Mr. Creed to find Uncle Hum. I promise, Mama. I swear it. I promise."

"I promise, too," said Creed solemnly. "I will keep my promise to you, Martha Doak. I will take Little Bee with me, and together we'll find his Uncle Hum." For good measure, he added, "No matter how long it takes."

The arm and leg beams of the light slowly withdrew into the body of the glow as it re-formed into an oval and then a ball. As soon as the transformation was complete, it danced upward, then from side to side. Up and down it went again, then it vanished as if someone had blown out a lantern.

"I guess she's satisfied for now," said Creed. "What do you think, kid?"

Little Bee was too scared to think of too much, except to say, "I think we ought to get out of here, Mr. Creed."

Creed glanced around warily, and suddenly an icy chill ran up and down his spine as if his vertabrae were so many piano keys being tickled by the bony fingers of the Grim Reaper. His shoulders scrunched together with a shiver. Then he said, "I think you're right, kid. Let's get moving."

5

The day dawned into another spring beauty. The sun was bright and warm, and a soft breeze blew up from the southwest. A good day for a leisurely ride in the open air.

After breaking camp and hitting the road, Creed and Little Bee crossed one creek a half mile from the stream where they had passed the night, then came to another three miles farther down the road. They stopped there to let Nimbus and the mule drink. The man and the boy ate strips of jerky for their breakfast.

"You said that you and your mother ran off about a week ago?" queried Creed between bites.

"Yes, sir, that's right," said Little Bee. He swallowed a half-chewed bite of meat, then continued to answer Creed's question. "Eight days back. Mama waited till old Hezekiah got himself all liquored up on corn and fell to snoring the night away, then we took all we could carry on our backs and lit out. We walked all night to get away. Mama thought we was heading east for Missouri like she planned, but we must've got turned around somehow 'cause when the sun come up we was almost to Salina. We hid out for the day, then started out again that night. Mama figured since we was already going south that we might as well keep going that way. So we did for two more nights when we come to the big river. Mr. Vann said it was the Grand River. We was getting powerful hungry by then, and that's when we smelled the smoke from Mr. Vann's house across the river. We swum across and found his house. He and Miz Vann took us in and fed us, and they told us that old Hezekiah come by there earlier that day looking for us. Mr. Vann said old Hezekiah headed on south toward Fort Gibson, so Mama decided we should go on back north. Mr. Vann said that the Texas Road was right outside his door and it would take us to Kansas. He gave us some food, and we lit out for Kansas the next evening because Mama wasn't sure we could let ourselves be seen by just anybody just yet. We was sleeping in that creek bottom where you come across us when old Hezekiah catched up to us yesterday."

"You say Mr. Vann's farm is three days south of there?" asked Creed.

"Yes, sir, three days, but Mama and me was on foot. I suppose it's closer on horseback."

Creed nodded in agreement with Little Bee's supposition. "Was there anything else along the way? I mean, any other farms or towns or anything like that?"

"Just one place that we saw for sure. Not too far south of here, as a matter of fact, Mr. Creed. It looked like a store, or something like that, and a plantation. There was a big log house there, and a barn and some pens and coops beside it. Mama and me stopped there to see if we couldn't get a bite of food. The man there—his name was Mr. Hawk. Cherokee man, I think. He gave us some corn mush, then we moved on."

"How far south was this place?"

"We come across it the night before old Hezekiah catched us yesterday," said Little Bee. "Early on that night, right around sundown."

"Good," said Creed. "Then we'll be coming to it soon. Well, we'd best be moving on now."

They mounted up, crossed the creek, then rode high ground for the next six miles until they came to Hudson's Crossing on the Neosho River, a few miles above where it merged with the Spring River to form the Grand River. They forded the river before noon, and two miles on the other side, they passed the weed-shrouded ruins of a plantation and trading post. Creed thought that this might be the place that Little Bee had mentioned earlier, but he concluded that it wasn't because this place was lifeless. He wondered what had happened here that such a fine homestead should be deserted and disintegrating. Had anybody been around to tell him, he would have learned that the place had an interesting and tragic history that was common to much of the Cherokee Nation, if not the entire Indian Territory.

Alfred Hudson had come to the Cherokee Nation from Georgia

with his Cherokee wife in the 1830s, bringing their slaves as well, and they had built a first-class farm and trading post on the creek that bore his name. During the war, the Union Army had occupied his home and confiscated all his livestock. The Federal commander allowed Hudson to move his family and personal possessions—but not his slaves, who were freed—to safety in Kansas, and as soon as the Hudsons had departed, he ordered the destruction of everything on the plantation except the house and trading post, sparing those buildings because he was residing in the Hudson home and his officers were quartered in the store. After the soldiers moved farther south, Hudson tried to return to his property, but as soon as his presence was discovered by the Keetoowah Society, a clandestine organization of full-blood Cherokees who opposed slavery and who thought to rid their nation of the peculiar institution by eliminating the slaveholders, Hudson was murdered by night-riders, and the house and trading post were vandalized.

Leaving the Hudson plantation behind them, Creed and Little Bee crossed another twelve miles of prairie before they came to the place that Little Bee had recollected earlier in the day as the one that resembled a store and working plantation. Just as the boy had said, it had one large frame building that appeared to be a business of some kind—an inn or a hotel, thought Creed, from the size of it—and the house was made of logs, as were the barn, corn crib, and shelters for chickens, hogs, cows, and horses. Two chestnut geldings, one distinctively marked by long white stockings on its left feet, were tied to one of the four hitching posts in front of the store. Both were saddled and had droppings piled behind them that appeared to be several hours old, which made Creed think that their owners had been visiting inside for a good part of the day, which probably meant that alcohol was being served there. In spite of that possibility, Creed decided to stop and rest there for a while—for the night, if lodging were available—and maybe get a hot, home-cooked meal, too. He and Little Bee rode up to an unoccupied hitching post, climbed down from their mounts, tethered Nimbus and the mule, then walked up the steps that led to the open door. Creed entered first.

Much as Creed suspected, the establishment was a tavern, Hawk's Tavern now, which had been originally constructed by a company of Cherokee Home Guards as a barracks during the war because of a large freshwater spring on the property and the site's militarily strategic proximity to the Texas Road, the main thoroughfare through the Cherokee Nation from Fort Scott, Kansas, to Fort Gibson on the Arkansas River.

Serving in that company was Second Lieutenant Alexander Hawk, who recognized the potential of the place as a stopover for travelers and a store for the people of the area when they returned to reclaim their lands after peace and order were restored. Hawk claimed the property after the war, but instead of living in the tavern, he built the log house for his family—new wife, Jane, and baby daughter, Lydia. The Hawks were mixed-bloods, but young Alex hadn't ever been a slaveholder, which was the only reason the Keetoowahs let him go about his business.

The tavern was divided into two sections: one was the sleeping quarters, a bunkhouse, for guests; and the other was the store-saloon-lobby. The bunkhouse was double the size of the store. Hawk maintained a small inventory of dry goods for sale behind a long plank counter that occupied one quadrant of the room. A handmade table and four chairs were placed to one side of the fireplace that was built into one end of the building. This end of the room was the saloon, although the manufacture and sale of alcoholic spirits for anything other than medicinal purposes was illegal in the Indian Nations. The remainder of the room was primarily open space.

The only occupants of the tavern when Creed and Little Bee entered the place were two men seated at the table. One was swarthy with long, black hair that covered his ears, and the other was pale with shaggy, blond hair that curled over his ears and down his neck. Both were drinking from a stoneware jug that sat in the middle of the table. They wore the butternut-colored coats of Confederate soldiers, but neither bore any insignia. They gave Creed a cursory glance, then glared at Little Bee through glassy eyes.

Creed did the polite thing by tipping his hat and saying, "Afternoon, gents."

"Niggers ain't allowed in here," said the light-skinned man. "Leave him outside with the other animals."

"Are you the owner of this establishment?" asked Creed, forcing himself to smile.

"Don't make no difference who I am," said the blond fellow. "Niggers still ain't allowed in here."

"This boy is Choctaw," said Creed.

"No, he ain't," said the other man. "He's a nigger. We seen him in here two nights ago with his nigger maw. They was begging food from Hawk."

"That's right," said the lighter man. "White man named Branch came through here yesterday looking for the woman and the boy. Said she was his squaw and had run off with the boy. You ain't Branch, so what are you doing with the boy?"

"I'm looking after him for his mother," said Creed.

"Not likely, friend," said the darker man.

Creed's anger flared at the insinuation that he was lying, but he controlled himself, as he grinned big and said, "What's your name, friend?" directing the question at the darker fellow.

"What's it to you?" asked the blond man.

"Well, nothing," said Creed with a slight snicker, "but I always like to know the name of a man before I go to stomping him into the ground."

"It's King," said the dark man, coming to his feet. "Ed King from Missouri, and where I come from, I usually do the stomping, friend."

"You know, Little Bee," said Creed, tilting, but not turning, his head to the side to address the boy, "the problem with drinking liquor is it makes you stupid, and right there is a fine example of what I'm talking about." As he spoke, he casually unbuttoned his coat with his left hand. "Mr. King over there doesn't realize that right now we're not anywhere near where he comes from in Missouri."

"Oh, a smart-ass, eh?" mumbled King. He reached inside his coat and pulled out a Bowie knife. "Let's just see how smart you really are, mister." He started to stagger across the twenty feet that separated him from Creed.

Damn! thought Creed. Not another dumb bastard with a knife. He pulled back the coat flap with his left hand and drew the Colt's with his right, all in one smooth motion. Cocking the revolver in the next instant, he brought the gun to bear at King, holding it at arm's length. "Hold your ground, Mr. King," he said loudly and firmly, but without shouting, "or I will hold it for you. Permanently. I am from Texas, sir, and I can kill you in the wink of a cat's eye, if I have to."

King wasn't so drunk that he didn't recognize the .44-caliber pistol staring its deadly eye at him. He stopped halfway across the room.

Creed heard footsteps behind him. He moved to his right, away from the doorway, pulling Little Bee with him, so he could see who it was that was approaching from outside, while he kept an eye on King at the same time.

"What's going on here?" asked a thin gent with a wisp of a black mustache and a sparse beard. His brown eyes shifted to King. "Ed, what are doing with that knife?" He stepped into the room and saw Creed. "And who are you, mister, and what are you gonna do with that gun?"

"Are you a friend of Mr. King there, sir?" asked Creed.

"I am not. I am Alexander Hawk, and this is my tavern. Now I repeat, sir, who are you and what are you gonna do with that gun?"

"My name is Slate Creed, Mr. Hawk, and I'm not going to do anything with this gun as long as Mr. King there doesn't do anything stupid with that Bowie he's holding."

"You heard him, Ed," said Hawk. "Put that knife away and he won't shoot you." When King didn't respond quickly enough for him, Hawk shouted, "Put it away, Ed, or I'll get my shotgun and shoot you myself!"

King replaced the knife in its sheath inside his waistband and said, "That nigger-lover brought that nigger brat in here, Hawk. I was just trying to get him out of here."

"Well, it looks like this gent was about to remove you instead," said Hawk. "Which ain't that bad of an idea. Why don't you and Harry take your jug and get on out of here? I've had my fill of you two for one day."

"You got no call to treat us like that, Hawk," said King, acting the injured party. "Corn and me are your best customers."

"And my worst when you're drinking," said Hawk. "Now go on and get out of here, Ed King. You, too, Harry Corn. And don't come back until you're both sober again. Do you hear me?"

Corn staggered to his feet and said, "We ain't the ones who brought a nigger in here, Hawk. You got no call to treat us this way. We ain't done you no hurt."

Hawk stepped over to the table, picked up the jug, and thrust it at Corn. "Go on, Harry. Take your whiskey and get out of here before you two do something we'll all regret later."

Corn took the jug, glared at Creed, and said, "Come on, Ed. Let's git, like he says. We can take care of the nigger-lover some other time."

"You hear that, nigger-lover?" grunted King. "We'll take care of you some other time."

"Shut up, Ed," said Hawk, "and get out of here."

Creed made no reply. He just kept his gun trained on them. King and Corn left.

Creed moved to the door to watch them mount up and ride away, glad to see them go. As soon as they were out of sight, he put his gun back inside his waistband, turned to Hawk, and said, "My apologies, Mr. Hawk. I did not come here with the intent of starting any trouble."

"No need to apologize to me, Mr. Creed," said Hawk. "Those two have been trouble ever since they started coming here."

"Who are they?" asked Creed.

"King is a Cherokee," said Hawk. "Mixed-blood. Corn is a white. Both of them are bushwhackers from Missouri. They're hiding from the law up there for what they done during the war. They've been hanging on here since the war ended. Occasionally, they ride out of here and are gone for two, three weeks at a time. I guess they ride back to Missouri to rob and kill somebody, then they come back here to escape the Missouri law. Leastways, every time they come back they've got fresh cash on them and several new jugs of whiskey."

"Will they be back?" asked Creed. "Soon, I mean."

"No, they'll stay away until you're gone," said Hawk. He looked at Little Bee for the first time. "Welcome back, Little Bee. Where's your mother?"

"She's dead," said the boy, glaring at the innkeeper.

Hawk's face twisted with concern and confusion. "Dead?" he queried. "How?"

"You ought to know," said Little Bee angrily. "You're the one who told old Hezekiah we was here and where we was going."

"Old Hezekiah?" asked Hawk. "Who's that?"

"Hezekiah Branch was the man they were running from," said Creed. "He killed the boy's mother yesterday."

"And Mr. Creed killed old Hezekiah," said Little Bee. "Didn't you, Mr. Creed?"

Hawk looked askance at Creed, and the Texan explained, "Do you recall how that fellow King was coming at me with that Bowie of his just a few minutes back?"

"Yes, of course."

"Well, Branch tried the same thing," said Creed, "but he didn't listen to me when I tried to warn him off. He's buried by the first creek on this road after you cross into the Quapaw lands. So's the boy's mother."

"I see," said Hawk, accepting Creed's explanation at face value. "So you brought the boy here to us?"

"Not exactly," said Creed. Then he related how he had promised Martha Doak to take her son to her brother in the Choctaw Nation.

"And you intend to keep that promise?" asked Hawk.

"Yes, sir, I do," said Creed.

"Well, I wish you luck, Mr. Creed. The Choctaw Nation is a big place, and finding one man could be difficult. Especially when you have so little information about him. I don't know if Armstrong's Academy is even there any longer. I think the Choctaws took it over for something. That's about all I can tell you about it."

"Well, it's a start," said Creed. "I promised the boy's mother that I'd find her brother, and I will, no matter how long it takes."

Hawk studied Creed's face, then said, "Yes, sir. I believe you will." Then thinking to change the subject, he said, "So what brought you into my tavern this afternoon, Mr. Creed?"

"I was hoping to get a hot meal," said the Texan, "and maybe a bed for the night. For me and the boy."

"Yes, of course," said Hawk. "You can sleep in the back, and Little Bee can sleep in the barn."

Creed smiled and said, "I don't think you understood, Mr. Hawk. I said I would like a bed for me, and I'd like one for Little Bee as well."

"Yes, sir, I heard you. He can—"

Creed sighed and interjected, "Mr. Hawk, Little Bee will have a bed in the back with me. That's one bed for me, and one bed for him." He pulled a silver dollar from his coin pocket in his pants and slapped it on the counter. "Now do you understand me, sir?"

"But he's a nigger, Mr. Creed," said Hawk, as if that made all the difference in the world.

The placidity of conviction relaxed Creed's facial features as his gaze met Hawk's eye-to-eye, and he said, "No, sir, he's not. He's a boy. A human being just like you and me. He's more white and Choctaw than he is Negro." Seeing that this wasn't getting through to Hawk's brain, he added, "And I'm almost half Cherokee and Choctaw myself. What about you, Mr. Hawk? How much Indian blood have you got?"

"Half," he said.

"So what does that make you, Mr. Hawk? Half white or half Indian? And does it really make a difference?"

Hawk thought for a second, then said, "No, sir, I suspect it doesn't make a difference." He picked up the silver cartwheel and added, "A bed for you, Mr. Creed, and a bed for Little Bee. Yes, sir." Then looking down at Little Bee, he smiled and said, "Mrs. Hawk will be glad to see you again, son. I believe she's serving molasses with the cornbread tonight." He looked back up at Creed. "You can wash up out back and join us in our home for supper, sir. I'll tell my woman to set two more places."

Creed nodded and said, "We'd be honored, sir."

6

The Hawks proved to be most hospitable hosts, considering the conditions that Creed had seen in the Indian Nations thus far. Since leaving the Fort Scott area in Kansas, he had seen much in the way of wild game: deer, raccoons, rabbits, geese, ducks, even a panther and a bear, but he noted very few stray cattle or roving swine in the countryside. More than that, the only habitations that he'd seen were some Indian huts clustered here and there in the Treaty Party Addition of the Cherokee Nation. Below there, in the Quapaw lands, he'd seen dozens of burned out farms, their stone chimneys standing as grim monuments to the now destitute families that had lived and laughed and loved within the walls of homes that war had turned to ashes. Littering the roadside were the skeletons of cows, horses, and hogs; the remains of broken wagons; the discarded possessions of refugees fleeing a war zone; and graves, hundreds of recent graves.

Recollecting the number of cemeteries that he had seen along the way, Creed felt shame for not erecting some sort of marker for Martha Doak. At the breakfast table the next morning, he told the Hawks about Martha's final resting place, then asked them to see that a headstone was placed over her. He paid them five dollars for the job, and they promised to take care of it. Creed wrote down an epitaph to be carved into the stone:

MARTHA DOAK
Mother
Killed by H. Branch
March 18, 1866

39

As an afterthought, Creed asked them to put a marker over Branch's grave, and he wrote an epitaph for it, too:

HEZEKIAH BRANCH
Womankiller
March 18, 1866

With that bit of business out of the way, Creed asked where he could find the nearest lawman so he could report the killing of Martha Doak and the subsequent killing of Hezekiah Branch. Hawk explained that no civil elections had been held in the Cherokee Nation since 1861 and from the early days of the war most of the districts had been without civilian law enforcement, that the Army—Union or Confederate, depending on which one was in control of the neighborhood—was the only law and neither of them was very adept at keeping the peace. If Creed wanted to tell a lawman about the deaths, then he would have to ride down to Fort Gibson to do it.

"But," said Hawk, "if I was you, I'd let it go. I'd put it behind me and get on with living. If I was you, that's what I'd do. Once we get some law and order and government around these parts again, I'll see that their deaths are put in the records. You can count on it. You just put it behind you, and let me take care of it."

Creed accepted the advice and finished the excellent food that Mrs. Hawk had prepared for them.

Although they weren't much better off than other people in the Cherokee Nation, the Hawks had gone all out to feed Creed and Little Bee, serving them a decent spread of cornbread and butter with sorghum molasses, pork steaks, and beans for supper, and an equally delicious breakfast of scrambled eggs and cornmeal mush sweetened with honey. Both repasts were washed down with fresh, sweet buttermilk from the family milch cow. The visitors had eaten like kings, and immediately after the morning meal, Creed and Little Bee bade the Hawks farewell and continued their southwesterly journey along the Texas Road.

The day was another beauty for traveling. For the most part, the trail that they traveled passed through grassy prairie, and occasionally a creek had to be forded. Always, the Grand River was to their left.

Throughout the ride, Creed recalled the events of the past two

days and nights. In less than forty-eight hours, he had killed a
man who had killed a woman; he'd seen a ghost, or at least he
thought the spooky light was the spirit of Martha Doak; he'd
taken a young boy into his charge; and he'd come close to
killing another man because the sonofabitch had insulted him
and threatened him with a knife. Every one of these incidents
troubled him. He didn't like killing, even when the victim
had left him no option. He was angry with himself because
he hadn't reacted quickly enough to save Martha Doak's life.
He was distressed to be responsible for the welfare of Little Bee
Doak, feeling that he wasn't capable of giving the boy the proper
care, attention, and direction. And an uneasiness over the episode
with King and Corn at Hawk's Tavern continued to haunt him, as
if he'd left something unfinished that would have to be concluded
later, but under more difficult circumstances, with even more tragic
results.

But most disturbing of all was the phantom light that he and
Little Bee had seen the night before. Was it really Martha Doak's
ghost like he'd told Little Bee? Was it a spirit at all? After the kid
had gone to sleep the night before at the tavern, he'd mentioned
the sighting to Alex and Jane Hawk, and they told him that they'd
heard tales about a spirit wandering that part of the countryside
for some years now. According to the legend, an irate squaw
cut off her husband's head after a nasty fight, then she hid it to
continue his punishment in the spirit world. Until the two parts
were reunited, the body would have to wander endlessly in search
of the head. Nice story, thought Creed, but he was still uneasy
over seeing the spooky light. It was as if it had intruded on his
own soul, refusing to permit him peace until he had fulfilled his
promise to Martha Doak. On the other hand, he tried to convince
himself that it was his duty, his Texan's honor to keep his word
to the dying woman, and it was this sense of integrity that was
his true conscience, not some ghostly glow dictating to him in
the dark.

At one point, near midafternoon, they came to a signpost beside
the road that indicated that the town of Salina was seven miles to
the east, Fort Gibson was forty miles south, and a place called
Alberty's Store was also south of there. Creed considered turning
off the trail there for Salina, thinking that it was a community
that probably had an inn of some kind where they could spend
the night comfortably, but Little Bee reassured him that the other

settlement, Alberty's Store, was closer and it was ahead of them on this very road. "Why should we ride all the way to Salina," said Little Bee, "then have to come back here tomorrow when there's a place down this road a piece where we can probably stop for the night?" The kid's logic registered with Creed, and they rode on, moving into the region generally known as the Three Forks because of the convergence of the Grand, Verdigris, and Arkansas Rivers just south of there, in the vicinity of Fort Gibson.

The settlement of the Three Forks country had begun as early as 1802, when Major Jean Pierre Chouteau induced the Osage Indians to move there from the Missouri River basin. Having an exclusive right to trade with the Osage, Chouteau established a trading post at Le Grand Saline, which eventually became the town of Salina. Two decades later, after the first contingents of Cherokees arrived from the East to start up their new nation in western Arkansas, war broke out between the two tribes, and the result was the Osages lost their Three Forks lands by treaty in 1825. Three years later, the territory was given to the Western Cherokees as a portion of their permanent home and as a new home for those Cherokees and Creeks in the East who wished to sell their lands to the government and move to the new lands in the West.

Several Eastern Cherokee families decided to take advantage of the opportunity that was given to them in the 1828 treaty, which allowed them to sell out and move away before the land-hungry, bigoted, white citizens and their equally bigoted government of Georgia drove them away without any compensation for their property. Among those choosing to leave were John Alberty, Sr., and his sons, Moses and John Alberty, Jr., from Hightower. They made the long journey with several dozen other families and arrived in the new land in 1830. The elder John settled in Illinois District with his son, John, and Moses opted to put down new roots in Neosho District along the Emigrant Road to Texas where it crossed Pryor Creek. The Alberty clan became part of the political faction in the Cherokee Nation that would be known as the Old Settlers.

Moses and his wife Sallie had seven children and twenty-five slaves when they left Georgia. They were blessed with two more sons after settling on Pryor Creek, just two and a half miles above its confluence with Grand River. In time, the Albertys built a bigger and better plantation than they had owned in the East.

As their sons grew to maturity, Moses gave each one a section of land for his own. The children married well: Nancy, the eldest, married Bluford West, who became a precinct superintendent and the first circuit court judge from their district; John and William married sisters, Jennie and Musidora Rogers respectively, whose Aunt Tiana had been Sam Houston's Cherokee wife; Delilah married Eli Harlan, the great-grandson of the Ghigau, the legendary Beloved Woman of the Cherokees; and Amelia married Thomas Lewis Rider, who was a great-great-grandson of the Ghigau. William West Alberty became known as an opulent and influential merchant with a store at Flat Rock.

But this was all before the war, which changed everything except the familial ties that bind so tightly in times of distress and need.

Moses's sons, John, William, and Bluford, served as officers in the Cherokee units that supported the Confederacy early in the war. John was a second lieutenant in the second regiment of Cherokee Mounted Volunteers; Bluford commanded Company I in Stand Watie's regiment of Cherokee Mounted Rifles; and William was the captain of Company F in Colonel John Drew's regiment of volunteers. They rode off to defend the only mode of living that they had ever known, but while they were absent, that way of life was swept away with the multiple defeats suffered by the very forces that they led. When they came home at the war's end, they discovered that everything had changed. Their parents were older and becoming decrepit, their once thriving plantations were overgrown with weeds, and their stock was all gone, including their slaves. Not all was lost, however. They still had the land, and they still had the will to survive.

In the Fifteenth Cherokee Treaty that was concluded at Fort Gibson on February 14, 1833, the United States government agreed to erect and equip four blacksmith shops, one wagon-maker shop, and eight patent railway corn mills for the Cherokees. This same provison, or one similar to it, appeared in many subsequent treaties between the United States and several Indian tribes, but unless the Indians forced the issue, the government was slow to keep its end of the bargain. The mills and shops were gradually set up, and almost always an enterprising fellow or two, people like Alex Hawk, would build a trading post, a general store, or a tavern nearby in order to accommodate the hunters, trappers, travelers, and settlers in the vicinity. Sometimes a permanent church would follow, and then would come a school. Thus, a town might be born. If nothing more, the few businesses formed the nucleus of a rural community with a radial stretch of five, six, even seven or eight miles, depending on the topography of the immediate area.

The Alberty settlement, designated on the maps as Alberty's Store because of William's business, had been the benefactor of one of those government mills and a blacksmith shop, and this had given the settlement the congeniality of a town. But that was before the war. The mill, the store, and the blacksmith shop had all failed to survive the conflict, thanks to raiders from both sides who had also senselessly destroyed most of the farms that dotted the landscape around the junction of Pryor Creek and the Texas Road. Only the presence and elderly condition of Moses and Sallie Alberty, both now in the eighth decade of their lives, had saved the main house from fire. It was to this home that the Alberty sons returned in 1865 to begin rebuilding their lives.

The first part of the settlement that Creed and Little Bee saw was the main farm that belonged to Moses and Sallie. It was a fine-looking residence, with an L-shaped, two-story frame building that had been painted within the past year and that had two chimneys. Behind the home were a stone spring house, a stone well, a log barn, and piles of ashes that had been slave quarters. Orchards flanked the buildings, and more than one hundred fruit trees—peaches, plums, pears, and apples—were just beginning to bud. Creed couldn't help thinking how much it reminded him of Glengarry, his own home back in Texas. With a touch of homesickness saddening him, Creed led Little Bee past the farm and across Pryor Creek to William Alberty's place.

Outwardly, Alberty's Store appeared to be no different than hundreds of other rudimentary settlements throughout the Nations. William and his brothers had rebuilt the store, a house for him and his wife Nancy, a barn, a corral, some pigpens, a chicken coop, a smokehouse, and a root cellar. They had also recovered the tools from the old blacksmith shop and had built a new one. In Creed's estimation, this settlement wasn't all that different from Hawk's Tavern, and to his chagrin, the similarities between the two outposts went further than their physical characteristics.

"Aw, hell," groused Creed, as he and Little Bee rode up to one of the store's two hitching rails. Tied at the other were the same two horses that had been tied up in front of Hawk's Tavern the day before.

"King and Corn?" queried Little Bee.

"Sure does look that way," said Creed, pointing to the horse with the white stockings on one side and recalling how he'd thought that he'd left something unfinished with those two the day before. Maybe they'll be sober today, he thought and hoped.

"What are you gonna do?" asked the boy.

Creed sighed, slouched in the saddle, and said, "I'm tired. I'm hungry. And I'm thirsty. And I suspect you are, too. So we're going in there to see about taking care of those things." He straightened up. "Come on. Let's go."

They dismounted, tied up their animals, then cautiously stepped up the four stairs to the porch on the front of the store. The door was open. They walked in. The room appeared to be almost identical to the one at Hawk's, with two exceptions—it contained more canned and bottled goods behind the sales counter, and it had a table for measuring and cutting cloth. The fireplace was in the same spot, and the table and chairs for loungers and card players were in the same location. And Ed King and Harry Corn were sitting there with the same whiskey jug between them. Creed had to wonder if he and Little Bee hadn't ridden in a circle and were once again at Hawk's. Convincing him that they hadn't been a couple of dogs chasing their tails all day was the presence of William Alberty behind the sales counter instead of young Hawk.

"Well, lookey here, King," said Harry Corn. "It's that nigger-lover from up to Hawk's."

"Why, I believe you're right, Harry," said King. "That is you, ain't it, nigger-lover?"

Creed decided it would be best to ignore them and hope that they weren't so drunk that they'd try something foolish again. He nudged Little Bee in the direction of the counter, and he addressed Alberty. "Good afternoon, sir," he said. "I'm Slate Creed, and this is Little Bee Doak. We're on our way to the Choctaw Nation to find the boy's family. Is it possible to get a hot meal and a place to sleep the night?"

Alberty was a tall, skinny man with a bushy, white mustache, weak chin, large ears, salt and pepper hair, and brown eyes. He wore a collarless white shirt, green suspenders that held up his homespun brown trousers, and black sleeve garters. He leaned on his palms on the counter and said, "I'm Will Alberty. I own this place. You can sit to table with me and my family, and we've got a room in the back of the store for sleeping." He eyed Creed's clothing, then added, "It'll cost you, though."

Creed dug a silver dollar out of his trousers coin pocket and placed it on the countertop. "Will that cover it, Mr. Alberty?" he asked with a friendly smile.

Alberty reached for the money, picked it up, examined it for authenticity, then said with a congenial grin, "More than enough, Mr. Creed."

"Hey, Captain Alberty," said Corn. "You ain't letting that nigger-lover stay here, are you?"

"That's right, Captain," said King. "That kid's a nigger."

Alberty cast a study on Little Bee's features.

"He's a mixed-blood," said Creed quickly. "So am I."

"He's a mixed-blood all right," sneered Corn. "Nigger and Injun, and that makes him a nigger."

Creed turned slowly until he faced the pair, then said, "I thought we'd settled this up to Hawk's yesterday."

Both men stood up and spread their coats open to show Creed that they had Bowie knives *and* revolvers this time, and that they'd drunk enough whiskey to make them braver and dumber than they really were.

"You got the drop on me yesterday, Creed," said King. "But you ain't gonna do it today. There's two of us, and only one of you, and today you're gonna be the one to ride on. So you and the nigger boy can just move on now."

"That's right," said Corn. "You just move on, but you can leave that big stud and that mule out there as a way of thanking us for not killing you." He moved his right hand closer to the six-gun tucked inside his waistband.

The Choctaw warrior in Creed was awakened—his face became as unreadable as that of a masked executioner. Without another word, without waiting for either Corn or King to make the first move, he pulled back the flap of his coat with his left hand, drew his Colt's with his right, brought the revolver to bear on Corn, cocked the hammer, and fired.

Will Alberty ducked behind the counter.

Little Bee jumped under the cutting table for protection.

The whiskey and the suddenness of Creed's attack froze King and Corn. Before either could move an inch, Creed's ball struck Corn just below his right clavicle, sending him staggering backward against his chair, which he toppled over. The outlaw landed on his back, with the wind knocked out of him for the moment.

As Corn gasped for breath, Creed shifted his aim at King, but the second villain, thinking that Creed had killed his companion, bolted for the open door. The Texan tried to draw a bead on him, pulled back on the hammer again, and fired, but the shot missed the target, ricocheting off a corner of the fireplace before lodging in the log wall. King leapt through the doorway, over the steps and landed on the ground, falling in a heap, which was all that saved him from being struck by Creed's third shot.

Corn gathered his wits enough to realize that he was shot, but not so seriously that he couldn't pull his gun and fire wildly at Creed.

Hearing the report of Corn's revolver, Creed turned his attention from King who had scrambled to his feet. He wheeled toward Corn, and dropped to one knee. He saw Corn propped up on his left elbow, the pistol in his right hand aimed shakily in Creed's general direction, blood dripping from his back where the ball had exited, hate twisting his face.

"Dirty son of a bitch!" swore the outlaw as he cocked his Remington again. He spoke his last words. "I'm gonna kill you for this."

Creed took careful aim and fired.

The Texan's ball tore into Corn's chest just to the right of his sternum. Because of the angle of the shot, it missed the breastbone and ripped through Corn's heart and left lung. The impact jolted the outlaw, causing his right arm to jerk upward as he pulled the trigger of his gun, firing harmlessly into the roof above Creed.

Corn's eyes glassed over, and a death sigh huffed from his mouth. He slumped onto his back. Dead.

Black powder smoke filled the room. Nobody moved until the sound of a horse's hooves beating a frantic retreat down the road intruded on the silence.

Creed stood up and turned around in time to see King riding his distinctively marked horse across the creek as if the Grim Reaper were close on his tail. He watched him until he was out of sight, then he turned back into the store and walked over to Corn's body. He stood over it, feeling no more remorse than he'd felt on that day long ago when he was a teenager and he'd shot a rabid skunk that had gotten into the chicken coop at Glengarry.

7

The sound of gunfire coming from the store brought all the Alberty men who had heard it on the run, weapons in hand, ready to defend their property against any outsider. Right behind them were their teenage sons, and beyond them the smaller boys who had escaped their mothers' clutches or had ignored their cries to stay at home.

Will Alberty, being in the store already, was the first to react. He stood up and surveyed the scene before him.

Little Bee crawled out from under the cutting table. Creed was standing over the bloody dead body of Harry Corn. The acrid odor of gun smoke hung in the air. The shouts of his relations filled the air.

What the hell happened here? Alberty asked himself. He knew Corn and King for what they were: two Missouri desperadoes with a penchant for making trouble. One or both of them getting killed was no reason for real concern. But this stranger? he wondered. Who is he? He said his name is Creed, and he looks like a friendly, peaceable sort. But he just up and killed Harry Corn. Of course, Corn and King did challenge him.

Before he could think or do anything more, Alberty was hailed from outside. "Will, you all right in there?" The caller was his brother Bluford, known within the family by his initials.

"I'm all right, B.W.," answered Will.

The exchange awakened Creed to the situation. He looked at the storekeeper, wondering if he posed a threat. Seeing Alberty standing calmly behind the counter, much as he had done before the affray had begun, he turned his attention to the doorway.

48

Through it, he could see Bluford Alberty, a younger version of
Will, with a shotgun in his hands, and to his right stood John
Alberty, also holding a scattergun, the image of his brothers
with the exception that his face was hidden behind a long, gray
beard. Beyond them were some teenage lads, one of them with a
revolver in his hand. Creed looked back to Will and said, "I sure
hope this man wasn't related to you or any of those fellows out
there, Mr. Alberty."

"No, sir, he wasn't," said Alberty.

"Just the same," said Creed, "I apologize for the ruckus."

"I can't see that you had much other choice in the matter, Mr.
Creed," said Alberty.

"I appreciate you seeing it that way, Mr. Alberty. Do you think
you might tell that to those boys out there before one of them
mistakes me for a deer?"

"Certainly," said Alberty. He came out from behind the counter
and went to the doorway. "It's all right, B.W., John. You can put
your guns down. It's all over."

"What happened in there?" asked John.

"Harry Corn's been killed," said Will.

"I saw Ed King riding out of here lickety-split," said B.W. "Did
he do it?"

"No, another fellow did," said Will. "He's still in here, but
it's all right. Corn and King challenged him, and he took them
up on it. Corn lost, and King ran off like his tail was on fire.
It's all right. You can come in." He stepped away from the
doorway.

Creed stuck his Colt's back inside his waistband and buttoned
up his coat as a way of showing the Albertys that he was no threat
to them.

Little Bee ran across the room and stood beside Creed. "Are
you all right, Mr. Creed?" he asked.

"I'm fine," said Creed. He smiled and asked, "What about you?
Are you all right?"

"I'm all right, I guess. I'm not hurt any." He looked down at
Corn's corpse. "Are you gonna scalp him, Mr. Creed?"

Creed frowned and said, "No, and neither are you."

Little Bee beamed up at Creed and said, "Don't worry, I won't.
But why ain't you gonna scalp him?"

Seeing the Albertys enter the store, Creed said, "Never mind
that now. We'll talk about that later."

"Mr. Creed," said Will, "these are my brothers." He introduced Bluford and John, then said, "I'm sorry, Mr. Creed, but I can't recall your first name."

"Slate. Slate Creed from Texas. As I said before all this happened, Mr. Alberty, I'm taking this lad to his uncle in the Choctaw Nation."

"Yes, I recall that," said Will. "But didn't you also say that you and the boy are mixed-bloods?"

"Yes, sir, I did. There's Choctaw on my mother's side and Cherokee on my father's. Little Bee here is a Choctaw on both sides. His father is a fellow named John Doak."

"John Doak," repeated Will. "I've heard of him. I believe he lives near Doaksville in the Choctaw Nation." Then a thought puzzled him. "If his father is John Doak, why are you taking him to his uncle?"

"Little Bee's mother was a half-blood," said Creed, making certain to keep solid eye-contact with Alberty. "Half Negro and half Choctaw."

The Albertys exchanged glances but said nothing about Little Bee's Negro blood. Instead, Bluford asked, "You say you're a mixed-blood, but you also say that you're from Texas. How do you come to be a mixed-blood from Texas?"

"My grandfathers came from back East right after Texas won independence from Mexico. They moved to Texas instead of moving to this country," explained Creed. "My Grandfather Dougald figured that as long as we lived in the United States that our family would always be treated like outcasts because of our Cherokee blood and that, no matter what land the government gave us to live on, eventually the government would want to take it back and give it to white settlers. So he moved to Texas where he thought he would be left alone, which he was because in Texas a man holds on to what's his—at the point of a gun if he needs to—and once folks see that he's willing to die for his land, they usually leave him be. My Grandfather Hawk McConnell went along with my Grandfather Dougald, but he preferred the old ways of the Choctaw over the ways of white men. A few years before the war he got tired of being away from his people, so he moved to the Choctaw Nation, and I haven't seen him since."

The Albertys listened politely, nodding at the appropriate times and exchanging looks occasionally. When Creed finished, they seemed satisfied that he was what he said he was, but they still had questions about Little Bee.

"This boy," said Bluford, "why is he with you and not with his mother?"

"His mother's dead," said Creed. Then he related the tragedy of two days earlier.

"Hezekiah Branch," said Will. "I knew him. He was a bad sort. Worse than bad. He won't be mourned. I can assure you of that, Mr. Creed."

"It's too bad about the boy's mother," said John, "but—"

Creed knew what was coming next, and he didn't want to hear it. He interrupted Alberty, saying, "His name is Little Bee, Mr. Alberty, and he's got more Choctaw in him than he's got Negro and white put together. As far as I'm concerned, he's Choctaw."

"Mr. Creed has a point," said Bluford. "Many Seminoles have Negro ancestors, and we accept them as Seminoles without questioning their heritage." He looked down at Little Bee. "Why should we look at this boy any differently? I see him as a Choctaw. What about you, Will?"

"Yes, I do, too," said Will.

"So do I," said John.

"As I said earlier, Mr. Creed," said Will, "you and Little Bee can join my family for supper, and you can share the room in the back for the night."

John turned to a boy standing at the door. "Jake, see to Mr. Creed's horse and mule," he said.

"Aw, Pa," whined the youth. "Why do I have to do it? Today's my birthday. Why can't Mose do it?"

"You heard me, boy!" snapped John. "Now get to it!"

"Hold on, son," said Creed to the younger Alberty. He dug into his coin pocket, pulled out a silver dollar, then flipped it to the lad. "Happy birthday, Jake."

Jake snatched the coin out of the air, looked it over, then beamed at Creed. "Thanks, mister. Thanks a lot." He vanished through the doorway.

"You didn't have to do that, Mr. Creed," said John, "but thank you, all the same."

"So what was the trouble between you and Corn and King?" asked Bluford.

Creed related his experience of the previous day up at Hawk's Tavern, then said, "I'm beginning to think I made a mistake coming through the Nations, what with all the trouble I've had so far, and I've only been here for four days."

"You've been here four days," said Will, "and you've already killed two no-good men. You stay too long in the Nations, Mr. Creed, and there won't be any bad men left before long."

"I'll try to pace myself a little better from now on," said Creed dryly.

8

Before the sun set that evening, every Alberty within three miles knew about the shooting of Harry Corn by a Texan named Slate Creed, and they looked forward with morbid anticipation to viewing the dead man's corpse and meeting the gunman who had done the deed.

Early the next morning family members began arriving at Will Alberty's store. The first were Moses and Sallie, Will's parents.

The patriarch and matriarch of the Pryor Creek branch of the clan heard the news soon after the shooting, but instead of hurrying over to Will's then and there to see Corn's body and meet Creed, Moses remarked sagely that "the body will keep until morning. We will go over tomorrow and have a look-see." They rose before dawn, which was their habit anyway, did the morning chores, which was also their habit, but they skipped breakfast because, as Moses put it so Scotly, "We fed Will all those years he was growing up. It won't be hurting him none to be feeding us this morning."

Although the distance between their home and that of their son was only a quarter of a mile, Moses hitched up the mules to the family wagon to drive the short stretch. It wasn't that he was lazy. Far from it. He was merely thinking of his health. "No sense in getting our feet wet at this time of the year," he told Sallie. "Get all wet and get sick. We don't need it." They drove casually across the creek and parked the wagon in front of the store.

The old man, whose seventy-eighth birthday was less than a month away, helped his equally elderly wife climb down from the seat, not so much because he was a gentleman but more

so because of her advanced age. Both were white-haired, and
Moses had a long white beard as well. Although the weather
was quite mild, they wore long, heavy, black woolen overcoats.
A high-crown hat adorned Moses's head, and Sallie had a knitted
red scarf tied around her chin. They were met at the steps by their
storekeeper son.

"Morning, Pa," said Will.

"Where's Harry Corn's remains?" asked Moses, foregoing any
greeting and coming straight to the point of their visit. "We want
to look at him first, then Nannie can feed us some breakfast, and
we can meet the fellow 'hat shot Corn."

"He's in the corn crib," said Will with a sheepish grin.

Moses gave his son a sideways glance, and Sallie snickered at
the pun that Will obviously intended. "Seems fittin'," said the old
woman.

Will scratched the nape of his neck and said, "John and me
put him in there for the night so the wild varmints and the hogs
couldn't get to him." He led his parents around the store to the
log corn crib in the rear. "It was pretty slick how Creed killed
him. One ball in the shoulder, and the second one right through
his heart." He threw open the door to the empty crib for them to
see the body.

The corpse rested on a wide slab of wood with the head end
resting on a sawhorse and the foot end on the floor so that the
body was at an approximate forty-five degree angle in order to
make viewing it easier from the outside. Will had left Corn's
clothes on him. He'd tucked the dead man's hands inside the
waistband of his trousers, put his hat over his groin, and opened
his coat so onlookers could see the bullet holes in his chest.

"Looks like a good clean kill," said Moses quite clinically.

"First time I can recollect Harry Corn looking peaceful," said
Sallie. She turned her head aside and spat on the ground. "It
shoulda happened to him sooner. Too bad this Texas fellow didn't
get Ed King, too. Then we'd be all the better off around these
parts."

"There's no need to carry on so, Ma," said Moses. "You know
it ain't right to speak ill of the dead."

"Why not?" she argued. "We sure spoke plenty of ill about him
when he was alive. What difference does it make now? He's dead,
and he won't be missed."

"That much is certain," said Will.

"Well, I've seen enough," said Sallie. "Let's get to the house. I want me some coffee."

Will closed the door and followed his parents to the house where he introduced them to Creed and Little Bee over the breakfast table. The men shook hands, Creed bowed politely to Mrs. Alberty, and Little Bee nodded his greeting, choosing to remain silent in the presence of so many adults. Moses sat down ahead of everybody; although it was Will's home, it was the old man's way, the family's way, because he was the head of the clan. Will sat next. Creed held a chair for Sallie to sit on. Little Bee remained standing behind Creed.

"Well, thank you kindly, Mr. Creed," said the old woman. She eyed her husband and son as she added, "Manners are one thing that our people could learn from the whites."

Her statement struck Creed oddly. These people think of themselves as Indians, he thought, but they look and dress like whites. Or is it that they think of themselves as Cherokees in the same way that Mexicans consider themselves to be Mexicans instead of mixed-blood Indians? That must be it.

Little Bee was the last to sit.

The first words out of Moses Alberty's mouth questioned Creed's lineage and heritage. "What kind of name is Creed?" he asked directly.

"It's not so much a name as it is a reminder," said Creed.

"A reminder?" queried Moses. "What does that mean?"

"It means Creed isn't my real name, Mr. Alberty," said the Texan, feeling that anything less than total honesty with these people would be considered an insult to them and a sign of weakness in him. "My real name is Cletus McConnell Slater."

"McConnell I recognize as a Scotsman's name," said Moses, eyeing Creed closely, "but this Slater. What's that? English?"

"No, sir," said Creed, smiling at the old man's inquisitiveness. "The Slaters are Scots. Clan MacDonald to be exact."

"We're Scots, too," said Moses. "I was born in Surry County, North Carolina. My mother—her name was Wa-Lee-Ah—she was a half-blood Cherokee, and my father was John Alvis Alberty. He was a full-blooded Scotsman. A Highlander. He fought for the British in the Revolution, then settled in America after the war. Sallie and me got married in 1810. Her daddy was the legendary Jack Wright—legendary because he was a foundling who was discovered washed up on a South Carolina beach, lashed to the broken spar of a ship, and was then adopted by a family named Wright. Sallie's ma was Jennie Crittenden, the granddaughter of a British officer named Major Downing and a full-blood woman of the Wolf clan."

Moses went on to tell Creed about his background in Georgia and how the state government had made it too hard for those people living as Cherokees to stay there, so he had sold out and moved to the new nation out West. "We came out in '30 and staked out this piece of land as our own. We worked a lot of land before the war. We ain't working so much now, but we will in due time. My brother John down to Going Snake District has fared better than us, I've heard. Probably because he seen fit to sidle up to John Ross instead of sticking with General Watie like we did. I don't know for sure." He scratched the back of his head. "What about you, son? You musta fought in the war. You said you was from Texas, didn't you?"

Will's wife, Nancy, poured coffee all around as Creed answered the old man's question.

"Yes, sir," said Creed, "I am from Texas, and I did fight in the war." As an afterthought, he added, "For the Confederacy."

Moses nodded his approval and said, "When my boy B.W. told us that you'd shot Harry Corn, he said you were a mixed-blood. Cherokee or Choctaw. Is that right?"

"Yes, sir, it is."

"Well, which is it?" asked Alberty. "Cherokee or Choctaw?"

"Well, both actually," said Creed.

"How can you belong to both tribes?" mumbled Sallie. "Who-ever heard of such a thing?"

"If that's so, how do you come to be from Texas?" asked the old man, ignoring his wife's questions as so much blathering. "It was my understanding that the Texicans killed off or chased off all the peaceful Indians on their side of the Red River long before the Mexican War. How did your people escape that?"

"Probably because we never told anybody that we didn't trust real well that some of our ancestors were already here when the Europeans started coming to America." Seeing that the Albertys were perplexed by his statement, Creed chuckled, then regaled them with his knowledge of his family background as much as he knew it.

9

The Slaters owed their feudatory allegiance to the chief of the MacDonald Clan, and the first freeman to bear the surname was Angus of Sleat, a man-at-arms in the service of his feudal lord, Donald MacDonald, Lord of the Isles.

At the bloody Battle of Harlaw in 1411, Angus lost the use of his blade hand when a foe's short sword slashed through most of the ligaments, tendons, and blood vessels of his right wrist. Dropping his shield, he wrapped the wound with a tartan swatch from his kilt and a rawhide thong from his leggings, picked up his sword with his left hand, and returned to the fight, screaming his anger and cutting a deadly swath through the stunned enemy forces. Seeing the valor in Angus, his chief cried out, "Behold! The Sleater! A real warrior!" The clansmen rallied around Angus and saved themselves from being annihilated by the forces of the Earl of Mar. The Lord of the Isles rewarded Angus for his heroics with a small parcel of land, a horse, two cows, and a bull, and designated him from that time forward as the one and only Sleater—*The* Sleater.

Angus's heir styled himself Donald mac Sleater as a matter of pride in his father and to make it known to everybody that he was the son of *The* Sleater. The distinction was important in that it set Donald above his first cousins in the clan.

Donald's only son Robert retained the surname, linking the words to MacSleater, and like his grandfather, he was a valiant warrior. For this reason, he was chosen to accompany the clan chief, John MacDonald, to the court of King Edward IV of England where the Scottish laird entered into a treaty with

57

the English monarch. When the other Scottish nobles learned about the conspiracy between Edward and John, they condemned MacDonald as a traitor, and Scotland's King James forced him to surrender his title to the Earldom of Ross. Although his role in the plot was minor, Robert MacSleater was denied his inheritance and his name, as King James said, "Since you are so enamoured with the English, you may go live among them, but if you choose to remain in this realm, you will no longer be known as Robert MacSleater but shall be forever known as Robert Slater the Traitor."

Nine decades later, Robert Slater's great-grandson Roderick redeemed the family name and regained royal favor when he fought valiantly for Queen Mary in the civil war of 1567. His reward was the return of his great-grandfather's lands from a cousin who had fought on the losing side. Roderick swore that the property would never again be taken from the Slaters. He determined that the lands would always remain in the family as long as one male member was on the winning side of any political dispute. To achieve this feat, the oldest son would ally himself with one side, and the next son in the line of inheritance would take the side of the opposition, no matter who that opposition might be or what it might represent.

Roderick's oath went unchallenged until 1715 when the Jacobite supporters of James the Pretender rose up in Scotland to drive the new king, Protestant and German George I, from England. When the Earl of Mar raised the standard against George and the English Whigs, one of the ten thousand men who responded to the call was Robert Slater, the younger brother of Fergus Slater, the heir-apparent to the family lands. Robert was killed at the Battle of Sheriffmuir, and the rebels were defeated. Just the same, the Slater lands were still in the family and in one piece.

Thirty years later, the Jacobites rose again under the banner of Prince Charles Edward Stuart. Fergus Slater's oldest son was named Robert for the brother who had given his life for the House of Stuart in 1715. The second son was Duncan, named for his mother's father. Fergus told his sons about Roderick's oath and how the family had met the challenge by dividing itself during the first rebellion against a Hanoverian king. He suggested that Robert remain loyal to the crown and that Duncan rally to Prince Charlie's standard. The nineteen-year-old Duncan eagerly marched off to war. After a few initial victories, the tide turned on the Jacobites, and their second rebellion was culminated at the Battle of Culloden Moor. Duncan was among the lucky who escaped the wrath of the English, but for six years he was an outlaw in his own land. Figuring he would never be free again in Scotland, he booked passage under an assumed name on a ship bound for Charleston, South Carolina, and landed there in 1752.

Once in America, Duncan Slater met a man named Knight who traded with the Indians who lived in the mountains to the west. The coastal plain was the hottest place that Duncan had ever known, and the oppressive heat convinced him that he would be wise to leave the area as soon as possible. He joined Knight in making the long journey to the cool uplands, but when it came time to make the return trip to Charleston, the merchant could do nothing to persuade Duncan to leave the foothills of the Blue Ridge Mountains. However, Knight did make Duncan a proposition before departing. "I've noticed," said Knight, "that you're quite proficient at dealing with the Cherokees, Duncan. It seems to me that you'd make a good partner. Suppose I return to Charleston for more goods, and you build a permanent post here in the hills? That way the Cherokees can come to us, instead of us wandering all over their nation looking for them. How does that sound to you?" Duncan was agreeable.

In a short time, loneliness took its toll on Duncan. A young Cherokee woman of the Long Hair clan named Quatie caught his eye. He fell in love with her and managed to convey his feelings to her through gentle words and kind attentions. When she didn't repulse him, he took it as a positive sign that she also had affectionate intentions toward him, and he let it be known to her family that he wanted her for his wife. They were agreeable to the match, and so was Quatie. They were married, and they set up housekeeping at the trading post.

Duncan bought a few cattle, a good horse, and a family of slaves—a man named Anthony, his wife Theodora, and their two small children, Cicero and Lavinia—and the Slaters took to the land. Quatie bore two sons and two daughters during the seven years of their marriage, then she died in the winter of 1761. Duncan's heart was broken, and he swore that he would never marry again, that he would devote his life to his plantation and the prosperity of his children.

Duncan's fortunes increased with the years. His herds grew. He acquired more land. He bought more slaves.

After Pontiac and his Indian allies were defeated in the mid-1760s, Duncan sold his mercantile business and devoted all his time to expanding his plantation and raising his four children. He imbued them with many values that he had brought with him from Scotland, especially the virtues of thrift and familial unity. And he taught them a few of his own principles, precepts that he had developed on his own, particularly that of his attitude toward slaves. "They're people," he told his children. "They have feelings just the same as everybody else in this world. The men love their women, and the women love their men, and they all love their children just as much as I love all of you. That's why I don't buy a field hand without buying his wife and children as well." Then he looked off in the distance and added, "It's not right to take a man away from his family."

He gave his slaves as much freedom as the laws allowed, and he treated them with kindness and dignity, making certain that no one ever abused them physically or verbally and giving them time to themselves for lives of their own by never working them after dark or on Sundays and holy days. He philosophized that "a healthy, well fed, happy slave will work harder for his master than one who is beaten with the lash. If he does turn out to be a shiftless, lazy lout, then he gets sold, which is no different a punishment than discharging a white man from the best work he'll ever know."

Living in the foothills of the Blue Ridge Mountains gave Duncan a sense of freedom akin to that of the lairds back in Scotland. In his own right, Duncan had become a feudal lord of sorts, a chief of the clan, only now it was the Slater clan, not the MacDonald clan. He had visions of being the founder of a great and long line that would one day be as powerful as any of those in Scotland, but before he developed too many thoughts and plans in that direction, the minutemen of Massachusetts refused to surrender their weapons to the Lobster Backs on Lexington Green, and Duncan was reminded that the tentacles of the English octopus could still reach out and dash his dreams into the infinite ether. As the war expanded and it became apparent to him that neutrality wouldn't be respected in this conflict, he recalled his own plight back in Scotland and decided that he would have to divide his sons in the same way that his father had forced a division between him and his brother.

"Lads," he said to John the older at twenty and William who was only sixteen, "this is a rebellion like the one I fought in

Scotland, and like my brother and me, you two must be on opposite sides so our land will remain in the hands of Slaters, no matter which side wins. John, you're the elder, you're my heir, so you have the right to choose because you have everything to lose and nothing to gain."

John, who had Loyalist tendencies, chose to remain true to the crown. William fell in with Francis Marion, the Swamp Fox, and fought the British, the Tories, and his brother who took up arms with other Loyalists. When the Americans won, John moved to Canada, as so many other die-hard Tories did, and William returned to his father's plantation.

Two years after the Colonies gained their undisputed independence from England, Duncan Slater was murdered by highwaymen on the road from Charleston where he had gone on a rare social call. William suspected that revenge rather than robbery was the motive. Although Duncan had declared himself neutral in the war, he did allow John to live at home and use some of the resources of the plantation for the Loyalist cause, and that was more than enough of a crime for many Patriots who wanted a pound of flesh for the wrongs done to them by the Tories and their British masters.

After Duncan's death, William inherited the plantation. He lived there like a white man, and he even married a white woman named Elizabeth Pace whom he'd met during the war. She proved to be too frail for childbearing, dying with her infant in 1787. William then married Isabel Gentry, the mixed-blood Cherokee daughter of blacksmith David Gentry and Mary Due. She bore him two sons, John and Dougald, and a daughter, Mary. Isabel died in 1794. William's third wife was a white woman named Rachel Harris, the mother of Duncan Slater, Jr.

William's third wife came from a crude but wealthy South Carolina family who owned hundreds of acres of land and several dozen slaves to work it. Rachel was mean, conniving, and deceptive. Although she knew that William was a mixed-blood Cherokee, she tried to hide the fact in social circles. Whenever her family or friends were coming for a visit, she would send John, Dougald, and Mary to stay with their mother's people in the mountains, presenting her son Duncan as William's only legitimate heir because he was white.

The absences of John, Dougald, and Mary from their father's plantation became longer and longer as they grew older. When

John turned fifteen, he decided that he'd had enough of his step-mother, and he chose to remain with an aunt and uncle in the Cherokee Nation. The following year Dougald did likewise, but Mary chose to remain in her father's home, living there to spite Rachel more than anything else.

Like many young Cherokee men, John Slater joined Andy Jackson's army and fought at the Battle of New Orleans. He died from a snake bite that spring of 1815, having never married.

Dougald Slater met Sallie McCoy in 1811. She was sixteen, pretty, and susceptible to the charms of the eighteen-year-old young man who was only two generations removed from Scotland. She was also a mixed-blood Cherokee whose parents were Daniel McCoy and Lucy Fields. Her uncle was George Fields, Dougald and John Slater's captain in the Cherokee auxiliary forces under General Jackson. Dougald and Sallie fell in love, but her parents refused to allow their marriage until she was eighteen. When Sallie did come of age, Dougald was off fighting the British in the War of 1812, so their wedding was delayed until 1816.

Mary Slater had an ordinary beauty that made attracting suitors difficult, but Rachel made it nearly impossible, discouraging any and all young men from courting her stepdaughter. As the years passed, Mary's fear that she might become an embittered old maid intensified. She ran off with and married the first man who asked. His name was Elijah Deaton from North Carolina, and he was six years younger than Mary. He thought he was marrying her for her money, but he was wrong. Rachel saw to it that Mary received nothing from her father's estate.

Rachel also convinced William to remove Dougald from his will because Dougald had married another mixed-blood. Duncan, she said, should be his only heir because he was white and had married a white girl. Old and frail and not in the best of spirits, William succumbed to her wishes, named Duncan as the sole beneficiary in his will, then died with a broken heart because he had forsaken his other children who he thought had forsaken him.

Dougald and Sallie lived in the Cherokee Nation for several years after they married, but when the Cherokee Treaty of 1828 was made, they sold out and moved, not to the Cherokee Nation West, but to Mississippi where they bought land on the border of the Choctaw Nation. It was there that Dougald met Hawk McConnell and befriended him.

As far as their neighbors outside the Choctaw Nation knew, the Slaters were whites, and they were treated accordingly. The McConnells and the other Choctaws knew differently, but they didn't mind the Slaters passing themselves off as whites because they understood the reasons behind this deception. Who could blame them for wanting to escape persecution?

Two events finally convinced Dougald Slater and Hawk McConnell to leave the United States and seek new homes elsewhere. Sallie Slater died in 1837, and that same year the federal government began rounding up all Indians in the East and moving them west of the Mississippi River. Dougald sold his land again, then helped Hawk McConnell and his family escape the soldiers. They took their families to Texas, where they carved yet another home out of the wilderness.

10

"Grandpa Dougald built a new plantation in Lavaca County," said Creed. "He called it Glengarry after his grandfather's home in Scotland." A faraway look crept into his eyes. "It's one of the most beautiful plantations in Texas." Realizing that he was waxing nostalgic, he added, "Or at least it was until the war came along." He heaved an involuntary sigh, then was silent for a moment.

"I had a couple of uncles that I never knew," he continued hesitantly. "One died from an axe wound. He chopped himself in the foot, and the blood poisoning set in. Another was killed in the war with Mexico. My father was killed when I was five years old. My other three uncles, my ma's brothers, they moved to the Choctaw Nation the year before the war with Mexico started. That left my grandfathers to work the place pretty much by themselves until I was big enough to help. When I was, Grandfather Hawk went to live with his people in the Choctaw Nation. Then the war came, and I went off to fight. My brother Dent was the only one left to help Grandpa Dougald then. Grandpa died while I was away fighting for the South. My brother Dent was killed by outlaws last year while we were trailing a herd of cattle to New Orleans. My sister and her husband own Glengarry now."

"Why do they own it and you don't?" asked Moses.

"My grandfather left Glengarry to my brother Dent because he thought I'd been killed at Shiloh," said Creed, "and Dent died without leaving a will."

"I don't understand," said Moses. "You were his brother. Why didn't you get the plantation or at least part of it?"

Creed sighed heavily again. "Well, they weren't sure that I'd been killed at Shiloh, and just in case that I did come back alive, my grandfather disowned me so Dent could have the place without any trouble. I guess that's what he was thinking when he did it. Disowned me, I mean."

"I still don't understand," said Moses persistently.

"I don't know that I understand it either, Mr. Alberty," said Creed. "All I know for certain is that I'm here in the Cherokee Nation and my sister and her husband have Glengarry all legal like."

"What about your ma?" asked Sallie Alberty. "Is she still living down to Texas?"

"Yes, she is, ma'am," said Creed, "but not at Glengarry. She remarried the year before the war with the North and moved to a place near Fort Worth. After I deliver Little Bee to his Uncle Hum, that's where I'm headed. I heard from my sister that my mother and her husband are having troubles and they need help. I thought I'd go see what I can do for them."

The older Albertys looked at each other, nodded their approval of Creed's words, then returned their attention to him. "This other grandfather of yours, the Choctaw one?" queried Moses Alberty. "What happened to him?"

"I don't know for certain," said Creed. "He left us back in '55. We never heard from him after that." He shrugged, then added, "I don't even know if he made it to the Choctaw Nation or not. Most likely, he's dead now. I guess he'd be about seventy or so now." He smiled. "Of course, Grandfather Hawk was a tough old bird, if you know what I mean. He probably made it to the Choctaw Nation, and he's probably living there with one of my uncles. Leastways, I'd like to think so until I find out different for certain."

"But you don't know exactly where your uncles settled in the Choctaw Nation?" asked Sallie.

"No, ma'am, I don't," said Creed, "but I guess I'll ask around when Little Bee and I get down that way." He looked at the boy and said, "And I suppose we'd best be getting along that way pretty soon."

"You said this boy is mostly Choctaw," said Moses, "but he was a slave. I heard stories about slaves who ran away and hid in the swamps back in Georgia and Florida, and they were taken in by the Creeks who lived there because they didn't want to live

like white men the way some of their brothers were doing. The
runaways married among the Creeks, and now they are called
Seminoles. They have a nation west of here. Maybe the boy
would be better off if he lived among them."

"I promised his mother that I'd take him to his Uncle Hum in
the Choctaw Nation," said Creed. "A Texan can't go back on his
word, Mr. Alberty."

"Neither can a Cherokee," said Moses. He stood up, which was
the signal that the visit was concluded. "I think you are a good
man, Slate Creed." He offered his hand. "I wish you well in your
travels."

Creed stood up, too. He shook the old man's hand and said,
"Thank you, sir, and I hope you get your place back the way it
was before the war." He released Alberty's grip and turned to
Sallie. "Ma'am, it's been an honor to meet you."

Before she could respond, Bluford Alberty burst into the house
with a frightening announcement: "Ed King is back, and he's got
company."

Everybody except Moses looked at Creed. The patriarch cast
his view on his sons. "Will," he said, "this is your place, and Mr.
Creed is your guest. This is your affair. You go out there and tell
Ed King to ride on and leave this man in peace. B.W., you get a
rifle and back him up."

"Pa, there's six of them and only two of us," said Bluford.

"Are you yellow, B.W.?" asked Moses matter-of-factly.

Creed interrupted, hoping to save Bluford the trouble of answering and suffering any further embarrassment. "Mr. Alberty, this
is my fight," he said. "I'll deal with Ed King and whoever else
he might have out there. I'm from Texas, Mr. Alberty, and we
Texans don't let others fight for us, and we don't back down from
cowards like Ed King."

"But there's six of them, Mr. Creed," said B.W.

"Pa's right, Mr. Creed," said Will. "This is my affair. You are
my guest, and I won't let Ed King or anybody treat a guest of
mine like this." He turned to his brother and added, "B.W., you
can use my rifle."

"I can't let you do this," said Creed.

"Mr. Creed," said Will, "you can go out there if you want to
go out there, but my brother and I are going out there, too."

Creed saw that Will was adamant on the subject and that further
discussion was pointless. "All right," he said. "Let's go out there

together. My guns are still with my gear in your store. So could I borrow one from you, Mr. Alberty?"

"I'll get your guns for you, Mr. Creed," said Little Bee.

Creed grabbed the boy by the shoulder and said, "Not a good idea, son. King's liable to shoot you just because you're with me. You stay in here out of sight."

"The only other weapon I've got in the house is my shotgun," said Will.

"Ed King won't shoot me," said Nancy Alberty. "I'll fetch your guns from the store for you, Mr. Creed." Her tone implied emphatically that she would tolerate no argument from anybody, that she was going after Creed's six-shooters, and that was that. "If you'll excuse me, please?" Nobody spoke as she exited the house and headed for the rear of the store.

As soon as his wife was gone, Will said, "I guess I'd better get my shotgun. Come on, B.W."

The two Alberty brothers left the kitchen and went to the bedroom where Will kept his weapons beside the bed, a custom of many Cherokees since the earliest days. They returned with a single-shot Remington 10-gauge and an Enfield Rifle Musket.

"Nancy's coming back," said Moses from the back porch. He moved inside. "It looks like she found your guns, Mr. Creed. She's walking with her hands tucked under her apron. Probably got your guns under there." He was right.

Nancy stepped onto the porch with her hands under her apron just like Moses had said, and when she entered the kitchen, she removed them and produced Creed's revolvers. "Here you go, Mr. Creed," she said, presenting them to him.

Creed took the six-guns, checked to make certain that the caps were in place on five of the six nipples, then said, "All right, Mr. Alberty. Let's go see what King wants here this morning."

Creed led the Alberty brothers through the house to the front porch. He stepped outside to find King perched atop his oddly marked horse a good twenty yards away. With the outlaw were five other men, all mounted and trying to appear menacing as each held a rifle in one hand and the reins to his horse in the other. King had no weapons visible. Creed stopped at the top of the steps, and the Albertys flanked him.

"This ain't your affair, Will, B.W.," said King. "We've come for Creed. He killed Harry, and we aim to make him pay for it."

"You ain't the law, Ed King," said Will Alberty.

"Neither are you, Will," said King. "So just stand aside, and we'll finish this business and be on our way."

Will leveled his shotgun in the direction of the riders, and Bluford did likewise with the Enfield. "No, sir!" said Will angrily. "This man is my guest, and you will not harm him. Now ride on out of here, Ed King, or there will be hell to pay."

King snickered, snorted, and said, "You ain't got the sand, Will. Neither do you, B.W."

Creed raised both Colt's and took careful aim at King's face. "But I do," said Creed. "Ever see what a .44 ball does to a man's face, Mr. King?" He cocked the hammers.

Before King could react, one of his comrades to his left lowered his rifle to shoot Creed. He was too slow, and his aim was poor.

Without flinching and barely shifting his eyes and right hand, Creed aimed and fired at the villain. Bang!

The man flipped over backward off his horse, simultaneously dropping his rifle and screaming. He landed on his back, grabbed at his face, and began rolling in the dirt. His horse reared up and whinnied in fright, stumbled, and nearly fell before righting itself again.

The report of Creed's six-gun, the victim's painful scream, and the animal's panic caused the mounts of the other outlaws to dance about wildly, preventing their riders from doing anything more than try to regain control of them. One man was thrown to the ground. Two others dropped their rifles.

Taking aim at King again, Creed shouted, "Last chance, Mr. King! Ride out now, or I will kill you in the next second!"

King spurred his horse and took flight. The one man who was able to stay in the saddle and hold on to his weapon was quick to follow him. The others threw up their hands in surrender. The wounded man continued to writhe in pain.

"Damn! you're quick!" said Will, looking at Creed in wide-eyed awe.

"Better see to the hurt man, Mr. Alberty," said Creed, without taking his eyes from the outlaws. "I'll watch the others while you do."

Will didn't move.

Moses stepped outside and said, "Don't just stand there like Lot's wife, Will. That man needs help."

Will still didn't move.

Sallie joined Moses. "You heard your pa," she said. "Get a move on, Will." She reached out and pushed him.

Will finally moved. "Here, Pa," he said, handing his shotgun to Moses. "Hold this for me."

Moses took the weapon and said, "Mr. Creed, you can be on your way now. My boys and me, we'll take care of this rabble. Go ahead. Take the boy and go."

Creed relaxed, lowered his revolvers, looked sideways at Moses, and said, "Yes, sir."

11

A half-day's ride down the Texas Road, Creed and Little Bee came to the farm of William and Hannah Vann on Brushy Creek, another tributary of the Grand River. Little Bee had told Creed about how he and his mother visited with the Vanns when they were running away from Hezekiah Branch. Creed figured that it wouldn't hurt any if he and the boy were to stop at their farm for a few minutes of rest and maybe a meal.

The Vanns took their surname from their former owners, the descendants of a white man named Avery Vann who married Margaret McSwain, a mixed-blood Cherokee of the Wolf Clan. Avery and Margaret had fifteen children: five sons and ten daughters.

Avery Vann was a slaveholder back in Georgia. He died before he was forced off his land during the Indian Removals of the 1830s. In his will, he left a young slave named William to his son David, who removed to the Cherokee Nation West with the Treaty Party of 1835.

In the new country, the Vanns established themselves in Flint District, where they raised cotton on the bottomlands and herded cattle on the hills. William, the slave, grew to manhood and was allowed to marry Hannah Chouteau, the daughter of Gyp and Martha Chouteau who were slaves that had belonged to Jean Pierre Chouteau, the first white settler in the area of the Three Forks.

When the War Between the States erupted, the Vanns fled to Texas, taking their slaves with them, until the Union army established some sort of order in Flint District. Upon their return,

70

David Vann was murdered by members of the Keetoowah Society, and his slaves were set free. William and Hannah packed up their meager possessions and their children and joined up with two other freedmen, Lige Rider and Bill Burgess, and settled on Brushy Creek.

In the short two years since their arrival, the three families had built log houses, barns, pens, and corn cribs, and they had planted and harvested two crops successfully. Having known freedom for only a scant time, they were still unsure of how to behave when whites and Cherokees came around, which explained why William Vann looked at Creed with such suspicion as the Texan and Little Bee Doak approached him that noon.

"That's Mr. Vann there," said Little Bee, pointing to the man standing behind the plow and oxen team in a small field beside the road.

Creed reined in Nimbus, and Little Bee did likewise with his mule. Wishing to stretch his legs and not wanting to show any disrespect to a potential host, the Texan dismounted as close as possible to Vann, then waited for the farmer to come to him. Little Bee also climbed down from the saddle.

Vann was a tall man, a little taller than Creed. He was well muscled, although he was narrow at the hips and shoulders. He had a broad, prominent nose set between high cheek bones. His strong jaw distracted the onlooker from his thick lips. From the deep, dark chocolate tone of his complexion and the rich, chestnut color of his eyes, Creed guessed correctly that this ex-slave had no whites or Indians in his ancestry, that Vann was a true son of Africa.

"Remember me, Mr. Vann?" asked Little Bee eagerly when the farmer walked up to the newcomers.

Vann smiled and said, "Sure, I do. You're Little Bee Doak, but when I saw you last, you was traveling with your mama. Don't tell me you done run off from her now."

Being forced to think of his mother brought tears to Little Bee's eyes and put a lump in his throat. He swallowed hard before saying, "She's dead, Mr. Vann."

"Dead?" queried Vann, his face twisting up with shock and dismay at the sad news.

"That's right," interceded Creed. "The man named Hezekiah Branch killed her."

Vann stared at Creed with eyes filled with disbelief and uncertainty. "Killed her?" he muttered.

"Yes, sir," said Little Bee, "but Mr. Creed shot old Hezekiah for it. Killed him dead, too." He beamed up at Creed with a touch of pride that bordered on familial.

Creed held out his hand to Vann and said, "Mr. Vann, I am Slate Creed."

Vann hesitated to accept the grip, but he finally realized that Creed was sincere with his introduction and shook hands with him. "Glad to meet you, sir," said Vann. Breaking the hold, he asked, "Is it true, Mr. Creed? What Little Bee said?"

"Yes, sir, it's true," said Creed. "I killed Branch because he killed Little Bee's mama. We buried them beside the creek where it happened. That was four days back."

"Mr. Creed came along just as old Hezekiah caught up to us, Mr. Vann," said Little Bee. "Old Hezekiah tried to kill Mr. Creed first, but Mr. Creed shot him instead."

Vann's brow furrowed in confusion. "I thought you said you killed old Branch?" he asked Creed.

Creed quickly explained how the tragic events of that day transpired, concluding his narrative by saying, "So Little Bee and I are on our way to the Choctaw Nation now to find his Uncle Hum."

"I see," said Vann. "That's right honorable of you, Mr. Creed. Ain't many white men who'd keep their word to a darky."

"Mr. Creed ain't white," said Little Bee. "He's Choctaw and Cherokee."

Creed could see that Vann was confused again. "I'm a Texan, Mr. Vann," he said, trying to clear up matters. "Some of my ancestors were Cherokees, and some were Choctaws, and some were Scotsmen. I don't know exactly what that makes me. I was born in Texas, and I guess that's all I consider myself to be. A Texan, and nothing more."

Vann nodded and said, "Yes, sir. That makes sense." He smiled and added, "Born in Texas, I guess that makes you a Texan, but are you a white Texan or a red Texan?"

"I'm just a Texan, Mr. Vann. With so many Indians and whites hanging on my family tree, where do I draw the line between them and declare myself to be white or red?"

The farmer pursed his lips, frowned with thought, then said, "I see what you mean now, Mr. Creed." He smiled and added, "I ain't got that problem. All my peoples come from Africa. We's Negro through and through."

"It's good that a man knows what he is," said Creed. "Let's him stand a little taller, I suppose."

"Yes, sir, it do," said Vann. "It sure do." He looked up at the sun, shaded his eyes, then announced, "Dinner time. Hannah be calling me soon." He glanced back at the Texan. "You and Little Bee is welcome to join us for dinner, Mr. Creed."

"I'd consider it an honor," said Creed.

"Me, too," said the boy.

Vann led them up to the two-room log house where he quickly explained the presence of Creed and Little Bee to his wife, then introduced her and their children: sons, Jim, William Junior, and Ben, and daughters, Rose and Lidion. All of the kids were younger than twelve, the youngest being two.

"Mighty handsome family you've got here, Mrs. Vann," said Creed. "You must be very proud."

"Thank you kindly, Mr. Creed," said Hannah. "I's sorry we ain't got much to eat except salt pork and beans and cornbread." Using potholders, she held the handle of a steaming kettle of pork and beans in one hand and a pan of hot cornbread, cut into neat squares, in the other. She set the food on the rough-hewn table near her husband's place.

Creed smiled, rubbed his belly, and said, "Sounds like a meal fit for a king, ma'am. It's an honor to sit at your table."

"Sit yourself down, Mr. Creed," said Vann, standing at the head of the table in front of his own chair, one of two covered with deerhide. He pointed to the other upholstered seat, which was situated to his right. Normally, it was at the foot of the table because it belonged to Hannah, but today it was Creed's chair. "Little Bee, you can sit here." He indicated one of the crude wooden chairs to his immediate left.

The guests sat, then Hannah and the children were seated. Vann remained standing for the moment. He bowed his head to say grace, and the others took their cue from him.

"O Lord, we thank You for this food we is about to eat," he said, "and we thank You for this house and this land that You is letting us work. We hopes that we been walking on the path of righteousness and that we is pleasing in Your sight. Today, we also wants to thank You for bringing Little Bee Doak back to us and for bringing Mr. Creed here, too. We knows You works in mysterious ways, Lord, and we hopes that we can see the Light that You shines for us each and every day and that we can do right by You, Lord, as You have done by us. Now we thank You again for this food, Lord. Amen."

Everybody else at the table said amen, but Vann did not sit down just yet. Nine pewter plates were stacked in front of him, as it was the custom in this household that the man dish up everybody's food. Vann took the ladle and the top plate and started portioning the pork and beans, passing the plate to Rose, the older daughter, who put a piece of cornbread on it before handing it to Creed who was the honored guest. Little Bee was the next to receive his dinner. Then Hannah. Then the children in the order of their ages, youngest to oldest. And finally the man of the house. No one ate or spoke until Vann was finished serving, had sat down, and had picked up his spoon. "Let's eat," he announced.

They dined quietly until Hannah said, "Mr. Creed, William say you is taking Little Bee down to the Choctaw Nation to find his uncle."

"Yes, ma'am, that's right," said Creed. "I promised his mother that I'd take him to his Uncle Hum in the Choctaw Nation. It was her last wish."

"Why you want to do that?" she asked.

"Hannah!" snapped her husband. "Mr. Creed already said he made the boy's mama a promise. He don't need to explain anything more than that."

Hannah lowered her eyes and said, "I didn't mean to be rude, Mr. Creed. I wasn't trying to dirty your honor or nothing. I was just wondering why you wants to drag Little Bee all over this country looking for his uncle when you could be leaving him here with us, and when you finds his uncle you could tell him where Little Bee is at, and he could come for him. That's all I was gonna get at, Mr. Creed."

"I thank you kindly for the offer, Mrs. Vann," said Creed, "but I promised his mother that I'd take him to his uncle."

"But it's so dangerous out there," said Hannah. "Little Bee would be safe here with us, and when you finds his uncle, you—"

Little Bee jumped in and said, "I want to go with Mr. Creed, ma'am." Then realizing that he might have offended the lady, he added, "I mean, I appreciate you all wanting to take me in and all, but Mr. Creed promised my mama, and I mean to hold him to his word."

"Mrs. Vann," said Creed, "I think I understand your concern for

Little Bee, but I don't think it would be right for me to leave him off with you kind folks. I know you could probably use his help around here, Mr. Vann, but I wouldn't be keeping my promise to his mother if I left him here."

"You is making this decision without giving it the proper time for thinking," said Vann.

"That's right," said Hannah. "Why don't you and Little Bee stay over the night and give it some real thinking, Mr. Creed?"

"I don't think that would be wise, Mrs. Vann," said Creed. "You see, I had some trouble yesterday with a couple of men back at Alberty's Store. I had to kill one of them, but the other one got away. He came back this morning with more men, and I had to shoot one of them."

"Shot him right in the face!" interjected Little Bee, who was all excited now. "You should've seen it, Mr. Vann! Broke his cheek and knocked out three of his teeth! Made a real mess of his face!"

"Is that a fact?" queried Vann.

"Yes, it is, Mr. Vann," said Creed. He sighed heavily, put his spoon on his plate, then added, "You see, this man doesn't like Negroes, and if he were to find Little Bee and me here with you folks, I fear that he'd do you and your family harm. Maybe not while we're here, but after we're gone. This man is no good, Mr. Vann. He's a bushwhacker, I've been told. In fact, I'd be on the lookout for him, if I were you. His name is Ed King, and he's—"

Hannah gasped, "Ed King?"

"Is you sure his name is Ed King?" asked Vann.

"Yes, I'm sure of it," said Creed. "Why? Do you know him?"

"I don't knows him, Mr. Creed," said Vann, "but I knows all about him and Harry Corn. Both bad apples, all right."

"Harry Corn is the man that Mr. Creed killed yesterday," said Little Bee.

"Is that a fact?" queried Vann.

"Yes, sir," said Creed.

"Then I believes you is right, Mr. Creed," said Vann. "You and Little Bee should be on your way as soon as possible. In fact, if I was you, I'd be getting myself out of the Cherokee Nation as fast as my horse could take me. You see, Mr. Creed, Ed King and that bunch he runs with is just what you was told they is. Bushwhackers. Killers. They shoots men in the back from hiding and for no more reason than they is black like me. I don't means to be rude, Mr. Creed, but—"

"Say no more, Mr. Vann," said Creed. "I understand completely. We thank you for the vittles, Mrs. Vann. The beans were mighty tasty. Come on, Little Bee. We'd better be going."

"Hold on there, Mr. Creed," said Hannah. "You haven't finished eating. We can't let you leave our table only half full. You sit yourself right there until you is done, and there's more if you wants it."

"Yes, ma'am," said Creed. He smiled and added, "Thank you kindly, ma'am."

12

Fort Gibson was established in 1824 as a deterrent to the wild, uncivilized Osage and other tribes of the Plains.

At the urging of Jean Pierre Chouteau, the Osage moved into the Three Forks region before Louisiana was purchased from France in 1803. They claimed exclusive hunting rights in the woodlands and prairies bordering the Grand, Verdigris, and Arkansas Rivers, and they resented the intrusions of other hunters, often challenging the interlopers to mortal combat whenever they came in contact with them, whether the intruders were white or Indian.

Without too much consultation with the Osage, the United States gave a large portion of their land to those Cherokees who were willing to leave their lands in the East and move to the West. As part of the Cherokee Treaty of 1817 and subsequent agreements between the United States and other Eastern Indian Nations, the federal authorities guaranteed the safety of all civilized tribesmen who immigrated to the new Indian Territory. The Army was to protect these immigrant Indians against the depredations of the Osage and other wild Plains Indians. To carry out this plan, the Army was to build cantonments and garrison them with soldiers who were to act as a buffer between the tribes.

The first of these forts was located on the Arkansas River and was known as Fort Smith. It was established in 1817, but it failed to stop the raids of the Osage on the more peaceful Cherokees. With the anticipation that more and more Eastern Indians would be removing to the territory, the Army sent Colonel Matthew Arbuckle and his 7th Infantry up the Arkansas to locate in the vicinity of the Three Forks the best possible site for a permanent military base. The primary prerequisite for the post was an excellent boat landing for the riverboats that would be bringing in supplies and people. Arbuckle learned that the very best place was already taken by Colonel Auguste Pierre Chouteau's trading post and settlement on the east bank of the Verdigris River a few miles above its confluence with the Arkansas. Forced to seek another locale, Arbuckle accepted Chouteau's suggestion that he might find a good place on the Grand River, which dumped its waters into the Arkansas only half a mile below the mouth of the Verdigris. The colonel directed his enlisted flatboatmen to return to the Arkansas, then to push up the Grand where a few miles upriver he found a wide ledge of shelving rock on the east bank which made a natural boat landing. The soldiers tied up their flatboats at this spot and began unloading their supplies, tents, tools, and other assorted baggage. Soon they were joined by another contingent from Fort Smith that had come overland with horses and oxen. Immediately, Arbuckle set his troops to work building Fort Gibson, which was named for Colonel George Gibson, a hero of the War of 1812 and the commander of the Army's commissary department.

Unlike Fort Smith, whose establishment failed to stop the Osages, Fort Gibson did achieve its goal; the presence of soldiers—and an attempt by the Cherokees to unite all the Eastern tribes against the Osages—worked to discourage the Osages from raiding their more peaceful neighbors. A treaty between the Cherokees and Osages was negotiated in 1825 in which the Osages agreed to leave the hunting grounds east of the Grand River to the newcomers from the East. Three years later the Osages agreed to withdraw farther west, and their lands in the Three Forks area were turned over to the Cherokees and Creeks who were then being forcibly removed from Alabama to the Indian territory west of the Mississippi. Colonel Chouteau sold his trading post on the Verdigris to the government, and it became known as the Creek Agency until the time came that the Cherokees were given the area and the Creeks moved farther south to establish a new agency.

Over the next three decades, Fort Gibson served as the training ground for many West Point graduates who were to become government leaders and generals during the Mexican War and the War Between the States. Among these were Winfield Scott,

Zachary Taylor, Robert E. Lee, George McClellan, Stephen Watts Kearney, Braxton Bragg, Albert Sidney Johnston, and Jefferson Davis. The post became the primary terminus for new arrivals to the Indian Nations, beginning with the Creeks in 1828. In succeeding years, more and more Creeks, then Choctaws, Chickasaws, and Cherokees, were deposited at Fort Gibson by steamboats, keelboats, flatboats, and bateaux, and from there they dispersed overland to their respective nations. These Eastern Indians came unarmed and unprepared to defend themselves against the wild tribesmen of the Plains, which made them dependent on the Army for protection. For that reason, many lingered in the area of the fort until they became acclimated to the weather conditions and adjusted to the emotional stress of relocation.

In 1857, the Army abandoned the post, and the Cherokees subdivided the land, platted a town, and started selling lots. The community of Keetoowah was still in its infancy when the War Between the States broke out and the Confederate Army possessed the fort. The Confederates didn't stay long because the Union Army, acting under the orders of General James P. Blunt, captured the fort on April 5, 1863. The Union commander, Colonel William A. Phillips, refurbished the dilapidated cantonment and renamed it Fort Blunt, for his superior back in Kansas.

After the Union forces took possession of the fort, it was surrounded by several thousand destitute Indian refugees and freedom-seeking slaves. They remained in sight of the fort for safety and for the food that was issued to them in small quantities. Some of them put in small crops under the protection of the guns of the fort. They would have gone farther away to their homes if not for the fear that they would be raided by predatory bands of bushwhacking guerrillas, both Union and Confederate, that ranged over the country indiscriminantly robbing and killing.

Although the war ended in the summer of 1865 with the surrender and disarming of the Indian regiments, the bushwhackers continued to menace the countryside, forcing peace-loving people to remain in the refugee camps around Fort Gibson. As many as seventeen thousand people crowded around the post through the winter of 1865–66, simply trying to survive until spring when they could return to their homes and begin rebuilding the lives that the recent conflict had all but destroyed. In their own way, some of these homeless were as dangerous as the outlaws roaming the hills and prairies. Fights and killings were almost daily occurrences;

theft was almost hourly, especially after dark when a thief could move about without being recognized.

Creed had been warned by the Albertys about the terrible conditions at Fort Gibson and was cautioned to avoid the post and continue southward to North Fork Town on the Canadian River. The danger from the refugees was of less concern to Creed than the fact that Fort Gibson was a military establishment and that he was wanted by the Army. Although it was likely that he would come into contact with the soldiers, he figured that none of them would have heard about him, and therefore they were unlikely to bother him. Even so, it was risky to go to Fort Gibson. Had there been another settlement on the Texas Road where he could purchase provisions for the next leg of his and Little Bee's journey to the Choctaw Nation, the Texan just might have accepted the Albertys' advice and bypassed the fort, but since no alternative place existed, he had no choice but to chance losing his freedom and ford the Grand River to Fort Gibson.

As soon as he and Little Bee were across the river, Creed asked the first man that they met to direct them to a local merchant. The fellow pointed to a large building a few hundred yards ahead on the south edge of the military grounds. Creed thanked him, and he and the boy rode ahead to the store.

Florian H. Nash was the post sutler. He'd come to Fort Gibson in '53 to work for William Denckla, but Denckla sold out to the firm of Shaw and Lanigan. After the Union Army regained possession of the fort in '63, Nash purchased the business from his employers and expanded it to fit some of the needs of the growing population of refugees—or at least those who had money. The storekeeper was a tall, thin man with a long, thick beard that covered his chin only. His gray eyes were separated by a broad, prominent nose, which was made all the more outstanding by a mouth that was little more than a slit between the thinnest lips.

When they entered Nash's place that afternoon, Creed and Little Bee found it full of people—mostly women, some children, and a few men—their ethnic circumstances revealed by their attire and, in some cases, by their complexions. The ladies occupied themselves with the prices of food, cloth, sewing thread, and the like; the men examined carpentry tools and farming implements. The kids huddled near the counter, wistfully eyeing the candy jars.

Although he employed three clerks, Nash still waited on customers. While he was helping two men—from the looks of them, a minister attired in a black frock coat, black tie, and a high, white collar, and an ex-slave wearing a Union Army foraging cap, light-blue trousers, a dark-blue coat that had no insignia or brass buttons, and Army-issue shoes—Nash spotted Creed and Little Bee at the door. More strangers just passing through, he thought. The man's probably a bushwhacker from Missouri who's just looking for trouble. Probably hasn't got more than a dollar to spend in here.

"I will take these, Mr. Nash," said the minister, holding up a pair of hammers and a crosscut handsaw. He was a thick-lipped, heavy-jowled, stout man in his late forties. A collar of black and gray whiskers hid a pair of chins and a fat neck. A wide-brim, low-crown straw hat covered his bald pate and shaded green eyes that had known the ecstasy of religious fervor.

"Yes, of course," said Nash, mildly embarrassed to be caught in reverie. "Very good, Reverend," he added with a faint smile.

"And I'll take those," said the former slave, pointing at a set of camp necessities: a blue speckleware cooking pot, a long-handled steel spoon, a blue speckleware coffee pot, a tin cup, a tin pie plate, a steel tablespoon, and a three-tined steel fork.

Nash's face turned sour as he shifted his view to the former soldier and said, "Yes, of course." When the buyer made no move to pick up the items he wanted, the merchant gathered them up begrudgingly and stomped to the counter to price them.

The minister and the ex-slave followed Nash.

Creed and Little Bee stepped up to the counter at the same time, unintentionally drawing attention to themselves.

"I'll be with you in a minute, sir," said Nash to Creed. He glanced down at Little Bee, then back at Creed as if he approved of something.

"I'm in no hurry, sir," said Creed.

Of course not, thought Nash, although he continued to appear pleased with Creed. He picked up a pencil and began writing a bill of sale for the minister.

Creed noticed that the ex-slave, a tall, wiry man with skin the color of rich topsoil, was looking down at Little Bee as if he were trying to determine who or what the boy's forebears might have been. Seeing the expression on the ex-soldier's face turn from curiosity to anger, Creed felt a warning raise the hackles on his spine from bottom to top. Damn! Creed thought. Now what? His eyes met the taller man's, and he recognized the hell-fire hate in them. He'd seen that look before—the previous autumn in Victoria, Texas, when he was caught up in events that were none of his doing. He was nearly lynched by a mob of Negro soldiers just because they thought he was as bigoted as his cellmate, the killer of a former slave and the real object of their rage. Thinking that he could head off trouble here and now with a show of force, Creed unbuttoned his coat to reveal the butt of his Colt's protruding from the waistband of his trousers.

The ex-soldier noted the weapon, then he spread his lips in a satanic grin as he also unbuttoned his coat, exposing the grips of a pair of Remington .44s sticking back-to-back out of his trousers. "You don't scare me none, white trash," he said in a tremulous bass that betrayed the agitation within him.

"I beg your pardon," said Creed evenly, his senses settling into the calm of impending combat.

"You heard me, white trash," said the ex-slave.

"What's this about, Mr. Tyler?" asked the minister, suddenly aware that something was amiss between Creed and his associate.

Nash looked up from his writing and saw the two men squared off with each other. Lord, no! he thought. A nigger and a Missouri bushwhacker! They're going to kill each other right here in my store. O Lord, no!

"Ain't much, Reverend," said Tyler. "We got us a white trash here who don't know that Mr. Lincoln done freed the slaves. That's all, sir."

Continuing to pinpoint his gaze on Tyler's eyes, Creed said, "So that's your problem, friend."

"No, it ain't my problem, white trash," said Tyler. "It's yours, and I got the solution to it right here." His hands started to move toward his guns.

Creed was quicker. Much quicker. He drew his Colt's, cocked it, and had it aimed at Tyler's nose, the deathly muzzle only a foot from the ex-slave's face, before Tyler could touch the handle of one of his six-shooters. "Don't do it, friend," he cautioned softly. In the next second, he realized that Tyler would heed the warning, and he said, "This boy with me is Little Bee Doak. His mother was a slave who was killed by the kind of man that you're imagining me to be, friend. I killed that sonofabitch for what he did to the boy's mother, and now I'm taking Little Bee to his uncle in the Choctaw Nation because that was his mother's last wish." He paused to make sure that his words had penetrated Tyler's senses. Assured by the change of the man's expression, he added, "Now you know my business, friend. Are you happy?"

The store fell silent as everybody's attention was focused on Creed and Tyler.

"There's no call for violence, sir," said the minister, stepping forward in the role of peacemaker. He huffed himself up and added, "I am the Reverend Mr. David Thayer, sir, late of Louisville, Kentucky; this is Mr. Britt Tyler, late of the 1st Kansas Colored Volunteers. I'm certain that Mr. Tyler meant no offense, sir."

"Reverend, you're either stupid or deaf," said Creed, annoyed by Thayer's patronizing tone. "Your friend here was just about to draw down on me because he thought I was some sort of Negro-hating white trash, and you say he meant no offense."

"You got no call to talk to the reverend like that," said Tyler defiantly. "He's a man of the cloth."

"That doesn't give him any right to insult my intelligence, Mr. Tyler," said Creed.

"I meant no offense, sir," said Thayer. He cleared his throat and added, "Would you mind lowering your weapon?"

"I will as soon as Mr. Tyler tells me that he'll mind his own business now," said Creed.

Tyler looked down at Little Bee and asked, "Is he telling true, son?"

"Mr. Creed wouldn't lie," said Little Bee. "He's a Choctaw warrior." Then for good measure—or so he thought—he added, "Just like me. I ain't no nigger like you."

Angered, Creed snapped around and growled, "What the hell's the matter with you, Little Bee? You've got no call to talk to this man like that. You've got no call to talk to anybody like that. Not anybody, you hear?"

Stunned by Creed's outburst, Little Bee cringed as if he expected to be struck about the head.

Tyler didn't know what to think. On the one hand, Creed had just chastised Little Bee for using abusive words, and on the other, the Texan had raised his voice and seemed to be ready to strike the boy. And what Little Bee had said also bothered him. He claimed to be Choctaw when Creed had just said that the boy's mother had been a slave. Which was it? What to do?

Thayer was as confused as Tyler. Here this young man had spoken to him disrespectfully, then he'd turned right around and told the boy to be respectful of a Negro. How odd.

"Gentlemen, please," said Nash. He aimed his words at Creed. "I don't want any trouble in my store."

Creed regained control of his anger, backed off a step, and uncocked his revolver, lowering it to waist level and pointing it at the floor. "Look, Mr. Tyler," he said, "Little Bee and I just came in here to get some provisions for our journey. We didn't come in here looking for trouble, so why don't you and the reverend there go about your business and leave us be?"

"I don't take orders from white trash," said Tyler.

Creed tightened his jaw, looked down at the floor, then slowly raised his view to Tyler's face again. "I'm from Texas, Mr. Tyler," he said, "and I can shoot you dead as quick as a cat can wink an eye. Now you either leave us be or that's exactly what I will do." To punctuate his statement, he brought the Colt's to bear on Tyler's face again.

Thayer stepped in front of Tyler and said, "You'll have to shoot me first, sir."

Creed cocked the six-gun and said, "All right, Reverend, if that's the way you want it."

"Reverend," said Tyler, looking over the minister's shoulder at Creed, "we'd better pay our bills and be on our way."

Nash took his cue and quoted the prices of their purchases, hoping to defuse the volatile situation.

Tyler dug out his money and paid for his items, and Thayer did the same.

Creed continued to hold his gun on the ex-slave and the minister until they started for the door. He uncocked it and replaced it in his waistband, but he continued to keep an eye on Tyler until he and the reverend were outside. Not until then did he turn to Nash and say, "I apologize for all that, sir. I meant no trouble when I came in here."

The other customers returned to what they were doing before the incident began.

"I thank you for restraining yourself, sir," said Nash, grateful for the return of normalcy to his store. "How may I help you?"

"In a second, sir," said Creed. He turned to Little Bee, took a deep breath, then let it out slowly and heavily. "I'm sorry for speaking to you in that tone, Little Bee. I had no right to raise my voice at you. I hope you'll forgive me."

The boy was stunned again, only this time it didn't hurt. "It's all right, Mr. Creed," he muttered. Then he was struck by a thought. "I'm sorry, too, Mr. Creed. I shouldn't have said those things to Mr. Tyler."

Creed smiled and patted the boy's shoulder. "Good," he said, then he turned back to Nash. "Now about those provisions we need."

13

Mr. Nash was relieved to hear that Creed was from Texas instead of Missouri or Arkansas. It seemed to him that every man from those two states who was now in Indian Territory had come there because he was dodging the law back home. For the most part, this was true, but exceptions were noted because not every male noncitizen in the Nations was from those two former slave states. Such as Creed.

"Could you tell me where I might find a place called Armstrong's down in the Choctaw Nation?" Creed asked Nash after he paid for the provisions that he had come there to buy.

"I believe you mean Armstrong's Academy," said Nash.

"Armstrong's Academy?" queried Creed, emphasizing the second word, wondering if he'd heard the storekeeper correctly.

"Yes, Academy," said Nash. "That was the name of one of the Choctaw schools before the war. It wasn't the only one, of course, but it was probably the best. The Choctaws took it over a couple of years back and moved their capital there. They changed the name of the place to Chahta Tamaha, which means Choctaw Town, of course."

"Where is it?" said Creed.

"Oh, yes," said Nash, laughing at himself for his omission. "It's south of here. In the Choctaw Nation. Down by Boggy Depot and Fort Washita. Down there somewhere. On the Blue River, I believe."

Creed grinned patiently and said, "How do I get there from here, Mr. Nash?"

"You ride south," said the storekeeper, as if Creed should have known that much already.

"Yes, sir. Of course, I do."

Finally realizing what Creed was getting at, Nash said, "Of course, you're a stranger in these parts. How silly of me, sir! You want to know how to get there, am I right?"

"Yes, sir," said Creed with a benevolent smile.

"Well, you ride south," said Nash, making a feeble attempt at humor. He laughed at his own joke, then seeing that it wasn't all that funny, he said, "You follow the road to North Fork Town, and from there you go to Perryville, or what's left of it, then to Boggy Depot. Once you get there, you should be able to find Chahta Tamaha. Somebody ought to be able to direct you from there."

"Thank you," said Creed, then he turned his attention to the supplies that he'd bought. "Give me a hand with this stuff, Little Bee." He picked up a twenty-pound sack of dried beans and the slab of bacon wrapped in cheesecloth and brown paper, and the boy picked up a ten-pound sack of flour. They carried the food outside where Creed tied a leather thong to the drawstrings of the two sacks and slung them over the back of Little Bee's mule. Little Bee put the bacon in a saddlebag, and they went back inside to get the remainder of their purchase.

"Mr. Creed," said Nash, as the Texan and his diminutive friend returned to the counter, "I'm wondering if you should be traveling all alone at this time."

"I'm not all alone," said Creed. He patted Little Bee on the shoulder and added, "I've got Little Bee to keep me company on the road."

"Yes, sir, of course, you do," said Nash, "but the roads are dangerous these days. What with so many Missouri and Arkansas bushwhackers hiding here in the Nations, one can never know when evil might befall one."

"Well, I appreciate your concern for us, Mr. Nash," said Creed, "but I think we'll be all right on the road. Right, Little Bee?"

"That's right, Mr. Creed," said the lad, smiling up at the Texan with love and respect in his eyes.

"It wasn't *your* safety that I was thinking about," said Nash. "It's Reverend Thayer and his family that I'm worried about, Mr. Creed."

Something was telling Creed that he shouldn't do it, but he couldn't help asking, "Reverend Thayer and his *family*?"

"Yes, sir. He has two daughters and a son traveling with him. I understand his wife passed away shortly before they left Louisville last fall. The Thayers are headed to Cherokee Village down by Fort Arbuckle in the Chickasaw Nation. That's just west of the Choctaw Nation. Reverend Thayer and his daughters will be opening a new school there in the fall."

"That's all well and good, Mr. Nash, but I'm in a bit of a hurry to find Little Bee's uncle and then be on my own way. I've got business to tend to down in Texas."

"Yes, of course, you do," said Nash, "but a peaceful man like Reverend Thayer, traveling with two young women and a teenage boy with only a nigger to protect them, is sure to become a victim of some band of bushwhackers along the way."

"What would Reverend Thayer have that a band of bushwhackers would want?" asked Creed.

"They have two covered wagons loaded with items that many people would pay for," said Nash, "and they have livestock. A Guernsey bull and three heifers, as well as the eight mules pulling their wagons. These are things worth killing for in the Nations, Mr. Creed." He paused to let that much sink into Creed's brain, then he added, "And, of course, there's the reverend's daughters. Neither of them are a hurt to the eyes, sir. Even if they weren't lookers, they're still women. Who knows what depravity bushwhackers are liable to stoop to?"

Nash was good at pouring guilt on a conscience. Already, Creed was imagining the worst for the Thayers, and the only one he'd met so far was the reverend. How much heavier would his soul become if he should hear sometime in the future that the Thayers had fallen prey to a band of bushwhackers and had suffered grievously, possibly losing everything, including their lives? How terrible would he feel if he heard this horrible news when he could have prevented such tragedy? He really didn't want to think about it.

"I was just thinking," said Nash, continuing, "that a man who is good with guns, a man like you, Mr. Creed, presuming your threats against the nigger were more than idle boasting—"

Creed frowned at Nash and interjected, "I believe, sir, his name is Tyler."

Nash flinched, then said, "Yes, of course, it is, but as I was saying, a man such as you, Mr. Creed, would provide the Thayers with much more protection than the nigger will."

Realizing that it would be useless to attempt changing Nash's prejudice toward Tyler, Creed sighed and said, "Mr. Tyler gave me every impression that he can handle himself adequately in a fight. I'm sure the Thayers will get along nicely without my help, Mr. Nash."

"I see," said Nash. "Well, if you change your mind—"

"I won't," said Creed with finality. Seeing that Nash had finally taken no for an answer, he asked, "Now, sir, could you tell me where I might find some lodging for Little Bee and me for the night?"

"We have no hotels here, Mr. Creed," said Nash a bit coldly, "but the Army does permit transients to keep their animals in the post corral for a night, and people are permitted to throw down a bedroll in the post barn or to camp nearby."

"Where would I find this corral and barn?"

"Just follow the Tahlequah Road," said Nash. Seeing that Creed didn't know which road was which, he added, "That's the road right out front. Just go east from here. The corral and barn are about half a mile down the road."

"Thank you, Mr. Nash," said Creed. "Good-day."

As he and Little Bee gathered up the rest of their provisions and loaded them on Nimbus and the mule, Creed noticed Thayer and Tyler going back into the store. Not wishing another confrontation with them, he and Little Bee mounted up and rode over to the post corral and barn.

Creed located the sergeant in charge of the post stables and made arrangements for their animals to be fed and kept in the yard for the night and for him and Little Bee to bed down in the barn. The sergeant showed them where they could sleep—a clean horse stall just inside the barn's front door—and advised Creed to keep all their valuables and supplies where they could be easily guarded. "Between the niggers and Injuns, I don't know which is the biggest bunch of thieves," said the soldier. Creed ignored the man, realizing that he could no more change this man's attitude than he could change Nash's. He decided it would be best to mind his own business and get out of Fort Gibson as soon as possible, at sunup the next morning.

As they unloaded their supplies in the stall, the two travelers soon discovered that they weren't the only occupants of the barn. Several spaces were occupied, some by whole families but most by lone men. At the other end of the building were two young women and a teenage boy. From the looks of them, they were sisters and brother. The Thayers? wondered Creed. Nash did say the minister had two daughters that were lookers and a teenage son. This is probably them. When he saw the parson and Tyler enter the barn through the rear entrance and approach the young women and the boy, he knew that he was right. Damn! he thought. I was hoping I'd never have to see those two again.

"There's the minister and Mr. Tyler," said Little Bee. "Do you think those are the minister's daughters? The ones Mr. Nash told us about?"

"I reckon so, Little Bee," said Creed, "but they're none of our concern. We'll be riding out of here first thing in the morning, leaving them far behind. Let's get us some food and then get a good night's sleep. All right?"

Little Bee was still looking at the two young women. Creed couldn't blame him; they were attractive. Both were tall and blonde, although the elder's hair was a shade darker than the younger's. Creed guessed their ages to be around twenty, give a year for the elder and take a year for the younger. He couldn't discern the exact color of their eyes—probably blue, he thought—from the distance that he was from them, but they did have the high cheekbones characteristic of many Indians. Maybe they're part Indian like me, he thought. Then he looked at their brother and changed that notion. He was shorter than both girls. He was blond like them, but he was round-faced with darker eyes and puffy cheeks. Where they were sleek and slender, he was stocky but not stout. He resembled their father, which they didn't.

"You know, Mr. Creed," said Little Bee, "Mr. Nash just might be right. Maybe we should travel with those folks."

Creed looked down at the boy, thinking Little Bee wasn't that much of a boy any longer, that he was more of a maturing youth now. He tried to remember what he was like at the same age, succeeded in recalling some of the feelings that he'd had in those days, then smiled inwardly, thinking, Yes, Little Bee is more than a boy now.

"I don't think so, son," said Creed. "Come on. Let's get Nimbus and the mule unsaddled and in the corral, then we'll find someone with a fire and get some of this grub into us." He headed for the nearest exit, leading Nimbus, but he didn't get to it soon enough.

"Mr. Creed?" called Reverend Thayer. "A word with you, sir? If I might?"

Now what? wondered Creed. He stopped and turned around to see Thayer approaching him. Tyler remained behind. At least I don't have to face him again, thought Creed. He bucked up a smile and said, "Sure, Reverend. Why not?"

Thayer smiled at Little Bee, stopped to pat him on the head, and said, "So you're a Choctaw. Isn't that nice?"

As grating as Thayer's patronization was, Little Bee was willing to overlook it because he knew the parson meant well. "Yes, sir," said the lad.

"Very good," said Thayer. He turned to Creed and said, "I was just speaking with Mr. Nash at the store—"

That's just great, thought Creed. Let me guess what you two talked about.

"—and he mentioned that you and the boy were traveling in the same direction that we are. He suggested that we might be wise to travel together as a matter of safety."

"Did he tell you that he also suggested the same thing to me, Reverend?" asked Creed.

"Yes, he did."

"Did he tell you what I thought of that idea, Reverend?"

"No, he didn't," said Thayer, "but I take it that you weren't very enthusiastic for the proposition."

"That's a polite way of putting it," said Creed.

As Creed and Thayer conversed, Tyler and the reverend's children came slowly closer until they were well within earshot. Tyler stepped forward of the Thayer siblings. "Mr. Creed," he said, "as much as I don't cotton to Rebs, I'm willing to forget all that for the time being, if you was to see your way clear to join us for the journey to Boggy Depot. Mind you now, I ain't asking for myself. I don't need you to help me protect these good folks on the road. I can do just fine without your help. It's for the reverend and his family that I'm asking. Reverend Thayer thinks we'll all sleep better if we gots another man riding with us. I tend to agree with him, but if it was up to me, I'd try finding somebody else instead of a Reb like you to ride with us."

"Mr. Tyler, I appreciate you laying your cards on the table like that," said Creed, "but the answer is still no. I'm in a hurry to get to Texas, but I have to find Little Bee's uncle first and see to it that Little Bee will be all right. Riding with you folks will only slow me down."

The older of the two daughters stepped forward and said, "That's a rather selfish attitude, sir."

"Down in Texas, ma'am," said Creed, "we call that minding one's own business."

Silence gripped the scene for a heartbeat before Thayer said apologetically, "My daughter meant no disrespect, Mr. Creed." Then realizing that introductions were in order, he quickly added, "This is my daughter Louise, and this other pretty young lady is my daughter Faye. And that handsome young man is my son Drake. Children, this is Mr. Creed from Texas."

"Pleased to meet you," said Creed.

Faye pranced ahead and offered her hand to the Texan, saying, "And I'm pleased to make your acquaintance, Mr. Creed."

Creed was unaccustomed to shaking hands with a woman. He hesitated for a second before gently taking her hand, bowing, and kissing it as he had learned to do in New Orleans when introduced to a proper lady.

"Oh, my!" gasped Faye, her free hand moving reflexively to her blushing cheek. "How gallant!" When Creed released her hand, she backed away, still flushed, now holding her hand over her mouth.

Drake was next. He shook Creed's hand vigorously and said, "Pleased to meet you, sir." Sincerity and true warmth were intoned in his words.

Louise held her ground, blandly saying, "Mr. Creed."

Creed looked hard at her. She did have blue eyes, blue the shade of lake ice. Just as cold as lake ice, too, he thought. "Miss Thayer," he said evenly, nodding in her direction.

Thayer cleared his throat, "Ahem!" then said, "I certainly appreciate your eagerness to find the boy's uncle, Mr. Creed, but don't you think that you are endangering the boy by taking him across this wild land? I mean, I'm certain that you mean well and you appear to be capable with a gun, but don't you think that the boy's life is at risk riding along with just you to protect him?"

"No, I don't," said Creed flatly.

"I don't think you're considering the boy's welfare here, Mr. Creed," said Thayer.

"No, Father, he isn't," said Louise. "It's quite obvious that Mr. Creed is strictly interested in ridding himself of this child as soon as he can and be done with him once and for all."

"I ain't no child!" said Little Bee testily.

Creed put a hand on the lad's shoulder to restrain him, saying, "Easy, son. The lady has a right to speak her mind, even if she doesn't know what the hell she's talking about."

"Sir, your language!" snapped Thayer.

"Sorry, Reverend," said Creed. "I forgot for a second that you're a man of the cloth." He aimed this last at Tyler.

"I was thinking of my daughters, sir," said Thayer.

Creed turned to Faye, bowed, and said, "A thousand pardons, Miss Thayer."

Faye could only give out a little giggle, blush, and cover her mouth again to hide her reaction.

"Father, considering this man's total disregard for the boy's welfare," said Louise, "perhaps you should take the matter up with the fort's commanding officer."

"Little Bee's welfare is nobody's business except mine," said Creed, driving a hard stare directly into Louise's eyes. "I gave his mother my word that I'd take him to his uncle in the Choctaw Nation, and the only thing that's going to stop me from keeping my word is my own death."

"Well, I can arrange that," said Tyler, opening his coat.

"No, Mr. Tyler!" snapped Thayer, turning and facing the ex-soldier. "There will be no violence here. Not now. Not ever. Is that clear, sir?"

Tyler looked down at Thayer and said, "Yes, sir, no violence, but I still say we don't need this Reb riding with us. I can take care of you folks just fine."

"I know you can, Mr. Tyler," said Thayer, "but we would all be a lot safer on the road if we traveled together." He turned to face Creed again. "Including Mr. Creed and young Mr. Doak."

Damn! he's right! thought Creed. We would be safer riding with them, and they'll sure be a lot safer with us riding with them. "All right, Reverend Thayer," he said, "we'll ride with you to Boggy Depot, but let me make something perfectly clear first. I won't take orders from any one of you." He fixed an eye on Tyler. "Is that understood?"

"Are you saying that you wish to be in charge, Mr. Creed?" asked Thayer.

"No, sir," said Creed, shifting his view to the parson. "I'm saying that we'll ride along with you as far as Boggy Depot, but if you give me any grief along the way, we'll ride on without you. Is that clear?"

"I understand, Mr. Creed," said Thayer. "Then it's settled. We leave first light tomorrow." He turned to Tyler and his children and said, "Come along now. We have much to do before morning."

Creed couldn't help thinking that his words had fallen on deaf ears. They hadn't even left yet, and already Thayer had given him an order. He probably doesn't even know it, thought Creed. He shook his head, then went about his own business.

14

The little caravan departed Fort Gibson at dawn on the third day of spring, 1866.

Tyler rode point because he was familiar with the road having marched along much of it during the war. He was mounted on a handsome chestnut gelding that he called Payday because of the rude way that he was mustered out of the Army. When he was discharged from military service, Tyler was allowed to keep his clothes, a pair of shoes, and a blanket, and he was paid his final month's wages: thirteen dollars. Nobody said thank you, nobody patted him on the back, or said farewell, or even shook his hand for a job well done. In fact, the disbursing officer said, "You got your money, so you're officially out of the Army now. There's the gate. Don't let it hit you in the ass on your way out." Figuring he deserved better treatment and more reward for the service he had rendered his country, he slipped back into the fort that night and appropriated the animal as a sort of bonus, then named him Payday as a constant reminder of his time in the Army.

Reverend Thayer drove the first covered wagon. Faye sat on the seat next to him, and the three heifers were tethered to the tailgate. Drake drove the second wagon. Louise rode with him, and the Guernsey bull was tied to the back because the stockman who had sold them the beast said that if they put the cows up ahead of the bull that he would be less likely to balk at being led along the road.

Creed and Little Bee brought up the rear, riding side-by-side and leading a pack mule that Creed had bought at Fort Gibson.

Creed had the thought that the extra animal could carry their provisions, relieving Nimbus and Little Bee's mule of their burdens and allowing them more freedom of movement, if the need should arise during their journey.

The morning passed without incident. Being fresh and eager to be on the trail, they traveled the two and a half miles to Nivens Ferry in little more than an hour and crossed the Arkansas River into the Creek Nation. Two miles more brought them to the ruins of Fort Davis, a post built in '62 by the Confederates and destroyed in '63 by the Federals. Just beyond the site, the road forked; the right arm led to the Creek Agency six miles due west, and the left turned southward toward North Fork Town. They chose the latter route, following it for another two miles before halting at the foot of a high hill to consume a modest noon meal of bacon strips that Louise had fried up that morning on slices of wheat bread that Faye had baked the previous day.

Faye invited Creed and Little Bee to eat with her family. Creed accepted but with reluctance because he suspected that fraternizing with the Thayers—at least, the females—would lead to trouble. He and Little Bee staked Nimbus and the mules in a patch of new grass, took their drinking cups from the pack animal, then joined the others in the shade of the first wagon.

Reverend Thayer said grace for all of them, then Louise served the sandwiches, while Faye poured water into their cups.

"Mr. Tyler is also from Texas, Mr. Creed," said the parson between bites. "Isn't that so, Mr. Tyler?"

Tyler nodded as he chewed on a mouthful of food. He allowed himself to glance at Creed, but he was wishing that Thayer hadn't brought up the subject of home states. The last thing he wanted was to get friendly with Creed, a fellow Texan, although he was positive that Creed wouldn't see it that way.

"The eastern part of the state, I believe," said Thayer. "What is the name of that town you're from, Mr. Tyler?"

Tyler washed down the dry sandwich with a gulp of water, then said, "Nacogdoches."

"What part of Texas are you from, Mr. Creed?" asked Faye.

"Lavaca County," said Creed. "That's farther south than Nacogdoches. Between Houston and San Antone."

"I'm not that familiar with Texas, Mr. Creed," said Thayer, "but I have seen some maps of the state. From what I can recall offhand, I would have to say that you are a great distance from your home."

"Pretty far, Reverend," said Creed.

"Did you fight in the war, Mr. Creed?" asked Faye. Already she was infatuated with Creed, and she was beginning to imagine him as some sort of knight in shining armor on a quest to rescue her from a life of drudgery.

Creed aimed his eyes at Faye, but he concentrated on Tyler with his peripheral vision, looking for any signs of hostility. He said, "Yes, ma'am, I did."

"For the Rebels?" queried Thayer.

"For Texas," said Creed. He swallowed a chunk of bacon and added, "At least, in the beginning I was fighting for Texas. After a couple of years, I was just fighting to stay alive, I guess. Not much else."

"You Rebs was fighting to keep my people in slavery," said Tyler bitterly. "That's what you was fighting for."

Creed pushed his hat backward on his head and scratched at his hairline with his free hand, not looking at anyone or anything in particular as he did. He lowered his hand, raised his head, sighed, then said, "Mr. Tyler, I'm not going to be so foolish as to try and make an apology to you or any other former slave for the past. I didn't cause it. I didn't put chains on anybody. I didn't take a whip to anybody—"

Tyler jumped in and said, "But you did own slaves, didn't you, Creed?"

"No, I didn't own a single slave, but my grandfather did."

"I thought so," said Tyler triumphantly. "Same thing."

"Mr. Tyler, my grandfather died during the war, but before he passed away, he freed his slaves. They all stayed on the plantation until the war ended and the Yankees came, but even then, some of them stayed because they wanted to stay, because they were treated like people when they were slaves, and they were treated like people after they were freed. That's the way it is with my family, Mr. Tyler. Until somebody gives us cause to do less, we treat everybody like we want to be treated." He looked at Thayer. "I believe that's called the Golden Rule, Reverend. Am I right?"

"Yes, sir, you are," said Thayer, "but you still owned slaves, and that, sir, was a moral indignation to the Lord."

Creed sighed, smiled, then said, "Reverend, I've had a lot of time on my hands during various episodes of my life, and I've had the opportunity to read and study the Bible. Now correct me here if I'm wrong, but didn't many of the patriarchs in the olden days own slaves? And weren't these men the Chosen of God?"

Thayer blanched because he knew that Creed was right, the old patriarchs did own slaves; the Bible said so, and he knew it. "Well, yes, I suppose," he blustered.

"And these men were pleasing in the sight of the Lord," said Creed. "Isn't that what the Bible says, Reverend?"

"Well, yes, I suppose," he blustered again.

"You know something, Reverend?" queried Creed. "I heard a Baptist minister and a Methodist minister spout that same line of horse droppings in church more than once, and as many times as I heard it, it never once made sense to me. I mean, those things that happened in the Bible happened a long time ago. As I heard one fellow put it, a lot of water has passed under the bridge since then, so who's to say that those men in the Bible really did own slaves? Who's to say that over all those years that somebody didn't just put that in the Bible to make it all right to own slaves? And that over the years, people have been using the Bible as an excuse to own slaves? Who's to say that isn't the way it happened, Reverend? You? Me? Well, whether those old patriarchs owned slaves or not, that's a part of the Bible that I just can't accept, Reverend. The God in Heaven that I believe in doesn't like one man owning another against his will.

"Now I didn't always think that way," he said, continuing. "There was a time when I thought slavery was all right as long as a master treated his slaves decently like we did back home. But I changed my thinking on that. I can't say exactly when I did it, but I did change my thinking on slavery. Mr. Tyler, can you read and write?"

"No, I can't," said Tyler. He glanced at Louise, then added, "Not yet, anyway."

"I didn't think so," said Creed, "but you can learn, you know. That's another thing, Reverend. I've heard ministers preach on how the Negroes aren't anything more than apes come down out of the trees to serve the white man. Can you believe that, sir? Can you believe that men of the cloth would actually preach such hogwash? And can you believe that some people actually believed them? I never did, because whoever heard of an ape that could talk like a man, walk like a man, or think like a man? I met a mulatto in New Orleans once who could read better than I could. Does that sound like an ape to you? No, sir. It doesn't to me either. Negroes are people just like any other people. Some of them are real dumb, and some of them are real smart. Some of them are ugly as sin, and others are some of the most beautiful folks on this earth." He looked straight at Tyler, smiled, and added, "Mr. Tyler, you fall somewhere in between there."

Tyler ignored the gentle dig and went on eating his lunch and listening to Creed's speech.

"My whole point here, gentlemen," continued Creed, "is this: I believe every man has the right to be free, no matter what color he is or where his ancestors came from. I believe in the Golden Rule, and I do my best to remain true to it. I will give you the same respect that I want you to give me. But if you can't see your way clear to return the courtesy, then I am no longer obligated to give you my respect. You see, gentlemen, the Golden Rule works both ways. Not only should you do unto others as you would wish them to do unto you, but what you do unto others will be done unto you. Leastways, that's how it is with me." He stood up. "Now I've had my say on the subject of getting along while we're on the road together. If either of you gentlemen has any objections to what I've just said, then tell me now, and Little Bee and I will go our own way."

When neither Tyler nor Thayer spoke up, Creed turned to Faye and Louise and said, "Ladies, thank you for the lunch. I apologize for spoiling your meal with my lecture. Now if you will excuse me, please?" He bowed toward them, waited a moment for their consent to leave, which Louise gave with a nod, then he walked away toward Nimbus and the mules.

No one said anything, but all eyes except one pair followed Creed. The exception was Reverend Thayer. His focus was on his children: all three were riveted on Creed, quite obviously awed by his speech. This worried the minister.

Tyler was the first to stir, starting to get up and go after Creed; but Thayer waved him off, popping erect as if a hornet had just then stung his backside. He followed the Texan, calling after him, "Mr. Creed, a word with you, if I may?"

Creed halted but didn't turn around as he waited for Thayer to catch up to him. He was beyond the second wagon, almost to the patch of grass where his horse and the mules were still grazing. When Thayer came around in front of him, he said, "Reverend, I don't wish to discuss the Bible and slavery any further. I've had my say, and that's that."

"Yes, sir," said Thayer, "but I would like to say one more thing about our journey together, if I may."

"All right, speak your piece, and be done with it," said Creed, folding his arms in front of him.

"I can tell, sir," said Thayer, "that you are a gifted speaker. I think you would have made a good minister if you hadn't gone to war."

"Is that it, Reverend? You just wanted to tell me that you think I'd have made a good minister? Is that all?"

"No, it's not. I'm impressed by your speaking talent, and I'm certain that my children are equally impressed, and that is what concerns me, sir. They are young and inexperienced in the ways of the world. I fear that they would look upon you as some sort of hero, a man to be admired and, dare I say it, to be adored. I've already noticed that Faye is quite taken with you."

"I doubt that they'll look on me so kindly, Reverend," said Creed. "I'm not exactly the dime-novel hero, if you know what I mean."

"Yes, Mr. Creed, I do know what you mean, but you are wrong about this. I know my children, sir. They are quite impressionable, just as much so as the boy, Little Bee, who is well disposed to your influence already."

"How Little Bee and I get along is our business, Reverend," said Creed a bit angrily. "His mother left him to me. Now maybe that wouldn't hold up in a court of law, but until some law does come along and tell me different, I'm taking care of the boy the best way that I know how, and I'm taking him to his uncle in the Choctaw Nation. Until then, I won't tolerate any interference from you or Tyler or anybody in your family as far as Little Bee is concerned. Is that clear, Reverend?"

"Little Bee is not the question here, Mr. Creed," said Thayer. "My family is. I agreed not to give you any orders on this journey, and with that in mind, I request that you keep some distance between yourself and my children."

"That's fine by me, Reverend," said Creed. "Why don't you tell them the same thing?"

"I will," said Thayer.

"Good. Now have we cleared up that point, Reverend?"

"Yes, I believe we have."

"Fine," said Creed. He looked up at the sky, then back at Thayer. "We've got about six hours of daylight left. The ferryman said there's a place about fifteen, sixteen miles up ahead called Honey Springs where we can make camp for the night, if we get moving now."

"Yes, I know," said Thayer. "Mr. Tyler told me about it already. He said the same thing about making camp there tonight."

"Then let's be moving, Reverend."

"Yes, of course."

15

An hour before sunset the landscape became more familiar to Britt Tyler. Honey Springs was still four and a half miles ahead, but Tyler recognized this locale as the place where the action had begun on a steamy July day in '63. He dropped back to the first wagon to suggest to Reverend Thayer that they halt there for the night, and the minister agreed.

They made camp on the far side of Coodey's Creek just in case it should rain during the night and make the stream impassable in the morning. Tyler and Creed picketed the animals between the tongues of the wagons, which were formed up in a wide V-shape with their end gates toward the water. Drake and Little Bee gathered wood for a fire, which the reverend started with a flint and steel kit. Louise set the pot of salt pork and beans that had been soaking all day to cooking, while Faye made a batter of corn meal for baking into cornbread.

In spite of her father's orders to the contrary, Faye wasted no time inviting Creed and Little Bee to join her family and Tyler for supper. The Texan was again reluctant to accept the invitation, fearing another confrontation with Tyler that might finally lead to a violent end, and he would have said no if not for the sorrowful plea in Little Bee's eyes.

With the last of the day's light fading to orange, they sat down to eat, each of them sitting on chests that Drake had gotten down from the second wagon and placed in a circle around the campfire. Creed, Little Bee, and Faye sat to one side, Tyler, Drake, and Louise to the other, and the reverend at the head between them. Much of the meal was quiet as the travelers were too tired to do

102

much talking while consuming their food, but after getting their fill, they became talkative.

Tyler was the first to finish eating, and seeing a golden opportunity to rub salt on what he thought were open Rebel wounds, he focused on Creed and began to relate his version of the Battle of Honey Springs. "This is the way it was," he said at the start, the firelight dancing devilishly in his eyes.

The Confederacy held sway over the Indian lands without serious challenge for the first year of the War Between the States, but the Union regained a foothold with the capture of Fort Gibson in '62. Even so, the Confederates under Stand Watie continued to imperil much of the countryside in the Cherokee Nation, and all of the other nations were firmly within the control of the South.

Wishing to strengthen the Federal position at Fort Gibson, General James G. Blunt dispatched a supply column of 218 mule-drawn wagons and an oxen train of forty wagons carrying confiscated goods, sutlers' merchandise, and soldiers' baggage. With the conveyances of civilians who were returning to their homes, the entire train was more than three hundred wagons long, stretching several miles along the Texas Road. They carried much-needed relief for the beleaguered forces at the old fort on the Grand River. The military unit consisted of companies from the 1st and 2nd Indian Home Guards, the 3rd Wisconsin Cavalry, the 2nd Colorado Infantry, the 6th Kansas Cavalry, the 2nd Kansas Battery, and the 1st Kansas Colored Volunteers, an infantry outfit in whose number was Private Britt Tyler.

After fighting a minor battle at Cabin Creek in which the Confederates under Stand Watie and Colonel D. N. MacIntosh, a Creek leader, were driven from the field by the Union artillery, the relief train arrived at Fort Gibson on July 6. A week later, fearing an impending attack on Fort Gibson by Rebels under General W. S. Cabell from Arkansas, General Blunt arrived with more reinforcements that turned the Union command from a mere defender of a strategic fortification into a potentially offensive army.

Taking the initiative, General Blunt sent a detachment of cavalry across the Arkansas River at Hitchiti Ford on July 15 that drove the Confederate pickets from the opposite bank, then the unit came down the south side of the river to find that the Rebels at the mouth of the Grand River had fled their posts. With the river crossings secure now, Blunt's army crossed the Arkansas in flatboats on the next day, then marched all night to attack the Confederate supply depot at Honey Springs.

"It was about eight in the morning," said Tyler, "when we came up on the Rebs here at Coodey's Creek. It was raining to beat the band, but we attacked them anyway. They didn't put up a fight, and we chased them all the way to Elk Creek where their main body was prepared to make a stand against us. The general put us coloreds in the center with the white boys from Colorado on our left. There was an Indian regiment to our right, and one to the Colorado Infantry's left, and outside of them was the cavalry. We figured the general put us that way because the Indians weren't much on fighting, especially when most of the enemy was also Indians, and the general must've figured that being flanked by the other units would help keep them in line when the battle commenced.

"Well, we rested for a couple hours before the general finally ordered the attack. We sent out skirmishers to draw their fire and see how strong they was. We drove the Rebs back to the creek where they made a stand at the bridge and three fords. A Texas outfit faced us coloreds. They put up a good fight, but we got the best of them in the end."

Realizing from the start what Tyler was trying to do, Creed listened politely and attentively, and he wisely refused to let Tyler arouse his anger. Instead, he chose to take a philosophical approach to the tale, hoping that it would frustrate Tyler into ceasing his prattlings on the past.

"We lost a lot of battles during the war," said Creed. "We also won a lot of them. A lot of good men died in those fights."

"And so did a lot of bad men," said Tyler. "And they was all Rebs."

"Not all of them," said Creed. He laughed intentionally, then said, "You know, we called the Yankees blue bellies, but for the life of me, I don't know why. You see, it was their blue backs that we saw mostly—when they were running away from us when the fighting got heavy."

"Is that so?" snarled Tyler. "Then how come we won the war like we did?"

"You know," said Creed quite seriously, "I've often wondered that myself." His head drooped, and he stared at the ground between his feet. "In fact, I've often wondered why that horrible war was ever started."

"It was the hand of God," said Thayer. "He knew that the only way to cleanse this nation of the evil of slavery was through the fire of battle."

Creed looked up at the minister and said, "You know, Parson, you just might be right." He stood up, and just as he did, a gunshot shattered the night, and a rifle ball crashed into the top of the chest where he had been sitting. Reacting without thinking, he drew his Colt's and dropped to one knee beside the chest, his eyes scanning the shadows for movement, his ears straining to hear the softest sounds.

Tyler also responded like a soldier, drawing his .44s and seeking protection behind the chest that had been his seat during the meal.

Little Bee followed Creed's example and made himself as small as he could behind a chest.

The Thayers were too shocked initially to move. Faye and Louise did gasp at the explosion in the night, but the reverend and his son simply froze where they sat.

A second shot splintered a corner of the second wagon's bed next to Drake. Faye and Louise screamed.

The cows bellowed, and the mules brayed. Nimbus danced nervously, eager for his master to take him into action.

"Bushwhackers!" shouted Tyler.

"Get down!" shouted Creed, noting the gun flash in the timber along the creek.

The women fell on the ground in obedience. Drake and his father scrambled for cover beneath the wagons.

A third bullet kicked up dirt near Creed. He saw the gunfire flare in a different spot from the first. There's two of them at least, he told himself.

All of this in a matter of five seconds.

Tyler fired in the direction of the last flash. His action only served to draw more shots at him.

Creed held back, choosing to estimate the strength of their attackers before retaliating. He counted the gun flashes. They came from six different locations on the far side of the creek. Yellow bastards! he thought. Too cowardly to come across the creek and fight! He figured four of the bushwhackers were using six-guns and the other two were shooting repeating rifles, probably

Henrys. Seeing that Tyler had drawn their fire, he decided that a flanking movement was called for here. He rolled under the wagon to the other side, losing his hat in the process, then crawled off to some bushes along the stream's edge. He could now make out the silhouettes of three outlaws, each behind a tree. The closest was only thirty or so feet away. Creed aimed his Colt's carefully at the villain and squeezed off a round. BANG!

"Ai-ee!" agonized the outlaw as the ball blasted through his ribcage into his left lung. He fell sideways, dropping his weapon and clutching at the fatal wound.

The bushwhackers ceased firing, their attention drawn to their fallen comrade. "Where'd that shot come from?" demanded one of them.

"Don't know," said another.

Creed was confident that he could get off another shot before they figured out where he was. He drew a steady bead on another black form and fired. BANG!

"Unh!" grunted the target as the ball ripped into his neck, lodging in his brain stem and killing him instantly. He crashed on the ground and thrashed about for a few seconds before settling into a deathly repose.

"Over there!" shouted an outlaw. He fired in Creed's direction, and two of the others did likewise.

The last man wanted no part of this fight. "Piss on this!" he shouted. "Let's get the hell out!"

Creed recognized the voice as being that of Ed King, the same son of a bitch that had run off from Hawk's Tavern and then had run off from Alberty's Store. Damn you, King! thought the Texan angrily. If I'd known you were going to be this much trouble, I would have killed you that first day. He raised up and emptied his gun in the general direction of the bushwhackers.

Tyler did the same.

The outlaws fled.

Realizing that King and his men had given up the attack, Creed returned to the camp, cautiously announcing himself as he approached the wagons. "It's only me," he said.

Faye ran to him. "Are you all right?" she asked anxiously, taking hold of his free arm and walking beside him back to camp.

"Yes, I'm fine," he said casually. He stepped into the firelight, sweat glistening on his face. "Anybody hurt?" he asked, looking from person to person.

Reverend Thayer and Drake were just then crawling out from under the wagons.

Little Bee ran up to Creed. "Did you kill any of them?" he asked excitedly.

"Mr. Tyler's been shot!" shouted Louise.

"It's nothing," said Tyler. Blood dripped from his left hand. He held out his arm. "Went clean through." He forced a chuckle, then said, "Sure do hurt though."

Everybody gathered around Tyler.

Louise took his arm and said, "Let me see." After a quick inspection, she said, "Let's get your coat off, Mr. Tyler."

"It's nothing, Miss Louise," said Tyler.

"Oh, posh, Mr. Tyler!" said Louise. "You just be quiet and let me take care of this." She looked at Faye, started to speak, but hesitated a mere second as she saw her sister clinging to Creed. She thought about voicing her disapproval, but discarded the notion instantly as being inappropriate at this time. Instead, she said, "Faye, get me that box of bandages and the bottle of medicinal alcohol."

Faye was pale with fright from the brush with death and from the sight of Tyler's blood all over his forearm. She was unable to move until Louise said firmly, "Get going, Faye!" Then the younger sister hurried off to retrieve the items the older sister wanted.

Tyler looked at Creed and said, "I reckoned there was six of them. What about you?"

"The same," said Creed. "But now there's only four."

"You killed two of them?" asked Little Bee.

"Go get your shotgun, Little Bee," said Creed.

The boy hustled off to retrieve the weapon.

"You aren't going after them, are you?" asked the minister.

Creed ignored the question, saying, "Mr. Tyler, I don't think they'll be back tonight, but just in case, maybe we should figure on doing a little guard duty."

"I think you're right," said Tyler.

Little Bee returned with the shotgun. "Are we going after them, Mr. Creed?" he asked.

"No," said Creed. "But let's go have a look at the two they left behind."

Creed and Little Bee waded across the creek and found the outlaws. The first was dead; the second dying but still conscious;

barely. Creed lifted the man's head and asked, "Was Ed King with you?"

"Help me!" gasped the villain. "Help me!"

"You're dying, friend," said Creed. "Now tell me, was Ed King with you?"

"Yes," said the outlaw. He gurgled, choked, spit up blood, and died.

Creed let the man's head fall back on the ground, then he turned to Little Bee and said, "I guess Mr. King's not going to let me alone, is he? Well, we'll have to keep a sharp lookout for him from now on, Little Bee. You and me."

"What about the others?" asked Little Bee. "Mr. Tyler and the Thayers. Shouldn't we tell them to watch out for him, too?"

"No, don't tell them anything about King," said Creed. "There's no need to worry them. He's after me, not them."

"But King shot Mr. Tyler," argued Little Bee.

Creed gave that a moment's thought, then said, "All right, I'll tell Tyler about King, but not the others. Understood?"

Little Bee nodded.

"Come on," said Creed. "We'd better get back to camp."

16

The next morning, Sunday, Tyler and Little Bee searched for and found the horses that had belonged to the two dead outlaws while Creed and Drake Thayer dug graves for the dead men. Reverend Thayer held a funeral for the villains, using the occasion to sermonize on the virtues of the Ten Commandments. Afterward, he performed a regular Sabbath service for his tiny congregation of family, Tyler, Creed, and Little Bee. The latter two attended more out of courtesy than a desire to hear preaching.

When Thayer finished with his religious duties, Creed took out a knife and began carving grave markers for the outlaws. Had it been his decision to make, Tyler would have let their bodies molder to dust in unmarked graves. "They wasn't nothing but white trash," he said. "They don't deserve to be remembered." Creed held different thoughts. He put up a simple argument that Tyler didn't like but completely understood. "Would you feel that way if they were colored?" he asked the ex-slave. Not knowing the bushwhackers' names, Creed put up a wooden marker over each one that simply stated the facts:

Bushwhacker
Killed
March 24, 1866

"Maybe their friends will come back here and find their graves and put up proper markers for them," said Creed.

"I doubt that will happen," said Tyler. "Their kind don't care nothing about such things."

Creed wanted to argue the point, but he realized that he'd be wasting his breath. Besides, they had more important matters to concern them now. He turned to Thayer and said, "You can sell their horses and trappings in North Fork Town and use the money for your school, Parson."

"I won't take blood money," said Thayer.

"Look at it this way, Parson," said Creed. "The Lord gave the Promised Land to the Hebrews, but He made them fight for it first. And if I recollect rightly, those Hebrews shed a lot of blood to get their own country."

Thayer stared at Creed with confusion distorting his facial features as he said, "You astound me, Mr. Creed, with your knowledge and understanding of the Bible. I still say—"

"That I'd have made a good minister," interjected Creed. He shook his head and added, "No thanks, Reverend. That's not my calling in this life."

"Then what is your calling, sir?" asked Thayer.

"I don't rightly know," said Creed. "Not yet anyway." He looked up at the sun, then turned to Tyler. "Maybe we should be moving on, Mr. Tyler."

Tyler nodded in agreement, turned to Thayer, and said, "Yes, I believe we should be moving on, Reverend."

"Today is the Sabbath," said Thayer. "We won't be going anywhere until tomorrow."

Creed heaved a sigh, then said, "Parson, those bushwhackers jumped us here last night. They're liable to come back here. If not them, then another bunch. We're vulnerable here, sir. I should think that we'd be wise to move on to the next settlement. What do you think, Mr. Tyler?"

"As much as I don't like doing it," said Tyler, "I have to agree with Creed, Reverend." He scanned the western horizon, then added, "Besides, it looks like it might rain. We'd be well advised to find some shelter, Reverend."

Thayer studied Creed then Tyler. He searched his conscience for an argument, but he found none that held water. "All right, we'll move on," he said, "but only to the next settlement. What did you say the name of that place was, Mr. Tyler?"

"Honey Springs," said Tyler.

"Yes, of course," said Thayer impatiently. "We'll stop there. Shall we go now?"

Everybody went into motion, packing up, hitching up, and saddling up. For all but Tyler, this was no problem.

Louise had sterilized and bandaged Tyler's wounded left arm the night before and again that morning. She had argued with him about putting the limb in a sling, but he had refused, saying it was all right the way it was. Then he went to saddle his horse. Seeing the great pain that it caused him, Louise went to her brother and said, "Drake, why don't you help Mr. Tyler with his saddle?"

"Yes, of course," said Drake, and he did the chore for Tyler, although the ex-soldier tried to talk him out of it.

Tyler was forced to face reality. Realizing that holding the reins in his left hand would be painful and that holding them in the right would be awkward for him, he said, "Why don't you ride Payday today, Mr. Drake, and I'll ride on the wagon?"

Drake smiled broadly and said, "Could I?"

Tyler offered a grin and said, "You'd be doing me a kindness, if you did."

"Thank you, Mr. Tyler," said Drake. He threw himself into the saddle and beamed down at Tyler. "Yes, thank you very much, Mr. Tyler."

"You lead the way now," said Tyler. "Just follow this road till we get to Honey Springs."

"Yes, sir."

Louise helped Tyler into the second wagon, but she wouldn't let him take the reins. "I'll drive, Mr. Tyler," she said. "You just rest that arm of yours."

"Thank you kindly, Miss Louise," said Tyler.

Creed and Little Bee took up their places at the rear of the little caravan, both regretting that the opportunity to tell Tyler about Ed King had failed to materialize just yet.

The travelers rode the rest of the morning, arriving at Elm Creek shortly after midday. They came to the toll bridge that the 20th Texas Cavalry had tried so valiantly to defend during the Battle of Honey Springs three years prior but had eventually lost to the 1st Kansas Colored Volunteers. After paying the price of a dollar for each wagon, a quarter for each animal, and a dime for each person, the travelers crossed to the south side of the stream and stopped for lunch. Creed hoped that this might be his chance to speak with Tyler about King.

As Faye and Louise made up some sandwiches, the men gathered at the bridge where Tyler told them more about the Battle of Honey Springs. "We was over yonder," he said, pointing at the trees north of the creek, "beyond them woods. We came at

those Texans at a slow walk until they broke and fell back to
the bridge. The Indians on the Confederate side was the first to
run. Most of them was across the creek long before the Texans
retreated." He turned to Creed. "I'll say this much for those
Texas white boys. They died like men." He turned around and
faced south. "We chased them all the way to Honey Springs and
beyond. They was in full retreat by then, but we was too late
to capture the supplies that they couldn't take with them. Most
of the buildings was already on fire." He chuckled, then added,
"Those Rebs wasn't all that dumb that day. They broke up two
hundred and fifty barrels of molasses and made this real big mess
that kept us from putting out the fires and saving the stores they'd
left behind." He looked down at the ground and concluded his
narration. "Yes, sir, it was quite a day for freedom. We buried
more than a hundred Confederates and captured some, too. We
only lost a few men. Nobody I knew."

"Lunch!" called out Faye.

The Thayers headed back to the wagons. Tyler started after
them. Seeing a chance to talk to the ex-soldier, Creed looked
at Little Bee, then nodded at Tyler. Little Bee understood. He
rushed up to Tyler and grabbed his good arm.

Stopping and turning, Tyler asked, "What is it, son?"

Little Bee placed an index finger to his lips to signal for quiet,
then pointed back at Creed. He motioned with his head for Tyler
to come back to Creed with him.

Tyler frowned, but he went along with Little Bee. "What is it,
Creed?" he asked when he was close enough.

"Mr. Tyler, I'd like to talk to you about the raid last night,"
said Creed.

"What about it?" asked Tyler belligerently.

"Those men weren't just after the cows and whatever else they
might have thought the Thayers have with them," said Creed.
"Their leader was a man named King. He's a bushwhacker from
Missouri."

"How do you come to know this?" asked Tyler.

"One of the men I shot was still alive when we found him,"
said Creed, "and he told me that King was the leader."

Tyler's brow furrowed as he peered quizzically at Creed and
said, "You sound like you know this man."

"We met him last week at a place called Hawk's Tavern. He
had a man named Harry Corn with him. We had trouble with them

from the start, but we ran them off that day. The next day when we came across them again they weren't so lucky. I had to kill Corn, and King ran off again. He was back the next morning with some other men. I had to shoot one of them before King would ride off and leave us be."

Tyler thought about what Creed was saying, then said, "So you think this King is after you now for killing his friends. Is that it?"

"That's mostly it," said Creed. "I showed him up for what he is: a yellow coward. And now I think he's out to kill me for it."

"So how come you're telling me all this?" asked Tyler.

"I thought you should know about the danger that you and the Thayers are in by having us with you," said Creed.

Tyler nodded and said, "I appreciate your concern for the Thayers, Creed, but you don't need to worry about me none." He patted the handles of his two Remingtons and added, "I can take care of myself."

"Yes, of course," said Creed, "but I thought you should know so you could keep a lookout for trouble. I think King will try bushwhacking us again. I'm telling only you because I don't want to fret the Thayers about it."

"I see what you mean," said Tyler. He stroked his chin, then said, "We'll be laying over at Honey Springs tonight. It's only a couple miles more from here." He scanned the western horizon, which had grown darker by the hour. "Rain's coming for sure. Those bushwhackers ain't likely to come near us in a storm or when we're camped in a settlement. Weather permitting, tomorrow we'll make for North Fork Town. Maybe there we can hook up with another outfit headed our way."

"Or maybe we'll just go our own way," said Creed.

Before Tyler could reply, Faye came up and said, "You'd best come and eat now." She took Creed by the arm to lead him to the wagons. "Father is getting real eager to say grace."

17

Tyler's prediction came true. It rained. Beginning late that afternoon and all that night. Almost until dawn, the rain fell. Hard and steady and cold, with little lightning and thunder. The storm didn't start until after the Thayers, Tyler, Creed, and Little Bee made it to Honey Springs with its shelters and its comforting semblance of civilization. A good place to rest.

The distance between Honey Springs and North Fork Town was eighteen miles. That meant an exhausting, day-long ride for Reverend Thayer's little caravan even under ideal weather conditions; after such a heavy rain, the road would be extremely muddy and thus quite difficult for travel. Taking the mileage and the mud into consideration, the minister opted to remain at Honey Springs for another day before proceeding to North Fork Town, and this relieved both Tyler and Creed. It also gave everybody a chance to become better acquainted with each other.

The Thayers were originally from New York State, the Mohawk Valley around Syracuse, a place called Taunton. Reverend Thayer was a fourth-generation American, the youngest grandson of the youngest son of the first Thayer to settle in New England after the French and Indian War. Like his brothers, he took up farming as his occupation, but unlike them, he failed at agriculture because it required more perspiration than inspiration. He took up teaching, but this occupation proved financially inadequate, especially since he was married and had a growing family. Therefore, he added Gospel preaching to his resumé in order to supplement his income with the collection plate.

The year before the War Between the States erupted, Thayer moved his family to Louisville where he hoped to join the Baptist Missionary Society and be assigned to a mission in one of the Indian nations. Much to his disappointment, the Society was no longer sending missionaries to convert and educate the Indians to Baptist Christianity and American civilization. Undaunted, he switched his religious allegiance and joined the Cumberland Presbyterians who were still sending out missionaries to the Indians in order to convert and educate them to Presbyterian Christianity and American civilization. But before he could be posted in the West, the war broke out, and his wife's health began to fail, delaying his mission for five years.

Louise, Faye, and Drake were each born two years apart. The Thayers had other pregnancies and other births, but these three were the only children to survive beyond their third year. Both girls were educated by their parents until they reached their sixteenth year, then Reverend Thayer packed them off to the Female Academy in Louisville for formal training and finishing. Drake would have gone to the Male Academy when he achieved the same age if not for his mother's death and his father's decision to accept a missionary position in the Chickasaw Nation. Mrs. Thayer's demise affected Drake profoundly, depressing him so deeply that he contemplated suicide for some time afterward until Louise finally convinced him that he would never see their mother in heaven if he took his own life. By the time Drake recovered from his depression, he was too late to begin classes at the academy. Reverend Thayer said that was all right, that Drake would help the family move to the West, then he could return to Louisville for the fall term in 1866.

Moving an entire household was a great undertaking for the Thayers; so much so that they eschewed employing public transport and opted to purchase wagons and mule teams for their emigration to the Chickasaw Nation. They left Louisville in early October with four wagons and high hopes, and they arrived at Fort Gibson in late February with two wagons and a low opinion of reality west of the Mississippi River.

At the military post, Reverend Thayer was advised against continuing their journey until later that spring when weather conditions would become more predictable—a contradiction in terms when applied to the climate of the Indian nations—and until such time that they could find someone, preferably another, bigger, well-armed wagon train, to accompany them for their mutual protection against the bands of bushwhackers that were then menacing the countryside. Seeing how weary his family had become from the long trek from Kentucky and concerned that they couldn't afford any more financial setbacks and still succeed with his mission, Thayer heeded the wise words offered to him and stayed put inside the fort until he met Britt Tyler.

Only a month before, on President Lincoln's birthday, Tyler was discharged from the 1st Kansas Colored Volunteers at Fort Scott, Kansas. Like many former slaves, he had fought valiantly for freedom during the war, and now he was looking for his rightful share of the American dream.

Tyler was born in the year of Texas independence on a plantation in the vicinity of Nacogdoches, Texas. During the last summer before the outbreak of the war, he helped his master trail a small herd of cattle to Missouri, and when they reached St. Louis, he ran away to freedom, crossing the Mississippi and disappearing in the Illinois countryside. In making his flight to liberty, he left a wife and two younguns back in Texas. He figured that he could sneak back to Texas and steal his family from his old master, but the war came and interrupted his plans. In the interim, he did manage to reach Kansas where he joined the Army and fought the rest of the war. With the conclusion of hostilities and his release from duty, he hoped to pick up his plans where he'd left them in '61, and he set out for Texas to find his family. At Fort Gibson, the Thayers found him.

Being staunch Abolitionists, the Thayers had no aversion to accepting former slaves into their society. Tyler, on the other hand, had a well developed distrust of whites, especially those who seemed willing to offer him something for nothing. When the Thayers asked him to join them for the journey to Cherokee Village, the ex-soldier was reluctant to accept the invitation, leery of the Thayers simply because they had light skin.

Seeing the suspicion in Tyler's eyes, Reverend Thayer said, "We are in need of a guide, Mr. Tyler, and I've been told that you have been down these roads during the war. I would pay you, of course, for your services, but I can only offer you fifty cents a day."

"White men get a dollar a day," said Tyler with a touch of belligerence.

"I'm sorry, Mr. Tyler," said Thayer. "I didn't know the going rate. I'll make it a dollar a day. Gladly." He held out his hand to close the bargain.

Tyler believed him, and he agreed to the deal.

Both Reverend Thayer and Tyler wanted to leave Fort Gibson behind them as soon as Tyler hired on, but their departure was delayed by several annoying impediments. First it was Drake's bout with the catarrh, then it was Louise's female misery. After that, one of the mules took sick and had to be destroyed; a replacement had to be found. And, of course, the weather was also a nuisance, changing dramatically from day to day, just as the minister had been warned it would.

On the day that Creed and Little Bee arrived at Fort Gibson, the skies cleared, Tyler found a new mule, and both Drake and Louise announced their complete recoveries. When Florian Nash told them that Creed and Little Bee were traveling in the same direction, Thayer looked upon their meeting the Texan and the boy as the work of the Lord. Tyler saw it as coincidence, but he wasn't about to tell the parson that. He was smart enough to realize that a single colored man riding across the Indian nations was fair game for the first white trash bushwhacker to catch him in his rifle sights and that he was safer riding with the Thayers. Having Creed along as an extra gun was just that much more insurance. Tyler would go along with the minister's confirmation that "the Lord works in mysterious ways" and allow Creed to join them.

Now they had been on the road for four days and forty-three miles. They had crossed the Arkansas River on a ferry, had forded Coodey Creek, had paid a toll to cross Elm Creek, had fought off outlaws, and had sat out a rainstorm at Honey Springs. Now they were passing over the Rock Crossing of the North Fork of the Canadian River with the hope that the worst of their travails was behind them. Less than a mile ahead was North Fork Town, officially designated in 1853 by the United States Post Office as Micco, the Muskogean word for king, a title given to the chief of a town.

The Creeks, also known as the Muskogee or Muskogeans, had their lands in South Carolina, Georgia, Alabama, and Florida treatied away from them gradually over a century. In 1732, colonist James Oglethorpe was given dominion over the land he named Georgia for his benefactor, King George II of England, and their land gradually decreased until the 1830s, when in 1832 the United States concluded negotiations with the Creeks to remove them from their ancestral country in the East and transport them to new lands in the West. By the terms of this latter agreement, the Creeks in Alabama would have their country surveyed and allotted to individual tribal members who could then either sell the land to whites or remain on it and become citizens of Alabama, gaining title to the ground after five years of continuous occupation. If they sold out, they could emigrate to the new nation in the West at the government's expense. Those who did sell and chose to move to the new lands were few, numbering but 630 souls of whom only 469 survived the journey to Fort Gibson. The thousands who refused to sell were oppressed by their white neighbors and by the officials of the government that had sworn to protect them. Finally getting their fill of abuse, a few Creeks were provoked to commit acts of reprisal against their tormentors, and this inaugurated what was called a "Creek war" against a peaceful people who wished only to be left alone. Over the next two years, the Creeks were herded by the military into concentration camps, and with many in chains, they were driven like cattle to steamboat landings for transport to the Indian territory in the West. Thousands died, but those who survived took up new homes in the area situated primarily west of the Verdigris River and north of the South Fork of the Canadian River. Their first principal settlement and agency was located near the tip of the triangle of land between the two major branches of the Canadian, and this place they called North Fork Town.

In time, whites moved into North Fork Town as owners of the permanent businesses, causing the Creeks to disperse into the countryside and to use the community as a supply point. Josiah Gregg, noted for the development of the Santa Fe Trail, laid out his own trail that originated at Webbers Falls on the Arkansas River and ran through North Fork Town, Edwards' Trading Post, and westward to Santa Fe. Captain Robert B. Marcy escorted a party of '49ers across the Indian Nations, passing through North Fork Town on their way to the California gold fields. With the north-south Texas Road and the east-west California Road intersecting here, North Fork Town continued to grow in importance, so much so that the Methodists built Asbury Mission, a four-story brick building, near there in 1849. During the War Between the States, the Confederate Army used the town as a supply base, which the Union Army captured and destroyed, including all of the outbuildings of Asbury Mission.

Like Fort Gibson, which became a refugee center for dispossessed Cherokees in the last years of the war, North Fork Town became a harbor of life for Creeks and Seminoles who had lost their homes when the war ended. Several thousand of these people were still camped around the settlement when Drake Thayer led his father's little caravan into town at twilight.

"Let's stop there," said the reverend, pointing to William Nero's store at the junction of the two branches of the Texas Road. The wagons halted in front of the establishment. The front door was shut tight, and the sign in the window said "CLOSED." But Thayer ignored these indications that Nero was finished with business for this day. A brace of saddled horses tied to the hitching post at the side of the wooden plank building and a corral in the rear with another pair of saddled horses tied to its rails told Thayer otherwise. Men were inside this place, even at this hour of the evening, which meant they were most likely drinking men. For that reason, Thayer climbed down from the first wagon and walked back to the second where he asked Tyler, "Would you mind inquiring within where we might find a suitable place to camp for the night?"

Tyler scanned Nero's store, the corral, the creek beyond the stable, and a double row of Army tents on the knoll above the stream, then reluctantly said, "Yes, sir." He jumped down from the wagon seat just as Drake rode up on Payday. Tyler nodded at young Thayer, then walked around to the rear of the building where he found another entrance. He hesitated at the single wooden step before opening the door and entering.

The production and sale of alcoholic spirits in any form other than medicinal were strictly prohibited in the Indian Nations, but the law applied only to Indians—in practice, if not in intent. Many storekeepers maintained small saloons in a back room of their stores in which they served white customers only, and the law, meaning the Army, looked the other way. At some saloons, the best customers were the soldiers whose duty it was to keep whiskey and beer out of the Nations. Usually, these watering holes were nothing elaborate: four walls with two doors for exiting in a hurry, a square window or two for light and ventilation, a bar that consisted of a thick plank stretched over two large cracker barrels, and a backbar that held a few stoneware jugs of corn whiskey and a keg of warm, often sour, but potent beer that had been smuggled into the Nations inside a barrel marked as flour, molasses, or coal oil. Some, such as Nero's drinking pit, might have a table or two for gambling.

Tyler entered Nero's and found it to be crowded with six white men, all of whom were typically nondescript with their sunburnt faces, light eyes, unkempt, tobacco-stained brown beards, and worn woolen coats and trousers that were black, navy blue, or dingy brown. Before Tyler appeared in their midst, the drinkers were engaged in several animated conversations, but these fell silent as the ex-slave stepped up to the bar. All eyes bore down on him.

The barman was Bill Nero himself, pale from working indoors all the time, with blue eyes, graying brown hair and beard. He was of medium height and stout from success that afforded him a healthy appetite. Wearing a white apron, maroon sleeve garters, and a collarless gray shirt, he moved to stand opposite of where Tyler stood at the bar and asked, "What are you doing in here, nigger?"

Tyler stiffened but maintained his composure as he said, "Just looking for some information, sir."

"I sell hard liquor and beer in here, nigger," said Nero, "and I only sell it to white men. So you just get your black ass back out that door and go looking elsewhere for whatever it is you want to know."

"The reverend sent me in here," said Tyler, "to find out where we might camp for the night." He looked around the room at the hateful faces looking back at him. "Anybody here that can tell me where we might camp for the night?"

Nobody answered him, but Nero did say, "You heard me, nigger! Get on out of here before I sic my dogs on you!"

In anger, Tyler spun around to face Nero again, and when he did, the flaps of his coat flew up, exposing the grips of the Remingtons in his waistband.

"Hey, look!" shouted a man at one of the two tables. "He's got a gun!"

Without thinking, Tyler grabbed at the butt of one revolver, but before he could draw it, the men standing at the bar, all four of them, seized him and threw him to the plank floor. He struggled, kicking and thrashing, but he was unable to free himself. His fight drew the man who had seen the .44 first and his drinking companion at the table into the affray. They pinned Tyler's arms to the boards with their booted feet, then they stooped and pulled his six-shooters from his pants.

"What are you doing with these, nigger?" asked the observant gent. "These are Army pistols. Were you in the Army, nigger?" When Tyler didn't answer him immediately, the man kicked the former soldier solidly in the ribs.

"Sure, he was in the Army, Stiver," said his drinking companion. "Look at that blue suit he's wearing. That's a soldier suit, ain't it?"

"Sure is," said Stiver. "Kill any white men in the war, nigger?" When Tyler again refused to answer, Stiver kicked him in the side again.

"Aw, let's just shoot the bastard and throw his black ass outside," said Stiver's friend. He aimed the Remington that he'd taken from Tyler at the ex-slave's head, but his hand was stayed.

"There'll be no killing in my place, Morris!" shouted Nero, grabbing him by the wrist and jerking it upward until it aimed skyward. He was in time to save Tyler's life but not in time to stop Morris from firing the weapon, the ball harmlessly lodging in the ceiling. Nero took the gun from Morris and said, "Nigger or not, a killing will bring the Army down on me, and I won't have that, Morris." He waved the revolver at Stiver and said, "If you boys want to make trouble, you can just go elsewheres and make it. Not in here, you hear?"

Creed had watched Tyler jump down from the second wagon and go into Nero's saloon, and he wondered about the advisability of such a venture, considering the enmity felt by many whites toward non-whites. "Stay here," he told Little Bee, then he rode up to the front of the second wagon to speak with Reverend Thayer. "Do you think that was such a good idea, Parson?"

"Do you mean sending Mr. Tyler into that den of iniquity, Mr. Creed?" queried Thayer.

"Yes, sir," said Creed.

"Would you suggest that I, a minister of the Gospel, should have gone in his stead, sir?"

"You'd stand a lot better chance of coming out alive," said Creed. He dismounted, and just as he did, a gunshot rang out from within the saloon.

The mule teams started, but Louise and Faye held them in check.

Creed drew and cocked his Colt's and handed Nimbus's reins to the minister. "Here, hold Nimbus," he said, ordering Thayer instead of asking him to do the job. Without waiting for any acknowledgement, he broke for the saloon door, gun in hand.

Drake jumped down from Payday and followed Creed's lead, handing the reins of Tyler's horse to his father and running toward the saloon door.

"Drake!" shouted his stunned father. "Come back here!"

The son didn't want to hear him. He kept on after Creed.

Little Bee jumped down from his mule and tied it and the pack mule to the end gate of the second wagon.

The shot from Tyler's Remington was heard across the creek by a sentry at the military encampment, and he reported it immediately to the sergeant of the guard, who passed on the report to the officer of the day. Lieutenant Bagley ordered Sergeant McGuire, a stout-hearted Irishman with a droopy black mustache, to round up a squad of armed men and go investigate the disturbance.

Louis Ross had a store across the road and down a ways from Nero's. He also had a saloon in the back of his place. Like his fellow merchant, he catered to whites only, mostly soldiers and transients, who were many considering the store's proximity to the crossroads and the Army camp on the knoll above Chapman's store on the California Road. Ross and his patrons heard the report of Tyler's Remington, and they poured outside to see what had caused the disturbance. Upon seeing the Thayer wagons in front of Nero's, they guessed that these newcomers were involved somehow with whatever trouble was afoot, and they hurried forth to learn whether their suspicions were true.

"Come on," said Stiver inside Nero's. "Let's take this nigger outside and teach him some manners."

The drunken men lifted Tyler off the floor, although he struggled to free himself, while Nero went to open the door for them. Still carrying Tyler's other Remington, Stiver led the way, followed by Morris.

Just as Creed reached for the saloon door, it opened. He withdrew his hand and backed away. Drake crashed into him, knocking him forward toward the doorway and, worse, causing him to pull the trigger on the Colt's. The ball disappeared into the mud at his feet, but the report scared the hell out of Drake.

The percussion of Creed's gun stopped Stiver, Morris, Nero, and the other men cold for a second, but only for a second. In the next instant, thinking they were being attacked by Creed and Drake, Stiver and Nero opened fire at them, which only frightened young Thayer all the more.

"Save me, Mr. Creed!" cried Drake, as he tried to use Creed as a shield against the flying bullets. He succeeded only in pulling Creed to the ground.

Creed tried to free himself from Drake, pushing the teenager away with one hand and trying to hold on to his Colt's with the other. He was only partially successful.

The blast from Tyler's Remington had done little more than put a start in the mules hitched to Thayer's wagons, but the shots that Nero and Stiver fired shook them into nervous prancing, forcing Faye and Louise to concentrate on holding them in place.

Louis Ross and his patrons didn't know Creed or the Thayers, but they knew Bill Nero and his customers. Ross assumed that the newcomers were attacking his friends, so he said, "Come on, boys, let's get those bastards!" as he led the rush to seize Creed and Drake.

Seeing Ross and his men coming to their aid, Nero, Stiver, and Morris rushed from the saloon to help them capture Creed and Drake. Much to their surprise, they had an unexpected ally in young Thayer who held on to Creed like a child clinging to his mother's skirt. They had no trouble grabbing Creed's right arm and taking his Colt's away from him.

"Mr. Creed!" yelled Little Bee. He started to run to the Texan's aid, but Reverend Thayer grabbed him in time to keep him out of harm's way.

"Gentlemen, gentlemen!" called out the minister, fully expecting that the brawlers would listen to him. "Please, gentlemen! There's no need for violence!"

Nobody heard him.

Tyler had stopped struggling at the sound of Creed's gunfire, allowing himself to go limp in the hands of his captors. As soon as it became apparent to him that they had focused their attention elsewhere, he gave a mighty twist of his body and managed to escape their grasp. Before they could react, he knocked two of them to the floor and was on his feet, prepared to kill all four, and he would have, too, if not for the fearful cry of Drake Thayer distracting him. He burst through the doorway and crashed broadside into Stiver, Morris, and Nero, sprawling them on the ground and freeing Creed for the moment.

Across the creek, Sergeant McGuire heard the shots fired by Stiver and Nero, then he spotted the melée outside Nero's saloon. "On the double, boys! March!" he commanded the armed squad of soldiers. He broke into a trot with them, and they splashed across the creek and up the opposite bank to Nero's corral.

Louise and Faye fought to hold their teams in check.

Reverend Thayer continued to restrain Little Bee and plead with the brawlers to cease their fighting, but to no avail.

Ross and his men jumped into the affray, attacking Creed, Drake, and now Tyler.

Stiver came to his feet. "Sonofabitchin' nigger!" he shrieked viciously as he kicked at Tyler.

As best as he could tell, Sergeant McGuire saw the riot as an attack on Tyler, a Negro who was wearing a Union Army uniform. In his mind, this made Tyler a fellow soldier in need of rescuing. "Let's get in there and help that colored fellow," said McGuire, a bit of the brogue still in his accent. "He's a soldier."

The infantrymen joined the brawl.

Creed grabbed Stiver's leg and pulled it out from under him, throwing the ruffian to the ground. The Texan scrambled to his knees but was knocked down again by a man stumbling backward and falling over him.

While prone, Stiver picked up the Remington that he'd dropped, cocked it, and took aim at Tyler's skull. "God damn nigger son of a bitch!" he swore like a madman.

Creed rolled over and saw Stiver aiming the six-gun at Tyler. He reached out just in time to grab the drunk's arm and slam it to the ground. The .44 fired into the dirt.

"Bastard!" screamed Stiver at Creed as he tried kicking him. He brought his gun hand up and tried shooting the Texan, but Creed wrenched the Remington away from him.

McGuire didn't see who had fired the shot. He didn't even see the gun until Creed had it in his hand. That was when he leaped on the Texan and drove the wind from Creed's lungs, rendering him defenseless. The sergeant picked up the revolver, stood up, fired it twice, and yelled, "That's enough now!"

The fighting stopped.

18

The shots that Sergeant McGuire fired sent the mule teams into a frenzy as they strained every muscle against the lines that restrained them from bolting, forcing Faye and Louise to work equally hard at keeping the beasts under control. Much to their credit and the relief of their father, the Thayer girls were successful at holding the mules in check.

"Help that man up!" shouted Sergeant McGuire, pointing a finger at Tyler. When Creed and some of the other men tried to rise, he raised a booted foot to Creed's backside, pushed him back to the ground, and said, "You hooligans stay right where you are until I sort this out and find out who's responsible for this little . . . brouhaha."

Creed rolled over and came to a sitting position with his knees bent up to his chest and his arms around them. He put on a blank expression, not wishing to show any emotion to McGuire until he figured out whether this Yankee soldier would be a friend or another foe.

Stiver piped up first. "It was the nigger that started it, soldier boy," he said from his kneeling position.

"That's right," said Morris, who was also still on his knees.

The others in their bunch chimed in with similar affirmations that Tyler was responsible for the fight, but commendably, McGuire recognized the untruth in their voices. He looked to Nero who was standing near the door of the saloon and said, "I don't know these roughnecks, Mr. Nero, so I don't know whether to believe them or not. So you tell me. Is what they say about all this true? Did this darky start the ruckus?"

If nothing more, Nero was honest; he wouldn't cheat a customer, and he wouldn't lie about a man, even if the man was a different color than he. "Not exactly," said Nero. "He came into my place, and I told him to get out. When he wouldn't leave right off, the boys here just tried to show him out. That's all there was to it, McGuire, until this fellow here," he pointed at Creed, "took a shot at us. We didn't know what else to do except shoot back at him."

McGuire leaned over Creed and said, "All right, mister, what have you got to say for yourself?"

"Mr. Creed didn't start it," said Drake, who was sitting in the mud near Creed.

"Who asked you?" spat Stiver. "You were with him."

McGuire studied Stiver for a moment and didn't like what he saw. Just the same, he kept his opinion to himself for the time being. "Both of you keep your yaps shut until I say you can talk to me," he said to Stiver, then Drake. Turning to Creed, he said, "What was it the boy over there called you, mister?"

Creed stared hard at McGuire and said evenly, although reluctantly, "My name is Slate Creed, Sergeant." He looked for any sign in McGuire's cobalt eyes that the soldier recognized his name as being on an Army Wanted list. He saw none.

"Well, Mr. Creed, what have you got to say for yourself?" asked McGuire.

"Not much, Sergeant," said Creed. "Only that I didn't fire the first shot."

"Then who did?" asked McGuire.

"I don't know," said Creed, shrugging. "Why don't you ask him?" He nodded toward Nero. "It came from within that saloon."

McGuire looked up at the saloonkeeper and said, "Is that true, Nero? Did the first shot come from within your saloon?"

Nero glanced at Stiver and Morris, then down at the ground, before he said, "Well, that was an accident. The nigger had a couple of guns on him, and the boys here took them away from him, and one went off when the nigger put up a fight."

"That's not how it happened at all, Sergeant," said Tyler.

"Is that so?" asked McGuire. "Since you seem to be the center of all this, why don't you tell me what happened here? What's your name first?"

"Britt Tyler, Sergeant. Recently of the 1st Kansas Colored Volunteers from Fort Scott. I was discharged just last month, and I'm now on my way to Texas with Reverend Thayer there and his family. We only just arrived here a little bit ago, and Reverend Thayer asked me to go into that saloon and ask where we might camp for the night. That's when these men jumped me and took away my guns. That one," he pointed to Morris, "was gonna kill me, but that man there," he pointed at Nero, "stopped him. That was the first shot, Sergeant. I don't know who fired the second shot or who did the shooting after that."

McGuire nodded, then turned to Nero. "Is that more like you remember it, Mr. Nero?"

"Yes, that's more like it, McGuire," said Nero, clearing his throat as he spoke, "except that man there," he pointed at Creed again, "started shooting at us when we opened the door to throw this nigger out."

Looking down at Creed again, McGuire said, "All right, now we're getting somewheres. Mr. Nero says you shot at them when they opened the door. Is that true, Mr. Creed?"

"I didn't shoot at anybody, Sergeant," said Creed. "My gun was discharged by accident."

"He's telling the truth," said Drake, as he scrambled to his feet against McGuire's order.

McGuire looked angrily at young Thayer but decided to let him stand, saying, "How do you know he's telling the truth, lad?"

"You see, sir," said Drake, "after we heard the first shot fired inside the saloon, Mr. Creed went to see what the trouble might be, and I followed him to see if Mr. Tyler needed any assistance. Well, when the saloon door opened, Mr. Creed stopped and backed up a bit, and I . . . I sort of ran into him. That's when his gun went off and the men in the saloon started shooting at us."

McGuire nodded his understanding, then looked around until he saw Reverend Thayer and Little Bee standing beside the second wagon. "I take it, sir," he said, "that you're this reverend that Tyler spoke about."

"Yes, sir, I am," said Thayer. He released Little Bee and stepped forward. "I am Reverend David Thayer, late of Louisville, Kentucky. This is my son, Drake," he pointed at the youth, "and these young ladies on the wagons are my daughters, Louise and Faye. Mr. Creed and Mr. Tyler you've met, and this young lad behind me is Little Bee Doak. We are travelers on our way to a place called Cherokee Village down in the Chickasaw Nation where I plan to start a mission on behalf of the Cumberland Presbyterian Mission Society."

"Good for you, Reverend," said McGuire, slightly annoyed at the lengthy introduction. "Did you see what happened here, sir?"

"It all happened just as Mr. Tyler and my son have told you, Sergeant," said Thayer. "The first shot came from within the saloon, and Drake did run into Mr. Creed, causing him to fire his weapon accidentally. All of the other shots were fired by the men in the saloon."

"Thank you, Reverend," said McGuire. "I think I see what happened here now." He turned to the other saloonkeeper and said, "Mr. Ross, what are you doing here?"

"We heard the shots," said Ross nervously, "and came to see what the trouble was. That's all, McGuire."

"Well, you can just go about your own business now," said McGuire. He thought about that for a second, smacked his lips a tad, and said, "Me and the boys'll be along shortly."

Ross nodded and headed back to his place with his gaggle of customers right behind him.

"Now, Mr. Nero," said McGuire, "since you don't seem able to run a peaceable establishment, I'm closing you down for the time being." He looked at Stiver, Morris, and their lot. "As for you, I've noticed you've been here in town for some time now. Where do you hail from and what's your business here in North Fork Town?"

"We're from Wisconsin, Sergeant," said Stiver, "and we're on our way to the goldfields in Arizona. We're just staying here until we can hook up with an outfit large enough to make it safely through the Indian territory west of here."

"I see," said McGuire. "Well, you can stay until then, but if I catch you causing another bit of trouble here in North Fork Town, I'll put you in chains and ship you back to Arkansas. That goes for the whole lot of you."

Stiver, Morris, and their friends knew exactly what McGuire meant by that: jail time for breaking the law in the Indian Nations. Like most whites, they figured that they were above the laws of Indians, and they resented being punished for such trivial transgressions. They also detested federal officials who took their jobs seriously and did their sworn duty to uphold the promises made by their government in the treaties with Indians. When men like

McGuire threatened them with arrest and deportation to Arkansas, men like Stiver and Morris took heed and danced to the tune of the law.

In no time, Stiver, Morris, and the rest of their party disappeared into the gloaming.

McGuire turned to Creed, and becoming cognizant of the fact that the Texan was still sitting on the ground, he reached out a hand to help him to his feet as he said, "You can get up now, Mr. Creed."

Creed accepted the aid and stood up. "Thank you, Sergeant," he said.

"What business do you have in Cherokee Village, Mr. Creed?" asked McGuire.

"None," said Creed. "I'm on my way to a place called Armstrong's Academy. Or at least, it was called that before the war. Now I understand that it's called Chahta Tamaha, and it's the capital of the Choctaw Nation."

"That's right, it is," said McGuire. "It's south of here, in the general vicinity of Fort Washita. So what business do you have there?"

"I'm looking for Little Bee's uncle," said Creed. "His name is Hum Doak. I'm taking Little Bee to him."

"Hum Doak?" queried McGuire. "What kind of name is that?"

"Choctaw," said Creed.

McGuire studied Little Bee for a second, then said, "You say the boy's uncle is an Indian? From the looks of him, I would have guessed he was a colored." He nudged Creed in the side, snickered, and added, "Probably a nigger in the wood pile somewheres, right?"

Creed ignored the crude jest and retrieved his hat.

Reverend Thayer was acutely desirous of being away from this place. "Sergeant," he said, "could you direct us to a good place to make camp for the night? We've traveled all day from Honey Springs to get here this evening, and we're quite exhausted from our journey."

"You'll probably be wanting fresh water," said McGuire, "so you might as well go on into the center of town to the well. That's up on the terrace, as they call it here. If you can't find a decent spot near the well, then go ahead and fill up your water barrels anyway. Then take the left fork past Stidham's store, and you should find yourself a decent place soon after that. Go too much farther, and you'll be among the Indians and the coloreds. You won't want that, of course. Not with your daughters being with you."

"Thank you, Sergeant," said Thayer abruptly. "Come on, children, let's be going." He offered the reins to Nimbus back to Creed and the reins to Payday to Drake.

Creed and Drake mounted up, while Tyler climbed aboard the second wagon with Louise. Little Bee joined Creed, and the reverend got up beside Faye in the first wagon.

"Good luck to you, Reverend," said McGuire. "I wish you a safe journey."

"Thank you, Sergeant," said Thayer. He snapped the lines over the mules, and the wagon lurched forward.

As the second wagon passed him, McGuire repeated his good wishes to Tyler and Louise, then he did the same when Creed and Little Bee rode by him. They, in turn, bid him a forced but polite farewell.

As soon as McGuire and his men were well behind them, Creed said, "What do you make of those men back there, Little Bee?"

"Including the sergeant?" asked Little Bee.

"Sure, him, too."

"Horses' asses," said the boy succinctly.

Creed laughed and said, "You got that right."

19

Reverend Thayer determined that a day of rest in North Fork Town wouldn't hurt any of them. "There's no sense in beating ourselves to death to get where we're going," he said. "Cherokee Village will still be there when we get there."

Creed wanted to argue with him, but he knew it would do no good. Ministers, he'd learned over the years, were some of the most stubborn, most mule-headed, most ornery, and most cantankerous people on this earth once they'd made up their minds about something. They could be told that the world was round, but if they'd decided that it was flat, nothing short of the Second Coming would convince them otherwise. Creed simply heaved a heavy sigh over the parson's decision and went about his own business, which was to rest up and stay out of Tyler's way.

Louise used the hiatus in their journey to teach school. Her two pupils were Tyler and Little Bee. Britt Tyler wasn't stupid, only illiterate. The same was true with Little Bee. Fortunately for both of them, Louise recognized this fact instantly and was not only able, but also quite willing and patient enough, to correct this unfortunate deficiency in them. She'd started teaching Tyler some of the basics of reading and writing back at Fort Gibson, and Little Bee joined the class the day that they arrived at Honey Springs. She found both of them to be eager and able students. She'd begun Tyler's education by teaching him the alphabet, which he picked up with no trouble at all; by the time Little Bee enrolled, the former slave was reading from McGuffey's *New Second Reader*. Little Bee's schooling followed the same curriculum that Louise had applied to Tyler. He learned his ABCs, then moved on to recognize simple words. Today, he would begin reading from McGuffey's *New First Reader*.

Faye wanted no part of teaching until she absolutely had to do it, which wouldn't be until they reached Cherokee Village and had the school set up for the fall term. Then, and only then, would she pick up a textbook of any kind. In the meantime, she had other thoughts of entertainment. She wished to visit all the stores in North Folk Town, but her father forbade her to leave their camp unescorted. "What if Drake goes with me?" she asked.

"Drake is hardly enough protection for you, Faye," said Thayer, without looking up from his Bible. "No, you can't go."

"What about Mr. Creed?" she asked petulantly. "What if he goes along to protect me? May I go then?"

"He won't do it," said Thayer, his voice beginning to show his annoyance with her. "He and I have an agreement on such things. There will be no fraternization with him. I forbid it."

"I won't be fraternizing with him, Father," argued Faye. "He'll only be along to protect me." Which was good enough for her, considering how she looked at Creed as some sort of medieval knight in shining armor.

"He won't do it, Faye."

"But what if he says he will?" she continued to plead. "May I go then?"

Feeling safe that Creed would say no, Thayer replied, "If he says he will accompany you, then you may go. Now leave me be, girl."

Joyous and excited, Faye kissed him on the cheek, said, "Thank you, Father," then ran off to find Creed and beg him to go with her to the stores.

Overhearing his sister's conversation with their father, Drake was hurt that his father thought so little of his budding manhood, but he buried the pain with a desire to traipse after Faye and Creed to the town. He approached the reverend with the same proposition that Faye had presented him. Annoyed by the second interruption, the minister told him to go with Faye and Creed, providing, of course, that Creed was agreeable to going through the town with both of them. Drake thanked him, then ran off to join his sister in her search for Creed.

Reverend Thayer had followed Sergeant McGuire's directions

perfectly when seeking a campsite the night before. He'd found the well in the center of the town, but no camping space was available there. They had drawn water, then moved on to Stidham's store on the terrace, where they were able to make camp beneath a stand of oaks just west of the business. Creed, Little Bee, and Tyler had picketed their mules and horses between the trees, then they made their usual sleeping arrangements—blankets, one under and one over the body—on the cold, hard ground near a fire that burned down through the night, throwing off less and less heat as it did. This wasn't exactly the most comfortable way to sleep, and it often only allowed intermittent rest as it had this past night for Creed.

After sunrise, breakfast, and Reverend Thayer's announcement that they would be staying put for the day, Creed figured out that four of the oaks were strong enough and close enough together for rigging up a pair of hammocks for him and Little Bee. He learned this trick during the war. He tied a knot in each corner of a blanket, then he tied a rope below the knots on one side of the blanket. He looped each rope around a tree that would suspend the hammock, making sure the lines went over a strong low branch or burl for support. He then tied the ropes below the remaining knots in the blanket. *Voila!* A hammock.

When Faye and Drake came along with their request, Creed was resting in his swaying bed, trying to get some of the sleep that had escaped him the night before. The weather was cool but not cold, which still made a top covering necessary, and because it was daytime, Creed had his grandfather's old brown felt hat over his eyes in order to keep the light away.

"Mr. Creed?" queried Faye, uncertain whether he was asleep or not.

Creed stiffened but remained silent, keeping his eyes closed and covered and hoping she would go away and leave him be.

Drake reached out, tapped Creed's shoulder gingerly, and said, "Mr. Creed?"

Coming to the realization that they wouldn't go unless he told them to leave, Creed said, without moving anything except his tongue and lips, "Go away."

"Mr. Creed," said Faye, "I'm sorry to bother you like this, but I have no choice."

"Yes, you do," said Creed, again without moving. "You can

choose to go away and leave me alone."

"Please, Mr. Creed," said Drake, "we can't go without you."

Faye looked at Drake and asked, "What do you mean we? You aren't going with us."

"Yes, I am," said Drake. "Father said I could go if Mr. Creed would go with us."

"Well, I said you can't go with us," said Faye.

"Mr. Creed hasn't said that he'll go with you yet," said Drake, "and I don't think he'll go with just you."

"I'm not going anywhere with anybody," said Creed. "Now go away and leave me be."

"Please, Mr. Creed," said Faye, her voice full of pathos, "won't you go with me through the stores. Father says I can't leave camp unless you accompany me, and there's simply nothing to do here."

Creed was surprised that Reverend Thayer would trust him with one of his daughters. Of course, Drake would have to come, too, thought Creed, but I suppose that's why the parson gave her permission in the first place. But didn't he tell me to stay away from his family? Did he change his mind about that now?

"Father was right," said Drake. "He said Mr. Creed wouldn't do it. Come on, Faye, let's go anyway."

Drake hadn't intended to stir Creed into agreeing to go with them by mentioning his father's negative attitude, but it worked anyway. Creed sat up suddenly. His legs straddled the blanket, and his hat fell to his chest, where he caught it. He looked at Faye and said, "Your father said that I wouldn't go with you, Miss Faye?"

Surprised, but quick to seize the opportunity, Faye said, "Yes, that's right, Mr. Creed. He said you weren't gentleman enough to accompany a lady in a tour of the stores. Isn't that so, Drake?"

Drake hesitated to confirm her prevarication until she nudged his foot with her own, and then he said, "Well, something like that."

Creed saw right through Faye, and he was a bit put out by her plot. He thought about lecturing her, but then he remembered his bargain with Reverend Thayer. Even so, he said, "How come I don't believe you, Faye?"

Caught in a lie, Faye's eyes widened with surprise, then they drooped into sadness.

As he gazed at Faye, a twinge of nostalgia, a feeling for

something long ago, put a chill into Creed. He tried to pinpoint it, and in the next second, he recognized the memory as it flashed through his mind on its way to his heart. He was Clete Slater back then, and he had his whole life ahead of him.

"Come on, Clete," said Texada, as she tugged on his hand. "Let's go down to the riverside. It's too nice a day to sit around here on the porch."

"Your grandmother didn't invite me here to run off with you, Texada," he said softly, hoping Mrs. Hallet couldn't hear them.

Texada was standing, and he was sitting in one of the rockers on Mrs. Hallet's front porch. The grand dame of Hallettsville had invited him to her house for Sunday dinner, which was only a formality because he was courting her adopted granddaughter, Texada Ballard, and he would have come by anyway to see her. They hadn't talked about it yet, but everybody who knew them, including Clete and Texada, pretty much felt that it would only be a matter of time before Texada became Mrs. Cletus McConnell Slater. Probably after he returned from trailing the herd to New Orleans. That would make it an autumn wedding. Neither of them suspected it that June afternoon, but their plans, unspoken though they were, would be thrown into limbo by events both past and future; their wedding would have to wait until many difficult situations were resolved.

"Oh, come on, Clete," begged Texada. Flaxen hair falling to her shoulders, pavonine eyes, and a few freckles sprinkled over tawny cheeks, she had become the woman of his dreams, although she still had moments, like this one, when she reminded him of the tomboy that he'd found so annoying when they were children.

"No, Texada," he said, refusing to move from his seat. "I won't be rude to your grandmother. Now stop asking."

"It such a nice day, Clete," she whined. "Granny won't mind if we take a walk down by the river. Come on, please."

"I said no, Texada, and that's that. Now leave me be."

She dropped to her knees in front of him, still holding his hand in both of hers. Her lower lip protruded in a pout as she batted sad eyes at him, not saying a word.

He frowned at her and said, "That won't work, Texada." When she intensified her expression, he let his head fall backwards in order to avoid looking at her. He gazed casually at the underside of the porch roof and started humming "The Song of the Texas Rangers."

"Please, Clete?"

To drown her out, he started singing the words:

"The morning star is paling; the campfires flicker low;
 Our steeds are madly neighing; for the bugle bids us go:
 So put the foot in stirrup and shake the bridle free,
 For today the Texas Rangers must cross the Tennessee.
 With Wharton for our leader, we'll chase the dastard foe,
 Till our horses bathe their fetlocks in the deep, blue Ohio."

Realizing that he wouldn't surrender to her pleading, Texada jumped up and stormed into the house.

Creed sighed, wishing that he had taken that walk with Texada on that warm June afternoon.

"All right," he said, "I'll go with you, but both of you have to promise me that you'll stick close to each other and to me. I don't want either one of you running off by yourself. Is that understood?"

"Yes," said Faye. She beamed at Creed. "Oh, yes."

"Sure thing, Mr. Creed," said Drake. "Anything you say."

They began their outing at G. W. Stidham's place, which was right beside their camp. Then they crossed the street and cut through Joe Coodey's property to the store owned by the firm of Coodey & Whitlow, which was out on the Texas Road. Coming back into town, they stopped by Charles Smith's general mercantile located opposite the town well. Ed Butler owned a business next to the village's water source. From there, they walked down the slope to Dr. A. J. Patterson's drug emporium, then to Mr. Seale's store. After that, the only two stores left were those of Louis Ross and Bill Nero.

"We don't need to go to either one of those," said Creed as they stood out front of Seale's. He glanced at the sun perched directly overhead. "It's time we were heading back to camp."

"Yes, I think you're right, Slate," said Faye. "Come on, Drake. We'd better be going."

Drake hesitated, his attention being drawn to two men on horseback riding by them and headed toward Nero's. "Say, Mr. Creed," he said, "aren't those the two men who caused all the trouble last night?"

Creed studied the pair, recognized them as Morris and Stiver, and said, "Yes, I believe you're right." He watched them ride up to Nero's, rein in their horses, and dismount. "Looks like they're planning on getting an early start with their drinking today." He started to turn away, but something caught his eye. Looking beyond Morris and Stiver, he thought he saw Ed King's oddly marked gelding hitched to the corral fence in back of the store. He squinted for a better view, but it didn't help. "Stay here," he said. "I'll be back in a second."

"Are you going after them?" asked Drake, excited by the memory of the night before and wishing to redeem himself for his lack of backbone.

"Never mind," said Creed. "Just stay here."

"Where are you going, Slate?" asked Faye.

"Just stay here," said Creed firmly over his shoulder. He didn't look back to see whether either of them obeyed him.

"Where is he going?" asked Faye, as she watched Creed cross the California Road to the schoolhouse.

"I think he's going to Nero's to have it out with those two varmints that caused all the trouble last night," said Drake. He was very agitated as he turned to face his sister. "I think I'd better go help him."

"I don't think so," said Faye, looking past Drake to Creed. "He's coming back already."

"What?" said Drake. He spun around hoping her report would prove to be false. He was totally disappointed.

Creed joined the Thayers and said, "Come on. We've got to get back to camp right away."

"Why?" asked Faye. "What's wrong?"

"Never mind," said Creed. "Just get moving." He took her by the arm to hurry her along.

Both Faye and Drake tried to question Creed about what he'd seen that had troubled him, but he refused to answer either of them, telling them to shut up and keep walking. Strolling leisurely, they would have covered the distance back to camp in fifteen to twenty minutes, but being in haste, they took half that time to reach the wagons.

As soon as they were within earshot of Reverend Thayer, Faye decided that she'd had enough of Creed's bullying. She pulled up short and said, "All right, Slate, I want to know what this is all about."

Reverend Thayer looked up from his Bible at the sound of his daughter's voice.

Louise was stirring a kettle of pork and beans. She stopped and shifted her attention to the arrivals when she heard Faye's angry demand.

Tyler and Little Bee were sitting in the shade of a wagon, practicing their reading. They closed their books and looked up at Creed, Faye, and Drake when Faye spoke up with such righteous indignation.

Creed ignored Faye and kept walking, right up to Tyler. "That bushwhacker I told you about yesterday?" he said.

"What about him?" asked Tyler, his face scrunched up with concentration and concern.

"He's here," said Creed. "I just saw his horse tied up at that saloon where we had trouble last night."

Tyler scrambled gracefully to his feet. "Are you sure it's his horse?" he asked.

"If it's not his," said Creed, "then it's one just like it."

"Two high stockings on the left feet?" asked Little Bee. When Creed nodded, the youth added, "That's Ed King's horse all right."

"What's this all about?" asked Reverend Thayer as he joined them. "Who's Ed King?"

Creed sighed, then faced Thayer. "He's a bushwhacker, Parson," he said.

Thayer wasn't sure that he understood, but once he did, his eyebrows shot up his forehead. "Do you mean he's one of the villains who attacked us the other night?" he asked.

"I think he's their leader," said Creed.

"How do you know this man?" asked Thayer.

Louise, Faye, and Drake came closer, and Little Bee stood up beside Tyler.

"Never mind that now, Parson," said Creed. "Just suffice it to say that this Ed King means trouble. All right?"

"What do you plan on doing, Creed?" asked Tyler.

"He attacked us, didn't he?" said Creed.

"Are you gonna turn him in to the Army?" asked Tyler.

"I think that's best, don't you?" said Creed.

"I'll go with you," said Tyler.

"Would one of you tell me what this is all about?" pleaded the minister.

"All right, Parson," said Creed. "I guess you have a right to know." He took a deep breath and let it out before beginning his explanation. "Ed King is a bushwhacker from Missouri. Last week Little Bee and I had a run-in with him and his partner, a fellow named Harry Corn. I ran them off the first time, but when we met up with them the next day, I had to kill Corn."

"You had to kill him?" queried Thayer, obviously distraught by this revelation from Creed. "What do you mean by that?"

"Just take my word for it, Parson," said Creed. "I had no choice at the time. I killed Corn, and the day after that King came after me with five others to help him. I had to kill one of them before King and his bunch finally rode off. I thought I was shed of him after that, but I guess I was wrong."

Thayer looked to Tyler and said, "What does this have to do with us?"

Tyler blew out a breath and said, "It seems that this King and his crowd were the outlaws who attacked us the other night."

"What?" gasped Thayer.

"Why didn't you tell us about this before?" demanded Louise.

When neither Creed nor Tyler answered immediately, Little Bee spoke up for them. "Mr. Creed didn't want you to worry, Miss Louise," he said.

"Never mind all that now," said Creed. "We've got to tell the Army about King. Are you coming with me, Tyler?"

"I'll go with you," said Thayer. "Mr. Tyler should stay here and take care of the children."

"All right," said Creed. "Come on."

20

Creed didn't look back to see if Thayer was following him as he marched off toward the Army encampment on the knoll next to the Chapman & Company store on the California Road.

Thayer scurried to catch up to Creed who had a good ten-pace start on him. He was able to overtake the Texan at the town well, but by the time he did, he was too out of breath to talk, which was just fine with the longer-legged Texan. From that point onward, Thayer had all he could do to match Creed stride for stride, and when they reached the cantonment on the low hill, his energy was nearly spent. Huffing and puffing and sweating profusely, he was unable to do little more than listen to Creed speak with a sentry who directed them to the mess tent where Sergeant McGuire was certain to be at this time of day.

McGuire was exactly where the guard had said he would be: in the mess tent, enjoying his midday meal. When Creed and Reverend Thayer stepped up to his table, he looked up at the Texan without recognizing him immediately, but a glance at the parson stimulated his memory. "What are you two doing here?" he groused. "I thought by now that you'd be on your way to wherever it is you're going and that you'd be out of my hair."

Choosing to ignore McGuire's insinuation, Creed cleared his throat and said, "Sergeant, our party was attacked by a band of bushwhackers the other night when we camped north of Honey Springs. We shot two of the vermin before the others rode off, but before they died, one of them told me that they were led by a Missouri bushwhacker named Ed King. I know this man, Sergeant, because I've had a couple of run-ins with him besides

the other night. He's a yellow coward who rides a chestnut gelding
that has two long white stockings, both on the left side."

"So why are you telling me this now?" asked McGuire.

"Because I just saw that horse tied up outside Nero's store,"
said Creed.

"I see," said McGuire. "So you want the Army to arrest this
King fellow. Is that it, friend?"

"If you don't, there's liable to be more trouble between him and
me," said Creed. "I'd prefer to avoid that sort of trouble, if I can,
Sergeant."

McGuire's head bobbed as he gave Creed's statement some
thought. He looked to Thayer and said, "Would that be what you
want, Reverend?"

Still pretty much out of breath, Thayer swallowed hard and
nodded a positive reply.

"All right," said McGuire. "As soon as I finish eating, we'll go
find Lieutenant Bagley and see what he wants to do about this
King fellow."

Thayer had his breath back now. He opened his mouth to
protest the delay, but Creed stopped him by saying, "Sounds
just find to me, Sergeant. Enjoy your meal. We'll wait outside
for you to finish. Come on, Reverend." He took Thayer by the
arm and guided him into the open.

"What are you doing, Mr. Creed?" growled Thayer, jerking free
of the Texan's hold. "I want something done about this fellow
King, and I want it done right now."

"So do I, Reverend," said Creed, "but we're dealing with the
Army here. The Army moves at its own speed, and the worst
thing you can do when dealing with the Army is try to make
them move faster. All that will get you is nowhere. Do you
understand?"

"That's preposterous, Mr. Creed," said Thayer. "They only
need some proper prodding. Watch and see." He started to go
back inside the mess tent.

Creed reached out, grabbed the minister by his coat collar, and
held him back. "Just hold on, Reverend," he said.

"Let go of me, sir!" snapped Thayer, as he struggled to free
himself from Creed's grasp. He was unsuccessful.

"Listen to me, Reverend," said Creed. "I know these men. Soldiers, I mean. They don't like taking orders from anybody except
their own officers, and even then, they don't always obey them.

Just be patient, Reverend. Sergeant McGuire is a good soldier. He'll see to this business for us in due time."

Before Thayer could protest further, McGuire made an appearance outside the tent. "All right, gentlemen," he said, "let's find Lieutenant Bagley now." He ignored the hold Creed had on the parson and headed off toward the camp's center where the flagstaff stood proudly.

Creed released Thayer and followed McGuire.

The minister straightened his coat, then shuffled after Creed and the sergeant.

In a minute, all three were standing in the presence of Lieutenant Bagley, a career man who had been a major during the war but, like so many other officers, had been reduced in rank when the Army was reduced in size after the war. He was a West Pointer, Class of '59. He had a full brown beard, a receding hairline, brown hair, and blue-gray eyes that disguised the intelligence behind them. The lieutenant sat in a camp chair at a small desk, a sheaf of papers spread out in front of him. "What is it, McGuire?" he asked, ignoring the two civilians.

"Lieutenant, sir, these gentlemen have come to report a bushwhacker they've seen here in town, sir," said McGuire.

"A bushwhacker?" queried Bagley. "Only one?"

"That's right," said Thayer. He wanted to say more, but Creed nudged him into silence.

Bagley glared at Thayer for intruding into his conversation with McGuire, but he said nothing.

"Yes, sir," said McGuire. "Just the one, sir."

"Get an armed squad together and go arrest him, Sergeant," said Bagley. "Then bring him back here and we'll see what he has to say for himself before we send him to Van Buren for trial."

"Yes, sir," said McGuire. He snapped to attention and saluted the officer.

Bagley waved off the military courtesy, dismissing McGuire and the civilians.

The sergeant led Creed and Thayer away from officers' country and quickly explained that it would take him a minute or two to assemble some men to carry out the lieutenant's orders. "You'll have to come along to identify the man," he said.

"Of course," said Creed.

McGuire was true to his word. He did take a couple of minutes to assemble a squad. When he had them ready, he gave the command, and the soldiers marched off toward Nero's saloon with Thayer and Creed walking alongside the sergeant. They cut across the low ground to the ford where the Texas Road crossed the creek. They waded through the stream, then climbed the hill to Nero's, halting outside the drinking den at McGuire's command.

"That's his horse there," said Creed, pointing to the chestnut gelding with the long white stockings on its left feet.

"Are you certain it belongs to the bushwhacker you told me about?" asked McGuire. "This fellow King?"

"I've seen him on it three times," said Creed. "If it's not his, then he stole it."

"Well, let's see if this fellow is in Nero's," said McGuire. "Reverend, you'd better stay out here."

"Yes, of course," said Thayer.

McGuire deployed his men to guard all the exits from Nero's, then he and Creed entered the whiskey pit to find Nero behind the bar, talking to the only visible patrons in the establishment: Morris and Stiver. "Afternoon, Nero," said the sergeant. Nodding at the two rowdies from Wisconsin, he added, "Boys," then he stepped up to the bar with Creed beside him.

"Afternoon, McGuire," said Nero. He acknowledged Creed with a stiff nod.

Neither Morris nor Stiver spoke to the newcomers, but they glared at Creed with hate in their eyes.

"Who owns that chestnut gelding outside?" asked McGuire, coming straight to the point of his visit.

"Which one?" asked Nero.

"There's only one out there," said McGuire.

Nero looked past him through the dirty window at the horse tied to his hitching post. "If you mean that one with the white stockings," he said, "it's mine."

"How long have you had it, Nero?" asked the sergeant.

"Not long."

McGuire nodded, then asked, "Where'd you get it?"

"Bought it off a fellow passing through here last week," said Nero. "Said his name was Smith and that he was going back East. Saw him get on a flatboat headed downriver. Let's see. That must've been last Monday or so."

"I see," said McGuire, nodding. He turned to Creed and said, "Well, I guess you were wrong, Mr. Creed."

"Yes, I guess I was," said Creed.

"What's this all about, McGuire?" asked Nero.

"Nothing much," said McGuire. "It doesn't make any difference now anyway. I'll be seeing you, Nero. Come along, Mr. Creed." He turned and left the saloon with the Texan.

Once they were outside and they were walking away from the saloon, Creed said, "You didn't really believe him, did you, Sergeant?"

"Of course not," said McGuire, "but let's pretend we did just for the fun of it. What say?"

Creed nodded and said, "I think I understand, Sergeant."

"Well, was King in there?" asked Thayer.

"Come on, Reverend," said McGuire, not answering the question. "We'll escort you and Mr. Creed back to your camp."

"Wasn't he in there, Mr. Creed?" asked Thayer impatiently.

"Come on, Reverend," said Creed. "We'd better be heading back to camp now."

McGuire formed up the squad, gave the command to march, and led the men off toward the town well with Creed and Thayer walking beside them. As soon as they were out of sight of Nero's, the sergeant halted the men. "All right, boys," he said, "the man we're after is hiding in Nero's saloon. It's my thinking that he's probably come out of his hole by now and he's having a good laugh at my expense. I don't like the thought of that, so we're going back after the son of a bitch." He noted Thayer's frown. "Sorry, Reverend." Then continuing with his orders, he said, "We'll spread out and sneak up on the saloon. As soon as I see that every man's in place, we'll rush in and take this man. He's probably got a gun, so don't anybody be afraid to shoot if he pulls a weapon on you. Understood?"

The six privates gave him affirmative's.

"What about me?" asked Creed.

"You just hang back, Mr. Creed," said McGuire, "and let us handle this. Once we've got everybody in there under guard, you can come in and identify this King fellow. Good enough?"

Creed smiled and said, "Sounds like a pretty fair plan, Sergeant. Reverend Thayer and I will wait behind the schoolhouse until you give the word."

McGuire and his men took less than five minutes to get into position for rushing the saloon. At the sergeant's command, all seven of them broke into the drinking pit, completely surprising the six men inside.

"What the hell's going on here, McGuire?" demanded Nero.

"Don't give me any shit, Nero," growled McGuire. "I'm closing you down for harboring bushwhackers."

"What bushwhackers?" demanded Nero. "There ain't no bushwhackers in here."

"Shut up, Nero!" said McGuire. "You men mind yourselves now and put your hands on the bar where I can see them plain as day, you hear?"

The five customers—Morris, Stiver, King, and two of the men who had been with King at Alberty's—obeyed the sergeant, their obedience prompted by the sight of a half dozen primed muskets pointed at them. McGuire proceeded to search each of them, finding weapons—six-guns and knives—on King and his henchmen.

"Now, you boys just stay put," said McGuire. "I'll be back in a minute." He went outside and called out for Creed and Thayer to come into the saloon.

Creed went inside Nero's with McGuire, but the reverend chose to look through the open doorway instead of entering the den of iniquity.

"Is this the man, Mr. Creed?" asked McGuire, pointing at one of King's cohorts.

"No," said Creed. He nodded at King and said, "That's him. That's Ed King. He's the one who led the attack on us the other night back at Coodey's Creek."

"He's a liar!" spat King. "He's a nigger-loving liar, I tell you!"

McGuire's right fist lashed out and bludgeoned King's jaw. The outlaw's head snapped backward then forward. It wobbled on his neck for a second as he stared cockeyed at McGuire with disbelief. Then his eyes rolled up, his knees buckled, and he dropped unconscious into a heap.

The sergeant turned to Creed and Thayer and said, "I don't think he'll be troubling you no more, gents. By the time he wakes up, he'll be on his way to the jail in Arkansas."

21

"You can come along with us back to the cantonment and prefer charges against him with Lieutenant Bagley," said McGuire. "Then the Army will ship him and these other two to the court in Van Buren for further disposition."

"Van Buren?" queried Thayer.

"Yes, sir," said McGuire. "That's in Arkansas. That's where the federal court is. We send all the criminals that we catch in the Nations there for trial if they've committed a crime here, but if they haven't done anything here to break the law and they're wanted elsewhere, we send them to Van Buren to be held in jail until some lawman who wants them comes for them."

"I see," said Thayer.

"If you like," said McGuire, "you can go along with this bunch to Arkansas and testify at their trial, and your testimony might help to get them locked up for a year or two. They might get a year or two in the penitentiary without your testimony. Who knows what the judge will do? You could be wasting your time because the travel and the trial could take the better part of two months. If I was you, I'd be on my way and let the Army and the court handle these vermin."

"I believe you're right, Sergeant," said Creed. "I know that I'd rather be moving on."

"So would I," said Thayer.

"Very good," said McGuire. He nudged King with his foot. "We'll just pack this one up with these other two and ship them off to Van Buren straightaway, and you won't have to worry about them troubling you no more this trip."

"Sounds good to me, Sergeant," said Creed. He and Thayer accompanied the soldiers back to their post, where each of them made a formal statement charging King and his henchmen with being bushwhackers and accusing them of the attack at Coodey's Creek three nights previous. Lieutenant Bagley had them sign the complaints, then dismissed them with the assurance that the outlaws would be dealt with according to the law.

Satisfied that the book on Ed King was closed, Creed and Thayer returned to their camp near Stidham's store. They related all the details of the arrest of King and his men at Nero's when the others pressed them for the tale, which Thayer concluded by saying, "That's the last we'll see of Ed King."

After eating their noon meal, Louise returned to teaching Tyler and Little Bee, the reverend resumed reading his Bible, and Creed strode off to his hammock where he still hoped to make up an hour or two of the sleep that he'd missed the night before. No such luck, however, because Faye and Drake followed him. Spinning around and squaring off with hands on hips and feet spread wide apart, he confronted the siblings, demanding, "Now what?"

Drake looked at Faye, then to the Texan. "Mr. Creed, I was wondering if you might show me how to shoot a gun," he said.

Creed was incredulous. "Show you how to shoot a gun?" he sputtered. He went limp as he thought about this naive young man from the East who wanted to learn how to shoot a gun. *How do I say no to him? How do I tell him that he's better off not knowing how to use a gun? Damn! How do I tell him to leave me alone without hurting his feelings?* Creed sighed, then said, "Really, Drake, I don't think your father would approve of you taking shooting lessons from me."

"Yes, he would," said Drake eagerly.

"No, he wouldn't," said Faye, acting the wet blanket.

"How do you know he wouldn't, miss smarty pants?" said Drake angrily. "He might."

"Until he does approve," said Creed, jumping in between the brother and sister before they got into a real fight, "my answer is no."

Drake's face crumbled with disappointment. "No?" he queried painfully.

"You heard him," said Faye. "No."

"That's right, Drake," said Creed. "No lessons unless your father gives his approval."

Young Thayer's eyes brightened as he said, "Do you mean to tell me that if Father gives his approval then you will show me how to use a gun, Mr. Creed?"

Aw, hell! thought Creed. What have I done? He'd let his tired mind and quick tongue back him into a corner. "Well, I suppose," he stammered. "But only if and when he gives his approval and not until then. Is that understood, Drake?"

A huge grin erupted on Drake's face. "Thanks, Mr. Creed," he said. "I'll go ask Father right now." He ran off without further ado.

"Father won't approve," said Faye.

"No, I don't think he will," said Creed. "But that's Drake's problem. What's yours, Miss Faye?"

"Me? I don't have a problem."

"Then what is it that you want from me?"

She smiled and said, "Oh, nothing much. I only thought we could talk for a while."

"Miss Faye, I'm real tired, and I'd like to get some sleep. We've got a long ride ahead of us tomorrow, and I'd like to be awake when I'm in the saddle."

"You can sleep later, can't you?"

"No, I can't," said Creed. He studied her for a second, then added, "But I'm getting the idea that I'll have to."

Faye smiled again and said, "I was only thinking that I hardly know anything about you, and you certainly don't know very much about me. I thought we might get better acquainted."

"Now why would we want to do that?" asked Creed.

"Well, it would be the friendly thing to do, wouldn't it?" she said. "Seeing that we're traveling together like we are and all, I mean."

"I see," said Creed. "All right, what would you like to talk about?"

"How about you?" she offered.

"Me?"

"Yes, you. Tell me all about you and your family and where you come from and where you've been and what you did in the war and what you've done since the war." She caught her breath and added, "Tell me everything there is to tell. Even your deepest, darkest secrets."

"I don't have any secrets," said Creed. "As for the rest, I'm not sure where I should start."

"Start by telling me when you were born," said Faye.

"February 27, 1842."

"That makes you twenty-four years old then."

"It did the last time I counted," said Creed.

"And who were your parents?" she asked.

Creed sighed and answered the question, then the next question, and the one after that, and the one after that, and so on for most of the afternoon until Faye had learned more about him and his family than he had related to any other person in his entire life.

While Faye was interviewing Creed, Drake approached his father about learning how to shoot a gun. The reverend was not pleased to have his Bible study interrupted. "What is it now, Drake?" he groused, closing his Bible and marking his place with a finger.

"Father, I was thinking that now that we're in the West that it would be appropriate for me to know how to shoot a gun," said Drake, coming straight to the point. "I mean, after all, we'll be living among Indians, and my knowing how to shoot a gun might save our lives some day."

"We'll be living among civilized Indians," said the senior Thayer. "I've been told that the Chickasaws and the Cherokees live in houses and that they wear clothes much the same as we do. You saw the Indians at Fort Gibson, Drake. Didn't they appear to be much like us?"

"Well, yes, Father, they did, but I wasn't thinking about the Indians that we'll be living among."

"But that's what you said," countered the reverend.

"Yes, I know," sputtered Drake. "But I meant the wild Indians west of the Chickasaw Nation. Mr. Tyler has told me that the Comanches and Kiowas are still uncivilized and still very dangerous and that they occasionally raid into the Chickasaw Nation for scalps."

"Yes, I've heard those tales, too," said Thayer, "but we'll have the Army to protect us. Fort Arbuckle is close to Cherokee Village. The wild Indians won't dare raid that close to an Army post, Drake."

Not ready to give up, Drake chose another tack, hoping to find a more favorable breeze from his parent. "What about bushwhackers,

Father?" he said. "They seem to be everywhere, and I understand that they rob and kill indiscriminately. Don't you think that I should know how to shoot a gun to protect us from bushwhackers and other such outlaws?"

Realizing that his son wasn't about to accept a negative answer very easily, Thayer sighed and said, "In the first place, son, we'll be living in a town, and I don't think outlaws or bushwhackers will bother us in a town. In the second place, I am a man of the cloth, and I don't think even a depraved bushwhacker would risk eternal damnation by harming a minister of the Lord or his family. In the third place, you will be leaving us soon after we are established in Cherokee Village to go back to Kentucky to college, and you won't have any use for guns there. In the fourth place, it has been my observation that men who carry guns are apt to use them."

"What does that mean?" asked the frustrated youth.

"It means," said Thayer, "that men who have guns within easy reach will use them to settle disputes instead of using their wits and their intelligence and the laws of God and the laws of this great nation of ours. Guns were meant for only one thing, son, and that's killing. Whether it's killing animals or it's killing people, it's still killing, and killing is against the Lord's will. Do you remember what our Lord said in Matthew when He was with His apostles in the garden of Gethsemane?"

"Yes, Father, I do," said Drake heavily. "But—"

"No buts, Drake," interjected Thayer, wagging a finger at his son. "Recite the Scripture, please."

Drake sagged but did as he was told. " 'All who live by the sword shall die by the sword.' "

"Quite correct," said the parson, pleased that Drake knew his Bible well. He'll make a fine minister for the Lord, thought Thayer.

"But, Father—"

"I said no buts, Drake. Killing is wrong, and you know it. Learning how to shoot a gun would be tantamount to learning how to kill, and I can't allow my only son to learn how to kill another human being. The answer to your request is no." Seeing the disappointment in Drake's face and wishing to soften the blow, he added, "Son, pick up your Bible and go off somewhere and speak with the Lord about what I've just said to you. Ask Him if I'm not right. Pray on it, son. Pray with all your heart, and ask the Lord for His divine guidance in this matter. Go on and pray, Drake, and you'll see that I'm only doing what is right for you. Go on now, and pray."

Drake was dejected by his father's attitude, but he did as he was told.

22

Louise had been so busy teaching Tyler and Little Bee to read, write, and cipher that she had hardly noticed Faye's absence from the family circle. Under normal circumstances, she wouldn't have thought much about her sister's truancy, but these weren't normal times for the Thayers. A young, impressionable girl like Faye spending an entire afternoon with a man like Slate Creed was no usual circumstance either.

As the sun reached the three-quarter mark in the sky, Faye finally left Creed to take his nap, and she returned to the wagons in order to help Louise prepare the evening meal. As she passed near her brother, she took particular notice that Drake was sitting by himself and reading his Bible, which was out of the ordinary for him. Recalling her own past experiences with their father when she had asked him for privileges or material items to which he would be ill-disposed, she recognized Drake's posture as their father's response to such requests. She shook her head slowly, feeling empathy for Drake. She then joined Louise at the makeshift kitchen at the end of the first wagon.

"Where have you been?" Louise asked testily, as if she didn't already know the answer.

"With Slate," replied Faye matter-of-factly. Her voice had a certain lilt to it that wasn't normally there, that betrayed the edge of annoyance.

A twinge of jealousy pinched Louise. She denied the real source of the pang, thinking it was a symptom of caring, the concern that a parent would have for the welfare of a precocious offspring.

"Do you think you know him well enough to be calling him by his first name?" she asked.

"I do now," said Faye gaily, sensing her sister's distraction and delighting in it.

"I see," said Louise, feeling within herself a growing frustration with Faye. "Do you think you should be spending so much time with Mr. Creed?"

"Yes, I do," said Faye, as she tied on an apron. "Especially since we're to be married."

Consternation flustered Louise. Her mind was filled with intertwining thoughts on the veracity of Faye's statement. She's pretending, thought Louise. She's making that up. She's dreaming. She's only hoping. She's lying. She's telling the truth. Aloud, she said, "Married?" permitting the inflection in her voice to express her disbelief.

"Well, not right away," said Faye. Then deciphering the doubt in Louise's tone, she added, "I mean, he hasn't asked or anything yet. But he will. I'm sure of it."

"I see," said Louise. She picked up a paring knife and began slicing onions into a pot of water that was sitting on the end gate that doubled as a work counter when let down onto its fold-up legs. "Are you saying that Mr. Creed has indicated that he has romantic notions about you?"

"Well, not exactly," said Faye. She took the other peeling knife and started whittling the skins off a dozen good-sized potatoes. "I mean, he hasn't come right out and said anything yet, but he will. He just doesn't know how he feels about me yet, that's all."

"He doesn't know how he feels about you yet," said Louise, trying to disguise the mockery in her tone but failing miserably, "but you're certain that he's going to marry you. Is that it?"

Although she was experiencing a touch of euphoric giddiness, Faye still had the percipience to realize that Louise's mocking summation of her pronouncement and her subsequent remarks were rather poignant. Even so, she refused to let Louise see that it had any effect on her emotions. "Yes, that's it," she said. Then employing the tactic that the best defense is a good offense, she added, "You may think I'm being silly, but that's only because you don't understand these things. But how could you be expected to understand romance? You've never had a romantic thought in your whole life."

That hurt. Louise knew Faye was right, and that made it hurt all the more. Faye could have slapped her in the face, and it would have been less painful. Fortunately, she had the onions to blame for her tears as she said, "Yes, I suppose you're right, but it's only because I've had to spend most of the last year looking out for you and Drake and Father, and for five years before that I had Mother to care for. I haven't had time for romantic notions." She wiped her eyes as she searched for some sort of consolation, found some, then said, "Now that I see what romance is doing to you, I'm glad that I haven't been afflicted with such foolishness. You go ahead and have your little dreams of love and such other nonsense. I've got much more important matters to occupy my life."

"Like Father's school?" chided Faye.

"Yes, like Father's school," said Louise firmly. "The education of the Indians is very important to me. Look how it's helped Little Bee already. And Mr. Tyler, too. You may feel that your duty in life is to marry a man like Mr. Creed, but I aspire to a much higher calling, my dear sister."

"Maybe so," said Faye, "but at least I won't die an old maid like Aunt Minerva."

"I don't plan to die an old maid either," said Louise. "I will marry some day, but it won't be to a drifter like Mr. Creed. My husband will be a man of God."

"Like Father, I suppose," gibed Faye.

"Yes, like Father," said Louise. "A minister was good enough for Mother. Why shouldn't a minister be good enough for me, too?"

"Will you also work yourself to death for your minister? Like Mother did for hers?"

Louise dropped the onion that she was peeling and used the back of her left hand to strike Faye on the right side of her face. Faye reacted only by taking a step backward and glaring at her sister.

"How dare you say such a thing!" Louise hissed through clenched teeth. "Father has worked hard all his life to give us a decent home and decent food and decent clothes. How can you imply that he has done anything less?"

"It's easy, Louise. Mother is dead." Now incensed by her sister's attitude, Faye squared her stance and added, "But I guess that's all for the better, isn't it? Now you can have Father all to yourself."

Louise tried to slap Faye again, but this time Faye was ready to defend herself. She deflected the blow with her right hand, her knife hand; then she pointed the blade at Louise as she said, "Don't ever do that again, sister dear."

Her eyes riveted to the now deadly weapon in Faye's hand, Louise said slowly, "Is that something you learned from your darling Slate?"

Realizing that she was threatening to do her only sister a grievous injury, possibly even to the point of taking her life, Faye lowered the knife but not her head or spirit. "Just keep your hands to yourself, Louise," she snarled.

Creed, Tyler, Little Bee, and Drake were all out of earshot of the arguing sisters. Reverend Thayer wasn't. He closed his Bible and strained to make out their words. Although he couldn't determine exactly what they were saying, he could discern the animosity in their voices. Unaccustomed to hearing his daughters argue, he moved quickly to intercede, joining them just as Faye finished her warning to Louise. "Now, now!" he said. "What's this all about, girls?" He looked at Louise and received no reply. He shifted his view to Faye and again got nothing but silence. Turning back to the older daughter, he said, "I heard you two arguing, Louise. What were you arguing about?"

"It was nothing, Father," said Louise, her eyes lowered.

"Nothing?" he queried.

"Nothing important," said Louise.

"I see," he said. "Is that what you say, too, Faye?"

"That's right, Father," said Faye, also casting her gaze at the ground. "It was just something silly." Then looking up at Thayer, she added, "I'm sorry we disturbed you, Father."

"I'm sorry, too," said Louise, also looking up now.

Realizing he would get no further with his questions, Thayer said, "Then I take it that you've settled the matter, whatever it was that you were arguing about?"

Louise stared at Faye and said firmly, "Yes, Father, it's all settled."

Faye returned the glare in her sister's eyes and said, "That's right, Father. It's all settled."

"Very well," said Thayer. "Then I take it that I can expect no more of these disturbances from you two. Am I right?"

Both girls said, "Yes, Father." But neither of them really meant it.

23

No further words passed between Louise and Faye until they had finished preparing the evening meal. Louise called out to their father that it was time to eat, and Faye said she would go fetch Creed and Little Bee for supper.

"No," said Louise, "I'll get Little Bee and Mr. Creed. You go tell Drake and Mr. Tyler to come and eat."

Faye thought about arguing but didn't. "All right," she said pleasantly. "Go ahead and get them. I know you're only doing it to spite me, but that's all right. You can't hurt me." That's what she said, but she was really thinking something else. As she watched her sister walk away toward the trees where Creed had hung the hammocks, Faye told herself, I know you, Alma Louise Thayer. You only want to tell Slate to stay away from me. Well, that's all right, too. Go ahead and tell him to stay away from me. It won't do you any good. You'll only make him want me all the more. So go ahead and tell him to keep his distance. You'll be doing me a favor, big sister.

Creed and Little Bee were both asleep when Louise approached them. She tapped the boy on the shoulder to awaken him, and he came around without a fuss. The Texan was another matter. When Louise tapped him, he shook like a bowl of gelatin, stiffened, then reached for the Colt's stuck in his waistband.

"Mr. Creed," said Louise firmly, "it's time to eat."

Louise's words didn't penetrate Creed's conscious mind, but the femininity of her voice did. He grabbed the butt of the revolver but didn't draw. His eyes came open and focused on Louise. She was frowning at him, but even so, he still liked what he saw. His next thought was to take her by the hand, pull her down atop him, and kiss her hard, lustily, with mouths open and tongues in excited urgency. It was only a thought, an arousement to be sure, but one that he suppressed—with great reluctance but also with a strong will.

"Oh, Miss Thayer," he said groggily. "What can I do for *you* now?" remembering that Faye and Drake had been around earlier, now he was certain that Louise wanted something from him as well.

"It's time to eat, Mr. Creed," she replied.

"Come on, Slate," said Little Bee eagerly. "Let's go eat." He was already out of his hammock and standing close by. He rubbed his stomach. "What are we having, Miss Louise? Not that it makes any difference. I mean, you sure do cook good, and whatever it is that you're serving has got to be good."

"We're having stew, Little Bee," she said, smiling involuntarily because she liked the boy so much, delighting in his simple joy for life. "You go ahead. I'd like to have a word with Mr. Creed first."

Little Bee looked at Louise, then at Creed. He knew that Miss Faye had more than a passing interest in the Texan, but Miss Louise, too? I sure hope the womenfolk cotton to me like they do to him when I get all growed up, he thought. He smiled at Louise and said, "Sure, Miss Louise, but don't take too long or I'll eat all that stew myself."

Louise tousled his hair, smiled back at him, and said, "If you do, you won't have any room for the dessert I made."

"Dessert? Oh, boy!" Little Bee dashed off for the wagons.

Creed swung his legs over the edge of the hammock, put his feet on the ground, and came erect. "What is it that you want to talk to me about, Miss Thayer?" he asked, his tone colored with suspicion.

"It's about my sister, Mr. Creed," she said, as soon as she was certain that Little Bee was out of listening range.

"What about her?"

"She's not as old as I am, Mr. Creed, and she doesn't have the experience in life that I have. She's actually rather naive about many things, and she's quite susceptible to the guiles of men like you."

"The guiles of men like me?" interjected Creed. She'd hit a nerve, and he was ready for a fight. His brow pinched together over his nose as he demanded, "Just what exactly does that mean, Miss Thayer?"

"Excuse me, Mr. Creed," she said evenly. "I thought you were better educated. Guile is another word for—"

"I know what the word means, Miss Thayer," said Creed, interrupting the lecture. "We had schools in Texas when I was growing up, and I did attend one for a good many years."

"Good for you, sir, but as I was saying, my sister is quite susceptible to the guiles of men like you."

"That's the second time that you've said that," said Creed, again breaking into her speech. "Just what the hell are you getting at, Miss Thayer?"

"Mr. Creed, there is no need for such vulgarity."

"There is when you go to impugning my character," countered Creed. Then realizing what he'd just said, he grinned sardonically and asked, "How's that for a word, Miss Thayer? Impugning. The present participle of impugn. To impugn: to challenge, to attack with criticism, to dispute the truth or validity of something. It's spelled I-M-P-U-G-N. It comes from the Latin, the exact word escaping me for the moment."

"Are you trying to impress me, Mr. Creed?"

"Hell no, I'm not trying to impress you. I'm just trying to get you to quit beating around the brush like a cowboy looking to make a dishonest dollar with somebody else's cattle. Come straight to the point. That's all."

Louise sighed with tolerance, then said, "The point is, Mr. Creed, you are putting ideas into Faye's head that will only lead her to unhappiness, and I want you to stop it."

"Ideas? What ideas?"

"Faye has the impression that you have romantic intentions toward her."

Creed was incredulous as he said, "Romantic intentions? Where in the world did she get such an idea as that?"

"From you, obviously."

Creed shook his head and said, "No, ma'am, not from me. I have made no such overtures to your sister. Not today, not yesterday, or at any other time since we met at Fort Gibson last week. And furthermore, I have no intention of ever making any such overtures to her in the future. Faye is a nice girl, but that's all she is: a girl."

"She's a nineteen-year-old woman, Mr. Creed."

"She may be nineteen in years," said Creed, "but in growing-up time, she's only about thirteen, maybe fourteen. She's far from being a woman yet."

"How would you know what a woman is?"

Creed leveled a scowl at Louise. "I don't think you really want me to answer that, Miss Thayer," he said evenly.

Louise stared into Creed's eyes. Yes, I would, her subconscious said, but to Creed, she said, "No, I suppose not."

"Look, Miss Thayer, I don't know what Faye has told you, but let me assure you that I have no romantic intentions toward her or any other woman except the one I left behind in Texas."

Shock and disappointment clouded Louise's face. "Do you mean to tell me that you're married, Mr. Creed?" she asked.

"No, I'm not married," said Creed, "but I do have a sweetheart waiting for me back in Texas. And someday, when my life is all straightened out, I plan on marrying her. But until that day comes—" He stopped himself from saying that he had remained true to Texada so far and that he would remain true to her in the future. He stopped himself from saying it because he would have been lying. He hadn't been as true to Texada as he wished he had been, and he doubted whether he would be strong enough to remain true to her in the future, especially with women like Louise around. "Well," he added, "never mind all that now. We're talking about your sister."

"Did you tell Faye about this sweetheart back in Texas?"

"She didn't ask," said Creed.

Louise smiled inwardly, delighted to possess this bit of knowledge about Creed that she would keep as a secret until she could use it to put Faye in her proper place. "I see," she said.

"Miss Thayer, I take it that your whole purpose in this conversation is to warn me to stay away from your sister," said Creed. "Am I right?"

"Yes, you're quite correct, Mr. Creed. I think it would be best for Faye if you stayed away from her for the rest of our journey together."

Creed burped a laugh and said, "Well, I'll be damned." Seeing that Louise was about to protest his use of profanity, he held up a hand and said, "Don't bother lecturing me again about what words I choose to use, Miss Thayer. Just let me say that I don't usually speak like this in front of ladies, but something about you, something you said or did—" He hesitated as he realized that he was getting himself into territory that he really wanted to avoid. "I mean, I don't know what it is for sure, but something has made me forget my manners, and I apologize for it."

"Apology acknowledged," said Louise.

"Acknowledged?" sputtered Creed. He was incredulous again; this time with Louise. "Don't you beat all now? That's something I would have expected to hear from your father. But not you." He shook his head, disbelieving she was taking this attitude. "You know, I feel like I've already had this same conversation, but I had it with your father. He told me to stay away from you and Drake and Faye, and I told him that he didn't have to worry about that, that I had no intention of cozying up to the three of you. The only thing was he forgot to tell the three of you to stay away from me. So maybe since he didn't I should. Or maybe you should do the telling. Sure, that's it. If you're so het up over Faye visiting with me, then you tell her to stay away from me."

"No, Mr. Creed, I think you should tell Faye yourself," said Louise, hoping she would anger him enough that he would do it and thus hurt Faye. That should teach Faye a lesson that she won't soon forget, thought Louise.

Creed snickered and said, "Like I said before, don't you beat all. I'm not the one who's so concerned about me talking to Faye. You are. Remember? You and your father. As far as I'm concerned, I didn't start one single conversation with Faye. Or with Drake, for that matter. I only mention that because I'm sure you're gonna tell me stay away from him, too."

"Only because Father has told you to stay away from Drake."

"I thought so." He shook his head with frustration. "Look, Miss Thayer. This conversation has gone far enough. If you've got a problem with Faye and Drake talking to me, then you can just take it up with them. As for me, I'm hungry, and I'm going to have some supper before it gets cold." He moved past Louise, then stopped and turned back to her. "Are you coming?"

"We'll continue this conversation later," she said, then she headed toward the wagons.

"No, we won't," said Creed, as he fell into step beside her.

Yes, we will, thought Louise.

As much as he hated it, Creed was having the very same thought.

24

Perryville, or what was left of it, was the next community on the Texas Road. For a lone rider, it was one day away from North Fork Town. For the Thayer wagons, it was two and a half days away. For Creed, the time and distance seemed like forever.

During the two-plus days that Reverend Thayer's party was on the trail to Perryville, Creed brought up the rear as usual, while Little Bee spent most of the time now riding in the second wagon with Louise in order to learn as much as he could before they would have to part company at Boggy Depot, because he wasn't sure whether he would ever get another chance at schooling. Like Tyler, who had declared that he was learning his three R's because he didn't "want to be no dumb nigger for the whole world to make fun of," Little Bee was quite determined to be an educated man when he grew up because he didn't "want to be no dumb Injun for the whole world to be funnin' with."

Because Little Bee was riding with Louise in the wagon, Drake Thayer rode the orphan's mule beside Creed, which was all right with the Texan because he knew it rankled Louise that her brother was spending so much time with him. Like Little Bee, young Thayer gravitated toward Creed because he considered the Texan to be the supreme example of manhood. Creed could handle a gun, he could face danger without fear, and he could kill bad men. In Drake's eyes, these were very admirable attributes in a man.

Of course, Creed didn't know that this was Drake's motivation for sidling up to him. He didn't know Drake well enough to see into his heart, and he hadn't really formed an opinion about the parson's son before riding with him much of the first day out

161

of North Fork Town. Before then, young Thayer was mostly a nuisance, starting with the incident at Nero's saloon, followed by his request to be taught how to handle a six-gun. Although he saw nothing wrong with a young man learning about guns, Creed was certain that the elder Thayer would be opposed to the idea of his son being taught the deadly art of shooting; therefore, he had side-stepped the question and had put the onus on the father to deny Drake his desire.

Early that first morning on the road to Perryville, Drake repeated his request for shooting lessons, and Creed answered him by asking, "How did that go with your father yesterday?"

"Not good," said Drake, looking forlorn. "He told me to go pray about it."

"Did you?" asked Creed.

"Yes, I did, but I don't think the Lord answered me. I mean, I didn't get any sort of inspiration from my prayers. I'm just as confused about guns as I was before."

"Is it the gun?" asked Creed. "Or is it what you can do with a gun that has you confused?"

"Father says that guns have only one use," said Drake, "and that's to kill. Whether it's animals that you kill with guns or people that you kill with them, it's still killing. That's what he said, anyway."

"That's true," said Creed, "but most people shoot animals for food or for their own protection. I've shot deer, ducks, geese, quail, rabbits, coons, squirrels, wild pigs. All sorts of animals. I killed them for food. I've also killed a few animals to protect myself. I once shot a dog with the hydrophobia. I've shot a few snakes, too." He paused, then intentionally added, "Both kinds."

"Both kinds?" queried Drake.

"Those that slither on the ground," explained Creed, "and those that walk upright on two legs."

"I see," said Drake. "Then you're saying that it's all right to kill people."

"No, that's not what I'm saying at all," said Creed. "I'm saying that some people are snakes, and when they become snakes, then killing them isn't the same as killing a man."

"I'm not sure that I understand."

"Let me tell you about some snakes I knew back in Texas," said Creed. "Their names were Harlan and Farley Detchen. They were twin brothers. They were probably born snakes, but we gave

them the benefit of the doubt until they murdered my best friend
Jess Tate. That's when they ceased being men and became snakes
permanently. From that day on, they were no different than any
two rattlesnakes or cottonmouths or any other poisonous snakes.
They deserved to be shot on sight. Then they murdered two more
friends of mine. They killed Kent and Clark Reeves in cold blood.
They had their hands up when the Detchens pulled the trigger on
them while they were standing on the pier down to Indianola this
past winter. I was on a ship going out to sea when it happened. I
ran and got my rifle real quick, and I shot Harlan Detchen dead,
and I would have shot Farley, too, if the ship hadn't taken me out
of range. I'll tell you this much, though. The next time I see Farley
Detchen I plan to shoot him dead, too, because he's nothing more
than a murdering snake and he deserves to be dead.

"But the Detchens are only one breed of slithering vermin,
Drake," said Creed, continuing. "There's this other outlaw who's
almost as bad as the Detchens. His name is Jim Kindred. He's
a United States deputy marshal now." Creed shook his head to
emphasize his incredulity. "Don't ask me who the genius was
who made him a marshal because I don't know anybody that
stupid. Anyway, Kindred was a deputy sheriff down to Lavaca
County. Lavaca County, that's where I'm from. Kindred led a
bunch of other outlaws in some raids on some freight wagons.
He was also the leader of a gang of thieving cowboys who killed
my brother. The Detchens were part of that gang, too. I've met
this Kindred on several occasions. He's nothing more than a
sawed-off runt with an axe to grind. Like most short fellows, he's
mad at God for making him short, but because he can't get back
at God for it, he's taking his anger out on every man who's taller
than he is. I've had more than a few chances to kill Kindred, but
I haven't done it yet because he's one of the most pathetic little
bastards that I've ever met. I probably won't kill him because
I figure he's living in hell already. His hate for taller men, his
resentment for being short, it eats at his guts, and that's his own
private little hell.

"You see, Drake, Kindred is a snake, too, but he's not the same
kind of snake that Farley Detchen is. Kindred is nothing more
than a garden snake. He's poisonless. He doesn't have the fangs
that Farley's got. He had several opportunities to shoot me, but
he didn't do it. If Farley had had those same chances to shoot
me, he would have done it in a cat's wink. But Kindred didn't

because he doesn't have the guts to kill anybody. He gets others to do his killing for him."

"Sort of like generals in the Army?" queried Drake.

"No, more like politicians and clergymen," said Creed. "You see, Drake, it's politicians that start wars. Not generals. They're just high-ranking soldiers who are following the orders of the politicians who are too yellow to fight themselves."

"But you said clergymen as well as politicians start wars," said Drake. "What did you mean by that?"

Creed wondered for a brief second about the wisdom of including religious leaders with political chiefs, then dispelled the guilt, asking, "Have you read about the Crusades, Drake?"

"Yes, I have."

"And who started those wars?"

"The popes."

"That's right," said Creed. "And what about the Hundred Years' War? Who started that one?"

"Some pope and some Protestant leader."

"Both were clergymen, though, weren't they?"

"Yes, I guess they were."

"Do you know anything about the Mohammedans?" asked Creed.

"I know that Mohammed started the Moslem religion, and the Moslems killed a lot of Christians over the centuries."

"That's right," said Creed, "but do you know why they killed so many Christians?"

"Well, no, I don't," said Drake.

"Because their religious leaders told them that Christians were infidels and had to be killed." Creed shook his head and added, "You know, I heard some ministers back in Texas say just about the same thing about Yankees. They told us that the Yankees would free our slaves and turn them loose on our women. Can you imagine that, Drake?"

"Yes, I can," said Drake dourly, "because I heard my own father preach things like that about you Southerners. He said it was the duty of every good Union man to kill every Confederate that came before his gun sights because Confederate men were sodomists, misogynists, rapists, and fornicators with the devil." He paused, sighed, then said, "I think I understand everything now, Mr. Creed. Politicians and clergymen get other men to do their killing for them. That's rather hypocritical, isn't it, when they're the ones who are always spouting off about peace and turning the other cheek and such?"

"Yes, it is," said Creed slowly.

Neither one of them spoke for some time after that as Drake mulled over everything that Creed had told him that morning. Finally, the youth said, "Mr. Creed, I think God won't mind if I learn how to use a gun. I don't think He'll mind at all." He nodded, then added, "I think I'll go tell Father." He kicked the mule in the ribs and rode off toward the first wagon.

Surprised by the suddenness of Drake's statement and by the rapidity with which he departed, Creed could do nothing more than watch him go and wonder if he hadn't made a bad situation worse, that maybe he'd made a mistake and misdirected Drake into thinking that killing another human being was acceptable behavior in a man. Damn! thought Creed, that's not what I wanted him to think at all!

But that was exactly what Drake was thinking as he approached his father with the announcement that God had given him permission to learn how to shoot a gun.

"Are you certain about this, son?" asked Thayer, agitated that his son would reach such a conclusion and then blame it on the Lord.

"Yes, Father, I am," said Drake confidently, as he rode alongside the covered wagon.

"But how do you know for certain that the Lord was telling you this and it wasn't the devil talking?"

"Because, Father, I recalled some of your sermons during the war when you preached against the evil Southerners and how it was the duty of every God-fearing Union man to shoot Confederates on sight, and I'm certain that God inspired you to preach those words to the congregation. If He made you preach those words, then He won't mind if I learn how to shoot a gun."

Thayer was trapped—and by his own words. Even so, he refused to give in. "Maybe I preached that during the war," he argued, "but the war is over now. This is a time of peace, and I expect you to be a man of peace. You have no need to learn how to shoot a gun, Drake."

"But you told me to pray to God about it," said Drake, "and I did, and He gave no sign that He was against me learning how to shoot a gun."

"He didn't have to give you a sign, Drake," said Thayer. "He gave it to me. And the sign was that you should not learn how to shoot a gun."

"But, Father—"

"No, Drake, no buts," interjected Thayer firmly. "The Lord has spoken, and the subject is closed."

Disappointed and angry, Drake pulled up on the mule's reins and let the two wagons pass by him. When Creed came along, he kicked his mount ahead and once again rode beside the Texan.

"I take it your father didn't agree with God," said Creed, trying to be gentle.

"Leastways, not with the God that I believe in," said Drake, his voice filled with bitterness.

I know exactly what you mean, thought Creed.

They rode on in silence for the remainder of the morning.

Reverend Thayer halted the wagons at noon, and everybody gathered around the endgate of the first wagon for lunch. No one spoke except the minister, and all he said was grace before they ate the meal of a cold bacon sandwich and a cup of water. Creed looked at Louise who was too busy to look back because she was watching Faye whose attention was focused completely on Creed. Little Bee let his eyes dart back and forth between the two Thayer girls and Creed, hoping that he might see some sparks fly, but he was only disappointed. Drake was so upset about his father's refusal to let him learn about guns that he was abjectly morose, and his aspect was totally downcast as he could only stare at the ground. Tyler's wounded arm hurt so much that he didn't want to talk, and he was grateful that no one else did. Reverend Thayer was too lost in his own thoughts to partake in any casual conversations with the others. Not until everybody had finished eating and the few utensils were washed and stored away did the minister break the quiet by ordering them to get moving again.

The subject of guns, and subsequently killing, came up again between Creed and Drake as they rode together that afternoon. Creed wished to let it rest, feeling Drake would only get his hopes up and go ask permission to learn shooting again, only to have his father disappoint him one more time. However, Drake refused to let it go as he asked Creed about his experiences in the war, making it nearly impossible for the Texan to avoid talking about shooting and killing, of course. Much to Creed's surprise and satisfaction, Drake didn't ask anything that leaned toward justifying the use of guns or the act of killing another human being. Instead, he kept his questions to points of information, such as: When were you in Kentucky? Was the Battle of Shiloh as fierce as the newspapers portrayed it to be? What sort of man was John Hunt Morgan? and the like. As the afternoon wore on and Drake continued to appear to have lost his interest in guns and killing, Creed began to take delight in being a firsthand history teacher, relating adventure after adventure until Reverend Thayer halted the party an hour before sundown.

That evening at supper, tension permeated the camp, just as it had when they stopped for lunch. Louise and Faye spoke to each other as little as possible, and Drake avoided his father. Tyler's pain kept him apart from the others, and Creed remained silent throughout the meal. Only Little Bee seemed prepared to socialize, but when he saw all the others were so sullen, he shrugged and minded his own business until it came time to hobble the horses and mules for the night, a chore he had been doing since Creed and Tyler had become satisfied that he could handle it alone. Seeing the downcast look on young Thayer and thinking to cheer him somewhat, he asked, "Do you want to help, Drake?"

"Sure," said Drake, "why not?" He stood and followed Little Bee to the outside of the second wagon where the eleven hobble straps were hung. He watched as the orphaned boy untied the fetter that held the others together in a bundle and was itself secured to a wagon bow.

"Here you go," said Little Bee, as he handed five of the hobbles to Drake. They walked to the little meadow where the animals had been staked out to graze until it was time to hobble them for the night as an added precaution against them wandering off or being stolen. "We only hobble the mules and Mr. Tyler's horse," explained Little Bee. "Mr. Creed says his horse doesn't need hobbling because Nimbus wouldn't stray in the dark and if any sneak thief tried to steal him, Nimbus would put up a fight and scare the varmint away."

As they went about the task, Drake asked, "That rifle on your saddle. Is it yours?"

"Yes, it is," said Little Bee. He caught up the reins to his mule, then as he held the animal steady, he tied one strap around its front fetlocks, effectively preventing it from walking away in the dark. Then straightening up, he said, "That rifle used to be old Hezekiah's. Then Mr. Creed killed the old son of a bitch and gave the rifle to me."

"Does he let you shoot it?"

"He did once," said Little Bee. He hobbled another mule as he spoke. "We come across some ducks on a pond before we met up with you folks at Fort Gibson. He let me take the first shot." He blushed and added, "I didn't hit nothing except water."

"But he taught you how to fire the gun, didn't he?" asked Drake as he tried his hand at hobbling a mule.

"Well, no, he didn't. I knew about guns before I met up with him."

"Where'd you learn about guns?" asked Drake, suspicious of the orphan's veracity.

"I watched old Hezekiah," said Little Bee truthfully. "Whenever he was going hunting, I watched him clean his rifle and load it up. He used to take me along to be his bird dog, only it was my job to scare up a deer instead of birds. When he went bird hunting, he used his shotgun. I watched him load it, too, but he would never let me shoot it or the rifle. Only Mr. Creed ever let me shoot the rifle."

"Did he ever let you shoot his handgun?"

"No, he didn't let me shoot one, but he let me clean and load one for him."

"One? Do you mean he's got more than one handgun?" asked young Thayer, as he finally succeeded in fettering a mule.

"Sure, he does. He keeps the other one wrapped up in an oilcloth in his saddlebag."

"Why doesn't he carry it on him like Mr. Tyler does?"

"I asked him the same thing after we met up with you folks and I saw Mr. Tyler with his two guns. Mr. Creed said that two guns inside your pants are a mite uncomfortable and that carrying one gun is invite enough for trouble to find you."

"What did he mean by that?" asked Drake.

"I guess he meant that a man carrying a gun is looking for trouble," explained Little Bee.

"Do you think Mr. Creed is looking for trouble by carrying his gun?"

"No, I don't think he is," said Little Bee. "I think he carries it because trouble has a way of finding him. Like he said it does. Like it did when we met up with Ed King and Harry Corn back up to Mr. Hawk's tavern. We wasn't bothering those varmints, but they were trouble just the same. Mr. Creed didn't start nothing with them, but they sure as hell wanted to fight. All he did was finish what those bastards started. That's all. It was the same with old Hezekiah. That son of a bitch didn't give Mr. Creed no choice but to kill him. I know Mr. Creed didn't like doing it, but he did it because it was kill or be killed. Like he said it was."

"I see," said Drake. They finished hobbling the last mule, then Drake fettered Tyler's horse to complete the chore. "Do you think you could show me Mr. Creed's other handgun?" he asked as they started back to camp.

Little Bee was slow to answer because, as much as he wanted to show off to Drake that he knew about guns, he knew that it would be wrong to get into Creed's saddlebags. "It ain't mine to show you, Drake," he said cautiously. "You'd better ask Mr. Creed about that. I think that would be best."

Surprised that Little Bee wouldn't jump at the chance to touch the weapon, to hold it and feel its power, its strength, Drake retreated, saying, "Yes, of course. You're right. I should ask Mr. Creed." But he knew that he wouldn't.

The last embers of daylight painted the western horizon as the boys returned to the wagons. Tyler and Reverend Thayer were already fast asleep, the ex-soldier on the ground near the fire, and the minister beneath the first wagon where Drake also slept. The Thayer sisters were in their beds beneath the second wagon, the space being enclosed with blankets, creating a kind of shelter from the weather and from the eyes of the male members of the party, but neither girl was asleep. Faye was waiting for Louise to drift off so she could slip away to sit with Creed as he stood the first watch of the night, and Louise refused to succumb to Morpheus until she was positive that Faye was deep in slumber. Taking Little Bee's .54-caliber Mississippi rifle with him, Creed had climbed an oak tree to stand his watch over the camp. Seeing that everybody else was where they should be for the night, Drake and Little Bee said goodnight to each other and headed for their beds, Drake beside his father, and Little Bee in his bedroll, which he had put down near the fire but opposite Tyler. Soon after the boys had fallen asleep, Faye gave up her duel with Louise and allowed sleep to overcome her. Louise soon joined her, satisfied that she had won this battle of wills.

Creed completed his first stint at guard duty, then awakened Tyler so he could take his turn watching over the travelers. At midnight, the former slave awakened the former master for his second watch, and they traded places again at three o'clock. When the first glow of pale light shone in the east, Tyler awakened everybody except Creed to begin another day that turned out to be a carbon copy of the day before, both in weather and in how the travelers played it out, from Drake riding with Creed on Little Bee's mule right down to Louise winning another skirmish with Faye at bedtime.

The third morning on the trail was different than the first two. The sky was overcast, and the air hinted that rain might be on the way. It was good that they were only eight miles from Perryville now.

Another difference was the order of travel. Faye decided that she was tired of riding in the first wagon with her father, so she asked him that morning if she couldn't ride Little Bee's mule instead of Drake.

"No," said Drake emphatically. "I'm riding Little Bee's mule again today."

"I wasn't asking you," said Faye. "I was asking Father."

"I'm not so sure Little Bee would want a young lady riding his mule," said Reverend Thayer.

"It wouldn't be very ladylike," said Louise.

"What do you say, Little Bee?" asked Faye. "It's your mule. Would you mind if I rode it today?"

"I don't mind," said Little Bee, smiling a wide grin, "if the mule don't mind."

"Well, Father, what do you say now?" asked Faye.

"I think I agree with Louise that it isn't very ladylike for you to be riding a mule," said the parson.

"Would it make a difference if I were to ride a horse instead of a mule?" countered Faye.

"Yes, it would," said Thayer confidently, knowing perfectly well that they didn't have another horse for her to ride.

"Fine," said Faye. "Mr. Tyler, may I ride your horse today since we have only a short distance to go until we reach the next town?"

Tyler wasn't quite certain what to say except, "Yes, I suppose it would be all right, if it's all right with you, Reverend."

"He's already said it would be all right," said Faye, not giving her parent the opportunity to refuse. "So that settles it. I will ride Payday today, and Drake, you can go ahead and ride the mule."

"So who will ride point?" asked Tyler, trying to save the situation for the minister.

"Drake rode point before," said Faye. "He can do it again." She shot a look of victory at Louise and said, "I'll ride in the rear with Mr. Creed."

"Maybe Mr. Creed would like to have something to say about that," said Louise.

"That's not my decision to make," said Creed, side-stepping the issue and intentionally frustrating Louise.

Thayer looked at the Texan, then to Faye he said, "As long as you don't pester Mr. Creed, I suppose it will be all right."

"Don't worry, Father," said Faye. "I promise not to pester him." She smirked at Louise, then went to the wagon to put on some riding clothes; in her case, an extra pair of pantaloons to protect her legs against the saddle and a pair of gloves to guard her fingers from the reins.

Within a half hour, they were under way, and Faye was riding beside Creed, imagining that she would be riding beside him on several occasions that would occur over a long and gloriously happy future that she was certain they would share together. Much to Creed's surprise, she remained silent for more than an hour after their departure, and when she finally did speak, it was to ask him if they couldn't dismount and walk for a short distance in order to let her exercise her legs. Of course, he consented, dismounted, then helped her down from Payday.

"Thank you, Slate," she said, turning to face him with the hope that he would try to steal a kiss, only to be disappointed when he didn't do anything except start walking down the road after the wagons that were beginning to put some distance between them already.

Still walking forward, Creed looked back over his shoulder to Faye and said, "Are you coming?"

She moved ahead slowly at first, but within a minute she was beside him again. "Louise told you to stay away from me, didn't she?" she said, coming straight to the point.

"Something like that," said Creed, fully expecting that she would ask this question sooner or later.

"What did you tell her?"

"I told her if she didn't want you and me together," said Creed, "then she ought tell you, not me."

Faye smiled and said, "That's kind of what I thought you might have told her. She was really upset when she came to supper the other night."

"I sort of gathered that already," said Creed. "You two aren't exactly getting along now, are you?"

"No, we're not."

"And it's because of you visiting with me so much, isn't it?" queried Creed.

"Yes, it is."

"You know, Faye, Little Bee and I will be leaving you folks in a few days to be on our way to Chahta Tamaha to find his uncle. We'll be gone, and you and Louise will still be living together with your father. With us gone, you two won't have any reason for all this fussing that you're doing now."

"That's not completely so, Slate," said Faye. "It's true that you and Little Bee will be leaving in a few days, but I'll be going with you, so there's no need to be concerned about Louise and me."

Creed had prepared himself for something like this. He had thought it out that she would make some sort of announcement that she wanted to go away with him, and he had come up with a plan to let her down easy. Such was his thinking, anyway. He halted in his tracks, smiled, and said, "You know, I could have sworn that you just said that you would be going with Little Bee and me when we pull out in a few days, but I know that I must have heard you incorrectly because there is no way in heaven or hell that you're going with us to find his uncle. Your father won't permit it."

Faye stopped beside him, smiled back at him, and said, "It's all right for you to say that now, but you'll think differently when the time comes."

This girl is plumb loco, thought Creed. But he could see that it was senseless to argue with her about the subject now. To do so would only cause her pain that she was sure to spread around to the other members of the party. For the time being, he would humor her. He said simply, "I guess we'll just have to see about that, won't we?" and he started walking again.

Falling in beside him, Faye felt quite confident, thinking, Yes, we will have to see about that, Slate darling.

25

Perryville was the first major community to spring up in the northwestern section of the Choctaw Nation. A post office was established there in 1841.

In 1858, the Butterfield Overland Mail started using two routes to cross the Choctaw lands. Both started at St. Louis and went to Fort Smith, Arkansas, where they split. One followed a southwesterly course to Boggy Depot, then south into Texas to El Paso, and from there across southern New Mexico Territory to southern California. The other road went west through Perryville and from there through the Texas Panhandle to Santa Fe, through northern New Mexico and the Mohave Desert, and on to central California where it linked up again with the other route to run up the San Joaquin Valley to San Jose and San Francisco.

The junction of the mail route with the Texas Road at Perryville made the town an important stop on both trails, and when the War Between the States erupted, Perryville became a strategic supply depot for the Confederacy.

After his victory at Honey Springs on July 17, 1863, Union General James G. Blunt felt relatively secure that he had ended the Confederate threat to his troops in the Cherokee Nation; therefore, he retired to Fort Gibson which had been renamed for him by his subordinate, Major William A. Phillips, who had captured the fort earlier in the war. However, Blunt underestimated the resilience of the forces opposing him. Within a few weeks, the Rebels repossessed Honey Springs, then they advanced as far north as Coodey's Creek, only a half-day's march from Fort Gibson. Thus, a second Union foray into the Creek Nation became necessary.

Blunt marched rapidly south with two regiments of cavalry, two batteries of artillery, and three thousand infantrymen, riding in three hundred wagons. He retook the Confederate warehouses at Honey Springs that hadn't been destroyed in the earlier battle. Continuing the march, he captured North Fork Town with its commissary and hospital, then he crossed the Canadian River and descended farther along the Texas Road to Perryville where he overtook the retreating Confederates on August 25. A sharp skirmish followed, and Perryville was taken. What Blunt's soldiers couldn't carry away, they burned, and this included every building in the town.

This was the Union Army's only major expedition into the Choctaw Nation during the war.

Unlike the Cherokee and Creek Nations, which had been divided by pro-slavery and anti-slavery factions, the Choctaw Nation had been nearly unanimous in its decision to align with the Confederacy during the war, and thus, the Choctaws didn't suffer the same level of civil strife that sorely afflicted the Creeks and Cherokees, whose lands became the major war zone of the region. Until Blunt's raid into their nation, the Choctaws hadn't known the sound of battle, the bitterness of defeat, or the desolation of war. Being at first terrified by the intrusion of Union troops, the people of Perryville scattered into the countryside, but as soon as it became apparent that the Federals were returning north again, taking dozens of Choctaw slaves with them, and stability would return to their region, they moved back to Perryville to rebuild their town and their lives.

Tyler had been among those Union soldiers who had burned Perryville in '63. As he led the little caravan into the town shortly after noon on the last day of March, 1866, he wondered how much of the town would be restored by now. He noted that very few of the businesses had rebuilt since the destruction of two and half years earlier. Of the other merchants who had tried to resume commerce, a few had merely constructed wooden facades in front of large tents, while most had put up slabwood shacks lined with construction paper to keep the wind out. Most of the houses weren't much more than Indian huts interspersed by several log cabins, some of two rooms with dog trots and porches, but most of the single-room variety. Most of the money in town was brought there by carpetbaggers and outlaws who the Army wasn't trying very hard to expel at this time.

Tyler found a good spot for the travelers to camp along Perryville Creek, and as soon as the wagons were in place, Louise and Faye started setting up their temporary quarters. Tyler staked out his space with his belongings, and Creed and Little Bee did likewise on the perimeter of the camp. Reverend Thayer took Drake with him and with the thought of offering his services on the morrow went in search of any local clergy. He found another Presbyterian minister in the town as well as a Baptist and a Methodist, two of the three preachers being itinerants from other communities. His fellow Presbyterian was also a missionary, having his post at Goodland Academy in the southern part of the Choctaw Nation. He invited Thayer to share his pulpit that Sabbath, and Thayer accepted eagerly.

Now that they were in the Choctaw Nation, Creed decided to begin looking for Little Bee's uncle instead of waiting until they reached Armstrong's Academy. "Who knows?" he said to the boy. "Your uncle might have left Armstrong's years ago and gone north to freedom. He might have been sold South. Who knows? I don't, so we might as well start looking for him now."

Creed had another reason for wanting to get away from the camp. Her name was Faye. He figured that the less time he spent with her the better, and looking for Little Bee's uncle was a good way of avoiding her. Without saying a word to anybody except Tyler about where they were going or what they would be doing, Creed and Little Bee began their search for Uncle Hum, which would be no easy task considering the circumstances in the Indian Nations after the War Between the States.

The United States government employed a system of dealing with Indians that was begun in colonial days when the English government recognized each tribe as owning its hunting lands, which in the English view made each tribe a separate and independent country just the same as all the minor principalities of Europe. Thus, like their British forebearers, American diplomats entered into treaties with each and every Indian tribe, guaranteeing the Native Americans explicit boundaries to their countries, payments for lands sold to the United States, and protection against outsiders who might threaten the peace and tranquility of the Indian Nations. Each of the Nations—the Cherokees, Creeks, Choctaws, Chickasaws, Seminoles, and several smaller tribes—had concluded such treaties with the United States before the War Between the States was begun. In those nations south of Kansas, slavery had been an unfortunate reality, but because the Nations were considered to be independent countries, the United States government didn't have the right to abolish the cruel institution in the Nations by proclamation, such as President Lincoln had done in the seceding states during the war, or by Constitutional amendment, which Congress had done after the war. The Federals figured the Indians would have to be coerced into ending slavery in their own lands, and the only way that could be done was by writing new treaties.

As far as the politicians in Washington were concerned, the Nations had broken their old treaties with the United States when they sided with the Confederates in their rebellion against the Union. The federal authorities completely disregarded the twin facts that, one, certain articles of those treaties were quite specific about how the U.S. Army was to protect the civilized tribes against the wild Plains Indians, against the intrusion of illegal whites into their lands, and against any other outsiders who might threaten the peaceful Nations; and that, two, this same U.S. Army withdrew from the Nations at the outset of the war, leaving the Indian Nations without the protection guaranteed to them by treaty. In the minds of the Indians, the United States, not the Nations, had broken the treaties. Therefore, when the Confederates came around with an offer to protect them and to pay the same annuities that the Federals were now foregoing, many leaders in the Nations accepted this new deal.

After the war, when the Indians voiced these facts during negotiations in Washington, the government's representatives completely ignored them. New treaties would have to be written, and until they were, the Nations would be considered to be vanquished countries to be occupied and policed by the U.S. Army.

As they conquered the Nations during the war, the Union Army freed the Indian slaves in much the same manner as they had in the Confederacy, but neither the Army nor any federal agency was allowed to set up and administer a bureau to deal with the freedmen in the Indian Nations as they had been allowed to do in the defeated Southern states. The former slaves of the Indians were without any controls, such as registration for share-cropping contracts or for the distributions of food and clothing; they were free to do much as they pleased as long as they acted within the limits of the laws of the Nations, statutes that weren't being enforced with any stringency in the first few months of 1866.

These people could wander anywhere without restrictions now, and no one would know who they were or where they had been because they would leave no written records unless they were arrested for some crime. Even then, the local authority might only record them as "niggers" or "black bucks" or as another contemptible designation.

Creed and Little Bee learned this distasteful lesson when they approached the military commander for the area and asked about Hum Doak.

"Choctaw nigger, you say?" queried the officer, a captain of infantry who had been a colonel during the war. He reminded Creed of his brother-in-law, Brevet Colonel Lucas Markham, back in Lavaca County. Stiff-necked, cold-eyed, the thin facial hair grown to give the aspect of maturity and strength of leadership, a slight sneer of the lips, probably the son of some wealthy Yankee businessman, most likely a banker, who had bought his son a commission.

"No, sir," said Creed, smiling friendly, "I said he was a former slave named Humma Doak or Hum Doak. Maybe even Red Doak if he decided to go by the English meaning of his name."

The captain glared back at the Texan and said, "It's not the Army's job to keep track of niggers in the Indian Nations, Mr. Creed. If you really want to find this buck, I suggest you ask another nigger. Good day, sir."

"Thanks for your time, Captain," said Creed. He turned and walked away with Little Bee at his side. As soon as they were clear of the Army camp, he said, "Yankee bastards! They fought like hell to free the Negroes from us Southerners because we were abusing them as slaves. And now that they're free, the Yankees treat them like dirt. At least, we cared for them and saw to it that they were fed and clothed and housed. What are these Yankees doing for them? Hear me good now, Little Bee. Don't ever believe any of their promises, and don't ever depend on them for anything. The Yankees, I mean. They're not all snakes like that one back there, but a lot of them are snakes. If you're going to survive in their world, then you'd better start learning right now how to tell the difference."

They spent the remainder of the day visiting through some of the town and inquiring about Little Bee's uncle. Nobody could tell them anything about him, although some people suggested that if he had been sold to missionaries before the war, then he most likely was sold South when the war started because all the missionaries left the Choctaw Nation at that time. This wasn't exactly what Creed wanted to hear, but Little Bee didn't mind it so much because the longer it took to find his uncle, the longer he could stay with Creed, and this made him happy, if not Creed.

26

After attending Reverend Thayer's church services on Sunday morning, Creed and Little Bee excused themselves from the other travelers and resumed their visiting through Perryville looking for former slaves who might have some information about Little Bee's Uncle Humma Doak. Once again they came up empty-handed.

"I could have told you that you wasn't gonna learn nothing from the colored folks around here," said Tyler when Creed and Little Bee returned to camp. He was sitting beside the campfire, carving an animal out of a piece of wood that he'd found. "They ain't gonna talk to a white man. Not even one like you, Creed, who talks nice to them. You're the kind that we're the most suspicious about."

"Do you think you could have done any better?" asked Creed.

"Maybe," said Tyler. He stopped carving to inspect his work. So far, it was discernible only as a four-legged creature, but whether it would turn out to be a dog or a horse or even a cow, only Tyler knew. "Maybe not. I'm a stranger in these parts, too. Folks might not want to talk me neither. It's hard to say who they trust around here these days."

"I see what you mean," said Creed. "Maybe it's too bad that you're not coming with us to Armstrong's."

"Got me better things to do with my time," said Tyler. And with that, he put his knife in its sheath, stood up, and said, "Like getting some sleep. Another long ride tomorrow."

Tyler was right. The next day was a long ride, and a lot of it was uphill.

An hour before sundown the next day the travelers approached a place known as The Gap, a natural slash through the Pine Mountains, a sandstone range that divided the drainage basins of the Kiamichi and Muddy Boggy Rivers. Cattlemen trailing a herd north on the Texas Road had learned early on that this was a good place for rustlers to strike. Riflemen could hide in the rocks and bushes on the hillsides and pick off unsuspecting drovers who had little protecting cover and practically no room to maneuver on the trail below. For the cowman, it was a matter of taking the chance that the outlaws were poor shooters and pushing the cattle through The Gap as fast as they would run, possibly losing a good many head, or finding a different route. The smart trail bosses did find another road, one that took them a little farther west, skirting the foothills of the Pines in a wide arc.

When he saw the ridges rising above both sides of the road, Creed's first thought was: Ambush! Then he embellished the thought: What a perfect spot for bushwhackers to be hiding! And immediately, Ed King appeared in his mind's eye. Thank God that son of a bitch is on his way to Arkansas to stand trial. Even so, King wasn't the only bushwhacker in the Indian Nations. Who knew what evil villains could be lurking in those rocks and bushes ahead?

Creed turned to young Thayer who was riding with him again and said, "Move up close to the second wagon, Drake. I don't like the looks of things around here. I'm riding up to Tyler to do a little chinning with him about this." He nudged Nimbus in the ribs, and the Appaloosa picked up his gait from a walk to a trot. When he came alongside the second wagon, Creed reined in the stallion to a walk again. "You might want to slow down here, Miss Louise," he said, his tone implying an order instead of a suggestion. "I'm not sure that I like the lay of the land ahead." Before she could reply, he tipped his hat to her, then he urged Nimbus into a trot again until he came alongside the first wagon where he repeated the same curt warning to Reverend Thayer. Not giving the parson a chance to argue, he spurred the stallion and rode ahead to join Tyler.

The former slave heard Creed coming, and when the Texan was beside him, he said, "You must be thinking what I'm thinking."

"Ambush?" queried Creed.

"Uh-huh," grunted Tyler without turning his head to look at Creed, his eyes being too busy searching the landscape ahead of them. "Could be bushwhackers in those rocks."

"Are you planning on having the wagons stop here, while you and I have a look up there?"

"Didn't you already tell them to stop?"

"I'm not the one in charge here, Mr. Tyler."

Now Tyler turned to study Creed. Seeing the sincerity in Creed's face, he reined in Payday to a halt, turned half-way around to look back at Faye and her father, then called out, "Best to hold up a minute, Reverend, while Creed and me see what's what up ahead."

Thayer brought his wagon to a rest, and Louise did likewise behind him.

"Would you prefer that I scout ahead, while you stick with the wagons?" asked Creed.

Tyler turned back to him and said, "I was thinking we should both go, but now that you mention it maybe one of us should hold back here to protect the Thayers."

"Do you think Little Bee should get his rifle from the scabbard on his mule?" asked the Texan.

"Can't hurt none, I suppose," said Tyler. "I'll see to that. You go on ahead as soon as you think it's right."

Creed nodded his understanding, then Tyler turned Payday around and rode back to fetch Little Bee's rifle for the boy. Creed opened his saddlebag and removed his other Colt's. He checked the chambers to make certain that all six were loaded and five nipples were capped. Seeing that they were, he turned the cylinder and capped the sixth. Holding the revolver upright as if he were preparing for a cavalry charge, he touched his spurs into the Appaloosa's ribs, and Nimbus stepped off at a walk to begin the scout of the rocks and bushes.

Tyler passed by both wagons without explaining anything to their occupants. When he came to young Thayer, he reached for the old Mississippi without speaking.

"What's going on, Mr. Tyler?" asked Drake.

"Could be trouble up ahead," said Tyler. "You stick close to the wagons where it's safe. If there's any trouble, get down from that mule and find some cover and be quick about it."

"What are you going to do with that rifle?"

"I'm gonna give it to Little Bee," said Tyler. "Creed says he knows how to use it." He checked the gun to make certain that it was loaded.

Although Tyler hadn't meant it to sound like an insult, Drake took his words to be a slap at his own manhood. "Oh, I see," he said meekly. Without saying anything more, he followed Tyler to the front of the second wagon.

"Here, Little Bee," said Tyler, handing the rifle to the boy. "You might need this." As an extra caution, he added, "Don't go getting too excited now and shoot before someone else shoots at us first."

"Are there bushwhackers ahead?" asked Louise.

"Don't know for certain yet, Miss Louise," said Tyler. "Creed's gone to take a good look in the rocks and bushes up in those hills before we go any farther. You just sit tight here, and make sure Little Bee don't shoot me in the back or nothing." He smiled broadly, then rode up to tell Reverend Thayer and Faye why they were stopped.

Creed made a thorough search of the terrain, looking mostly for fresh tracks, made either by men or horses. He found none. Satisfied that no bushwhackers were concealed among the rocks and bushes, he returned to the first wagon to report to Tyler and Reverend Thayer.

"See anything?" asked Tyler.

"No signs of anything except some deer spoor," said Creed. "Even so, I think we'd be wise to wait and ride through in the morning. The road slopes downward on the other side."

Tyler nodded and said, "Creed's probably right about that, Reverend. I think we'd best camp here tonight and go through in the morning."

Thayer's head bobbed as he said, "Yes, of course. We'll camp here tonight."

When first light shone in the east, they rose to a breakfast of fried cornmeal mush, bacon, and coffee. By sunrise, they were moving through The Gap, encountering no danger, and an hour later the wagons started down into the valley of Atoka Creek. They crossed the stream at noon, then stopped for lunch. After eating and a short rest, they were under way again until an hour before sundown when they arrived at the ford of Muddy Boggy River and crossed to the far side before dark. They made camp for the last time as a party of seven people; the next day they would reach Boggy Depot, and Creed and Little Bee would be leaving them.

Fully cognizant of where they were and where they would be

the next day, and concerned that Creed had made no commitment to her about the future, Faye decided the time had come to force the issue and bring the Texan to the understanding that she intended for him to marry her and take her away to a life of excitement and adventure. Knowing that Louise would oppose any attempt by her to get Creed alone, Faye conceived a simple ruse that would keep her sister occupied while she slipped away to be with Creed. She saw Little Bee sitting by the campfire, reading from his McGuffey's. She went over to him and suggested that he ask Louise about the Latin language and the ancient Romans.

He put the book down, looked up at Faye, and asked, "Ancient Romans? Who were they?"

"Great warriors," said Faye, sweetening the plot. "They conquered the world a long time ago. But you'd better ask Louise. She knows much more about them than I do."

"All right, but what was that other thing you said?"

"Latin?"

"Yes, that's it," said Little Bee, smiling.

"That was the language of the Romans," explained Faye. "A lot of our language, English, comes from the Latin. Louise can tell you all about that, too. She knows a lot of Latin."

"Thank you, Miss Faye," said Little Bee. "I'll go ask Miss Louise to tell me all about it." He left the campfire and went to Louise who was sitting by the second wagon reading a dog-eared copy of *Uncle Tom's Cabin* for the fifth time. "Miss Louise?" When she looked up, he asked, "Would you tell me about the ancient Romans and the Latin language?"

Louise was surprised by the question. She smiled and said, "Whatever makes you ask that, Little Bee?"

"Miss Faye told me that you know all about the Romans and their language," he said.

Suddenly suspicious, Louise said, "I see." She looked around for Faye and was even more surprised to see her come up behind Little Bee.

Faye placed her hands on Little Bee's shoulders and said, "I thought he would enjoy hearing about Julius Caesar and all those other Romans, and you know so much more about them than I do. I only thought he should ask you to tell him about them."

"I see," said Louise, still a bit suspicious of Faye's motive. "Well, I suppose I could tell you about the Romans and the

Latin language, Little Bee. Why don't you sit down? You, too, Faye. Then you'll know more about them."

"Oh, that's all right, Louise," said Faye. "I've got things to do in the wagon. If you'll excuse me, I'll get to them." With that, she climbed into the back of the wagon, opened a trunk of clothes, and began sorting through them, all the time listening to Louise begin her lecture to Little Bee. As soon as she was certain that her sister was wrapped up in her discourse on ancient Rome, she climbed down again, taking a dress and her sewing kit with her to the campfire. She didn't look back, but she was positive that Louise was watching her. She sat down on a chest near the fire and began to stitch the right sleeve of the garment, continuing to do the work until she was certain that Louise was no longer keeping an eye on her. As a test, she rose and went back to the wagon to replace the first dress and retrieve another. Returning to the fireside, she was happy to note that Louise hadn't batted an eyelash in her direction, but as an added measure, she sewed on the second garment for a few minutes. At last, she was convinced that Louise had ceased her watchfulness and the time had come to slip away to be with Creed. She carried the second dress back to the wagon, leaving her sewing kit behind. She put the dress inside the wagon, then quietly went to find Creed.

Neither Reverend Thayer nor Tyler noticed Faye's departure. The minister was too intent with his Bible study, and Tyler was concentrating on his woodcarving.

The only person who saw Faye leave the vicinity of the wagons was Drake. He knew what she was up to, and he got a small chuckle from the thought. Small because it was interrupted with another idea.

As was his evening routine, Creed had left camp to look for a good place to set up a nightwatch post. He was still looking for the right tree that would afford him a good view of the wagons and the surrounding area when he heard Faye approaching. Unsure of who was coming, he ducked behind a huge cottonwood and waited to pounce. When he saw that it was Faye, he decided to teach her a lesson about sneaking around in the bushes in the dark, or in this case, in the twilight. As she passed by his position, he jumped out behind her, placed his left hand around her mouth, and wrapped his right arm around her waist.

Faye was terrified. She hadn't expected anything like this. She struggled violently until she heard Creed's voice in her ear.

"You're lucky it's only me, Faye," he said sternly.

She relaxed, relieved that Creed was the one holding her. She leaned on him, feeling his steely body pressed hard against her. A fiery sensation flashed through her, warming her all over, making her feel something that she had never felt before but that she wanted to experience again—and soon, right away, now. She squirmed a little, rubbing her backside on him. Oh, yes, she thought, that's it! That's glorious!

Creed felt Faye go limp against him, and his first thought was that she had swooned. Then she wiggled. Little minx! he thought. He'd had women this close to him before and in this same position and without so much clothing. The pressure of her buttocks against his groin was an arousement. It felt good, but this wasn't right. She's only a girl, he thought. He released her and pushed her gently away from him.

Faye turned around instantly, smiling impishly, her eyes alight with a newfound passion. "You didn't have to let me go, Slate," she cooed.

"Yes, I did," said Creed.

Faye moved closer to him and said, "No, it was all right. I was safe in your arms. You could have held me longer."

"No, Faye, I couldn't. It wouldn't be right."

She moved closer still and said, "Yes, it would. It would be very right. For me and for you."

Temptation struck Creed where he was most vulnerable. If she was only a real woman, he thought, a grown-up woman like . . . like . . . like Louise. An image of Louise flashed through his mind. She was breathing heavily, sweating profusely, her face twisted with savage desire. She was fully clothed, but she was grappling with a man, him, and he wanted her, all of her, completely. He washed the vision from his brain, replacing it with a mental picture of the girl he'd left behind in Texas. He saw Texada standing on the bluff above the Lavaca River, her flaxen tresses falling over the shoulders of a sky-blue dress. She turned to look at him, her pavonine eyes questioning, filled with uncertainty. Creed squeezed his eyelids tightly together, dissolving Texada from his conscious thoughts, then he popped them open again. Texada was gone, but Faye wasn't. He backed away from her and said, "No, this is wrong. You shouldn't be out here with me."

"It's all right," she said coyly. "I know how you really feel about me."

"No, you don't."

"Yes, I do," she argued, "and I feel the same way about you." She took two giant steps forward and threw her arms around his neck. "I love you, Slate," she whispered, closing her eyes and pursing her lips for him to kiss.

Creed took her wrists firmly in his hands and pulled her arms from around his neck.

Startled and confused and disappointed, Faye opened her eyes, relaxed her mouth, and said, "What are you doing, Slate? I'm allowing you to kiss me." She tried to resume the embrace.

He was having none of that. "No, Faye," he said, gently pushing her away but not releasing her wrists. "I don't want to kiss you."

She refused to understand, laughing nervously and saying, "Of course you do. You love me."

"No, Faye, I don't. I love a girl back in Texas. Her name is Texada, and I plan to marry her one day."

Faye giggled, then said, "No, Slate. You love me, and you're going to marry me."

Realizing that words were superfluous, Creed let go of her wrists, stared hard into her eyes, set his jaw, and shook his head very slowly from side to side.

At last, she admitted the folly to herself. Pain flooded her eyes, overflowing down her cheeks. Without saying anything, she spun around and ran away, but not toward the wagons.

Impotence gripped Creed. He felt powerless to help her. What could he say that would comfort her? He didn't know. Not at this moment, anyway. He lowered his head, feeling guilty that he could do nothing. Damn! he thought. How do I get myself into these things?

Before he could consider an answer, Faye screamed.

Damn! now what? he wondered. Then he realized that Faye had run off in the wrong direction. He drew his Colt's and bolted after her.

27

Faye's scream was heard by everybody in camp. It scared all of them into action.

"What was that?" asked Reverend Thayer, his attention drawn away from his Bible study.

Louise glanced around quickly, realized that her sister was absent, then said, "It was Faye."

"It came from over there," said Tyler, pointing toward the trees north of the camp. He started off in that direction with Reverend Thayer, Louise, and Little Bee following him.

Drake had slipped away from the wagons earlier, much the same as Faye had done, but instead of looking for Creed, he went in search of Creed's saddlebags and the revolver that was hidden in them. He had found the gun and was examining it when Faye screamed. His first thought was that he had been discovered, and his guilt made him want to hide.

Creed found Faye lying in a heap beside a large rock in a small clearing; she was unconscious. He started to go to her, but the fluttery *chicka-chicka-chicka* warning of a rattlesnake stopped him stone dead still. Moving only his eyes, he scanned the ground in search of the snake and spotted it not more than six feet beyond Faye's motionless body. The diamondback was coiled, its tongue darting out, its rattles sounding like a pair of Mexican maracas. Carefully, slowly, Creed leveled the Colt's at the venomous reptile, squeezed the trigger, and shot it, the ball tearing through its body in two places. The rattling stopped, but the snake wasn't dead yet. It tried to strike out, but it was powerless to deal much of a blow because its spine was severed. Creed moved closer and fired again, this time putting a ball through the rattler's head and effectively killing it.

Satisfied that the snake was no longer a threat, Creed went to Faye's aid. He dropped onto his knees and began examining her for a snakebite. He found none on her arms, face, or throat. That left her legs. He pulled up her dress and undergarments, and just above the top of her high-button shoe, he found the twin holes where the rattler had struck. Knowing that the poison must be stopped from reaching her heart, he took his small knife from its sheath, cut a long strip from her petticoat, and tied it as tight as he could around her knee. Then he went to work on getting some of the venom out of the wounds.

The two shots from Creed's gun stopped Tyler for a few seconds as he tried to figure out what was happening. He recognized the explosions as pistol fire, then he surmised that bushwhackers were in the vicinity and had grabbed Faye or something worse. He drew one of his Remingtons and broke into a run in the direction of the blasts.

Reverend Thayer stopped when he heard the gunshots. He held back Louise who held back Little Bee.

When he heard the gunfire, Drake thought, Bushwhackers! He looked at the Colt's in his hand, nodded to himself, then started off to join the fight.

Tyler burst into the little clearing just as Creed was making the small cuts through the snakebite holes in Faye's leg. He stopped short of the Texan. He couldn't see what Creed was doing, but he did see that Faye's skirt was pulled up. "What the hell are you doing, Creed?" he yelled angrily.

The tone of Tyler's voice put a caution in Creed. He twisted to look over his shoulder at Tyler standing behind him, exposing the knife in his hand.

Tyler saw the blade that Creed was holding, and he saw the blood on Faye's leg. He did some quick addition, came up with the wrong answer, thought of shooting the Texan, but didn't for fear of hitting Faye. Instead, he kicked at Creed, his foot catching the Texan's left elbow, knocking him over and sprawling him beside Faye. He stepped closer to Creed until he was standing over him, his feet between Creed's and Faye's legs. He cocked the .44 and took aim at the Texan's head as he muttered, "White trash."

Creed wasn't ready to die. Reacting instead of thinking and talking, he let his instincts take control. His right foot shot upward, catching Tyler in the knee, buckling it.

Tyler's gun hand jerked to the side as he pulled the trigger on the Remington, sending the ball harmlessly into the dirt several feet away. He tried to right himself, but Creed struck him again with another kick in the same leg, knocking him down.

Seeing his opening, Creed scrambled to his knees and flopped onto Tyler. He grabbed the ex-slave's right wrist and slammed the hand holding the revolver to the ground.

Thinking that Creed would try to stab him, Tyler seized the Texan's right wrist with his left hand and twisted it away from his body. His next move was to roll to the right, putting Creed on his back and himself on top of the Texan, straddling his torso.

Reverend Thayer came into the clearing. His attention was drawn first to the two men rolling on the ground. "Mr. Tyler! Mr. Creed!" he barked. Then he saw Faye lying unconscious a few feet away from them. The minister went to his daughter's side.

Drake entered the clearing, saw Creed struggling with Tyler, then saw his father on his knees, holding Faye's hand. What's happened here? he asked himself. Because he admired Creed to the point of hero-worship, he suspected Tyler had done some harm to Faye and that Creed was defending her honor. Yes or no, the ex-slave was on top of his friend and threatening to kill him. What should I do? he wondered. Suddenly, he was cognizant of the deadly Colt's in his hand. He raised the gun, cocked the hammer, and took lethal aim at Tyler.

Louise came up behind Drake. Little Bee was behind her. She saw her father with Faye. She saw Tyler atop Creed. She saw her brother about to kill Tyler. "No, Drake!" she shrieked, grabbing at his right arm, spoiling his aim.

The Colt's fired.

Reverend Thayer fell forward across Faye, his head striking the rock beside her and knocking him unconscious.

"Father!" screamed Louise. She pushed Drake aside and ran to the fallen minister.

Tyler ceased his struggle with Creed, dropping his gun but not releasing Creed's wrist.

Creed stopped struggling as well. He looked at the parson lying face down over Faye.

"Damn, Drake!" swore Little Bee. "You shot your pa!"

"Oh, God, no!" cried Drake, realizing that Little Bee had spoken the truth. He stared at the Colt's as if it were Satan's tool. Horrified, he cried again, "Oh, God, no!" Then feeling that the six-gun was made of red-hot metal and was burning his hand, he dropped the weapon at his feet and stumbled backwards away from it, terrified that it was alive and might be following him. He bumped into Little Bee who pushed him forward again. Trying to avoid the Colt's, he tripped and fell down beside Louise just as she was rolling Reverend Thayer from atop Faye. "Oh, Father!" he bawled. He raised up on one knee but could do nothing more than cry and stare at the bloody wound that he had inflicted in his father.

Seeing that the minister was badly hurt, Tyler released Creed's wrist, jumped up, and went to help Louise.

Little Bee picked up the Colt's that Drake had dropped and went to Creed. "You all right, Slate?" he asked.

"I'm fine," muttered Creed. He scrambled onto his hands and knees and crawled over to Faye.

Tyler saw Creed approaching Faye. He turned to strike him with an angry fist, but the click of the hammer being cocked on Creed's Colt's stayed his hand. He looked up to see death lurking in Little Bee's eyes and was instantly convinced that the boy would shoot him if he tried to harm Creed.

"Rattler," said Creed, looking up at Tyler.

"Rattler?" queried Tyler.

Louise and Drake were both crying over their father.

"Got her on the leg," said Creed. He drove his knife into the ground beside Faye, then he bent over to suck the poison from her wounds.

"Get away from her!" screamed Louise. She lurched at Creed and pushed him away from Faye. "Get away from her, you fiend!"

Tyler grabbed Louise and pulled her back. "No, Miss Louise," he said. "Miss Faye's been snakebit. Creed's only trying to help her."

"See to your father, Louise," said Creed firmly. Without waiting to see if she obeyed him, he returned to Faye, put his mouth to her wounds, and sucked as hard as he could. He turned his head and spit out the blood and poison that he'd drawn from the injury. In the next several seconds, he repeated the sucking and the spitting twice more, then said, "Little Bee, put that gun away and help me get Miss Faye up so I can carry her back to camp."

"Creed," said Tyler, "the reverend is hurt real bad. You best come see."

Creed frowned and moved reluctantly toward the minister.

"No!" screamed Louise. "You've done enough!" She broke free of Tyler's grasp and tried to prevent Creed from coming closer to her father. She was being irrational, which was too bad for her.

Creed made a fist and slugged Louise solidly on the chin, snapping her head backward, knocking her unconscious, and sprawling her on the ground beside Thayer.

"How come you did that?" asked Tyler.

"She was in the way," said Creed, as he bent over the parson to examine his wounds. First, the one on Thayer's head, a superficial cut that was bleeding nastily but didn't appear to be life-threatening. Then he saw bubbles in the blood coming from his chest wound. "You're right, Mr. Tyler. He is hurt bad. It looks like the ball went through his lung. Help me roll him onto his side."

"Roll him onto his side?" queried Tyler. "What for?"

"Beats the hell out of me," said Creed. "All I know is that during the war I saw an Army surgeon do this once to a fellow who had the same kind of wound and that fellow lived to ride again. He said it had something to do with keeping the blood from filling up the good lung and drowning him."

Tyler nodded and helped Creed roll Thayer onto the same side as his wound.

"All right," said Creed. "Drake, you hold him like this for me, while I try to stop his bleeding." When Drake didn't move immediately, Creed shook him to get his attention, saying in an even, firm, authoritative tone, "Help your father, Drake, or he'll die for sure."

Louise began to stir, and so did Faye.

"Don't let Faye get up, Little Bee," said Creed. "Keep her on her back. She shouldn't be moving about."

"They need a doctor, Creed," said Tyler.

"I know it, Mr. Tyler!" groused Creed. "But do you know where we can find one right this very minute?"

"Boggy Depot," said Tyler.

"And how far is that from here?" asked Creed.

"Ten, maybe twelve miles," said Tyler.

"And who's gonna ride ten or twelve miles in the dark to get these people a doctor tonight? Drake? You?" When Tyler didn't reply, he added, "No, it's got to be me. Drake would get lost, and no white doctor's gonna come out in the middle of the night to help a darkie. Come on, Mr. Tyler. Let's get them back to camp, so I can get after that doctor."

28

Boggy Depot was started in 1837 when a log cabin was built by an early Chickasaw settler on the divide between the Clear Boggy River and Sandy Creek. Because the site was somewhat near the center of the more populated area of the Choctaw-Chickasaw holdings before the War Between the States, the Chickasaws located their annuity grounds in the vicinity. Also, as routes of travel from Fort Smith to the west and south joined those from the north at this location, the village grew into a place of considerable importance. Streams of immigrants followed these roads to Texas and California.

In the early '40s a brick church was built and a school started. Some travelers called the place the Depot on the Boggy, or the Chickasaw Depot, although it wasn't situated on the Clear Boggy River nor located in the Chickasaw Nation. A post office was established there in 1849, officially designating the town as Boggy Depot, Cherokee Nation, Arkansas, which was an error because it should have been Choctaw Nation, and the area hadn't been a part of Arkansas for twenty-one years. A star mail route from Fort Smith was authorized through Boggy Depot in 1850, and the Butterfield Overland Mail and Stagecoach Line established a route through the town in 1858.

No battles were fought there during the war, but one raid on Boggy Depot by Union forces did end in failure. After the Battle of Honey Springs, the church was turned into a hospital to care for the sick and wounded who were brought to Boggy Depot.

After the war, a toll bridge was built over the Clear Boggy River about a mile east of the town. It was the only obstacle facing Creed as he went in search of a doctor for Reverend Thayer and Faye.

Creed had been gone from the camp on the Muddy Boggy River for a little over two hours when he saw a lantern glowing in the road ahead. He slowed Nimbus to a walk from a cautious trot, the only gait that a wise rider would use in the dark in unfamiliar territory. Coming closer to the light, he discovered that it was hanging from a tollbar across the foot of a bridge. A few feet away at the side of the road was a one-room log cabin that Creed figured belonged to the toll collector. Since no light shone from the house, he figured the tollman had already gone to bed for the night. Waking the man would take unnecessary time away from finding a doctor, so Creed decided to let himself through the gate and figured he'd settle up with the collector later. He dismounted and tried to lift the bar, only to discover that it was locked in place with a heavy padlock. That left the Texan with two choices: shoot the lock and risk being shot by the tollman or jump the bar with Nimbus. He remounted, rode back fifty feet or so, turned around again, spurred Nimbus into a steady lope, and at the precise second, horse and rider jumped the bar, landing with a resounding clippity-clop on the plank bridge, then thundering across the structure in the dark to another lantern-lit tollbar at the far end, over which the Appaloosa also leapt.

As he passed another log cabin that appeared to be identical to the tollhouse on the east side of the river, Creed kicked Nimbus into a gallop and didn't bother to look back as the stallion sped off toward Boggy Depot.

Hearing the rumble of a horse's hooves pounding on his bridge, a half-dressed man carrying a shotgun emerged from the second tollhouse just in time to catch a glimpse of Creed and the Appaloosa before they vanished in the darkness. He jumped into the middle of the road, leveled the shotgun at the fleeing rider, and fired a load of buckshot, nearly all of it scattering in a wide pattern and falling harmlessly short of its target. "You son of a bitch!" shouted the toll collector, shaking his fist at Creed. "You come back here and pay up!" His words were barely discernible to Creed who continued on to Boggy Depot.

At the outskirts of town, Creed rode past one darkened cabin on his right, then another, and a cemetery on his left. He passed three more houses on his right, then saw a lantern hanging on the porch of a home to his left. The light illuminated a sign that read: Albert Moore, M.D. Creed reined in Nimbus and guided the stallion to the hitching post in front of the residence. He climbed down, tied the horse's reins to the post ring, then went to the front door and knocked hard, hoping that the doctor was at home and only asleep.

"Who is it?" called a woman from within.

"My name is Slate Creed, ma'am," replied the Texan. Then, feeling that the woman would want more explanation than that, he added, "I'm traveling with a party of missionaries bound for the Chickasaw Nation. One of the ladies has been snakebit, and the parson has been shot by accident. They need a doctor real bad, ma'am."

The window nearest the door came alive with a yellow glow. The door opened, and a middle-aged lady wearing a gray nightcap, a gray nightshirt, and a navy-blue shawl and holding a lantern presented herself. She held up the light to get a better look at the late-night caller.

Creed removed his hat and held it at his side.

"My husband isn't home right now, sir," said Mrs. Moore, satsified that Creed posed no threat to her. "He's gone to Wapanucka to tend to the sick children at the boarding school, and he won't be back until tomorrow afternoon. Have you tried Dr. Bond down the road?"

"No, ma'am," said Creed. "We're camped east of here on the Muddy Boggy River. I came from that direction, and this is the first place that I've tried."

"Well, Dr. Bond's house is right in the middle of town on the square," said Mrs. Moore. "He might be there now. I know he didn't go with my husband to Wapanucka, but he might be out on another call. Lots of sickness around here at this time of the year, especially this year. Dr. Bond might be home, though."

"Thank you, ma'am," said Creed. "I'll try him." He nodded, then replaced his hat, tipped it, and left.

Dr. Thomas J. Bond's residence was next door to Reuben Wright's store, a two-story structure that had a saloon in the back. Wright's watering hole and Colonel Guy's Hotel, which also had a bar, were the only places on the square with lights in their windows. A few horses were tied up beside each building when Creed rode into town. Like Dr. Moore, Dr. Bond had a sign with his name on it and a lantern to light it up at night hanging from the roof of his front porch.

Creed hitched Nimbus to the post out front and knocked on the door much the same as he did at Dr. Moore's place, and just like Mrs. Moore had done, Mrs. Bond called out, "Who is it?" from the dark interior. The Texan's first thought was that the doctor wasn't home, but he stated his name and reason for being there anyway, almost exactly as he had done at Dr. Moore's.

"My husband is next door at Wright's," said Mrs. Bond through the door. "You can talk to him over there."

"Next door, ma'am?" queried Creed.

"That's what I said. He's in the saloon, playing cards. He might be drunk, too, so I wouldn't count on him doing your people much good tonight."

Wonderful, thought Creed sardonically, but to Mrs. Bond, he said, "Thank you, ma'am." He left, untying Nimbus and walking the Appaloosa to Wright's saloon, where he hitched the stallion to the rail with two other horses. He entered the whiskey den, stopped just inside the door that he closed behind him, and had a look around the place.

Not surprising, Wright's saloon wasn't much different than Nero's back in North Fork Town. The bottles, jars, and bar were practically the same; even the position of the card table to the rest of the room was the same. Reuben Wright resembled Nero in attire and general looks, but the three customers playing poker with Wright weren't much like Nero's, though. Each wore a dark brown suit of similar cut, black string tie, and a hat, two of them plug hats and the third a straw hat. Two of the gents had wispy black mustaches, black hair, and brown eyes, and they were slightly swarthy in coloring, which suggested that some of their ancestors had been Indians. The third man was older with white hair, a thick salt-and-pepper mustache, bloodshot blue eyes, and a ruddy complexion that was accented by a bulbous, veiny nose that suggested he was a heavy drinker.

Wright and his trio of patrons ignored Creed until the Texan walked up to the last man and said, "Dr. Bond?"

"Who wants to know?" asked Bond, without looking up from the cards in his hands.

"My name is Slate Creed, and I'm traveling with a party of missionaries on their way to the Chickasaw Nation. One of the ladies has been snakebit, and the preacher was accidentally shot in the chest. They need a doctor real bad."

Bond put his cards facedown on the table, shifted in the chair to face Creed, and said, "You say the preacher was shot in the chest? What happened? Did he cross the wrong sinner somewheres?" He joined the other players in a good guffaw at the joke.

"It was an accident," said Creed firmly.

Bond cleared his throat and said, "When and where did all this happen, my young friend?"

"It happened about ten or twelve miles from here a couple of hours ago," said Creed. "We're camped on the Muddy Boggy River."

Bond nodded, then looked up at Creed for the first time and said, "You don't need a doctor, son. By the time I could get to those folks, you'll be needing an undertaker. Snakebite and a chest wound. Not much chance in either one surviving, I'm afraid to say."

"I take it you're Dr. Bond," said Creed.

"That's right. I am he."

"Have you got a horse, Dr. Bond?" asked Creed.

"Son, I don't think you understood me," said Bond.

Creed pulled his Colt's, cocked it, and put the muzzle to Bond's nose. "Have you got a horse, Dr. Bond?" he repeated.

Looking cross-eyed at the gun barrel, Bond swallowed hard and said, "Not saddled and ready to ride."

"That's all right," said Creed. "I'm sure one of your friends here won't mind loaning you one of those two tied up out front. How about it, gents? Who's willing to loan his horse to the doctor here?"

Both men spoke up at the same time. "He can have mine," they said.

"All right, Dr. Bond," said Creed. "You heard your friends. You can take the one you want."

"I'll have to get my bag from my house," said Bond, still staring at the gun.

"That's just fine," said Creed. "We'll just go over there and get it on our way out of town." He backed up, waved toward the door with the revolver, and said, "Let's go, Doc. You gents can go on with your card game."

Bond stood up shakily and wobbled slowly toward the door.

Creed heaved a sigh and said, "Dr. Bond, if either of those people die because you took your time getting there to tend to them, I guarantee you won't be late for your own funeral."

Bond stepped a little livelier through the door, with Creed following him outside to the hitching rail where they stopped by the two horses tied up beside Nimbus. The doctor tried to climb onto the first one, but he was approaching it from the wrong side.

Damn! thought Creed. Why am I doing this? I only wish I knew. He put his Colt's away, grabbed Bond by the arm, led him around to the left side of the horse, and helped him climb into the saddle. "Just hold on, Doc," he said. "I'll take care of the rest." He mounted the Appaloosa, took the reins to Bond's horse, and led him back to his house where he rode right up onto the porch.

The *clop-clop* of the stallion's hooves on the wooden porch disturbed Mrs. Bond. "What's going on out there?" she demanded through the door.

"It's me, Margaret," said Bond. "Bring me my bag."

"Why can't you come in and get it yourself?" she asked.

"Mrs. Bond, this is Slate Creed again. Your husband is coming with me back to our camp to tend to my friends. I'd be much obliged if you'd bring his doctoring bag out to him right quick. I've already warned him about what might happen if either of my friends die because he was late getting there to help them. I'd hate to have to make good on that warning and for you to become a young widow."

"Get the bag, Margaret!" shouted Bond. "This fellow's got a gun, and he's threatened to use it on me."

In the next second, the door opened, and a faded flower of womanhood who looked like she had spent her youth entertaining the troops during the Mexican War stepped outside holding up a lantern to see if her husband and Creed were telling her true. "Oh, my!" she gasped when she saw Nimbus blocking the way. The middle-aged lady looked up at Creed, liked what she saw, and said, "If I was twenty years younger, you could go ahead and make me a widow, as long as you came around personal to comfort me for my loss."

"Just get the bag, Margaret," said Bond.

She returned inside and was back in a few seconds with the black medical valise. She handed it up to Creed. "Here you go, Mr. Creed," she said.

"Thank you, ma'am," said Creed, taking the bag. He hooked the handle around his saddlehorn, then said, "I hope to send your husband back to you on the morrow, ma'am."

"If you do send him back alive," she said, "please see to it that he's sober."

"Yes, ma'am," said Creed. He tipped his hat, then led Bond off toward the toll bridge over the Clear Boggy River. They rode at a trot to the tollhouse where they stopped, and Creed hailed the tollman inside to come out and let them cross the bridge.

"Hurry up, Chiffey!" shouted Bond impatiently.

Wearing only his boots and a pair of trousers that were held up by one suspender, Osgood Chiffey came outside carrying the same shotgun that he'd fired at Creed earlier. He pointed the scattergun at the Texan and said, "That horse looks like the one that rode through here a while back and didn't stop to pay the toll."

"I'm sorry about that, Mr. Chiffey," said Creed.

"You're gonna be a lot sorrier, friend," said Chiffey, raising the shotgun to his shoulder.

"Hold on there, Chiffey," said Bond.

Chiffey shifted his focus and his aim to Bond. "You butt out, Doc," he said.

Creed used the opening to draw his Colt's, cock it, and put it up close to Chiffey's head. "I apologized to you once, Mr. Chiffey," he said. "I won't do it again. Now if you'll just put that shotgun down on the ground, I'll gladly pay you."

"You will, huh?"

"That's right."

"Just do it, Chiffey," pleaded Bond. "There's hurt folks over on the Muddy that need my help."

Chiffey nodded and complied.

As soon as the shotgun was on the ground, Creed dug into his coin pocket and pulled out a silver dollar. He flipped it at Chiffey who caught it out of the air. "Will that cover it all, Mr. Chiffey?" he asked.

"It'll do," said Chiffey. He walked over to the tollbar, took a key from his pants, unlocked the padlock, and pushed down on the counterweight, lifting the gate. After Creed led Bond onto the bridge, he lowered the bar again. "Come on," he said. "I'll go with you to the other side so my brother don't shoot you by mistake." He led them across the bridge, unlocked the second padlock, lifted the tollbar, and saw them on their way to the camp on the Muddy Boggy River.

29

When Creed returned to the camp on the Muddy Boggy River with Dr. Bond, Faye and Reverend Thayer were still unconscious but alive and resting in their beds. Louise was attending her father, while Tyler looked after Faye. Drake and Little Bee were dozing by the fire, but they came alert at the sound of horses entering the camp.

The two-hour ride had sobered Bond considerably. He was able to dismount without any assistance from Creed.

The Texan alit, handed the medical bag to the doctor, then pointed the physician toward his patients. He allowed Little Bee to take charge of Nimbus and the borrowed mount, then he saw Drake stand up, looking as dreadful as Creed was certain that young Thayer felt. Poor kid, he thought. He patted the youth on the shoulder and said, "Just remember what your father said about putting your faith in the Lord, Drake. It'll be all right. You'll see."

Drake could do nothing more than nod his droopy head.

Bond went to Reverend Thayer first, getting down on his knees beside the injured clergyman opposite Louise. "How do you do, miss?" he said. "I'm a doctor. Thomas Bond at your service."

"How do you do, Doctor Bond? I am Louise Thayer, and this is my father, Reverend David Thayer."

"Yes, I know," said Bond. "Mr. Creed told me everything on the way here." He focused on the darkening bruise on her chin, then pointed at it. "He told me about that, too. Does it hurt to move your jaw?"

"No," said Louise, putting a hand to the spot where Creed had struck her.

"Well, it will," said Bond. He shifted his attention back to the reverend, felt Thayer's pulse, then his cheek. "Pretty rapid heartbeat and a smidgen of temperature. That's to be expected, of course, with this sort of injury. Has he come around since the accident?"

"No," said Louise.

Bond grimaced. "That's not good," he said. "He must have hit his head pretty hard on that rock. His skull could be fractured." He lifted the minister's right eyelid. "Bring that lantern closer, Miss Thayer." As she did, he kept a close watch on the patient's pupil. "Uh-huh," he muttered. Then he checked the other pupil. "That's good news," he said. "You can take the lantern away now." He lifted Thayer's head just enough to peek under it at the pillow, then lowered it back in place. He peered into Thayer's left ear and up his nostrils. "I don't think his skull is fractured. No bleeding from his ears or nose, and his eyes react to light. Those are good signs." He reached for the bandage covering the exit wound in Thayer's chest. "May I?" he asked, but he didn't wait for an answer. He removed the dressing to look at the injury. "That's a nasty hole there. Handgun did this, you say?"

Creed, standing beside him now, said, "Colt's .44."

"Yep. Just as I thought." Bond replaced the bandage. "Whose idea was it to put him on his side like this?"

"Creed's," said Tyler, joining them.

"Probably saved his life," said the doctor. "For now, anyway. Funny thing about chest wounds like this. They can get you almost anytime." He looked at Louise. "Better put a new bandage on there. On his back, too. But not just yet. First, let's have a look at the young lady."

"She's over here," said Tyler.

Bond had trouble rising. Creed grabbed his arm, helped him up, then led him to Faye.

"She's been in and out of sleep since we put her down here," said Tyler, standing over Faye.

Louise joined the three men. She and Bond knelt down beside her sister, one to each side.

"That's good and bad," said Bond as he felt Faye's pulse, then her forehead. "Not much of a temperature. Heartbeat is a little fast, but that's to be expected. Let's look at that snakebite now." He glanced at the other men, trying to give them the idea that it would be improper for them to watch this part of the examination and that they should at least turn their backs to Faye. As soon as they caught on and turned away, Bond raised her skirt until he could see the bandage over the injury that was inflicted initially by the rattler then compounded by Creed. "Who did this? These cuts, I mean?" he asked.

"Mr. Creed," said Louise.

"You're a pretty smart fellow, Mr. Creed," said Bond. "You'd make a good doctor."

"You know," said Louise dryly, "my father said something very similar to that, Dr. Bond. He said Mr. Creed would make a good minister."

"I take it that you disagree with your father's opinion as well as mine," said Bond.

"He's better at killing than he is at saving souls and lives," said Louise.

"I wouldn't be so sure about that, Miss Thayer," said Bond. "Well, we'd better get back to your father. I think this young lady will be just fine for now. Keep her still for the time being, and don't let her eat anything except broth. She'll probably be just fine in a day or two, but we'll have to keep an eye on her all the same." He lowered Faye's skirt, and Louise helped him to his feet.

They returned to the reverend.

"It looks to me that the ball passed right through his chest," said Bond, standing over Thayer. "That's good because I'm not much of a surgeon. I sure do hate having to go into a man's chest after a ball." He shook his head and shuddered to emphasize his distaste for such an operation. He rubbed his chin, then added, "What we have to worry about is infection, but I'm afraid there's not much we can do about that until first light in the morning."

"Why do we have to wait until daylight?" asked Louise.

"We'll need daylight to see the trees," said Bond.

"Are you talking about collecting tree moss?" asked Creed.

"Yes," said Bond. "Do you know about that, too?"

"My grandfather told me about it," said Creed.

"Your grandfather?" queried Bond. "I thought only Indians knew about that sort of thing."

"My Grandfather Hawk is a Choctaw," explained Creed.

"Funny," said Bond. "You don't look like an Indian. Must be an awful lot of white folks on your family tree."

"A few," explained Creed.

"Excuse me, Dr. Bond," interjected Louise, "I don't understand. What's all this about tree moss?"

"I don't know for sure," said Bond, "but there's something in certain tree mosses that prevents infections. The Indians have been using this remedy for centuries. Whites won't use it because they think Indians don't know diddly about medicine." He shuddered and shook his head. "The things I could tell my colleagues back East, if I thought the bastards would listen." Then seeing that Louise was offended by his use of the expletive, he cleared his throat and added, "Sorry about that, Miss Thayer. I'm not real used to being around young white women. I sometimes forget my manners."

"I understand, Dr. Bond," said Louise. "You're forgiven, but why can't we look for this moss now?"

"For the same reason that Faye shouldn't have wandered away from camp the way she did," said Creed. "Snakes. They're liable to be hiding in the very places that we'll be looking for the moss. I don't know about you, Miss Louise, but I'd rather not put my hand into a place where a snake could latch on to it."

"Then what are we going to do for Father?" she asked anxiously. "We just can't do nothing."

"I told you to change his bandages, Miss Thayer," said Bond firmly. "That's the best we can do for now. That and prayer. As for everybody else, I suggest you folks get some sleep."

"I'm not leaving my father," said Louise.

"I'll sit with Miss Faye," said Tyler.

"No, I'll sit with her," said Bond.

"Go ahead and get some sleep, Mr. Tyler," said Creed. "I'll stand the first watch." He headed off to do the duty that he had started to do earlier that evening before the tragedy happened.

Tyler, Little Bee, and Drake slept fitfully by the fire. Bond dozed near Faye, and Louise kept a vigil beside her father. Whenever either patient stirred, the whole camp jumped with fear and hope—fear that Faye or the reverend might be breathing their last, and hope that their activity was a sign of recovery. The reality rested somewhere in between.

Creed let Tyler sleep through the night, choosing not to awaken him until first light. He made the coffee, while Tyler fried up some bacon and cornmeal mush for breakfast. By the time everybody had eaten, the sun was above the horizon providing enough light for Creed and Bond to search for the tree mosses that

Bond had mentioned the night before. Within an hour, they had scraped enough lichen from the trees to make poultices for Bond's patients.

Because Reverend Thayer's wounds were the more serious, Bond tended to him first. "There's no change in his condition since last night," said the doctor. "I'm not sure if that's good or bad. Good, I suppose. At least, he hasn't gotten worse." He applied poultices to Thayer's chest and back, then said, "Better keep him on his side for the time being. Hopefully, he'll come around soon, and when he does, try to keep him from moving. I don't want the bleeding to start up again. Now let's see about the young lady."

While Bond was applying a medicated bandage to the snakebite on her leg, Faye awakened. She was startled to see a stranger so close to her bed and thought to shrink away from him until she saw Louise beside him. "What are you doing?" she asked hoarsely. She tried to sit up, but a wave of nausea kept her from making any sudden movements.

"It's all right, dear," said Louise, restraining Faye. "Dr. Bond is only putting a bandage on your leg."

"A bandage?" queried Faye. "What for?"

"Snakebite," said Bond. "Rattler got you last night."

"What?" muttered Faye, then she remembered what happened and was terrified all over again. She grabbed her sister's arm and begged to know, "Am I going to die, Louise?"

"No," said Bond firmly. He looked up so she could see his face. "You're going to live, young lady, but you'll be sick for quite some time, I'm afraid. This poultice will keep you from getting an infection in your leg."

"Just be still, dear," said Louise.

Faye noticed the bruise on her sister's chin and asked, "What happened to your face, Louise?"

"Nothing," said Louise. "Are you hungry?"

"No, I feel sick to my stomach," said Faye.

"That's normal," said Bond. "You should still try to eat some broth and drink a little water. You might not be able to keep it down at first, but keep trying. The stomach sickness will pass in good time, and when it does, you can have a little soup at first, before you start eating solid food again." He tied off the bandage, then added, "You're a lucky girl, Miss Thayer. If Mr. Creed hadn't known what to do about a snakebite, you'd be dead now."

"Slate saved my life?" queried Faye.

"Yes, he did," said Louise reluctantly.

"Then he does love me after all," said Faye. She smiled and asked, "Where is Slate? I want to tell him how much I love him."

"You just rest easy now, Miss Thayer," said Bond. "I'll look in on you again before I go back to town."

"Do like the doctor says, Faye," said Louise. "Just lie back and rest. I'll go find Mr. Creed."

She went looking for Creed but not to tell him that Faye wanted him and that he should go to her. She had other thoughts to share with him.

Creed was gathering more tree moss for Dr. Bond when Louise caught up with him at the edge of the river. He tried to ignore her, hoping that she wasn't looking for him and that she would go away. He was greatly disappointed.

"Mr. Creed, I would like to speak to you about Faye," said Louise tersely. "She's awake, and the doctor says she will be all right in time."

"That's good news," said Creed.

"That part is," said Louise.

"What's the bad news?" asked Creed.

"Faye thinks that you saved her life because you love her," said Louise.

"Where did she get an idea like that?" asked Creed. "I would have done the same thing for anyone else in this party. I don't have any romantic inclinations toward Faye. I've already told you that."

"Yes, you told me, but have you told her?"

"Yes, I did. Last night. Just before she wandered off into the brush and got herself snakebit. Truth is, she probably went that way because she was upset by what I told her."

"That's exactly what I thought," said Louise, breaking into a tirade. "You're the cause of all this trouble, Mr. Creed. I told you to stay away from Faye and from Drake, and if you had, Faye wouldn't have gotten such silly romantic notions in her head about you, and Drake wouldn't have disobeyed Father. Faye wouldn't have been out there for that snake to bite, and Drake wouldn't have been playing with that gun of yours, and he wouldn't have shot Father with it. You, Mr. Creed. You are the cause of all our troubles. You and that gun of yours. I wish we had never met up with you. I wish you would leave us, and the sooner, the better."

Creed studied her for a moment, then calmly said, "All right, if that's the way you feel, then Little Bee and I will be on our way this morning."

"No, not Little Bee. Just you."

"Little Bee is my responsibility, Miss Thayer," said Creed. "He goes with me until I find his uncle. Then the boy becomes his responsibility."

"I don't think you're a very good example for Little Bee," said Louise.

"Frankly, Miss Thayer, I don't care what you think. Little Bee is going with me, and that's all there is to that."

"We'll just see about that," said Louise, and she stormed off toward the camp.

Creed walked cautiously after her, being in no hurry for another argument with her. When he came among the others, he saw Louise talking animatedly with Tyler. Now what? he wondered.

In a few seconds, Louise quit talking to Tyler, and the ex-slave approached Creed. "Miss Louise says she doesn't want you taking Little Bee with you when you leave, Creed," he said.

"And what do you say?" asked Creed.

"I think I agree with her," said Tyler. "The boy would be better off with these people."

"You might be right about that, but I gave my word to Little Bee's mother that I would take him to his uncle, and I still intend to keep that promise."

"I can't let you take Little Bee away from these folks, Creed," said Tyler. He reached for one of his Remingtons.

Creed pulled his Colt's and beat Tyler to the draw, hoping that the ex-slave wouldn't try to go through with the gunfight. Seeing Tyler clear leather and raise his gun at him, the Texan figured that he had no choice but to kill the man.

Little Bee had been sitting with Drake and Dr. Bond beside the campfire, listening first to Louise and Tyler, then to Tyler's exchange with Creed. Bond and Little Bee knew what was about to happen, but Drake didn't have a clue before Creed and Tyler drew down on each other. Bond ducked for cover, while Drake sat perfectly still. Hoping to prevent another tragedy, the orphan jumped between Tyler and Creed.

30

Creed held his fire.

Tyler didn't. He was startled just enough by Little Bee's sudden intrusion into the gunfight to have his aim spoiled. The ball from his Remington snapped off a limb from a cottonwood sapling behind Creed. The ex-slave cocked his revolver to take a second shot, which he might have taken, if Little Bee hadn't placed himself in front of Creed, shouting, "I don't want to stay with you people! I'm going with Slate!"

The explosion from Tyler's revolver had paralyzed Louise, Drake, and Dr. Bond, but it had the opposite effect on Faye and her father. Both of them stirred for a few seconds, as if they were having a mutual nightmare, but none of the others noticed.

"You don't know what you're saying," said Tyler. "He's a killer, son. You don't want to be tied up to a man like him."

"I know I'd rather be with him than with you," said Little Bee. "I'm going with Slate to look for my uncle, and nobody's going to stop me."

At last, Louise stirred and came forward, positioning herself in front of Tyler. "Little Bee, don't you think you'd be better off with us?" she asked. "We'll take good care of you. You can live with us at the mission and go to school and learn how to be a farmer, or you could learn a useful trade." She glared at Creed and added, "Anything would be better than going with him. He can only teach you to kill."

Little Bee glanced down at the ground, then he looked up at Louise. "Well, I don't agree with you, Miss Louise. I'm going with Slate to find my uncle, and that's all there is to that." He swallowed hard, glad that he'd said what he did. "Thank you for the learning that you did give me. I promise I'll keep on reading the book you gave me, and I'll practice my writing, too." He let his eyes drift downward again, only to have them refocus on Louise as he reiterated his first statement. "I'm going with Slate, Miss Louise."

Louise and Tyler were too dumbfounded to speak. Drake and Dr. Bond also remained silent, and Reverend Thayer and Faye were once again calm in their beds.

"Mr. Tyler, you can put that gun away," said Creed evenly from behind Little Bee. He continued to hold his six-gun at the ready. "Unless, of course, you think this matter isn't settled just yet. If not, I will still oblige you. But not here where we might hurt one of these other people. We can go have it out down by the river, if you like."

"No!" said Louise emphatically, her anger still aimed at Creed. "There will be no more shooting and killing. Little Bee can go with him if he wants, Mr. Tyler. Just let him go. He'll see soon enough that he's made a mistake."

Tyler put his gun away and turned to see about Reverend Thayer.

"Don't you beat all," said Creed. He stuck his Colt's back inside his waistband. "You know, I was beginning to feel guilty about punching you last night, but now I'm wondering why I didn't hit you a lot harder and knock some real sense into you."

"Just get your things and leave, Mr. Creed," said Louise. She turned and went back to her father.

Dr. Bond came forward and said, "If you don't mind, Mr. Creed, I'd like to ride back to Boggy Depot with you."

"What about Reverend Thayer and Faye?" said Creed.

"There's nothing more that I can do for them now," said Bond. "Miss Thayer can give them as much care as I can at this point. She can look after them."

"No, Doc," said Creed, "I think you better stay with them. At least until Reverend Thayer comes around." Then another thought struck him. "If you're worried about returning your friend's horse to him, I'd be happy to do that for you, Doc." He smiled and added, "In fact, it'd be my pleasure to take that horse back to Boggy Depot for you." Seeing that Bond was about to protest, Creed held up his hands and added, "You don't have to thank me, Doc. I'm just glad to help out." Turning away from the speechless physician, he said, "Come on, Little Bee. Let's get moving. I don't think we're appreciated around here anymore."

While Creed and Little Bee packed up to leave, Drake approached the Texan with an unexpected request. "Take me with you," he said.

Creed suppressed a laugh and said, "You Thayers are all on the unpredictable side, aren't you? Take you with us? Either you're loco or you think I am. Take you with us? Not on your life, Drake. You belong with your family. Your father needs you more now than he ever did in the past. And your sisters . . . ? As much as neither one of them will ever admit it, they need you, too. Especially Louise. She won't say so, but she needs a man to lean on once in a while. And you? You need a woman to lean on once in a while, just the same as every other man does. Don't be ashamed to lean on a woman now and then, Drake. Even if that woman is your sister. I haven't met a person yet who doesn't need someone to lean on every so often."

"Even you, Slate?" queried Drake.

"Hell, especially me." He sighed, smiled, and said, "You don't know how badly I wish I was back in Texas right now and had my Texada to lean on. Now I'll admit she still had some growing up to do when I last saw her, but she was already a lot of woman, too. Enough for me, anyway." He paused as he pictured Texada waiting for him back in Hallettsville, but the vision soon faded. "No, Drake. You can't go with us. You stay with your family. You'll be better off."

Drake was dejected, but he made no more argument. He left them to finish their packing.

Before he and Little Bee could depart, Creed figured he had one more chore to finish. He had to say good-bye to Faye.

"Where do you think you're going now?" demanded Louise, placing herself between the Texan and her sister.

"You know exactly where I'm going," said Creed, "and what I have to do. It's what you want, isn't it? For me to hurt Faye one last time before I ride off?"

"Yesterday, I would have said yes. But not today. Faye doesn't need that kind of pain now."

Creed hesitated for a second as he contemplated her words, wondering about their sincerity. Convinced that Louise was being honest with him and herself, he said, "I don't intend to hurt Faye. I only want to say good-bye." He paused to let that soak into her stubborn brain. Realizing it had no effect on her, he said, "Step aside, Louise, and let me see her."

"And what if I refuse? Will you strike me again like you did last night?"

"All right, I'll apologize for that," said Creed. "That is what you want, isn't it? An apology? All right. You got one. Now step aside."

"No."

Creed studied her again, wondering what it would take to make her move, other than another fist to her chin. When the right words came to him, he said, "If I leave here without saying good-bye, Faye will always blame you for ruining her life. Is that what you want, Louise?" He knew the answer before he asked the question.

Louise stepped aside and let him pass.

Faye was sleeping when Creed knelt down beside her bed. He touched her hand and spoke her name gently to awaken her. Her eyes fluttered open, blinked a few times, then focused on the Texan's face. "Slate darling," she rasped. She sat up, as if she intended to allow him to embrace her.

Creed shook his head and said, "Don't talk, Faye. Just listen to me. Please listen to me because I only want to say this once." He cleared his throat, then continued. "I'm leaving now, Faye. The time has come for Little Bee and me to be going our own way." When she looked like she would protest, he put his fingers to her lips and said, "No, don't talk, Faye. It won't do any good."

He took another deep breath and let it out slowly before continuing. "I told you last night that I love another girl back in Texas and that some day I plan to marry that girl and settle down and have a family. You don't know all there is to know about me, Faye. If you did, you'd know that I'm something of a rough cob most of the time. You'd know that I usually go my own way and I do what I want to do. You'd know that the only woman who can ever tie me down has got to be part wildcat, part mule, and part cottontail with just a tiny bit of alley cat thrown in to make her real interesting."

He smiled warmly at her and went on. "You're just too much cottontail, Faye, and there's absolutely no alley cat in you at all. But that's all right. You'll still make some lucky fellow a good wife one day. But I'm not him. I know you don't believe that now, but when you meet up with the right fellow—the right gentleman because you deserve a real gentleman instead of someone like me—well, when you meet him, you'll wonder what you ever saw in someone like me. Believe me, Faye, that's what will happen, and when it does, you'll be the happiest woman on earth because then you'll really be in love."

He leaned forward, kissed her on the forehead, then added, "You get well now because you never know when that gentleman will show up in your life."

He stood up, smiled down at her, and said, "Good-bye, Faye. It's been a real honor knowing you." He tipped his hat, turned, and walked away.

Louise had stood within earshot of them, listening intently. Her anger had been foaming inside her when Creed began his farewell, but it dissipated slowly as she had hung on his every word. When he was finished and he passed by her, tipping his hat to her and saying simply, "Miss Louise," she could do nothing except watch him go and wonder why he so vexed her, why he perplexed her, and yet moved her to experience every emotion in the extreme. She felt a tear course down her cheek as she thought, I hate you, Slate Creed. But before she could feed that hate, she heard Faye whimper behind her. Drying her eyes first, she turned and said, "Oh, you poor dear!"

Louise and Faye were sisters again.

31

The first order of business for Creed and Little Bee when they arrived in Boggy Depot that afternoon was to return the horse that Creed had forced Dr. Bond to borrow.

They found the owner at Wright's store, imbibing with a few cronies and regaling them with the tale of the young gunman who had abducted their good friend, Thomas Bond, the night before. Seeing Creed enter the saloon and being filled with the ubiquitous courage that is so easily obtained from a jug of potent moonshine liquor, the fellow became righteously indignant and demanded satisfaction. Creed obliged him by buying him and Wright's other patrons a round of drinks and by paying the gent two dollars for the loan of the mount.

"And if that's not good enough," said Creed, displaying the butt of his Colt's prominently, "then we can always step out into the street and settle this another way."

The gentleman's bloodshot eyes were fixed on the gun's handle as he said, "I think you've been chastised enough, sir. Now be gone with you and count yourself fortunate that I'm letting you off so easy."

Creed smiled and said, "Yes, sir."

With that task completed, Creed found lodging for them at Colonel Guy's Hotel, and he boarded Nimbus and the two mules with Tom Brown, the blacksmith who also ran the hotel's barn. The next morning at breakfast Creed asked the hotelkeeper for directions to Armstrong's Academy. The colonel informed him that the proper name was Armstrong Academy, for Captain William Armstrong, the popular government agent to the Choctaws back

211

before the Mexican War and that the place was now known as
Chahta Tamaha or Choctaw Town. "Depending on whether you're
a Choctaw or a white man," said Guy.

Creed bought some more supplies at H. C. Ford's store, then
he and Little Bee struck out for the Choctaw capital before
midmorning. The road took them south-by-southeast a full
twenty-five miles. They arrived at the former mission town
just before sunset and made camp on Bokchito Creek because
the hotel had no vacancies.

Armstrong Academy was founded by Baptist missionaries in
1844 as a boarding school for Choctaw boys. The first classroom
buildings and dormitories were made of logs, but in the late 1850s
after the Cumberland Presbyterians assumed the operation of the
school, a two-story brick structure was built. As the school grew,
so did the community around it. A trading post that evolved into
a regular mercantile, a blacksmith shop, and the Ramsey Baptist
Church were among the first establishments.

During the War Between the States, the Choctaws sided with
the Confederacy, and the academy was closed because most of the
missionaries running it were vehement Abolitionists who decided
to leave the Choctaw Nation. In 1862, the Choctaw Council
in Doaksville voted to shift the national capital from there to
Armstrong Academy and rename the place Chahta Tamaha, and
a year later this move was executed. On arriving in their new
capital, the council took over the main school building as its
headquarters.

Because the Choctaw government was seated there, thousands
of refugees from the Cherokee and Creek Nations found their way
to Chahta Tamaha during the war. Hundreds more camped and
slept on the ground near Blue River because cane grew there and
stayed green most of the winter. Disease was rampant. Deaths
and funerals were almost daily occurrences, and little cemeteries
of unmarked graves grew up everywhere. Many of these dispossessed people were still living in the area in the spring of '66.

Creed and Little Bee returned to town the next morning and
entered the Choctaw administrative building, hoping they had
enough facts about Humma Doak for someone to lead them to
him. They knew that Uncle Hum was a slave whose mother was
named Tabby and who had a sister named Martha; that his first
owner had been John Doak, a planter with a farm near Doaksville;
that John Doak's son, Titus, had sold Humma when he was only a

boy to some missionaries who took him to Armstrong Academy; and that the sale must have happened before 1853, because Little Bee said Uncle Hum was sold before he was born. They went from office to office, repeating these few details, but no one seemed willing to offer them any information about a slave. Angry, but not discouraged, they left the building.

As they walked along the street toward the mercantile, Creed wondered why people were reluctant to give them any help finding a former slave. Had Humma Doak done something so terrible that no one wanted to talk about him? No, most folks were usually quite willing to tell a bloody story, no matter how horrifying it might be. Was it because he was a slave? That was a very distinct possibility. Indians as well as whites were developing a deep resentment of Negroes, thanks mainly to Northern Abolitionists who were attempting to force the Indian Nations to assimilate their freedmen into their tribes. Could it be Hum's last name that was a problem? Maybe that was it. Maybe I should be asking about Titus Doak, he thought, instead of one of his former slaves. Or maybe I should be asking about the missionaries who bought Humma Doak. Now there's a thought, but that means I've got to talk to preachers again. Oh, well.

At the mercantile, Creed asked where he might find someone who could tell him about the missionaries who founded Armstrong Academy, and he was directed to a farm outside of town. "Brother Moffitt should be home today since it's Friday," said the storekeeper. "He usually comes to town on Saturday, if you care to wait till then, and if you miss him here in town, you can find him at the Philadelphia Baptist Church over on the Blue on Sundays. He used to be the pastor for that church when it was located here in town. Brother Hogue took over as pastor when they moved the church to where it is now, but he left for Texas right after the war ended. Brother Moffitt is leading the prayers over there again."

Creed thanked the storekeeper, then he and Little Bee rode out to the Moffitt farm west of Chahta Tamaha. They found a man of medium build and height, wearing a wide-brimmed straw hat, a red bandanna around his neck, trousers held up by suspenders, no shirt over his sweat-soaked longjohns, and knee-high boots. He was walking behind a mule that was pulling a single-blade steel plow, turning over the topsoil in a small, fenced field south of a log house, barn, granary, corn crib, and chicken coop. They alit, tied Nimbus and the mules to the top rail of the fence, and waited for the farmer to finish the furrow and come to them.

Seeing the newcomers standing beside the fence was excuse enough for Andrew Moffitt to halt his labor. He tied off the mule's reins to the plow handles, then removed his hat with one hand and took the neckerchief and wiped his face and neck with the other. After covering his head but still holding the bandanna, he walked through the field to greet Creed and Little Bee, shaking hands with the Texan but barely acknowledging the boy's presence. "What can I do for you, Mr. Creed?" he asked.

"I was told in town that you would know about the missionaries who started the school," said Creed.

"That's true," said Moffitt, wiping his neck again. "I was here when the academy was started back in '44. What would you like to know?"

"Well, I guess I'd like to know who started the academy," said Creed.

"Brother Ramsey Potts was one of the founders," said Moffitt. "Him and his wife founded the Providence Mission School near Fort Towson back in '35, then they came here from Doaksville back in '44 and got things going." He glanced at Little Bee before continuing. "He brought some Negro slaves with him to help build the school, but he didn't bring enough of them. They were long on building the classrooms and dormitories, and the school didn't open till December of '45. Brother Potts was the superintendent until he left here in '54. That's when I took over for a year. I was one of the teachers. Then Reverend A. S. Dennison took over in '55 for the Cumberland Presbyterians. He left when the war came, and the academy was closed down."

"I see," said Creed. "This Brother Potts that you spoke about, did he take his slaves with him when he left?"

"They weren't his slaves to take," said Moffitt. "They belonged to the mission. Besides, he sold all of the ones that he could once the school was built. The ones that he couldn't sell were passed on to the Philadelphia Baptist Church."

"Passed on?" queried Creed. "I don't understand. What does that mean?"

"They were signed over to the service of the pastor of the church," explained Moffitt. "Brother Potts passed them on to me, and I passed them on to Brother Hogue."

"Brother Hogue? I've heard that name before. I think the store-keeper in town mentioned him. He said that he went to Texas when the war ended. Is that right?"

"Brother Hogue came here from Georgia back in '58," said Moffitt. "He was sent here by the Indian Missionary Society of the Southern Baptist Board of Missions. I stepped down as pastor of the Philadelphia Baptist Church when he came because it seemed to me at the time that Brother Hogue could do the Lord's work a mite better than I could. After seeing him at his labors, I'm proud to say that I did the right thing. He was a fine pastor, a most righteous man, a fine example of the Lord's teachings. I dare say most of our congregation would have followed him to the ends of the earth or even to Texas, if he had asked us to do it in the name of the Lord."

"So he did go to Texas?"

"When the war ended, word came around that the Union soldiers would be rounding up all the Southern missionaries who helped turn the Nations against the United States. Brother Hogue and Brother Murrow took their families and went down to Texas. I don't know exactly where they went down there."

"Did he take the slaves with him?" asked Creed.

"There was only one left by that time," said Moffitt, "and she ran off when she found out that the Union Army was freeing all the slaves in the Nations."

"She?" queried Creed.

"That's right," said Moffitt. "Negress named Tash."

Little Bee's eyes brightened with recognition. "Slate," he said eagerly, "Mama once told me that she had an aunt named Tash, but she never said what happened to her."

"Is that what this is all about, Mr. Creed?" asked Moffitt. "You're trying to find this boy's family?"

"That's right, Brother Moffitt," said Creed. "We're looking for Little Bee's uncle. His name is Humma Doak."

"Humma Doak?" queried Moffitt. He stared at Little Bee for a few seconds, then said, "Yes, sir. I can see the resemblance now. Light-skinned Negro with red hair. Not a fiery red, but red like rust. You look a lot like him, boy, except for that. You having black hair, I mean. He was a good slave. Smart, too. There wasn't nothing we couldn't teach him to do."

"You know my Uncle Hum?" asked Little Bee, greatly excited.

"I *knew* him," said Moffitt. "He's dead now."

Little Bee's excitement vanished.

"Dead?" asked Creed. "Are you sure?"

"Pretty sure, Mr. Creed. I helped lower his coffin into the ground, and I helped fill in the hole. He's dead, all right."

This wasn't what Creed wanted to hear. Still hoping that Moffitt was mistaken, he asked, "When did he die?"

"During the war. We had a lot of sickness around here. Too many people trying to live too close together. Lots of folks got sick, and not all of them got better. Hum Doak was one of them that didn't get better. He died just before Christmas of '64. Right after the first real cold spell we had that year. He came down with the skitters, then the catarrh set in, then pneumonia. He went real fast after that." Moffitt's eyebrows pinched together as if he were trying really hard to remember something. "You know, I think Tash was his aunt," he said. "Seems I recall her carrying on pretty good at the funeral, and I recollect her saying something about her being the last one now. Of course, I could be wrong about that. She was a Negress, and nobody paid her much mind. Dark as she was, she probably wasn't his aunt. Just another Negress, I guess."

"You said that she ran off," said Creed. "Do you know where she went?"

"No, I don't, and I doubt that anybody else in these parts would know either. The Hogues might know, but they're living down in Texas now, and nobody around here knows exactly where they are down there."

"Yes, you said that before," said Creed. He looked at Little Bee and only one thought came to mind: Now what do I with you, son?

32

Upon learning that Humma Doak was dead, Creed and Little Bee were saddened somewhat, but they were also secretly relieved that their search for him was at an end, even if it had really only just begun. Even so, neither told the other how he really felt.

At the outset of the visit with Brother Moffitt, Creed had hoped that he was close to finding the orphan's only known relative and that he could finally fulfill his promise to Martha Doak to take her son to his Uncle Hum in the Choctaw Nation. When Moffitt told them that Humma Doak was dead, the Texan was disappointed, but at the same time, he was glad that he wouldn't have to be separated from Little Bee just yet, if at all. He had become quite fond of his young traveling companion; the boy had begun to fill a void in his life that had been created five years earlier.

Creed was Clete Slater back then, and he had a younger brother named Dent. They were only teenagers, and they were about as close as two brothers could be. When he rode off to fight in the war, Clete left Dent behind at Glengarry Plantation, and although he didn't realize it at the time, a sinkhole was opened in Clete's soul. The gap was temporarily filled when they were reunited after the war, but it was made wider and deeper later that year when Dent was murdered on the cattle trail to New Orleans. His brother's death was one of the most terrible pains of Creed's life, a wound that he thought would never heal.

Then came Little Bee.

Creed couldn't explain exactly what it was that he was feeling for Little Bee, but he knew that the emotion was something greater than a casual friendship. If he could have elucidated on the turmoil within him, he would have described it as a mixture of parental caring and brotherly love. One thing he knew for certain: his attachment to Little Bee was growing stronger with each passing day. When the time did come to part, he would have a tough time going his own way alone.

Little Bee felt the same as Creed about the news of his Uncle Hum's demise. He had been looking forward to meeting this man that he'd heard so much about nearly all of his short life. His mother had held her absent brother out to him as the best example of what a good boy was, speaking of Hum in terms and tones that were reverent and idolizing. Little Bee had tried to live up to this ideal, often falling short of the mark—or so he thought. Maybe that explained why the orphan experienced a bit of triumphant glee at Brother Moffitt's report. Not that he was happy that the flesh-and-blood person of Humma Doak was dead, but that the phantasmal image, the legend, was still just that, a legend. He wouldn't have to meet this Uncle Hum, this man that he had always imagined as some sort of hero that he had loved and had tried to emulate and that he had also hated because he, Little Bee, couldn't be that perfect. He wouldn't have to meet him and discover that Humma Doak wasn't everything that Martha Doak had portrayed him to be; he wouldn't have to meet him and see Uncle Hum as a real person with many of the minor faults and little imperfections that made him as human as the next fellow. Being dead now, Uncle Hum could remain the Uncle Hum that Little Bee's mother had planted in his imagination.

But better than not having to meet Uncle Hum, Little Bee wouldn't have to be separated from Creed now. Or so he hoped.

After visiting Humma Doak's grave in the Philadelphia Baptist Church cemetery, Little Bee and Creed headed back to their camp on Bokchito Creek. Little Bee asked the question that was plaguing Creed as well as him. "What do we do now, Slate?"

"I'm not quite sure, Little Bee. I thought we were at the end of the trail today when we met up with Brother Moffitt. I thought sure he was going to tell us that Humma Doak was living somewhere near here and that all we had to do was ride over and introduce ourselves, and he would take you into his house, and you would have a home again. Then I could be on my way to Texas to see what I can do about helping my mother and my stepfather on their ranch. Now . . . ?" Words failed him.

"What about Tash?" asked Little Bee, secretly hoping that they would go in search of her now.

"Tash?" queried Creed.

"Sure. Didn't Brother Moffitt say that she was my Uncle Hum's aunt?"

"He said he *thought* she might be his aunt," explained Creed. "He didn't say positive that she was related to Humma Doak. Of course, it does seem to add up to that, doesn't it? I mean, she was a slave belonging to the same folks, and she had come here from Doaksville with your uncle. It seems to reason that she was his aunt, but we can't be certain about that. We'd need to look at her chattel papers to see who owned her before and see what sort of bloodlines she had, but we can't do that because the last people to own her, the Hogues, are living down in Texas now."

"So why don't we ride down to Texas and look for them?"

"I don't think you understand how big Texas is, Little Bee," said Creed with a grin.

"Well, how big is it?" asked the orphan.

"Pretty big."

"How big?"

Creed gave that a minute's thought, then said, "Do you know how far we've ridden to get here from where we buried your mother and Hezekiah Branch?"

"Well, not in miles," said Little Bee, "but I know it's a pretty fair distance."

"Well, to ride across Texas would take us about five times, maybe six times longer," said Creed. "What that means is we could be looking for the Hogues for months, maybe longer. I don't have that sort of time, Little Bee. As much as I like you, son, I have to be moving on, and you need a place to live permanent."

"Why can't I just go with you to your mother's place in Texas?" asked Little Bee.

"That thought crossed my mind, too, and I've given that careful consideration." He shook his head, then continued, "To be honest with you, Little Bee, because we've been honest with each other all along and I don't see any reason to stop being honest now, I don't know that my mother and her husband would cotton to the idea of having you around. I could be wrong, but I don't think so."

"It's because of my Negro blood, isn't it?" said the boy.

"That's part of it, son," said Creed. "The other part is your Choctaw blood."

"I don't understand. Didn't you say that you're Choctaw on your mother's side, and don't that make her Choctaw, too?"

"Yes, I did say that," said Creed. "I am Choctaw. So is my mother, but I don't know that her husband knows about it. That's beside the point, though. I don't think Indians, no matter what tribe they belong to, are all that popular in Texas. I recollect before the war how this Colonel Baylor did his best to wipe out every Indian in the state. I don't think folks have changed their minds about Indians since then."

They rode on in silence for a while before Little Bee asked, "So what do we do now?"

"I was thinking that we could go to Doaksville," said Creed, "and try to locate your real father. What was his name again?"

"Titus Doak," said Little Bee heavily.

"Well, I thought we might find this Titus Doak and see if he'll take you in. After all, he is your real father. He might take you in. Even if he doesn't, maybe we can find out about Tash there and see if she really was your Uncle Hum's aunt. I think it's worth a try, anyway."

Little Bee didn't argue the point, but he wasn't exactly thrilled with the idea either. He merely went along with Creed, and the next morning they set out for Doaksville.

33

Josiah Doak was a white man living among the Choctaws when their nation was mostly within the state of Mississippi. It was at his trading post, Doak's Stand, that the United States government concluded the first treaty of removal with the Choctaws in 1820.

Figuring that the tribe would soon emigrate to the new country west of the Mississippi River, Doak and his brother loaded all their trade goods onto flatboats and took them down the Mississippi to the Red River, then up the Red to the mouth of the Kiamichi River. From there, they went inland to a place called the Witch's Hole and built a new trading post. After the U.S. Army built Fort Towson a few miles northwest of the store in 1824, the Doaks moved their operation to the bluffs overlooking Gates Creek about a mile west of the cantonment, and this place became Doaksville.

As the Choctaws left their lands in the East and came to the new country, they landed initially in one of three areas: Tamaha, the port town on the Arkansas River in the northern part of the nation; Osi Tamaha, a place also known as Eagle that was nothing more than a wide spot in the eastern sector of the Little Rock–Fort Towson Road; and Doaksville, which grew rapidly as a trading center for hunters in the central portion of the country and for the wild Plains Indians to the west and from Texas to the south. Of the three, Doaksville became the most prominent, in time surpassing Skullyville, which lost the capital to Doaksville in 1850.

Doaksville's importance continued to grow until 1862 when the Choctaw tribal council voted to move the capital to Armstrong Academy, fifty-five miles to the west.

The Cherokee leader, General Stand Watie, gave Doaksville its final distinction in history. He was the last rebellious general to lay down his arms when he surrendered at Doaksville on June 23, 1865. His capitulation effectively brought the War Between the States in the Indian Nations to an end.

Doaksville was a two-day ride from Chahta Tamaha for Creed and Little Bee. They arrived in the former Choctaw capital late in the evening of the second Sunday in April and found a room with a bed for the night in the back of V. B. Timms's store.

Returning to Doaksville was something of a homecoming for Little Bee. He had left there with his mother some six years earlier when Titus Doak sold them to Hezekiah Branch, who then took them north to his farm in the Cherokee Nation. When he and Creed rose the next morning and went in search of something to eat, Little Bee scanned the muddy streets and wooden buildings with vague familiarity, barely recalling any of them, although he did feel a definite affinity for the cloudy memories that the sights stirred in his mind.

When Creed asked him about Titus Doak, Little Bee could only recall that his natural father owned a farm somewhere in the vicinity of Doaksville. With just this to go on, Creed and he began searching for Doak right after breakfast, and within an hour, they learned that Doak's place was west of town on the Kiamichi River. They rode out to call on him.

Titus Doak was the son of John Doak, a nephew of Josiah Doak, the trader. John was half-Choctaw and half-Scots, and he married a mixed-blood woman. When Josiah moved to the new country after the Treaty of Doak's Stand in 1820, John sold his land in Mississippi to a white man and followed his uncle to the West, taking his few slaves with him. Titus was his first son to be born in the new country. When John passed away in 1857, Titus inherited the farm, its livestock, and fourteen slaves.

Doak was sitting in a homemade rocker all alone on the gallery of his double log cabin, smoking a cigar when Creed and Little Bee rode right up to the house. He had a long, black beard that hung down to the middle of his chest. His black hair was cropped short and hidden under a brown felt hat that had a high, rounded crown and wide brim. He wore a tattered brown coat that was unbuttoned to expose a collarless, yellowed cotton shirt over a pair of dingy red longjohns. Unpolished, square-toed leather boots covered his feet up past his ankles to the ends of the legs of his soiled undergarment. He wore no socks. His dull, dun-colored eyes studied the visitors with a great curiosity because the boy seemed familiar to him, while the man had the look of law about him, which gave Doak cause for concern, considering that his major source of income since before the war was the distillation and sale of corn liquor.

"Good morning, sir," said Creed, tipping his hat and smiling to show Doak that his intentions were friendly. "Mind if we climb down?"

"State your business, stranger," said Doak in a tone that bore absolutely no resemblance to hospitality.

Without dismounting, Creed said, "We're looking for Titus Doak." He broadened his smile, hoping to soften the man's attitude toward them.

"What for?" demanded Doak.

"I am Slate Creed from Texas." Then nodding toward his companion, he added, "And this boy is Little Bee Doak. We're looking for Titus Doak, his father."

Doak frowned at the latter and said, "You still didn't say what for, Mr. Creed."

"Are you Titus Doak?" asked Creed.

"That's him," said Little Bee without any enthusiasm.

Doak's eyes showed a sparkle of delight as he cackled and said, "So you recollect me, boy. Now ain't that something? Where's your mammy, boy?"

"She's dead," said Little Bee.

"That's why we're here, Mr. Doak," said Creed, still trying to be friendly even though he sensed that Little Bee would just as soon shoot this backwoods bastard as look at him. Creed summed up how he came to have Little Bee in his care and how they had gone in search of Uncle Hum only to discover that he was now deceased. "So we've come here."

"What for?" demanded Doak.

"Well, Mr. Doak, Little Bee is your son," said Creed.

"No, he ain't," said Doak angrily. "He's a nigger whelp, and that's all there is to it. My sons and their maw are over to Wheelock visiting."

Creed's head bobbed a bit as he realized that he might be talking to a real son of a bitch here. "I see," he said. "Well, sir, I was just thinking that with times changing as they are that you might be willing to take Little Bee into your household because . . . well, because you are his natural father."

Doak stood up for the first time, jabbed his cigar at Creed, and said, "Well, you thought wrong, mister."

"I don't understand your attitude, Mr. Doak," said Creed. "Little Bee is your son."

"I already told you, mister, he ain't my son."

"Mr. Doak, Little Bee told me that your father sired his mother and uncle and that you are his natural father through his mother, a slave named Martha. Are you telling me that he was lying to me?"

Doak took another step forward and said, "I'm telling you to get off my property and to get off right now, or I'll get my shotgun and get you off it, or I'll put you under it. The choice is yours. Get or else."

Creed opened his coat casually, drew his Colt's, cocked the hammer, and aimed it straight at Doak's nose, which was only a few inches from the muzzle. "You have pushed me across the line with your rude behavior, Mr. Doak," he said. "You will either take a different attitude this very second, sir, or I will put a ball through your brain and make you quite dead for your lack of manners and courtesy."

Doak swallowed hard as he glared at the black eye of death leering back at him. "Now listen here, mister," he said. "You ain't got no call to act this way."

"The hell I don't," growled Creed. "I came here hoping that you would be a decent man who was willing to take responsibility for his own son, but I guess I was wrong."

"Listen, Mr. Creed," said Doak, his tone now whiny and pleading. "When I took me a wife back in '59, she insisted that I make a few changes around here. She didn't want me having any of my nigger whores or their whelps around here. So I sold them all." He smiled with a bit of self-satisfaction and added, "Turned out to be a right smart thing to do, considering what happened with the war and all. Made me some real dollars off them wenches and their brats."

"You lousy son of a bitch!" swore Creed. It was everything he could do to keep from killing Doak right then and there. "How can you be so low as to sell your own children?"

"They was niggers, Mr. Creed," said Doak, once again anxious for his life. "Niggers is niggers. They ain't people like you and me."

Creed controlled the fury raging within him. As much as he wanted to shoot Doak dead, putting a ball through this bastard's head would be too quick, too painless; he wanted him to suffer more for his stupid bigotry. With that thought in mind, he raised his revolver slightly, squeezed the trigger, and shot a hole through the peak of Doak's hat, setting the cloth afire, the bullet lodging in the wall behind the farmer.

"Oh, Christ, mister!" cried Doak, throwing up his hands to plead for his miserable life. Then realizing that his hat was burning, he ripped it from his head, threw it on the porch, and stomped out the flame. When he looked up at Creed to protest this treatment, he saw the cocked Colt's staring at him again. "Christ, mister, don't kill me!" he whined.

"God only knows why I shouldn't," said Creed. "No, Mr. Doak, I don't wish to kill you, but I will, if you don't tell me a few things I want to know."

"Anything, Mr. Creed. Anything at all. You just name it."

"Little Bee's mother was Martha Doak," said Creed.

"That's right," said Doak eagerly. "Martha Doak. That was her name."

"Shut up, Doak," groaned Creed. "You make me sick, and I'll kill you just for that. Understand?"

"Yes, sir. I'll shut up."

"Fine," said Creed. "Little Bee also told me that his grandmother was a slave named Tabby. Is that correct?"

"Yes, sir. Tabby. She was Martha's mammy."

"Did Tabby have a sister named Tash that you sold to some missionaries with his Uncle Hum?"

"Tabby died right here back before the war," said Doak.

"I know that," said Creed. "I'm asking about whether she had a sister named Tash who you sold to some missionaries."

"I didn't sell any slaves to any missionaries," said Doak, "but my daddy might have sold some to the missionaries. Let me think about that for a minute."

"It would have been back about twenty years ago," said Creed. "The missionary's name would have been Potts, Reverend Ramsey Potts. Does that stir up your memory any?"

"Yes, sir, I recollect it all now. Daddy sold a whole bunch of slaves to Reverend Potts who was going off to start a new mission west of here. He needed niggers to build the place for him, and Daddy sold him some young bucks and a couple bitches to cook for them. I can't be certain for sure, but one of them could have been named Tash. I know that one of the bucks was Humma because he was my playmate when I was a boy, and I was sort of sorry to see him go. Daddy said it was for the best, though, because he said I'd never be able to whip Humma when he needed to be made to work when he was full growed." He hesitated in thought and let his eyes drift downward. The recollection of his childhood friend had actually stirred some sort of positive emotion in him. Looking up again, he said, "You say he's dead now?"

"That's right," said Creed.

"Too bad. He was like a brother to me when we was boys."

He was your brother, you dumb son of a bitch! thought Creed. You had the same father. Knowing it would do no good to say this aloud to Doak, he kept to the subject at hand, saying, "But you don't remember Tash being Tabby's sister?"

"Like I said, she could have been one of the bitches Daddy sold to the missionary. I can't say for sure."

"All right, Mr. Doak, I believe you," said Creed. He eased the hammer of the Colt's back to safety, but he didn't put the gun back inside his waistband.

Doak relaxed a bit and asked, "Why are you so interested in this Tash, Mr. Creed?"

"Other than you," said Creed, "she's Little Bee's only other relative that we know of. I was thinking that we might find her and see if she'll take him in."

"I see," said Doak. "Well, she probably will if you find her." He gave Little Bee a peremptory glance and added, "The boy's better off with his own kind."

"You son of a bitch!" snapped Creed. "Your blood runs in his veins! How can you stand there and not see that?"

"He's a nigger, Mr. Creed," said Doak, as simply as he would say that the sun comes up in the east.

"Give it up, Slate," said Little Bee bitterly. "He ain't my relation." He jerked on the reins to his mule and rode off toward Doaksville.

Creed watched Little Bee ride off, thought about stopping him, but knew it would be useless to try. He turned back to Doak and said, "He's right. You aren't related to him. He's too decent a kid to have a father like you. Even so, I don't want you to forget him. Ever." With that, he raised the Colt's, cocked it again, aimed at Doak's left ear, and fired.

As the ball tore off the lobe and the flame set his beard and hair afire, Doak screamed in pain and grabbed the side of his head, burning his fingers but extinguishing the fire. "Jesus! Jesus! Jesus!" he cried as he danced around, holding the side of his head.

Calmly, Creed replaced the revolver inside his waistband and said, "Good-bye, Mr. Doak." He turned Nimbus and rode after Little Bee.

Doak didn't hear Creed's farewell. Not in his left ear, anyway, and not above his own cries of agony.

34

"Did you kill him?" asked Little Bee when Creed caught up with him. His tone was flat, emotionless, cold.

Creed didn't answer immediately. He was incredulous as he stared at Little Bee who sat ramrod straight, looking directly ahead, his face as stoical as that of any Choctaw warrior who didn't want anybody to see what he was really feeling inside. The Texan wondered whether the boy had expected him to murder Doak in cold blood. Had Little Bee seen so much killing in recent weeks that he had come to think of it as the only way to resolve a confrontation? Damn! he thought. Was Louise Thayer right? Is killing the only thing that I've taught this boy? Lord, I hope not.

"No," said Creed uneasily. "I just left him with a little keepsake of our visit."

Little Bee didn't inquire about what that was. Instead, he asked, "Where do we go from here, Slate?"

"Good question," said Creed. "I'll have to think on that for a while, and when I figure it out, I'll let you know."

That was good enough for Little Bee.

As they rode on toward Doaksville, Creed came to the conclusion that they couldn't stay around these parts for long because, son of a bitch or not, Titus Doak was still a member of one of the most important families in the region and this meant that he was liable to come after them, most likely with a posse of several relatives and friends. Either way was trouble, and Creed had had enough of that already. He figured that they should move along as soon as possible. The question, as Little Bee had already asked, was where.

Of course, where they went depended on why they would be going there. Creed wanted to get to Texas to his mother's home near Weatherford, but he had an obligation to Little Bee because of his promise to Martha Doak. Or did he? He wondered about that, too. Have I kept my promise? he asked himself. After all, I did find Humma Doak, and I did take the boy to him. Was it my fault that his Uncle Hum was dead? I didn't promise to care for the boy beyond that, to find him a home. He looked at Little Bee riding beside him. But I can't leave the boy to fend for himself in this country. He's still a boy, although he's leaning real hard toward being a man soon. No, I've got to find him a home.

Creed considered how Little Bee might have had other family, someone besides Humma Doak. It was his opinion that the other woman, Tash, who had been owned by the missionaries at Armstrong Academy, was most likely Little Bee's great-aunt, that she had been his grandmother's sister. Probably the only way he could prove this for certain was to find Tash. That could take months, though, maybe years, and even then he had no guarantee that she was Little Bee's great-aunt or that she could or would take him.

No, Little Bee needed a home now, and Creed needed to be on his way to Texas. That left Creed with only one alternative, and he wasn't so sure that he liked it.

"Little Bee, I think we should go back to Boggy Depot and see if the Thayers still want you."

Little Bee's head snapped sideways to look at Creed with a face that was filled with surprise, hurt, and anger all at the same time. "The Thayers?" he muttered.

"That's right," said Creed. "Miss Louise did say that she wanted you to live with them, and right now, I can't think of any better place to leave you."

"Why do you have to leave me anywhere?" asked Little Bee.

"We've been over that before, son," said Creed. "I can't be sure that you'll be welcome at my mother's home in Texas, and I'd rather that you didn't have to face that situation. No, we've got to find you a home here in the Nations. That's all there is to it."

"But why do I have to go to the Thayers?" asked Little Bee. "Couldn't I go back to live with the Vanns? They wanted to take me in when we were at their place."

"If they lived as close as Boggy Depot, I'd take you to them in an instant, Little Bee, but they live several days' ride away from here. Then I'd have that many days' ride back this way again. No, the Vanns are out, son. It has to be the Thayers. We're going to Boggy Depot."

And they did.

The Thayers weren't in Boggy Depot.

Dr. Bond was.

Creed and Little Bee visited Bond in his office where he told them about what happened after they left the Thayer camp on the Muddy Boggy River a week before.

"Well, sir," said Bond, "Reverend Thayer came around shortly after you two departed. He was hurting pretty bad, and he was quite weak from all the blood he'd lost. Even so, it was plain to me that he would probably make it through the day, and if he did, he was most likely to survive to preach another sermon or two. Of course, that wasn't much of my doing. You putting him on his side right away to keep the blood out of his good lung is what saved his life. That and the care Miss Louise gave him. Anyway, he's gonna live.

"Miss Faye was real down after you left," he continued. "That girl has a real case of the sweetness for you, Mr. Creed, but I suppose she'll get over you in good time. She'll get over that snakebite first, though. Her leg will probably be weak for a long time to come, but she's alive. Again, thanks to you. Most rattlesnake bites are fatal in these parts. If you hadn't done what you did so fast, she might not have made it.

"Well, after you left us, we stayed there on the Muddy Boggy for another two days, then I felt my patients were strong enough to travel again, and we came on to town. The Thayers and Tyler stayed the one night, then moved on to popi-kuli, the salt springs northwest of here beyond Wapanucka. The Chickasaws call them oka-alichi, medicine water. I told Miss Louise about the springs and how the Indians swear that they speed up healing, and she said they were going there right away. I didn't see anything wrong with that idea, and besides, the springs are on the same trail that they'd have to take to Cherokee Town. So they left here for the springs. I haven't heard anything about them since, so I assume they made it."

Creed and Little Bee struck out the next morning for the springs known locally as oka-alichi or popi-kuli. They passed through the Choctaw school town of Wapanucka at midday and arrived at the springs late in the afternoon. The Thayers and Tyler weren't there, but Creed found their campsite, studied it, and figured they had pulled out of there the morning before. "That puts them only two days ahead of us," he told Little Bee. "I feel like a good swim, so we'll stay here tonight and start out again tomorrow."

They continued to ride west the next day, coming to a two-day old campsite at noon that Creed assumed had been made by Tyler and the Thayers. Early that evening they arrived at some more oka-alichi, but these weren't popi-kuli. They were medicine waters, but their pungent odor stated plainly that they were sulphur springs and not salt springs. The Thayers had camped there, too, and from the looks of the site, Creed guessed that they had left only that morning for Cherokee Town, which was still a half-day's ride away for Little Bee and him. Not wishing to be separated from the orphan too soon, the Texan opted to sleep one more night on the trail before catching up with the Thayers and placing Little Bee in their charge.

35

In the early days of the Choctaw Nation West, a small trading post was set up near Little Sandy Creek about a mile from where a much-used trail crossed the Washita River. The store remained unnamed until a band of Cherokees who were driven out of Texas shortly after the Texas Revolution settled in the vicinity. Because the Cherokees built homes and farms in the area, the trading post with its blacksmith shop became known as Cherokee Town and the ford of the Washita River as Cherokee Crossing.

Cherokee Town was situated at the junction of two roads: the east-west route from Boggy Depot to Fort Cobb and the south-north route from Fort Arbuckle to the Seminole Agency above the South Fork of the Canadian River. The village was made up of a few typical stores, a blacksmith shop, a livery stable and barn, and a few dozen log and slabwood houses.

Although the village remained small, Cherokee Town was the best known place west of Fort Washita until Fort Arbuckle was built in 1851. Hunters, trappers, and Indians as well as local farmers traded at the settlement's stores. It was here, prior to the War Between the States, that Confederate General Albert Pike met with the Plains chiefs and asked them to align themselves with the Confederacy against the Union. Pike's only achievement was to alert the wild Indians to the weakness of the settlers in the area, and they used this knowledge to turn the region into a bloody war zone known as "Scalp Alley" among the Nations.

With the end of the War Between the States and the return of Union soldiers to Fort Arbuckle, Fort Cobb, and Fort Washita, the Plains Indians were driven back and their depredations along the lower Washita River ceased. Those people who had moved away to avoid the savage attacks of the Comanches, Kiowas, and other untamed Indian bands to the west started coming back to their homes and farms as early as the spring of 1865. It was this restoration of peace and tranquility that Reverend Thayer had hoped to abet with the establishment of a mission and school at Cherokee Town, thus was his reason for choosing this locality.

As they approached the town, Creed and Little Bee were wishing that the minister had chosen a community that wasn't so remote from the beaten trails. Even so, they figured that finding Tyler and the Thayers wouldn't be that difficult in a place as small as Cherokee Town. Two covered wagons with white women and an ex-slave should have stood out prominently, or so they thought. When they didn't see any sign of the Thayers or Tyler in town, Creed decided to dismount and ask around. They tied up Nimbus and the mules in front of Jack Grant's general store, and Creed went inside, while Little Bee stayed with the animals.

The interior of the store was very dark after the bright midday sunshine outside, and Creed's eyes had difficulty making an immediate adjustment to the dimmer light. He blinked them rapidly as he tried to focus and walk at the same time, hoping that he wouldn't bump into something or someone as he moved toward the cash counter. Finally able to discern more than shadowy figures, he saw two Indian women examining some cloth on a table in one front corner and a couple of Indian men eyeing the rows of hammers, axes, and saws in the implement section. A handsome, young white man wearing an apron over his shirt and trousers stood near, waiting for them to make up their minds about their purchases. Creed started to approach the clerk, but a voice behind him stayed the move.

"May I help you, sir?" asked Jack Grant. He appeared to be a typical storekeeper: tall, thin, pale complexion, with a full beard that seemed to have every possible color of hair in it, brown hair that was slicked down with brilliantine. He approached Creed from a short hallway that led to the saloon in the rear of the building.

"Yes, sir," said Creed, looking Grant straight in the eyes and not noticing anything or anybody beyond the merchant. Of course, even if he had tried to see through the passageway into the watering hole, he couldn't have distinguished any of the drinkers because that room had less light than the store.

"My name is Slate Creed, and I'm looking for some people who might have passed through here in the last day or two."

Creed's conversation with Grant wasn't going unnoticed by the other customers in the store, and the five patrons in the saloon were also listening with keen interest. One drinker in particular strained to hear Creed talk.

"That's him," said Ed King.

"I believe you're right, King," said Stiver.

"Looks like he's alone, too," said King. "Let's finish the son of a bitch once and for all. How about it, boys?"

"Sure, let's kill the son of a bitch," said Stiver. Like King, he'd had enough liquor to make him braver—and a lot dumber—than he really was.

"I'm in," said Morris, "but let's make sure he's alone first." He wasn't as drunk as his friends. "How about it, King?"

King smiled evilly and said, "Sure, we can do that. Stiver, you and Morris stay here and keep low and keep an eye on him. When he leaves, you follow him out the front door. I'll take Mackey and Starr with me now, and we'll go out the saloon door and around to the front to see if that nigger is with him. If he ain't, we'll bushwhack him when he comes outside. You got that?"

"Sure, King," said Stiver.

"Good," said King. "Come on, boys." He drew a revolver from inside his coat and headed for the door with the two mixed-blood youths following him.

The town was pretty much vacant except for a few old men who were relaxing in the shade of McGilray's store across the street and Little Bee, who was sitting on the edge of Grant's porch, pawing the dirt with his foot, waiting for Creed. The orphan paid small attention to the quiet scene in front of him until he heard a stir around the corner of the store. Turning his bowed head to the side, he saw King and the two young men with him standing at the side of the building holding revolvers at the ready. Nobody had to tell him what their intentions were. He jumped up and started for the door just as King saw him.

"There's that nigger brat!" shouted King. He raised his weapon and fired off a round that missed its target.

At the sound of King's gunshot, Creed's instincts controlled his actions. He opened his coat and reached for his Colt's.

The men across the street hurried inside McGilray's for protection as King cocked his piece again, only to hold his fire as his target eluded him.

Little Bee crashed against the door, fumbled the latch, then finally lifted it and burst into the store, shouting, "Slate! It's Ed King!"

Hearing Little Bee's warning, Creed drew his gun, cocked it, and dropped into a crouch to survey the scene. He saw the orphan standing just inside the doorway, panting and scanning the room for him. "Get down, Little Bee!" said the Texan.

Little Bee looked in the direction of Creed's voice, thought he could make out the Texan's form, and said, "He was coming around the corner of the store with two others, Slate."

"Fine! Thank you!" snapped Creed. "Now get down!"

"What's this all about, Mr. Creed?" demanded Grant.

"There's no time to explain, Mr. Grant," said Creed. He looked back over his shoulder just in time to see Stiver and Morris in the hallway to the saloon. Both were pointing their revolvers at him. He had no time to take aim and shoot at them. Instead, he ducked behind the counter just as the two villains fired at him.

The two Indian women shrieked in fear and hid behind the piles of cloth. Their menfolk bent down behind another counter, and the young clerk did likewise. Grant dropped down beside Creed. Little Bee sought protection behind a cracker barrel.

Before Stiver and Morris could cock their weapons again, Creed popped up, took quick aim, and fired at them. The ball caught Stiver in the left shoulder at the joint, shattering the end of the collarbone.

The man screamed and fell backwards against Morris, knocking him back into the saloon. "I'm hit!" he cried as he stumbled after his companion. He cocked his gun and fired another wild shot in Creed's direction before retreating completely out of the Texan's view.

Creed crouched down behind the counter again.

"Lord Jesus, Mr. Creed!" said Grant. "What's this all about? What are you doing here? Why are these men shooting at you like that?"

"No time to explain now, Mr. Grant," said Creed, all of his senses straining for signs of King and his fellow villains. "Little Bee, are you all right?" he called out.

"I'm all right, Slate," the boy called back. "How about you? Are you all right?"

"Doing fine, son," said Creed. "You keep low, you hear?"

"Yes, sir," said Little Bee. He was close enough to the window to the left of the door to see through it to the street out front. "King and his two friends are taking cover behind the corner of a building across the road," he informed Creed.

"The son of a bitch shot me!" whined Stiver, as he and Morris hid around the corner of the saloon. "He shot me, Jimmy! The son of a bitch shot me!"

"We'll get him, Dick," said Morris softly. "Don't worry yourself none. There's five of us and only one of him. We'll get the bastard."

Stiver flattened against the wall and slid down it until he was sitting on the floor. He was breathing heavily and bleeding copiously, though not fatally.

Morris took a dirty red bandanna from a coat pocket and put it over the wound. "Hold that, Dick," he said.

Stiver complied, using his gun hand.

Creed peeked over the counter at the hallway to the bar. He couldn't see either Morris or Stiver, but he heard their muffled voices as they talked to each other. "How many men were in the saloon when I came in, Mr. Grant?" he asked.

"Five," said Grant.

"Just like I thought," said Creed. Damn! he thought. How did they get away from the Army? Dirty bastards! I should have killed King when I had the chance back at Hawk's Tavern. Well, I didn't, and now look at the fix I'm in. Damn! "You men in the saloon," he called out. "You quit this now, and I won't kill you. If you don't quit now, I promise you that you will not live to see the sun rise in the morning. Do you hear me?"

"We hear you, Creed," Morris called back, "but we ain't listening to you. We're gonna kill you, Creed. You're the one who won't live to see the sun rise in the morning."

"You know," said Creed softly, to himself more than to Grant, "I almost believe him."

36

Britt Tyler preceded the Thayer wagons into Cherokee Town late in the early evening of Friday, April 13, 1866. After a quick look around for a place to camp and not finding one, he asked a fellow on the street where they might find fresh water and a campsite, and he was directed to follow the road through the town to Little Sandy Creek. Tyler thanked the man, then he led the Thayers to a shady spot along the stream where they set up temporary quarters.

Satisfied with Tyler's choice, Louise determined that they would remain there until her father was well enough to be up and around on his own, and then he would decide what they should do next. In the meantime, Tyler was free to leave them, having fulfilled his contractual obligation to the minister. The ex-slave said he preferred to remain with them for a few days to rest up for the next leg of his homeward journey, the trip south to Texas.

Tyler was doing just that, resting, dozing after lunch in the shade of a cottonwood, when he heard a gunshot echo the half-mile down the road from Cherokee Town. He recognized the sound instantly as revolver fire, and his first instinct was to sit up and take hold of the Remingtons in his waistband. He gave the immediate vicinity a quick scan for trouble.

Louise was kneeling beside Reverend Thayer who was sitting up in his bed so his daughter could change the bandages on his chest wound. He was healing nicely, thanks to her constant attention to him.

Faye was also healing rapidly because of the care she was

getting from Louise. She was napping in her bed, the gunshot not having disturbed her rest.

Drake was—Drake was what? No Drake!

Where is that boy now? wondered Tyler. He let go of his gun grips and came erect, straining his other senses for a bad sign. Neither hearing nor smelling anything foul, he walked casually over to Louise and Reverend Thayer.

Seeing Tyler approaching, Louise said, "You heard it, too, didn't you?" She tied off the last wrap of cloth around her father's chest.

"The gunshot?" queried Tyler. Seeing Louise nod, he said, "Yes, ma'am, I heard it. It came from town. Must be trouble."

"Well, it's none of our concern," said Louise.

"No, I guess not," said Tyler, although he was curious enough to want to ride into town and see what was happening there, his business or not. He surveyed the camp again and still couldn't see Drake. "Where's Mr. Drake, Miss Louise?"

She glanced at Drake's bedroll, but he wasn't there. She stood up, looked toward the creek, but still didn't see him. "I don't know," she finally admitted. Her eyes met Tyler's. "He did say that he wanted to go into town. You don't suppose he went there without asking first, do you?"

Tyler didn't say it, but he was thinking, Oh, hell no, Miss Louise! Why would he be that foolish?

"Of course, he went into town," said Reverend Thayer. "You told him he couldn't go, didn't you?"

"Yes, of course, I told him that he couldn't go," said Louise defensively. "I wouldn't give him permission to go into town without Mr. Tyler going along with him."

"Well," said the parson, "that's why he went."

"You don't think he went into town, do you, Mr. Tyler?" she asked, hoping that he would have some other explanation for Drake's absence.

"Yes, ma'am, I think he did."

"Mr. Tyler," said Thayer, "would you be so kind as to fetch him back here before he gets himself into trouble?"

"Yes, sir," said Tyler. "Be glad to do it." He went to saddle Payday.

"You don't think that gunshot we heard had anything to do with Drake, do you, Louise?" asked Thayer.

"No, Father, I don't," said Louise. "I don't think Drake wants anything to do with guns now."

"I certainly hope you're right, Louise," said Thayer, as he leaned back on his bed.

She was.

Drake wasn't anywhere near Cherokee Town. He'd gone for a walk along Little Sandy Creek, following it downstream, being curious about how far it was to the next stream and hoping that he might be able to fish there. When he heard King's gunshot, he didn't realize that the sound had come from the village. Instead, he thought it had come from the area around the wagons, and this worried him, made him think that bushwhackers might be attacking them again. He spun on his heel and hurried back to camp, but he didn't arrive there in time to stop Tyler from riding off to look for him.

"Drake, where have you been?" demanded Louise when her brother returned.

"I've been down by the creek," he said. "Are you all right?" He looked around and noted that their company was one man and one horse short.

"Of course, we're all right," said Louise. "But what about you? Are you all right?"

"Where's Mr. Tyler?" asked Drake.

Reverend Thayer propped himself onto one elbow and said, "I asked him to go into town to look for you."

"I didn't go to town," said Drake. "Louise said I couldn't go without Mr. Tyler, and I didn't think he would want to go, so I went for a walk along the creek to look for a fishing hole." Then it struck him that his father was implying something else. "You thought I'd disobeyed her, didn't you?"

"Yes, son, I did," confessed Thayer, his voice betraying the guilt that he felt.

Drake hung his head. "I see," he said. "I suppose I'm not to be trusted anymore, am I?"

"Drake," said Louise, rising and going to him, "it's not that we don't trust you."

"No, Louise," said the reverend firmly. "Leave him be." He waited for her to stop, then he gave another command. "Drake, I want you to come here this instant."

Louise stepped aside, and Drake drifted past her toward his

father. "Yes, sir?" he said once he was standing over him.

"Please, son, kneel down here beside me. Please."

Drake complied with the request. "Yes, sir?" he said, not willing to look directly at his ailing father.

"Son, I'm sorry," said Thayer. "I'm sorry that I drove you to disobey me. I'm sorry that I didn't have enough confidence in you to let you learn about guns."

Drake's head shot up as he stuttered, "What?"

"Hear me out, Drake," said Thayer.

Drake nodded and remained silent, although riveted to his father's words.

"While I've been laying here in my sickbed," the parson continued, "I've had plenty of time to think and reflect on my own thoughts, and I've had plenty of time to pray and listen for God's voice. And you know, I think I've heard Him on more than one occasion these last few days or so. I think I've heard Him tell me that it isn't the gun that is evil. Only the man holding the gun can be evil. What is a gun, anyway, but a tool? What is a hammer but a tool? Both have the potential to kill, but they only kill when the hand holding them makes them kill. It's the man that's evil, son. Not the gun.

"I didn't realize this right off," he continued. "I didn't come to this understanding until . . . until I heard . . . until I thought I heard your mother's voice telling me that I couldn't die yet because my work here wasn't finished." He swallowed hard, then began again with more urgency, with a desire to be believed. "It was the strangest thing, Drake. I saw her standing in a misty cloud. She was young and beautiful again. The girl I married so very long ago." Tears welled up in his eyes, and he had to stop speaking for the moment.

Louise couldn't believe what she was hearing. She said nothing, merely standing there and listening with an open heart and wanting to believe that her father's vision was more than a fading dream. As he spoke, her eyes burned with tears.

The father cleared his throat and continued saying, "I wanted to go to her, to be with her. So much I wanted to go to her, but she wouldn't let me." Tears spilled from his eyes as he began to sob. He could only blubber, "I miss her so much sometimes." He wept for a moment, then wiped his eyes and went on. "She told me that I couldn't come to her until my work here was finished. I argued with her. I begged her to let me go to her, but she said no.

I couldn't. Not until I had finished my work here. What work? I asked. Our children, she said, and then she was gone, and I was still here." His head drooped, and he wept uncontrollably for a minute or so. Finally, he regained control of his emotions and looked up at Drake. "I'm sorry, son, that I thought that you might have some evil in you. I'm sorry that I didn't have enough faith in you. I'm sorry that I failed you, Drake. Will you ever forgive me?" The father took the son's hand and squeezed it.

Drake wept and returned the affectionate touch.

Louise wanted to kneel between Drake and her father and take their hands in her own and weep with them. But she didn't move. This is their time, she told herself. And she was happy for them, all of them, happy that they were becoming a family again.

Thank You, God, she prayed silently.

37

Creed had been caught between more than one rock and a hard place in his lifetime, but he was usually alone when it happened. Not this time. This time he had seven other people caught with him, and none of them liked the idea anymore than he did.

"Mr. Grant," said Creed, "do you know these men who are shooting at me?"

"They're all strangers to me," said Grant. "They rode in here yesterday morning from the north. They were in my saloon drinking last night, and they came back first thing this morning for breakfast and started drinking right away. They said they were on their way to Arizona to prospect for gold."

"Well, that tells me who that is back there," said Creed. "Couple of no-goods from Wisconsin named Stiver and Morris. I had a run-in with them at North Fork Town. And one of those men in the street, like Little Bee said, is named Ed King. He's a bushwhacker from Missouri. I don't know the other two with him, but I'll bet they're the two fellows who were with him back in North Fork Town." He shook his head. "I knew I should have killed that son of a bitch then, but instead, I did the right thing and turned him over to the Army. They said they'd take him and those other two to the court in Arkansas. I guess they escaped, and now they're here." He twisted his mouth to one side as another thought came to him. "I don't suppose you have any law around here, do you?"

"The Army at Fort Arbuckle is the nearest law," said Grant. "The Cherokees and Chickasaws in these parts are usually pretty much on the right side of the law, and when they do get out of line, they usually take care of their own problems. The Army only gets

242

involved when folks like those fellows in back come around here causing trouble for peaceful folks."

"Well, Mr. Grant, I'm sorry to have brought this trouble on you," said Creed. "Believe me, that was not my intention when I came in here."

"I believe you, Mr. Creed," said Grant. "So what do you plan to do about this trouble?"

"First off, I'd like to take this fight elsewhere," said Creed, "but I don't expect King or those two in back will let me do that. So the next best thing is to get you and those other folks out of here so I can get this business finished once and for all time."

"I would certainly appreciate that, Mr. Creed," said Grant. "Getting out of here, I mean."

Little Bee peeked through the window and saw one of the two young men with King come running across the street, making a wide circle as he did because he thought Creed might take a shot at him and he was keeping out of pistol range. "Slate," he called, "one of them is heading this way. I think he's going around back."

"Thanks, Little Bee," said Creed. "Keep an eye on King."

"Sure thing, Slate."

"You men in the saloon," called Creed. "There's other folks in here who might get hurt if we start throwing lead at each other careless like. I want you to hold your fire while they clear out of here. All right?"

"It's all right by us," said Morris, "but you'd better ask King about that."

"No, you tell him," said Creed. "One of his boys—" He didn't get to finish the sentence.

As Creed was speaking, the youth named Mackey burst into the saloon, startling Stiver and Morris who were listening intently to Creed. Without thinking, the two turned and fired at the unannounced newcomer, wounding him seriously as one ball caught him in the left pelvis and the other shattered his upper right arm. Mackey staggered backwards against the door, then ricocheted from it, falling forward to the floor. He kicked a bit, then he felt the pain and began to cry.

"Oh, shit, Jimmy!" said Stiver, forgetting his own injury. "We just shot one of King's boys! He'll be madder than hell about this."

"Shut up, Dick!" barked Morris. His face was twisted with

anger, but his eyes were filled with fear. As a plan struck him, he lowered his voice and added, "We'll just tell him Creed did it. He'll never know the difference."

Mackey wailed.

"He will if that boy lives to tell him the difference," said Stiver, his eyes bulging with fright.

Without another word, Morris walked over to Mackey, put the muzzle of his .44 to the youth's ear, said, "Sorry, friend," and pulled the trigger, killing Mackey instantly.

The explosion of Morris's gun intensified Stiver's fear. He pressed himself harder against the wall and wet his pants involuntarily. "Jesus, Jimmy!" he whined. "Why'd you do that?"

"So he couldn't tell King we shot him," said Morris. "Now he won't tell nobody that we killed him."

"I didn't kill him," said Stiver. "You did."

Curious about the shooting in the saloon, Creed came out from behind the counter and slipped into the hallway. He overheard the last exchange between Morris and Stiver and saw a golden opportunity to get the jump on them. He leveled his Colt's at Morris and said, "Don't move, boys."

Both outlaws were too scared to do the smart thing.

Morris raised his gun at the Texan, but he never got a shot off as Creed fired and put a ball into his chest, the force of the bullet knocking him backwards against the wall. He covered the wound with his free hand, felt the warm wet, then with disbelieving eyes he looked at the blood on his fingers. "Jesus, Dick," he said, his voice rising an octave. "He's shot me now. The son of a bitch!" His knees buckled, and he slid down the wall, still looking at his bloody hand and holding his revolver. He squeezed off a harmless round into the floor boards and muttered his last words, "I'm killed, Dick."

Stiver tried to stand and aim at the Texan at the same time, but he couldn't do either as Creed shifted, cocked his Colt's again, aimed, fired, and shot Stiver in the neck, the ball lodging against a vertebra and snapping his head against the wall. He gagged on the surge of blood as he dropped his pistol and grabbed his throat. In the next instant, the blow to the back of his skull took its effect. He slumped sideways into unconsciousness and eventually into death.

With three of King's gang out of the game now, Creed returned to the store, hurrying to the front window to look for King and Starr.

"King's still across the street," said Little Bee, "but the other fellow went around behind the building. I think he'll come out on the other side."

"You're right, Little Bee," said Creed, pointing with his left hand. "There he is now." He turned to the storekeeper. "Mr. Grant, I suggest you get these people out through the saloon now, and take Little Bee with you. If anything should happen to me, I'd appreciate it if you'd take him to Reverend Thayer, the parson I was asking you about before all this started."

"I ain't leaving, Slate," said Little Bee.

"Yes, you are, son," said Creed firmly, without looking at the boy. "Now don't give me any grief about this and get going with Mr. Grant."

"Come on, folks," said Grant, motioning to the two women and their men. "Let's do what Mr. Creed says." Then, seeing his clerk, he added, "You, too, Johnny."

"Sure thing, Uncle Jack," said Johnny.

The customers and Grant's nephew kept low as they moved toward the saloon doorway. The women were crying hysterically, and the sight of three dead men in the bar did nothing to calm them. Their men tried to comfort them as they hurried through the saloon and exited through the back door. Johnny stopped at the doorway and waited for Little Bee and his uncle.

"Mr. Creed," said Grant, "there's powder and ball and caps beneath the counter there. Help yourself."

"Thank you, Mr. Grant," said Creed.

"I ain't going, Slate," said Little Bee with more determination that ever.

"Didn't I just tell you not to give me any grief, Little Bee?" said Creed. He peered deep into the orphan's eyes and saw into his soul. He felt the love there, and it touched him. His eyes burned as he said, "Look. I've already lost one little brother. I don't want to lose another. Now go with Mr. Grant until I finish this business with King." Anticipating Little Bee, he added, "I promise you that I'll be all right." Then for emphasis and to reassure the boy, he said slowly and deliberately and softly, "I will . . . be . . . all . . . right. Now go."

Without another word, Little Bee turned and walked out with Grant. They joined Johnny in the saloon, where they hesitated to leave, preferring to watch the two Indian couples through the window as they made good their escape.

Creed heaved a sigh of relief that they were gone, then he reloaded his gun with the powder and ball he found under the counter where Grant said it was. He capped all six nipples, then moved to the front of the store to spy out King and Starr.

Feeling it was safe to leave now, Grant gave his approval for his nephew to lead the way to the blacksmith shop next door. Johnny looked toward King's position, then feeling that it was all right to leave, he moved out at a trot. Little Bee followed a few steps behind him, and Grant brought up the rear with lanky strides. They had made it halfway across the thirty yards of open ground when Little Bee saw Britt Tyler riding into town from the north. Recognizing the ex-soldier immediately, he broke ranks and ran into the street, yelling, "Mr. Tyler! Mr. Tyler! It's Ed King! It's Ed King!" He pointed to where the bushwhacker was hiding across the road.

Tyler reined in his mount when he heard his name being called, then he saw Little Bee running toward him shouting a name that he didn't recollect at first. Perplexed, he looked in the direction that Little Bee was pointing and saw King emerge from his hiding place.

"Little nigger brat!" shrieked King. He aimed his .44 at Little Bee and fired.

The boy went down.

Creed heard and saw all of this transpire in front of him, and he remained motionless until Little Bee landed face down in the dirt. "NO!" he screamed as loud as he had ever screamed before in his life. He threw open the door, leapt from the porch to the road, and started running toward King, yelling, "You dirty son of a bitch!"

King heard Creed yell, and he was struck with terror. Every muscle in him rigidized, making him the perfect target.

Tyler jumped down from Payday to go to Little Bee.

Creed fired before he was halfway across the street. The ball nicked the outside of King's left thigh, stinging him more than anything but also stirring him to action. Seeing King turn to run away, the Texan stopped, took careful aim, and shot the cowardly bushwhacker in the back of the same leg, dropping him in the dirt.

Seeing King go down, Starr panicked and ran off in the other direction. He wasn't going to die for a worthless no-account like Ed King.

When he fell, King's revolver bounced from his hand and slid away from him. He saw the weapon a few feet in front of him and tried to get to his knees to retrieve it.

"You dirty son of a bitch!" cried Creed. He moved closer, aimed at King's other leg, and squeezed off another round.

The second ball tore into the back of King's other thigh and flattened him in the dirt. He writhed in pain, rolled onto his back, and was faced with the black eye of death.

Creed stood over the wounded bushwhacker, aiming his Colt's at the outlaw's stomach. "Ever seen a man who's been gut-shot, King?" he growled. "It may be the slowest, most painful way to die that there is." He fired and hit King in the lower right side of his abdomen in the area of his appendix.

King screamed and grabbed the wound.

"It gets worse, King," said Creed, his face twisted with maniacal revenge.

"Creed!" It was Tyler. "Stop it, Creed!"

"Leave me be!" shouted the Texan.

"That's enough, Creed!" said Tyler.

"NO!" Enraged by the man's interference, he turned to face down the ex-soldier, aiming his Colt's at Tyler, prepared to shoot him dead, if it was the only way to make him stay out of this affair.

Tyler was only twenty feet away, holding the reins to his horse. Standing in front of him, apparently unhurt, was the orphan boy that Creed had come to love like a brother.

Creed couldn't believe his eyes. He let his arm slump low. "Little Bee?" he muttered, not yet comprehending that the boy was alive and all right. He started to go to him, but the clicking of a gun hammer being cocked into firing position stayed his feet. He spun on a heel, dropped to a knee, and saw King with a .44 pointed in his direction. The Texan didn't hesitate another heartbeat. He fired the fatal bullet that sent that bushwhacking bastard to hell where he belonged.

38

Nobody was more surprised to see Creed and Little Bee again than Louise Thayer was, and nobody was more surprised that Creed was asking her to take Little Bee than she was.

"I'm glad to see that you finally came to your senses," she said haughtily.

"It's only temporary," said Creed.

They—Creed, Little Bee, and Louise—were standing apart from the others. Tyler and Drake were tending to the animals, and the reverend and Faye were asleep in their beds.

"Only temporary?" queried Louise. "What do you mean by that?"

"I mean, I'll be back for him," said Creed. He put his arm around Little Bee's shoulders and hugged the boy to him. "Isn't that right, son?"

"I rather doubt that you'll ever come near him again," said Louise, "once you ride out of here."

"Is that right?" said Creed.

"Yes, it is," said Louise.

"Well, let me set you straight on that, Miss Thayer," said Creed. "You're wrong. You see, I'm a Texan, and Texans keep their word." He smiled and added, "Because if they don't, they know that's a sure-fire way to get a one-way ticket straight to hell." He turned serious again. "I gave Little Bee my word that I'd be back for him just as soon as I get things set straight on my mother's ranch. I gave him my word just the same as I gave his mother my word a month ago up in the Cherokee Nation, and I don't think I have to say anything more about that."

"Well, we'll just have to wait and see what happens in the future, won't we?" said Louise.

"Yes, we will, won't we?" he said. "In the meantime, you can see to it that he learns to read and write and cipher real well, because I don't want to come back here and find out he's still some kind of uneducated tumbleweed." He looked at Little Bee, hugged him again, and said, "You understand that, son?"

"Sure, Slate, I understand," said the orphan.

"You needn't worry about his education," said Louise. "I'll see to it personally. That much he can depend on."

Creed had had enough of his woman's attitude. "Will you excuse us for a minute, Little Bee?" he said.

"Sure, Slate," said the youngster. He walked away to visit with Drake and Tyler.

"All right, Louise," said Creed. "Let's have it."

"Have what?" she queried.

"Let's have it out. I want to know what it is about me that you detest so much that you have to speak to me like I'm so much horse dung stuck to the heel of your shoe."

"It isn't only one thing, Mr. Creed. It's *everything* about you that I detest. From the crown of your hat to the toe of your boots, I loathe everything about you."

For an instant, she lowered the veil of her soul and allowed Creed to see into heart. Her lips might have been speaking hateful words, but she was feeling the opposite.

"You're a liar," he said.

"What?" she gasped.

"You heard me. You're a liar."

"How dare you call me a liar!" she snapped. She raised her hand to strike him, but he caught her arm and twisted it downward. Even so, she remained defiant, gritting her teeth and saying, "You're hurting me."

"Not as much as you're hurting yourself, Louise."

Her face scrunched up with confusion. "What?" she rasped.

Creed released her and said, "You're hurting yourself by not being honest, Louise. You're not being honest with yourself or anybody else. You aren't fooling anybody with this bit of play-acting that you're doing."

"Play-acting? What does that mean?"

"You know perfectly well what that means." He chuckled, then said, "You've been play-acting since the moment I met you. Prob-

ably before that, too. You've probably been play-acting for years.
Probably so long that you don't even know that you're doing it
anymore. You'd better stop it, and stop it soon, or you just might
miss out when the right man for you comes along."

"The right man? Someone like you, I suppose."

"Maybe."

"Don't flatter yourself, Mr. Creed."

"No, don't you flatter yourself, Louise. Do you remember what
I told Faye when I said good-bye to her on the Muddy Boggy
River?"

"I wasn't listening."

"There you go again. Lying. You've got to stop that, Louise,
and start being honest. If you don't, you'll wind up either as an
old maid or as a very unhappy woman with a man that you really
will detest."

Creed had finally struck the right nerve. She winced, being
taken aback by his statement, but she recovered immediately.
"Just who do you think you are to talk to me this way?" she
said fiercely.

"I'll give you your choice on that one," said Creed. "I'm either
a man who feels sorry for you because you're pathetic, or I'm a
man who cares about you, a man who would come a-courtin' if
things were different with the rest of my life. But things aren't
different with the rest of my life, so let's just say I'm someone
who cares about you, and I don't want to see you unhappy for
the rest of your life.

"Now I've already seen that you've made up with Faye," he
continued, "and I see that you're getting along better with Drake
and your father. But what I don't see is you getting along with
yourself. Until you start doing that, you'll be unhappy, and worse
than that, you'll wind up making everybody around you just as
unhappy as you are. Do you really want that, Louise?"

"No," she said softly, "of course not."

"Then you'd better start being honest with yourself," he said,
"and start letting your feelings out. Your true feelings. Not what
you think everybody expects from you, but what you really want
to feel and say and do. Once you start doing that, you won't
have to look for happiness, Louise. It'll look for you." He turned
to walk away, then stopped, standing sideways to her. "I didn't
mean to preach to you like that, but you just bring that out of me,
I guess."

"No," she said rapidly, urgently, "it's all right." She sighed, then continued. "I guess you really do care . . . about me, I mean."

Creed blew a smile across his face, shook his head, and said, "You really do catch on quick, don't you?"

Louise lowered her eyes and said, "Yes, I suppose I am a little slow sometimes." Looking up again, she asked, "Did you really mean what you said about courting if things were different in your life?"

He smiled and said, "You caught that part, did you?"

She smiled back at him and said, "Yes."

"Well, let me put it this way," said Creed. "I told Faye that the only woman who could ever tie me down would have to be part wildcat, part mule, and part cottontail with just a tiny bit of alley cat thrown in to make her real interesting. She doesn't have that alley cat in her. But you do." He tipped his hat and said, "I'll be going to say good-bye to Little Bee now." He turned and walked away toward the meadow where the animals were staked out.

Louise watched him go, wishing that he would come back and take her into his arms and never leave again. But she knew that couldn't be. Not now, anyway. Maybe when he came back for Little Bee, whenever that should be. She could wait until then, or so she told herself.

Creed caught up to Little Bee, Drake, and Tyler in the meadow. "I'm going now," he said. "I just came to say good-bye." He offered his hand to the ex-slave. "Mr. Tyler, I hope we'll meet again one day and the next time we do we can get off to a friendlier start."

Tyler shook his hand and said, "I think I'd like that, Mr. Creed. You watch out for yourself now."

"Write me a letter, Mr. Tyler, and let me know if you find your family. I'd like to meet them someday."

"I'll do that," said Tyler. He released the grip.

Creed turned to Drake. "You had a hard lesson about guns, Drake," he said, "but I think you learned it well." He offered his hand to young Thayer. "You hurry up and get that education back in Kentucky and get back here. This country needs more people like you and your father. Peaceful folks. Good men to lead the way."

"Thank you, Slate," said Drake. He finished the handshake and walked off with Tyler so Creed could say his farewell to Little Bee.

"I'm going to miss you, son," said Creed.

Little Bee threw his arms around Creed's waist, squeezed him as tight as he could, and said, "Please take me with you, Slate."

Creed held the boy close to him and said, "We've already talked this out, Little Bee. I won't go into it again. You're going to stay here like we agreed. And I'll come back for you as soon as I can."

"When?" cried the orphan.

"As soon as I can," said Creed. He squeezed his eyelids tight, trying to hold back the tears. "I'll tell you what, Little Bee. When I come back, we'll go look for my Grandpa Hawk, and we'll stay with him so he can teach you how to be a real Choctaw warrior. How would that be, son?"

Misty-eyed, Little Bee looked up at Creed and said, "I'd like that, Slate."

"Then it's a promise," said Creed. "I give you my word that's what we'll do when I come back for you. Texan's honor."

America's new star of the classic western

GILES TIPPETTE

author of *Hard Rock, Jailbreak,* and *Crossfire*
is back with his newest, most exciting novel yet

SIXKILLER

Springtime on the Half-Moon ranch has never been
so hard. On top of running the biggest spread in
Matagorda County, Justa Williams is about to become
a daddy. Which means he's got a lot more to fight for
when Sam Sixkiller comes to town. With his pack of
wild cutthroats slicing a swath of mayhem all the way
from Galveston, Sixkiller now has his ice-cold eyes
on Blessing—and word has it he intends to pick the
town clean.

Now, backed by men more skilled with branding irons
than rifles, the Williams clan must fight to defend
their dream—with their wits, their courage, and their
guns. . . .

Turn the page
for an exciting preview of
SIXKILLER
by Giles Tippette

Coming in May from Jove Books!

IT WAS LATE afternoon when I got on my horse and rode the half mile from the house I'd built for Nora, my wife, up to the big ranch house my father and my two younger brothers still occupied. I had good news, the kind of news that does a body good, and I had taken the short run pretty fast. The two-year-old bay colt I'd been riding lately was kind of surprised when I hit him with the spurs, but he'd been lazing around the little horse trap behind my house and was grateful for the chance to stretch his legs and impress me with his speed. So we made it over the rolling plains of our ranch, the Half-Moon, in mighty good time.

I pulled up just at the front door of the big house, dropped the reins to the ground so that the colt would stand, and then made my way up on the big wooden porch, the rowels of my spurs making a *ching-ching* sound as I walked. I opened the big front door and let myself into the hall that led back to the main parts of the house.

I was Justa Williams and I was boss of all thirty thousand deeded acres of the place. I had been so since it had come my duty on the weakening of our father, Howard, through two unfortunate incidents. The first had been the early demise of our mother, which had taken it out of Howard. That had been when he'd sort of started preparing me to take over the load. I'd been a hard sixteen or a soft seventeen at the time. The next level had jumped up when he'd got nicked in the lungs by a stray bullet. After that I'd had the job of boss. The place was run with my two younger brothers, Ben and Norris.

It had been a hard job but having Howard around had made the job easier. Now I had some good news for him and I meant him to take it so. So when I went clumping back toward his bedroom that was just off the office I went to yelling, "Howard! Howard!"

He'd been lying back on his daybed, and he got up at my approach and came out leaning on his cane. He said, "What the thunder!"

I said, "Old man, sit down."

I went over and poured us out a good three fingers of whiskey. I didn't ever bother to water his as I was supposed to do because my news was so big. He looked on with a good deal of pleasure as I poured out the drink. He wasn't even supposed to drink whiskey, but he'd put up such a fuss that the doctor had finally given in and allowed him one well-watered whiskey a day. But Howard claimed he never could count very well and that sometimes he got mixed up and that one drink turned into four. But, hell, I couldn't blame him. Sitting around all day like he was forced to was enough to make anybody crave a drink even if it was just for something to do.

But now he seen he was going to get the straight stuff and he got a mighty big gleam in his eye. He took the glass when I handed it to him and said, "What's the occasion? Tryin' to kill me off?"

"Hell no," I said. "But a man can't make a proper toast with watered whiskey."

"That's a fact," he said. "Now what the thunder are we toasting?"

I clinked my glass with his. I said, "If all goes well you are going to be a grandfather."

"Lord A'mighty!" he said.

We said "Luck" as was our custom and then knocked them back.

Then he set his glass down and said, "Well, I'll just be damned." He got a satisfied look on his face that I didn't reckon was all due to the whiskey. He said, "Been long enough in coming."

I said, "Hell, the way you keep me busy with this ranch's business I'm surprised I've had the time."

"Pshaw!" he said.

We stood there, kind of enjoying the moment, and then I nodded at the whiskey bottle and said, "You keep on sneaking drinks, you ain't likely to be around for the occasion."

He reared up and said, "Here now! When did I raise you to talk like that?"

I gave him a small smile and said, "Somewhere along the line." Then I set my glass down and said, "Howard, I've got to get to work. I just reckoned you'd want the news."

He said, "Guess it will be a boy?"

I give him a sarcastic look. I said, "Sure, Howard, and I've gone into the gypsy business."

Then I turned out of the house and went to looking for our foreman, Harley. It was early spring in the year of 1848, and we were coming into a swift calf crop after an unusually mild winter. We were about to have calves dropping all over the place, and with the quality of our crossbred beef, we couldn't afford to lose a one.

On the way across the ranch yard my youngest brother, Ben, came riding up. He was on a little prancing chestnut that wouldn't stay still while he was trying to talk to me. I knew he was schooling the little filly, but I said, a little impatiently, "Ben, either ride on off and talk to me later or make that damn horse stand. I can't catch but every other word."

Ben said, mildly, "Hell, don't get agitated. I just wanted to give you a piece of news you might be interested in."

I said, "All right, what is this piece of news?"

"One of the hands drifting the Shorthorn herd got sent back to the barn to pick up some stuff for Harley. He said he seen Lew Vara heading this way."

I was standing up near his horse. The animal had been worked pretty hard, and you could take the horse smell right up your nose off him. I said, "Well, okay. So the sheriff is coming. What you reckon we ought to do, get him a cake baked?"

He give me one of his sardonic looks. Ben and I were so much alike it was awful to contemplate. Only difference between us was that I was a good deal wiser and less hotheaded and he was an even size smaller than me. He said, "I reckon he'd rather have whiskey."

I said, "I got some news for you but I ain't going to tell you now."

"What is it?"

I wasn't about to tell him he might be an uncle under such circumstances. I gave his horse a whack on the rump and said, as he went off, "Tell you this evening after work. Now get, and tell Ray Hays I want to see him later on."

He rode off, and I walked back to the ranch house thinking about Lew Vara. Lew, outside of my family, was about the best friend I'd ever had. We'd started off, however, in a kind of peculiar way to make friends. Some eight or nine years past Lew and I had had about the worst fistfight I'd ever been in. It occurred at Crook's Saloon and Cafe in Blessing, the closest town to our ranch, about seven miles away, of which we owned a good part. The fight took nearly a half an hour, and we both did our dead level best to beat the other to death. I won the fight, but unfairly. Lew had had me down on the saloon floor and was in the process of finishing me off when my groping hand found a beer mug. I smashed him over the head with it in a last-ditch effort to keep my own head on my shoulders. It sent Lew to the infirmary for quite a long stay; I'd fractured his skull. When he was partially recovered Lew sent word to me that as soon as he was able, he was coming to kill me.

But it never happened. When he was free from medical care Lew took off for the Oklahoma Territory, and I didn't hear another word from him for four years. Next time I saw him he came into that very same saloon. I was sitting at a back table when I saw him come through the door. I eased my right leg forward so as to clear my revolver for a quick draw from the holster. But Lew just came up, stuck out his hand in a friendly gesture, and said he wanted to let bygones be bygones. He offered to buy me a drink, but I had a bottle on the table so I just told him to get himself a glass and take advantage of my hospitality.

Which he did.

After that Lew became a friend of the family and was important in helping the Williams family in about three confrontations where his gun and his savvy did a good deal to turn the tide in our favor. After that we ran him against the incumbent sheriff who we'd come to dislike and no longer trust. Lew had been reluctant at first, but I'd told him that money couldn't buy poverty but it could damn well buy the sheriff's job in Matagorda County. As a result he got elected, and so far as I was concerned, he did an outstanding job of keeping the peace in his territory.

Which wasn't saying a great deal because most of the trouble he had to deal with, outside of helping us, was the occasional Saturday night drunk and the odd Main Street dogfight.

So I walked back to the main ranch house wondering what he wanted. But I also knew that if it was in my power to give, Lew could have it.

I was standing on the porch about five minutes later when he came riding up. I said, "You want to come inside or talk outside?"

He swung off his horse. He said, "Let's get inside."

"You want coffee?"

"I could stand it."

"This going to be serious?"

"Is to me."

"All right."

I led him through the house to the dining room, where we generally, as a family, sat around and talked things out. I said, looking at Lew, "Get started on it."

He wouldn't face me. "Wait until the coffee comes. We can talk then."

About then Buttercup came staggering in with a couple of cups of coffee. It didn't much make any difference about what time of day or night it was, Buttercup might or might not be staggering. He was an old hand of our father's who'd helped to develop the Half-Moon. In his day he'd been about the best horse breaker around, but time and tumbles had taken their toll. But Howard wasn't a man to forget past loyalties so he'd kept Buttercup on as a cook. His real name was Butterfield, but me and my brothers had called him Buttercup, a name he clearly despised, for as long as I could remember. He was easily the best shot with a long-range rifle I'd ever seen. He had an old .50-caliber Sharps buffalo rifle, and even with his old eyes and seemingly unsteady hands he was deadly anywhere up to five hundred yards. On more than one occasion I'd had the benefit of that seemingly ageless ability. Now he set the coffee down for us and give all the indications of making himself at home. I said, "Buttercup, go on back out in the kitchen. This is a private conversation."

I sat. I picked up my coffee cup and blew on it and then took a sip. I said, "Let me have it, Lew."

He looked plain miserable. He said, "Justa, you and your family have done me a world of good. So has the town and the county. I used to be the trash of the alley and y'all helped bring me back from nothing." He looked away. He said, "That's why this is so damn hard."

"What's so damned hard?"

But instead of answering straight out he said, "They is going to be people that don't understand. That's why I want you to have the straight of it."

I said, with a little heat, "Goddammit, Lew, if you don't tell me what's going on I'm going to stretch you out over that kitchen stove in yonder."

He'd been looking away, but now he brought his gaze back to me and said, "I've got to resign, Justa. As sheriff. And not only that, I got to quit this part of the country."

Thoughts of his past life in the Oklahoma Territory flashed through my mind, when he'd been thought an outlaw and later proved innocent. I thought maybe that old business had come up again and he was going to have to flee for his life and his freedom. I said as much.

He give me a look and then made a short bark that I reckoned he took for a laugh. He said, "Naw, you got it about as backwards as can be. It's got to do with my days in the Oklahoma Territory all right, but it ain't the law. Pretty much the opposite of it. It's the outlaw part that's coming to plague me."

It took some doing, but I finally got the whole story out of him. It seemed that the old gang he'd fallen in with in Oklahoma had got wind of his being the sheriff of Matagorda County. They thought that Lew was still the same young hellion and that they had them a bird nest on the ground, what with him being sheriff and all. They'd sent word that they'd be in town in a few days and they figured to "pick the place clean." And they expected Lew's help.

"How'd you get word?"

Lew said, "Right now they are raising hell in Galveston, but they sent the first robin of spring down to let me know to get the welcome mat rolled out. Some kid about eighteen or nineteen. Thinks he's tough."

"Where's he?"

Lew jerked his head in the general direction of Blessing. "I throwed him in jail."

I said, "You got me confused. How is you quitting going to help the situation? Looks like with no law it would be even worse."

He said, "If I ain't here maybe they won't come. I plan to send the robin back with the message I ain't the sheriff and ain't even in the country. Besides, there's plenty of good men in the county

for the job that won't attract the riffraff I seem to have done."
He looked down at his coffee as if he was ashamed.

I didn't know what to say for a minute. This didn't sound
like the Lew Vara I knew. I understood he wasn't afraid and
I understood he thought he was doing what he thought was the
best for everyone concerned, but I didn't think he was thinking
too straight. I said, "Lew, how many of them is there?"

He said, tiredly, "About eighteen all told. Counting the robin in
the jail. But they be a bunch of rough hombres. This town ain't
equipped to handle such. Not without a whole lot of folks gettin'
hurt. And I won't have that. I figured on an argument from you,
Justa, but I ain't going to make no battlefield out of this town. I
know this bunch. Or kinds like them." Then he raised his head and
give me a hard look. "So I don't want no argument out of you.
I come out to tell you what was what because I care about what
you might think of me. Don't make me no mind about nobody
else but I wanted you to know."

I got up. I said, "Finish your coffee. I got to ride over to my
house. I'll be back inside of half an hour. Then we'll go into town
and look into this matter."

He said, "Dammit, Justa, I done told you I—"

"Yeah, I know what you told me. I also know it ain't really
what you want to do. Now we ain't going to argue and I ain't
going to try to tell you what to do, but I am going to ask you
to let us look into the situation a little before you light a shuck
and go tearing out of here. Now will you wait until I ride over
to the house and tell Nora I'm going into town?"

He looked uncomfortable, but, after a moment, he nodded. "All
right," he said. "But it ain't going to change my mind none."

I said, "Just go in and visit with Howard until I get back. He
don't get much company and even as sorry as you are you're
better than nothing."

That at least did make him smile a bit. He sipped at his coffee, and I took out the back door to where my horse was waiting.

Nora met me at the front door when I came into the house. She
said, "Well, how did the soon-to-be grandpa take it?"

I said, "Howard? Like to have knocked the heels off his boots. I
gave him a straight shot of whiskey in celebration. He's so damned
tickled I don't reckon he's settled down yet."

"What about the others?"

I said, kind of cautiously, "Well, wasn't nobody else around. Ben's out with the herd and Norris is in Blessing. Naturally Buttercup is drunk."

Meanwhile I was kind of edging my way back toward our bedroom. She followed me. I was at the point of strapping on my gunbelt when she came into the room. She said, "Why are you putting on that gun?"

It was my sidegun, a .42/40-caliber Colt's revolver that I'd been carrying for several years. I had two of them, one that I wore and one that I carried in my saddlebags. The gun was a .40-caliber chambered weapon on a .42-caliber frame. The heavier frame gave it a nice feel in the hand with very little barrel deflection, and the .40-caliber slug was big enough to stop anything you could hit solid. It had been good luck for me and the best proof of that was that I was alive.

I said, kind of looking away from her, "Well, I've got to go into town."

"Why do you need your gun to go into town?"

I said, "Hell, Nora, I never go into town without a gun. You know that."

"What are you going into town for?"

I said, "Norris has got some papers for me to sign."

"I thought Norris was already in town. What does he need you to sign anything for?"

I kind of blew up. I said, "Dammit, Nora, what is with all these questions? I've got business. Ain't that good enough for you?"

She give me a cool look. "Yes," she said. "I don't mess in your business. It's only when you try and lie to me. Justa, you are the worst liar in the world."

"All right," I said. "All right. Lew Vara has got some trouble. Nothing serious. I'm going to give him a hand. God knows he's helped us out enough." I could hear her maid, Juanita, banging around in the kitchen. I said, "Look, why don't you get Juanita to hitch up the buggy and you and her go up to the big house and fix us a supper. I'll be back before dark and we'll all eat together and celebrate. What about that?"

She looked at me for a long moment. I could see her thinking about all the possibilities. Finally she said, "Are you going to run a risk on the day I've told you you're going to be a father?"

"Hell no!" I said. "What do you think? I'm going in to use a little influence for Lew's sake. I ain't going to be running any risks."

She made a little motion with her hand. "Then why the gun?"

"Hell, Nora, I don't even ride out into the pasture without a gun. Will you quit plaguing me?"

It took a second, but then her smooth, young face calmed down. She said, "I'm sorry, honey. Go and help Lew if you can. Juanita and I will go up to the big house and I'll personally see to supper. You better be back."

I gave her a good, loving kiss and then made my adieus, left the house, and mounted my horse and rode off.

But I rode off with a little guilt nagging at me. I swear, it is hell on a man to answer all the tugs he gets on his sleeve. He gets pulled first one way and then the other. A man damn near needs to be made out of India rubber to handle all of them. No, I wasn't riding into no danger that March day, but if we didn't do something about it, it wouldn't be long before I would be.

Classic Westerns from
——— *GILES TIPPETTE* ———

Justa Williams is a bold young Texan who doesn't usually set out looking for trouble...but somehow he always seems to find it.

__BAD NEWS 0-515-10104-4/$3.95

Justa Williams finds himself trapped in Bandera, a tough town with an unusual notion of justice. Justa's accused of a brutal murder that he didn't commit. So his two fearsome brothers have to come in and bring their own brand of justice.

__CROSS FIRE 0-515-10391-8/$3.95

A herd of illegally transported Mexican cattle is headed toward the Half-Moon ranch—and with it, the likelihood of deadly Mexican tick fever. The whole county is endangered . . . and it looks like it's up to Justa to take action.

__JAILBREAK 0-515-10595-3/$3.95

Justa gets a telegram saying there's squatters camped on the Half-Moon ranch, near the Mexican border. Justa's brother, Norris, gets in a whole heap of trouble when he decides to investigate. But he winds up in a Monterrey jail for punching a Mexican police captain, and Justa's got to figure out a way to buy his brother's freedom.

For Visa, MasterCard and American Express orders ($10 minimum) call: 1-800-631-8571

FOR MAIL ORDERS: CHECK BOOK(S). FILL OUT COUPON. SEND TO:	**POSTAGE AND HANDLING:** $1.50 for one book, 50¢ for each additional. Do not exceed $4.50.
BERKLEY PUBLISHING GROUP 390 Murray Hill Pkwy., Dept. B East Rutherford, NJ 07073	**BOOK TOTAL** $ _____
NAME_____	**POSTAGE & HANDLING** $ _____
ADDRESS _____	**APPLICABLE SALES TAX** $ _____ (CA, NJ, NY, PA)
CITY_____	**TOTAL AMOUNT DUE** $ _____
STATE_____ZIP_____	**PAYABLE IN US FUNDS.** (No cash orders accepted.)
PLEASE ALLOW 6 WEEKS FOR DELIVERY. PRICES ARE SUBJECT TO CHANGE WITHOUT NOTICE.	350